Praise For
New Harmony

———◆———

"Pettiway's haunting novel explores the generational trauma of racism through the story of a Black mother's quest for justice, truth, and peace.

"The story, framed by the 1949 funeral of 16-year-old Thad Butler, unfolds in the grief-stricken voice of his mother, Margaret, as she revisits the events that shaped her life—and ultimately, her son's tragic fate. Told in a rich Southern vernacular, the novel stretches back to 1915, when Margaret was a 10-year-old girl growing up in New Harmony, South Carolina. As the daughter of Black sharecroppers, Margaret came of age amid stark racial hierarchies, grinding poverty, and gendered expectations. A pivotal moment arrived when she was invited to live in the 'Big House' of the white Demmings family—a gesture of apparent kindness that concealed deeper power dynamics and exploitation. Through Margaret's eyes, readers witness the tension between survival and dignity, love and injustice. Her friendship with White Candy, the plantation owner's daughter, adds complexity to the novel's portrayal of race and intimacy. As Margaret's story winds through her adolescence, marriage, and motherhood, she tries to shield her children from the pain she carries from her past. However, when her child is murdered in an act of racist terror, she's forced to confront the forces that shaped them all. Over the course of this novel, Pettiway's richly voiced prose is lyrical and immersive, grounded in emotional precision and a tone of oral tradition. The narrative structure, which effectively interweaves past and present events, emphasizes the enduring weight of memory and trauma; as Margaret notes early on: 'The threads of our lives—the decisions, dreams, and hopes that wove in and out, over and under each other—crafted my boy's demise.' Overall, this is a story not just of loss, but of truth-telling, resistance, and the burden of inherited injustice.

"A moving debut that honors the enduring power of love and reflection."

—*Kirkus Reviews*

NEW HARMONY

NEW HARMONY

A MOTHER'S STORY OF LOVE AND LOSS

LEON E. PETTIWAY

New Harmony: A Mother's Story of Love and Loss
Leon E. Pettiway

Produced by Spoonbridge Press
Book design by David Provolo
Family tree design by Anwar

First U.S. Edition, 2025

ISBNs:
979-8-9891820-4-6 (hc)
979-8-9891820-5-3 (pbk)
979-8-9891820-6-0 (ebk)

Library of Congress Control Number: 2025918943

Printed in the U.S.A.

CONTENTS

PART ONE

ONE

Be Merciful Unto Me

The day belonged to the dead, and our lamenting floated down the worn steps of Calvary Baptist Church, past grave markers and upturned stones, drifted down Chestnut Street and onto Main, around the bend, and down into the next hollow. From where I sat on the front pew, I heard Pastor Jones scream,

"Nigga, you're a dead man!"

It was 1949, and while "nigga" conveyed the lies, bigotry, and terror nursed in New Harmony, South Carolina, the word had the power to turn the mourners' whimpering into silence. That word and the reality it conveyed encouraged them to imagine the deafening truth of what had happened one night in the dark. And so, in Calvary's stillness, Pastor Jones unleashed the pain of our loss, the death of our baby boy. Perhaps with those words, my family's misery became tangible, and folks could feel the sadness we experienced every time we recalled his death and remembered his blood splattered, now absorbed, in that ditch.

As he recounted that night's horror, my grief deepened, but he continued and said,

"*Yes.*

"From alongside New Harmony Road, Thad Butler's murderer screamed, 'Nigga! You're a dead man.'"

Draped in mourning, parts of me yearned for him to stop. I desired no more reminders because, sheathed in a mother's misery, I hankered for him to soothe me like Mammy did when the boogeyman stalked my dreams. But Pastor Jones sidestepped reassurance, nourished outrage, and hinted at other sins. When he captured the winds of folks lamenting, however, his voice shifted from its tone of condemnation and drifted into a breath of words, into a soft stream of sounds, to question,

"Are *we* decent enough to mourn this, our fallen angel?"

But it made me uneasy—I required no more overtones of unworthiness or guilt. I longed for somebody to calm the whispers whipped up by self-reproach. But instead of coddling my desire for pity and support, Pastor Jones continued with the horrors of loss. He demanded that the reluctant and those sheltering denial consider that evening's nightmare. He said,

"Mothers and fathers, consider how you would feel if death snatched your child's breath, leaving him lifeless in a ditch—a shotgun blast tearing him asunder." And with that, I fought back the tears, wrestled with his appeal, and coaxed "Breathe, Margaret" into a whimper.

His demands for us to reminisce forced me to ask, "Where is the justice?" while somebody in the Amen corner begged him to "Preach!" He snatched that bait, danced the preacher's bounce, and stiffened his sermon's resolve, heightening the mourners' outrage. So, like a biblical crooner, he hummed,

"Just *sixteen* years ago, God *blew* the freshness of *His* spirit into that boy's soul." But pointing to his stolen youth and reminding me of his age cut me to the quick, and my anguish deepened, inflaming the cauldron of my sorrow. In the depth of that misery, Pastor Jones scooped the air with his right arm, cradled it with his left, and rocked our emptiness into the lament of mourners. His "empty cuddle" was a mother's gesture, one I remember well, but he merely bred more misery, and when he uttered, "Now he's gone," I sat breathless.

But he stoked my pain enough for me to snag some of his fury, and I demanded to know who or what spawned my baby's nightmare, to which Pastor Jones announced as,

"Evil!" but with that decree, the church crowd grew mighty incensed, which forced them to pitch their prayers straight to the heavens, prompting Pastor Jones to lean over the pulpit a little ways to validate the cause—the demon of their outrage. He said,

"The devil snatched that boy's life under the cloak of darkness, where only a choir of whippoorwills and hoot owls bore witness alongside New Harmony Road."

I nodded and gave a silent "Amen!"

But in his failure to recognize that my baby stood alone, like an orphan before wickedness that night, Pastor Jones stood oblivious to the trials of mothering and a mother's loss, and his failure compelled me to flick my head way back and ask,

"Oh, Lawd! Why didn't you take *me*?"

I wanted to scream, "Only if *they* could have taken the witness stand," lamenting that God hadn't empowered them whippoorwills and hoot owls with the ability to divulge what they had seen. "*Sweet Jesus!*" I longed to jump up and holler, shuffle my feet like the preacher's prance and jig, but Pastor Jones kept me tethered to that evening's horror.

"Can you sense the boy's agony, his pain? Do you see him struggling to breathe alongside that road?" he asked.

Perhaps others fancied the pastor's dramatic accounts so that they could picture Thad dying—the explosion of buckshot and pellets piercing his body, rendering him desperate and breathless, gasping for air.

I required none!

As the choir began to sing, Pastor Jones's soulless blessing and patting landed cold on my shoulder. Without sorrowful bloodshot eyes, a sniffling nose, or a tearful voice to accompany his touch, the gesture was akin to attempting to satiate the belly of a starving and emaciated orphan with a thimbleful of milk. Yet it was that insufficiency that forced me to remember what nourished and comforted me most: family.

My other children, Tilda, Ruth, Helen, and Henry, sat on the front pew alongside me and William. My only grandbaby, William Alexander, nestled close to his granddaddy—resembling his white father, white as any white person. Tilda, his mammy, was pregnant by a colored man I thought she shouldn't have married. She was due to deliver soon, but no one could prevent her from attending her brother's home-going. She lolled motionless, seemingly not breathing, lost in a trance, I suspected, gazing somewhere far off—away from New Harmony—straight and endless miles into the distance.

I scanned the church for the others: close friends like Zora Mae and other family members (Pappy, my father; my brothers, Joshua and Neddy; and my younger sisters, Lena and Violet). Aunt Sarah and my oldest sister, Fannie, held on to each other. They resembled me in accepting life's hardships but were unlike me in their outspokenness. But today, they sat silent and humbled, grief-stricken. I saw Nate. Marlene comforted him just as she had always done, both inside and outside the Big House, where she worked as a servant. She cradled him, humming a spiritual that resonated with the same sacred gentleness she carried. As my son's best friend, Nate ached, and it showed when he walked to the casket and placed a red rosebud next to my baby.

As a bereaved mother, I wished for Pastor Jones to speak the truth about a colored woman's loss, but outrage consumed him. From that crippled state, he could only dole out a *"Help* me, Jesus!" when the choir's exuberance, signaling the song's end, prompted the Hallelujahs, the Amens, and the clapping hands to accompany the slapping of leather soles against the hard church floor. These incited the dips and sass of the organ's flurry that he quelled into the benediction.

"Let us pray for the Butler family: his mother, Sister Margaret; his father, Brother William. Plead that the murderer of innocence be found and brought to justice.

"Let the church say Amen."

Pastor Jones raised his hand to heaven and showered blessings onto Thad. At the same time, the funeral helpers sealed the casket and oriented it for the pallbearers and the recessional. The pastor positioned himself behind the casket as the piano's flourish and the organ's moans introduced Brother Jacob's voice.

He began singing with "Master, the tempest is raging," which accompanied the organ and piano's slow, syncopated rhythms. Brother Jacob urged the turbulent seas to obey Jesus's command as the organ's constant gospel beat nursed and rocked the church folks in the soothing chant of "Peace be still." It filled the church, and I hungered for it, but the choir sang of storm-tossed seas, demons, and men. We were familiar with the wrath of storms. The deeds of wicked men had acquainted my family with misery and sorrow. But turmoil and grief always fell with God's grace, which the choir intoned as sweetly as the "peace" we sought. I lifted my head in the promise of that peace. Brother Jacob and the choir sang "Peace be still" over and over until they fell into a whisper and then into a silence interrupted by the peal of Calvary's bells. We stumbled to our feet, and with our steps matching the clang of the church's bells, we followed behind Thad's casket, laboring toward his plot of ground.

We laid my baby to rest in the colored churchyard.

It was the hardest thing I had ever done, and I intended to leave that nightmare buried as William tugged on my arm and pulled me away from that box. Neither his father nor I wanted to see earth tossed upon our Thad. So, as I walked from his fresh ground, outraged by this scheme of the devil, this injustice, this atrocity, I turned my indignation into disbelief and wallowed into denial as if it were a featherbed. The only resolution to my sorrow, disbelief, and outrage was the hope found in prayer.

"Be merciful unto me, Oh God," spun in my head as we walked to the car. Then, the Spirit reminded me of my promise to Thad when William laid his body on our bed that night. When I held his hand, I vowed I would never forget this time.

As New Harmony Road stretched before me, I renewed my vow to capture what happened to a curly-headed colored boy who had departed life a few hundred yards from his home. I would tell the story of the handsome colored boy who loved his family but who encountered hatred and met death in a ditch. I prayed for folks to know why someone slaughtered our piece of hope before he grasped life's essence. I wanted folks to understand how he died all alone—his mother and his father, the ones who had sparked his life from their embrace, had no idea that malice waited for him along New Harmony Road. And if we were to learn who killed our boy, I would count our kin among the blessed.

———————◆◆———————

Now that we have learned the truth, I want everyone to know what happened to my beautiful, silky-skinned lad. I was forty-four when Thad was taken from us and fifty when we learned the truth. During those six years, from 1949 to 1955, I had ample time to ponder the events leading up to his death. I realized that a multitude of decisions and actions, both innocent and profound, created a web of hatred that justified murder. However, the threads of this story extend beyond my generation, long before I turned ten and met Hollis and Ophelia Demmings. My life, and the lives of others who intersected with my family's, resembled a frame used by a weaver, with its interlacing warps and wefts, producing the weaver's cloth and, in this case, fating his death. The threads of our lives—the decisions, dreams, and hopes that wove in and out, over and under each other—crafted my boy's demise. Our sixteen-year-old son died because of bigotry and ignorance— the inescapable consequences found in the conflict of black versus white and male versus female. I pray that we learn better. I ask us all to try harder and do better for one another.

What you will read in the coming chapters is the result of my recollections, which I completed in the fall of 1957. To help you understand a mother's story of love and loss—how my family's dreams and decisions intersected with those of others to seed Thad's demise—I decided to begin this tale of treachery in 1915, when I was a pullet and there wasn't even a hint of him.

TWO

Pappy's Gal

I heard my mammy yellin' clean 'cross that field, but I ain't say one word, nuthin' at all. I sat right still, like that walkin' stick bug I seen yestiddy, hidin' on some tree bark.

Mammy yelled again.

"Margaret!"

By then, I saw her 'vancing 'round that big old oak tree.

She was full of wind and festooned with shiny beads of water on her forehead. They dribbled into false tears that streaked her face and sparkled in the sunlight.

She'd been in the sun picking tobacco since dawn, and her eyes flashed a warning when she said,

"Gal, yuh gots sump'em crammed in them ears of yourn?"

She acted like she could've wrung my neck like Tom, the rooster who scratched past me in the yard. It was rare for her to raise her voice or rumble with anger. Rather, her voice, by its nature and her temperament, forced itself to flutter like the arched winds of a hen striving to shoo her clutch, gathering her chicks into her protection. But she picked up some more wind and blew,

"Gal, yuh ain't hear me callin' yuh?"

I still hunched down behind the cabin, trying mighty hard to pretend I wasn't there, but Mammy's footsteps assaulted the broom-swept yard and puffed a flurry of dust in my direction, and she said,

"Git up from there! Child, you's the *laziest* thang I ever did see."

I was never sassy, but I was right good at pouting, though. Besides, the switch taught me what it meant to be unladylike.

Her feet carried her only a little ways before she pulled up to ask, "Whut's the matter, baby?"

"Mammy, it be's too hot. The sun gonna turn me in'tuh uh tar baby."

"Gal, yuh gots a long ways 'foe you's uh tar baby. Quit yo' fussin', git off yo' tail, and go on yonder and give yo' pappy and the boys a drank of water. Tar baby, my *foot*! . . . Margaret Long, yuh's almos' white."

I pouted so that my bottom lip was way bigger than the top one, and I changed the subject and said,

"Mammy, Fannie ain't done nuthin' all day."

She stared at me, and with her eyes wide in disbelief and her fist firmly planted in the natural curve of her hourglass figure, she said,

"Fannie in the house wid baby girl."

But before I could stop myself, "Ain't Lena 'sleep?" flung out my mouth.

"Quit axin' so many questions. Jest does whut I axes yuh, gal. Git on *up*, and *don'tcha* be movin' like molasses, neither. Pappy and the boys hankerin' for sump'tem tuh drank. Yuh hear me?"

"Yessum."

Mammy walked toward the house to check on Lena and Fannie. Before the screen door blurred her silhouette, she removed the wrap that covered her head, and her raven-silk hair whisked at her shoulders. Mammy's hair once reached the middle of her back, but she'd cut it short. It had reached a point of being in-between, neither long nor short, but magnificent all the same.

Folks said I resembled Mammy when she was ten. I was thin, high in color, and had long, slender fingers like hers. Her eyes were brown, but mine held the hue of ripened hazelnuts mixed with green, brown, and gold that shifted in the sunlight from a nutty brown to a lighter brownish-green. But what I liked more than anything else was Mammy's long eyelashes and her dark, thick eyebrows. With the flutter of those lashes and the arch of one brow, Mammy spoke volumes. She was short, and folks said I'd take after her.

Lula was Mammy's name, but her beauty and presence should've been granted a more regal name. She was the prettiest woman I knew, but I was the second.

Mammy noticed my rapt gaze and shooed me up with "Gal, move yo' tail!"

Well, it took a mighty hefty thing to rouse me from my hidey hole, 'cause I hated summer as much as a snowman did. Summer meant field work, more housework, and caring for the young ones in the sweltering Carolina heat.

I despised all of it.

My desire to read and write consumed me day and night. Candy, the twelve-year-old daughter of the white man whose place we cropped on, had inspired me. She'd done the unforgivable and let me peep at her school-books. Like most colored folks, though, I only caught glimpses of her schoolhouse 'cause nary one of us could set even our little toe inside that piece of whiteness. Back then, most Negroes, like Pappy, signed by making their marks, but Mammy did more than scribble, and she could read.

I kept asking Mammy about schooling, but she always said,

"Ask yo' pappy."

And Pappy always said, "No."

"Boys need them kinda thangs," he said. "'Sides, yuh only ten."

Pappy's views mirrored the beliefs of people who lived in 1886 when he was my age and Mammy was seven. But it was 1915, and Pappy still believed girls didn't need any book learning. So, as I walked to do Mammy's bidding, I thought about school, and I uh'tempted to chide God, thinking, *Why did'ja make me uh girl, and why did'ja make me uh nigga on top of that?* And that caused me to blurt out, "Hmmph, one day I ain't gonna be livin' in this-here used-up town."

As I strolled 'round the bend, the spring burbled its closeness. Joy sprang loose when some of its cool water ran 'cross my hands and bare feet as I filled the jug. It felt so good, but I remembered Mammy's words: "Don't lemme git back there 'foe you does," so I filled the jug right-quick, put some pepper in my step, and headed to the fields that always scared me to death. Those tobacco plants were so tall and the leaves so big that they hid everything from me; I'd feared getting lost 'cause I couldn't see which way to go. This time I was lucky. Turning at the end of the third row, I spotted Pappy hunched over, cutting a plant and splitting the stalk.

Listen up: Pappy was handsome and made the womenfolk pant. The ladies admired a face that looked like somebody had chiseled it perfect, which he hid with a beard for a spell to hide his youthful face. But now, he only sported what he called his crumb duster, which allowed the dimple in his chin to bear an extra little smile. He had light skin, but it was a bit more brown than Mammy's. His straight hair was similar to Mammy's but not as black. I smiled at him and said,

"I brung yuh sump'em tuh drank," before cutting my eyes up at Mammy, who had walked up on us.

He put one hand on his backside and brought the jug to his mouth. Some water drizzled out from the corners of his lips, met down around his chin, and dribbled onto his bib overalls. Between gulps, he said, looking down at me, "Yo' mammy been lookin' for yuh. . . . Where yuh been at?" He handed the jug to Joshua.

I couldn't tell him I'd been daydreaming about reading and writing, knowing what he'd say: "Gal, where yuh git them ideas from?"

So I said, "Sitting . . . watching the chickens chase each other."

But just as I uttered those words, my knucklehead brother, Joshua, said,

"Her daydreaming again."

"Hush yo' mouth," I said.

Oh, Joshua was a know-it-all; thought he could put his pesky mouth where it ain't have no business since being fourteen made him "grown." I hankered to cut the legs out from under him, but Neddy cut his eyes at me, and it kept me quiet just like him 'cause he was different that way.

Pappy, looking at me and then Joshua, said,

"Joshua, mind yo' business . . . Margaret, gon' back tuh the house and tell Fannie tuh start fixin' sump'em t'eat," which caused Joshua to cut his eyes at me right fast.

I knew what he thought: *Pappy's gal.*

Confident, I stuck out my tongue and began to strut away. I intended to douse him with heaping doses of peacock pride until Mammy said,

"And yuh help Fannie fix them vittles. Yuh hear?"

Shucks.

I set foot on the road as if I carried a lazy man's load. Rounding the bend, I noticed a man struggling with his wagon stuck in a ditch. A pretty lady sat in it, and I hadn't seen either of them before that day. He sweated like he had done a full day's work, huffing like a bullied horse. She, looking as though a spring breeze had just hit her, sat perfect.

"Hey," I said.

He peered up with his forehead gathered in pleats and murmured a funny-sounding grunt from behind pinched lips, with the trappings of frustration twisting his face.

She smiled.

Huh! *Chocolate and cream,* I thought.

He was a shade lighter than pitch, but she could've been my Mammy— she was way lighter than "high yellow."

"Hello," she said.

After hearing her voice and seeing her lips stretch into a perfect smile, I wanted to be like her. She sounded so sweet, but she didn't sound like folks from these parts. So, I asked,

"Where y'all from?"

"Philadelphia," she said.

"Where that at?"

"Up north. You've never heard of it?"

"Nome," and with my eyes on her fancy white dress stitched with eyelets of lace, I said, "That sho' be's a pretty dress yuh gots on."

A smile the size of South Carolina adorned her face.

"Thank you," she said. "You know, Philadelphia is a very historic city—the birthplace of our nation."

This-here woman talkin' right funny, but I likes her.

I spotted the picnic basket in their wagon.

"Where y'all gwine?"

Her puzzlement jumped into "Excuse me?" and I remembered they weren't from around these parts, so I said,

"Where y'all headed?"

"To the schoolhouse," she said. "I am the new colored schoolteacher."

"Hillary," said the man, "this is too difficult for me alone."

"That's my husband, Mr. Jefferson Collins. Do you live nearby? I think he will require a little assistance. Would your father or someone be able to assist him?"

Yeah, I know they ain't from 'round these parts. Not talkin' like that. Her must mean they needs some help.

I glanced from him to her and considered their situation. Well, I wanted to shake my head and click my tongue up against the roof of my mouth like a tapping woodpecker to mark the sound of pity. I itched to say,

Yuh cain't git out'ah no ditch wid her still sittin' in that wagon. What in the world yuh thankin' 'bout?

But these were grown folks, and Mammy's home training had plenty of no-nos, so I said,

"Yessum. Jest left my pappy in the 'bacca field. I go git him."

I set out lickety-split, and near-about ran over a squirrel as I raced up on Pappy, panting and barely able to talk, nearly passing out in his arms. I pushed out,

"Pappy, Pappy, come quick. This-here lady and her husband done broke down wid they wagon. They needs help."

"Who?"

"I don't know whut he do, but his wife be's the new colored school-teacher."

"Margaret, us right in the middle of finishin' this-here row."

"Jake," Mammy said, "they's in need. Yuh go 'head; me and the boys'll make do. Almos' lunchtime anyways."

Nobody could move Pappy like Mammy.

"All right. Gal, show me where they at."

When Pappy and I reached their wagon, Miss Hillary sat under a tree with her parasol.

Pappy took one look at those folks and figured they didn't know nothing 'bout nothing, but he remained polite.

"Jake Long," Pappy said. "Look lac y'all in uh mess of trouble here."

"Horse got spooked," Mr. Collis said.

Extending his hand, he said, "I'm Jefferson Collins." Then, nodding in her direction, he said, "That's my wife, Hillary."

As she walked toward us, she smiled, and as smooth as silk, Miss

Hillary said, "Thank you so much for coming to our assistance. We are in your debt." Then, she took off her perfect white glove and reached to shake Pappy's hand.

Gloves in August, and it ain't even Sunday?

Her sho'nuf not from 'round here.

Pappy slapped his hands on his overalls, wiped off some of that 'bacca juice, and shook her hand. Then he said,

"You most welcome."

I thought, *Where that come from? Pappy done caught what they has!*

Well, Pappy laid so much loving onto the spooked horse that it settled into calm. After stroking the horse's mane and letting the po' thang rest a spell, Pappy coaxed the horse enough to free the wagon from that ditch. Before they took off, Mr. Collins tried to give Pappy some money, but he didn't know my pappy.

"Don't need it," Pappy said, waving it away. "Us helps one 'nuther 'round here."

"Thank you," Mr. Collins said, prompting Miss Hillary to glance at me with gentle doe eyes and say,

"Now, Margaret, I want you to come and visit me before the summer ends."

I glanced at Pappy, seeking a twinkle or smile that suggested his approval. Pappy didn't flicker until she added, "If that is all right with your father?"

"We gon' see," but I threw my arms around his legs, turned my face up to meet his (so I could look like Duke when he was a puppy), and coaxed, "I 'pose it be all right."

"Where y'all live at?" I asked, with excitement stamping my voice and glee brightening my eyes.

"We took over the old Henderson place next to the church," Mr. Collins said.

"Come by any time, and Mr. Long, please tell your wife to visit as well," she said.

"Yessum. I gonna sho' do that," Pappy said.

They set off down the road, and she turned and waved as Pappy said,

"Reckon yuh done made yo'self a friend."

I beamed. Butterflies, ruby-throated hummingbirds, little chickadees, and everything bright and light flew up in my chest.

Maybe Pappy gon' lemme go tuh school. I'll learn tuh read, and then White Candy won't get in no mo' trouble.

THREE

Just a Bee 'Round Honey

White Candy and her folks, the Demmings—her mammy, Ophelia, her daddy, Hollis, and her brother, Floyd—lived in what my mammy's mammy called the Big House and what the Demmings called Pleasant Bluff Plantation. Their three-story wooden residence perched high on the bluff, right next to Pleasant Ridge, and faced the east side of the Ashley River. Great hefty columns supporting two eye-catching balconies bolstered a grand gable and roof that protected the porches below. The Big House sat way back from New Harmony Road, and from there, the family had to travel Pleasant Bluff Avenue's long stretch to enter the plantation's gate. Entering the grounds, they could marvel at their wealth, and others could envy what they had.

Cherry, dogwood, and magnolia trees lined both sides of the lane, and they always made spring delightful. When their pink, white, and lavender tones faded, one could appreciate the faithful pines, beeches, and cedars dotting the rolling earth. Massive willow oaks shaded the stubble of green fields enclosed by four-plank wooden fencing that stretched and undulated along the avenue.

The Demmings family owned the Pleasant Bluff Plantation years before the Yankees blew through South Carolina. During the slave days, the "niggras" (that was how they said it back then, according to Mammy's mammy) lived in quarters close to the fields where they worked. That was way before Mammy was born, but her mammy told her all about those times. Only one of those shacks remained. The Yankees had burned the others to the ground but spared the Big House, that piece of whiteness they didn't touch. Hollis Demming ran roughshod over it, and folks rumored he'd wrestled the pennies from a dead man's eyes. His cunning ways made him slicker than snot, folks said. His neck didn't resemble a sunburned farmer's, but colored folks called him a redneck 'cause he pampered the ways of po' white trash and spouted their words. Even Pappy said, "He gots plenty money, but his mind so full of nastiness when it come to us colored folks, he'd put po' white trash to shame." And that was because Pappy believed, "Yuh ain't gots tuh be no white field hand to be a redneck." But when I was ten, "redneck" didn't seem to fit the pink and olive skin tones of folks whom some colored children called "white soda crackers" and colored men addressed as "Mr. Charlie" on the sly.

But his daughter, White Candy, ain't act nothing like her daddy. You should've seen how we use'ta play, giggle, and get into mischief. Lawd, she would sneak from the Big House, unbeknownst to Mr. Hollis. We'd meet on the path before it unfurled into our secret place down by the spring. Within that cloister, she'd whisper every kind of hidden truth, and we would be full of giggles. It was there that White Candy revealed she didn't share her father's traits. She had finished gathering the last of my hair in a plait when Kearns, a piece of white trash who worked for the Demmings, confronted me. On seeing her, a white youngin, slick down the last part of a colored youngin's hair, his redneck ways flared up, and he grabbed me up in the collar of my print dress and spoke his hot breath and hatred down my throat. White Candy changed the direction of his outrage—she jumped up and kicked him in the shin. When he reached out to place his gnarled hand on her perfect dress, she said, "You like ham, don'tcha, Kearns?" The question rolled out as delicately as the halo of blond curls Marlene had spiraled on her head. Kearns stiffened because he understood what she meant—she'd seen him stealing from the smokehouse.

"Daddy dud'en need tuh know 'bout this, does he?" she added.

She didn't have to throw a hissy fit 'cause she'd learned to sweeten intimidation well enough from Mr. Hollis. That Kearns was a stallion, and she was a filly, carried no weight—a Demmings sired her.

As for Miss Ophelia, Candy's mammy, folks said she donned two hats: one for the white folks who recognized her as a highfalutin' white woman, a real white woman's woman, and the other hat for the colored folks she ruled. "Mean as the day was long and held the venom of thirty copperheads," folks said, and I heard Mammy say, "You don't wanna cross Miss Ophelia. She'd snatch the taste right out yo' mouth." Yessiree, plenty of folks rumored caution about her.

One morning, I went with Mammy to the Big House to help fetch some clothes to wash, and after returning home, Mammy began sweating over the pile. When Pappy walked up, with dusk nearing, and with her still toiling over the pile, he asked,

"Where this mess of wash come from?"

"Ah, Miss Ophelia po' mouthin' 'cause Agnes done had 'nuf sense tuh leave her high and dry."

"Why'd her quit?"

"Tired bein' Miss Ophelia's house nigga I 'magine."

"The last time yuh calls yo'self tryin' tuh help her, she said the clothes wan't clean. You 'members that?"

"'Course. Had tuh wash 'em twice that time. Woman done had the gumption tuh fix her mouth and say, 'They *dingy.*'"

"But why yuh pullin' the slack Agnes done left?" Mammy stopped washing to place her hands on her waist in disbelief and asked,

"Where yuh been at—or did'ja have monkey paws over yo' eyes for the last twenty-nine years?"

"Nah, but I've been ailin' from bein' sunstroke, though," he said with a peck on her cheek.

"Got us here lac they had my mammy and them. So now, I's saddled wid 'least two days washin' and 'least three mo' days ironin' and foldin'."

"Best git Margaret out here tuh help yuh then."

Yeah, it was another one of those jobs I hated, and I figured it was Miss Agnes's fault.

But Mammy said Miss Agnes "done been rode hard and put up wet," and I heard Miss Effie say, "Miss Ophelia done worked Agnes dry and then had the gumption not tuh pay right." Some other colored women rumored tales of tragic mishaps that befell colored folks who didn't do Hollis and Ophelia Demmmings's wishes. But because Miss Agnes caught some quick wit, Mammy stuck me with helping her wash, iron, and fold this hateful white woman's clothes. To make things worse, when Mammy pressed and folded the last of the wash, we had nary a wagon to deliver two days of washing and three days of ironing. The boys and Pappy had the wagon in the field, and me and Mammy had to *tote* that mess of laundry to old Miss Hateful. I was at my wit's end, and I rocked between losing my religion and fuming—madder than a mule chewing on a mess of bumblebees. I don't remember how many trips it took, but I thought, *Why don't her fetch these clothes? They her clothes!*

On our last trip, Miss Hateful started fluttering around Mammy like a bee 'round some honey, saying, "Lula this and Lula that," talking all fast— grinning and stuff. Yeah, she scurried around Mammy like she was fixin' to kill up a mess of snakes, but I caught her looking in my direction, too. She stared at me like a preacher hankering to devour a piece of chicken, gnaw- ing the bones 'til they were slick as a ribbon. Even back then, I understood that winking was equivalent to nodding for a blind horse.

She finally turned to Mr. Hollis and said,

"Look here. Lula has done such a marvelous job! Now, pay her well 'cause she deserves an ample reward for all her fine work."

Mr. Hollis reached into his pocket, tossed six dollars on the wash pile, and left after looking me up and down. But I ain't paid him much attention. I watched Candy, who peeped from another room. She looked down and out—like she had a tough row to hoe. I couldn't right out comfort her (any attention would get me the switch), but I caught her signal, remembering what she told me: "When yuh see me pull my nose, you need to meet me by the spring. Margaret, it's really important when I do that."

I winked.

When we left, I asked Mammy, "Ever been in the rest of they house?"

"Many a time."

"Sho' is big."

"Uh-huh. It's a grand house, a lively old plantation. Durin' the slave days, they has sixty tuh seventy slaves all bunched up on this-here place. Po' souls, they worked 'em like they animals. . . . Bet if yuh listen right good, yuh can hear the old ones, the Great Spirits, the ones they planted after they drap dead."

We stopped then, and she cranked her head with her ear up to the sky to listen. "Yuh hear 'em?" she asked, and my eyes turned as large as fifty-cent pieces. Mammy threw her arms around me and said,

"Baby, they's good spirits. They's us'es flesh and bones, the greatest of all the spirits," and she smiled in a way only Mammy could.

"Whut grandmammy use'ta say 'bout them days when she lived here, Mammy?"

"They hard . . . real hard times. I tells yuh mo' when you's uh little older."

When we reached the shortcut by the spring, I asked Mammy if I could stay.

"I wants tuh play in the water. It so hot and all," I said.

Mammy had disappeared when White Candy approached on the dirt path. She breathed heavily and fretted as if haints chased her, appearing whiter than usual. She said,

"Cain't stay long. Got'tuh git back b'foe they miss me." Then after she sucked enough breath to say, "They're gon' send me away, Margaret. I leave tomorrow," the tears inched to her lips.

I stood up then. "Where yuh gonna go?"

"Uh'lanta."

"Ain't heard of such a place."

"Jaw'ja," she said, "Tuh uh all-girls' school."

Her down-in-the-mouth ways made me notice how different she was from colored folks. It wasn't just her skin, eyes, and hair, but for the first time, I noticed the way she talked. Her voice had more than a twang. She had a drawl that pulled sounds out like she had all day long for them to unwind, so that corn became "cawn" and horse turned into "hawse." I ain't care. She was my friend, and I held on to her for a spell until she leaped to her feet and darted off almost as quickly as she had come.

As she rounded the bend, I thought, *I gon' miss yuh,* just as Fannie snuck up on me and slapped such a notion clean out my head. She yelled,

"Why yuh always wid that white gal? Don'tcha know her pappy wears that Klan's hood, ridin' through these parts burnin' crosses and hangin' colored folks left and right? He the ringleader!"

I sucked my teeth at her, but before I could sass her good and proper, she had me by my cotton dress and walloped me so hard I fell to the ground. She was sixteen, and I was ten, so it wan't no kinda fight.

Trapped, I cast a fierce, piercing stare, took a deep breath, and screamed full-throated.

"*Git off me* 'foe I . . ."

But what would make her turn me loose? All of a sudden, I remembered just the thing, but she needed a teaser first to get her attention. So, being devilish, I said,

"'Foe I tells Mammy whut yuh done did . . . the uh'ther night!" as I struggled to wrestle her off, but she held on.

"Whut'ja mean? Tell Mammy whut?"

"I sees yuh . . . wid that boy—"

"*Whut* boy? You ain't seen *nuthin'*."

"Did *too* . . . that Gardner boy. The one wid them white folk's eyes!"

She let me go then. I raised myself high enough from the ground to sling, "Whut y'all *doing* down there? *Kissing?*"

"Bet not let on tuh Mammy . . . if'n yuh knows whut good for yuh," she said as she got up.

Her threat softened toward sadness, and her face stretched so far into the gloom that it would have made Mammy say, "She could eat oats from the bottom of a churn."

And looking down at me 'bout ready to squeeze some tears into that churn she could've eaten from, she said, "*Please* don't blab whut'ja done seen."

She pulled me to my feet.

Speaking with her *I-got-a-secret voice*, she said, "Now, if'n I tells yuh this, yuh *gots* tuh promise, yuh ain't gon' let on tuh-uh soul. Yuh *gots* tuh promise me now."

Walleyed, I said, "Cross my heart and hope tuh die."

"Yuh sho' now?"

I nodded my head and crossed my heart one more time.

"Robert done axes me tuh marry."

A startled "*Nah!*" flung out my mouth.

"Uhhh-huh," she said with a peacock's pride.

"Pappy ain't gon' let'cha," I said in a high-pitched voice, which I reinforced with "Both Mammy and Pappy say they folks ain't no good" in a faster cadence.

I nodded my head for extra emphasis.

She stomped her foot. "I loves Robert, and he loves me. Us gon' git hitched," she said, pulling her skirt tail to dab at her eyes. I didn't know what to do, so I threw my arms around her waist and held her like I had held White Candy moments before.

"Don't cry," I said. "I ain't gon' breathe it tuh uh soul."

The sun perched on the horizon, so we headed home. When we reached the house, Lena, who was six then, ran in the yard until Mammy caught her and tickled her into giggles. Fannie ran toward the barn, opening the door as Pappy came in from the fields. Joshua led the mule, and Neddy carried a sack full of corn slung over his shoulder to feed the hogs.

Mammy and Pappy were neither the village pets nor country hicks who couldn't prize beauty. Most of all, we didn't behave like some Negroes who humbled themselves before white folks, bowing and scraping with their hats in their hands.

Dignified? Yes.

Arrogant? No.

We lived a simple life squirreled up on New Harmony Road, where we sharecropped, but Pappy and the boys also worked at the sawmill to make ends meet. Our place sat on a patch of ground large enough for the chickens and geese to run free. But our larger critters dotted and pranced behind corral fencing of various designs. We tended to five hogs, two horses, four mules, and two milk cows. Except for where we grew vegetables and yellow roses, Mammy kept the yard swept clean. Her sweeping broom stood right beside the rocking chair. The old kettle, where she made soap and boiled the clothes, sat near the door. At one end of the house, Pappy stacked the woodpile high. Wood stoked the cookstove; coal fueled the fireplace and potbelly stove, both of which kept us warm during the winter.

A fireplace dominated the cabin's large front room where Mammy cooked on a wood stove, whose flue pipe ran into the fireplace chimney. We took our meals in that room, and Neddy and Joshua slept there. Eventually, Pappy built them another space so they would have more privacy. Mammy and Pappy roosted next to the front room while Lena, Fannie, and I occupied the shed room.

Unlike farmsteads in other small towns in those parts of South Carolina that some folks call the "sticks," our place was charming. Our cabin wasn't an unpainted or unkept lean-to, our barn didn't require timbers to steady it, and we didn't leave the fields cluttered with dead corn or tobacco stalks. Mammy and Pappy said the Demmings insisted that their sharecroppers toe the line. And unlike other nearby villages, the buildings in New Harmony were well kept, too. They weren't unpainted, the warehouses weren't rickety, and the streets weren't weedy. Town folks didn't plaster advertisements on every post or building with enough wood to hold a piece of paper, and folks in New Harmony lived in time-mellowed houses nestled under oak trees, guarded by picket fences that protected private gardens. We had shops filled with sweets like peanut brittle, jawbreakers, licorice, gingersnaps, and homemade sweet potato pies. Stores sold pickles that you could pick from a barrel. The square and park downtown were well-tended—professional and volunteer gardeners maintained a tremendous variety of flowers, trees, and shrubs. The Demmings insisted on that, and they made sure New Harmony was charming, clean, and perfect.

New Harmony and its surroundings were beautiful, but even besieged by such beauty, nothing was as lovely as the Big House.

FOUR

The Big House: Missus and a Snake in a Dress

Candy's mammy's pappy was one of the wealthiest men in South Carolina, and the Big House was part of his treasure. So, Pleasant Bluff Plantation had been in Miss Ophelia's family for as long as cruelty had masqueraded as chivalry and strutted as honor in South Carolina. Ophelia and Hollis Demmings kept to the family's traditions, which also included having a small brood of two children—Candy and her knuckle-head brother, Floyd. But Candy would soon shift her position and become the knee-baby. Her mammy was in the family way.

One day, Miss Ophelia sent her colored gal, Marlene, to the cabin to fetch Mammy. Back then, Marlene probably weighed a hundred pounds soaking wet and was no bigger than a bar of soap after a good day's washing. As she stood before Mammy, who was hanging clothes on the clothesline, Marlene tried to catch her breath. She huffed and puffed like a train engine, but she didn't want to end being a fox forced to eat a mess of yellowjackets, so she said,

"Miss Lula, Miss Ophelia axes me come fetch yuh. She gots sump'tem that be's mighty important."

"Tell her I'll come de'reckly . . . soon as I git done hangin' these-here clothes," Mammy said as she reached for another one of my print dresses.

Marlene shot Mammy a look that was as rare for her as a hen cutting teeth. Most times she'd crack in her shoes and cut and run, but the weight of her task demanded that she cut to the last row, and she was hell-bent for leather.

"Nah, that won't do, Miss Lula," Marlene said, pursing her lips. "Yuh gots tuh come *right now* . . . 'foe two shakes of a sheep's tail, 'cause Miss Ophelia done told me over and over: 'Now, yuh make plenty sho' her comes right away.' Now, y'all knows how Miss Ophelia is."

"Tarnation. For the life of me, whut be so important? My word, it ain't like we burning' daylight," but Mammy turned toward the house and yelled,

"Fannie, finish hangin' these-here things."

Fannie ran to Mammy's side, grabbed her apron, took the blue and white lard can filled with clothespins, and started hanging clothes before Mammy reached the swinging gate.

Off they went.

With her cornrows cinched tight to her head, Marlene strode forward, swinging her arms and slicing the air like two butcher knives. She walked as if those yellowjackets she'd avoided earlier had stung her in the hind parts. Mammy tried to keep up, but she soon gave up. Marlene stepped like a wild woman who wouldn't have known what *Whoa!* meant if somebody screamed in her direction.

When Mammy returned, peakedness veiled her.

"Whut's the matter?" I asked.

"Come. Sit by me for a spell," she said from the front porch steps.

"You all right, Mammy?"

"Oh, fine as rain," she said. "Lemme tell yuh whut Miss Ophelia wanted." She stroked the side of my head, and she surveyed my face when she said,

"I don't wants yuh tuh fret none. Yuh hear?"

"Yessum."

"When I gits to the Big House, Miss Ophelia sittin' in the parlor, wrapped up lac'uh papoose—her face, the only thang pokin' from under the covers, lookin' mighty poorly too. Yuh could'ah knocked me over wid a feather 'cause Marlene ain't say one word 'bout Miss Ophelia's condition. So I axes her, 'Yuh seen Doc James, Miss Ophelia?'

"'He just left,' she said, but Doc James ain't gots no 'pinion 'bout whut be ailin' her. Her look up at me and say, 'Lula, please sit down.'

"Well, right then I knowed sump'tem be mighty wrong—when a white lady axes a colored woman tuh sit next to her—that's when they axes for part of yo' soul, yuh know. So I sucks in my breath a little bit, 'cause I figured the earth gon' tremble when she cracks her lips.

"When she let 'Lula' come cross her dry lips lac sweet butter, I knowed I has her pegged right. Then her say, her need me tuh do sump'tem for her. Oh, she say her ain't gots no right tuh axes me this, partic'ly since us ain't been close over the years. . . .'Tain't stop her none though.

"I shifted a little in the seat, but have yuh ever seen them chairs that look like they done sprouted wings on they sides?"

"Yessum."

"Well, I sits way back, way back 'tween them wings.

"'Don't know how long this sickness gonna last,' Miss Ophelia say, but her knowed her gon' need some mo' help 'cause Marlene cain't do everythang her gon' need done.

"So, I axes her whut kinda help her reckon her gon' be needin'. Oh, her go all 'round the barn b'foe her ketches her senses at the front door."

"Whut her say?"

"Her say in August, Candy done gone off tuh that schoolhouse in Uh'lanta; only Floyd and Mr. Hollis in the house wid her now. Her misses Candy sump'em fierce, and her need somebody, a gal, tuh keep her company for a spell."

Mammy paused a bit to gauge my mood before she said, "Her wants yuh tuh come—yuh know, stay wid 'em in the Big House."

"Me? Whut'ja say?"

"I be's flabbergasted, but I wan't too walleyed tuh look her square in the eyes, and axes her whut Mr. Hollis say 'bout this.

"'Don'tcha worry 'bout him.' Her say Mr. Hollis thanks the extra help gon' be good, but I tells her I ain't know if'n yo' pappy gons like the idea—yuh bein' a youngin and all.

"Then curiousness slapped me hard upside my head. Miss Ophelia reached out from under her blanket and . . . her took my hand."

Then Mammy started talking about Miss Ophelia's hands. Back then,

I didn't know what she meant. Only as an adult could I imagine Miss Ophelia's hands, pale and frail, reaching out from under the blanket and taking a-holt of Mammy's hand. As an adult, I understood that it wasn't the frailty that made Mammy jump with surprise—she jumped because of Miss Ophelia's direct-and-front-door tenderness. 'Cause back then, work had been the only lopsided solidarity Mammy had seen between white and colored women. White women demanded that she wash their clothes, mother their children, clean their houses, and fix their food. She had known of no other kind of sanctioned union until their eyes met.

"I figure 'twas her need, and not her wantin', that prodded her tuh take my hand—let her cross over . . . you know, cross the color line that done always smothered respect and decency tuh colored folks.

"She still had a-holt of my hand when I tells her, 'Jake not gon' like it. I cain't promise, but I axes him.'

"She thank me and tell me I 'minds her of my mammy. I leaves wid my head buzzin' all the way here, but I couldn't help wonderin' out loud, Whut Miss Ophelia knowed 'bout my Mammy? Whut any white person knowed 'bout any colored person?"

"Does I haf tuh live wid them?"

"Now, don't fret. It's gon' be all right."

"You sho', Mammy?"

"Sho'. Gon' be all right," she said, hugging me. "'Sides, 'pends on whut yo' pappy gon' say."

Evening twilight crawled toward darkness, but Mammy waited until we had started dessert before she let the shoe drop and told Pappy and the others. Peach cobbler should've clued them that something earth-shattering was forthcoming. We only had dessert to celebrate special occasions or after Sunday dinner. And just before we mashed the last crumbs of flakiness between fork prongs, Mammy started telling everybody the story. But in the middle of Mammy's tale, Pappy jumped to his feet and set to pacing like a caged tiger wanting to go somewhere but couldn't. He looked at me, then Mammy, and then paced some more. Back and forth, back and forth, before he asked,

"How long this be for?"

"'Til her feelin' better," Mammy said. "Almos' time for her youngin tuh come."

He stopped pacing, and this was one of the times I remember hearing my pappy say the word "cracker." He turned to us and said,

"Crackers ain't got no kinda heart. Sometime I even wonder if blood runs in they veins. Same as yuh washin' her clothes—If'n us says no, then us ain't got no way tuh make ends meet, got no place tuh live."

"Nah, Jake. Her say us ain't got'tuh do this; her ain't gon' make no trouble," Mammy insisted. Pappy tightened his eyebrows, grabbed the straps of his bib overalls, and said, "I 'pose yuh believes that. Whut her or her no-good husband ever done for us? Made livin' in New Harmony a livin' hell, is all," which set him to pacing again.

"Jake, maybe if'n us helps this-here time, thangs might git mo' better. 'Sides, yuh know all that done happened tuh her." But Mammy's caring forced him to turn, fix his gaze on her, shove his hands into his pockets, and say,

"Woman, yuh must be crazy as a betsy bug. I ain't care whut done happened tuh her. Ever seen a redneck done anythang for us coloreds? *Have yuh?*" This time, Pappy raised his voice. I could count on one hand the number of times Pappy raised his voice to Mammy. This news had pushed his uneasiness and worry into an overpowering rage. He was hotter than a goat's behind in a pepper patch. Veins stuck out from his neck, and the one in the middle of his forehead began beating right fast. Even Pappy's eyes glowed red hot as anger crammed wind into his jaws.

"Everythang that means sump'em tuh us, they gots tuh have, tuh use up, and then chunk it back tuh us when they done sapped all the life out of it."

"She gon' be fine."

But anger forced him to speak way faster than any hummingbird flapping its wings in retreat. I had never seen Pappy catch such a fit.

"How yuh know for sho'? Got all them redneck boys up yonder—don't thank much 'bout no colored women, no ways. Whut'ja thank they gon' care 'bout our child? Whut 'bout old man Hollis? Yuh know whut they says 'bout him: soon as kill one of us as he'd kill a hog. Man hates us so much—he gots that sickness, that disease that all of 'em ketches, that creeping crud. He full of it! Then again—nah, he ain't caught no disease. His sorry ass done been lac that all his damn life."

Had never heard Pappy cuss. *Ever!*

"Whut kinda man cain't protect his own?" Water started building up in his right eye, and he left on out of there, with that night's darkness having consumed him fully.

Mammy and I strolled to the Big House the next day.

Pappy was nowhere in sight. I reckon he couldn't bear seeing me leave, you know. Joshua, Neddy, and Fannie acted like I was headed off to the jailhouse or something. Lena cried straight out. But even with their moping, I thought it was a right pretty day. Birds scampered and flew off into the morning sun at each hinted menace. The wind rustled tree branches and set leaf colors of amber, russet red, lemon, and brown to flounce against the blue Carolina sky. The autumn wind hit my face and blew the two braids Mammy had plaited, each accented with bright yellow bows. They matched the barrette Mammy had slapped across my head. My pea-green cotton dress sported little bitty yellow daisies, and white crocheted lace edged the white collar. I felt terrific, almost choked chock-full of excitement, that October morning. I longed for White Candy's friendship, but Marlene was there, and I felt less worried knowing I wasn't gon' be the only colored person in their house.

As we approached, it shone in a grove of trees, full of the glory folks said came with being painted white. Like always, we knocked on the back door. Marlene opened it, and Mammy instructed her to protect me before Marlene closed the door to familiarity.

As a child, I couldn't appreciate what I had walked into. Only as an adult did I understand what I saw that October morning. From the advantages of age and from that perspective, if anyone had doubts about this family's position, their wealth and status, crossing the threshold quickly settled those. The white marble imported from Italy stamped these folks rich as all get-out. A serpentine staircase hung in the air and emptied onto an alabaster floor, sparking visions of gussied-up ladies descending the staircase's red-draped treads and risers. Most folks would never behold a house with such tall ceilings or see such beautiful wood floors. A dazzling design of dark and light pieces of wood edged the floor, enshrining luxurious carpets.

I felt tiny in there. Our cabin could've fitted into their living and dining rooms, and the Demmingses would still have ample space to swing tons of cats. But as we made our way to where Miss Ophelia sat, questions consumed me.

"Whut's that?" pointing to a shiny glass thing hanging from the ceiling.

"They calls that a crystal chandelier," Marlene said. I had never seen anything like it. From it, aided by the morning's shifting sunlight, red, green, blue, and yellow fought and lost their places on walls that felt like silk and shined as if the moon had kissed them real light-like. When we reached the living room, the fireplace, standing at one end, had this bright, shiny stone all around it, and when I felt its smoothness, I asked Marlene,

"What these curly-head women made out'ah?"

"That mantle, they brung from way over yonder someplace—made from whut'cha call, alabaster marble." I peeked inside the fireplace's firebox.

"It sho' is big!"

"Big uh'nuf tuh burn a quarter-cord of wood all at once."

Leaving the living room, we entered the dining room. The table, which sparkled like the glistening crystal ball in its center, had at least twenty chairs sitting around it. Chandeliers, smaller yet identical to the one in the entryway, hung from the ceilings of the living and dining rooms. The ceilings were adorned with designs resembling sweetbriar, wild jasmine, and winding vines as graceful as Spanish moss in the breeze. I asked Marlene what they were.

"Oh, them thangs. They calls 'em medallions. They's made from plaster—the stuff they puts on the wall so they can paint," she said. Looking down at the delicate patterns in the floor beneath her feet, she added,

"That be's a medallion, too, but all them made from cherry, maple, and walnut."

One was in the living room, but the one in the dining room—what Marlene said doubled as a ballroom—was even grander, stretching out into the room with its swirls and loops to suggest it was meant for twirling gowns and dancing feet. Prettiest things I'd ever seen.

The dining room had two doorways. One led to the kitchen, and the other to a hallway. Across the hall, a library overflowed with books stacked to the ceiling. In the sitting room, called the parlor, Miss Ophelia sat propped up in one of the wing chairs Mammy spoke of. I reckon she had a chill because a fire blazed in the fireplace, and I took to sweating like a sinner in church.

The fireplace's carved black eagles, perched and staring, protected the painted image of a little girl about five years old that hung above the mantel. I wondered who she was, but I turned my attention to Miss Ophelia. She was heavy with child, and she acted like it sho' wan't agreeing with her. I thought she looked like she was at death's door with her pasty white skin and lips that looked like they hadn't had a drop of water on them in weeks. Thank God she ain't smell, bless her heart.

Miss Ophelia had been dozing, and her eyes, resembling the shape of almonds, peeked out from under their lids. She pert near looked as if a Chinese man had been kin. She motioned for me, but I was almost scared to approach, the way she looked nestled between those wings.

Caution guided my legs.

When I reached her chair, it seemed she couldn't whip a gnat! Yeah, she was feeble all right, frail as a newborn kitten, and she spoke only in a faint whisper that sounded like a purr. I swallowed, and with courage by the throat, I leaned in closer.

"Margaret, I'm so glad you've come. Thank you."

Then she smiled.

Maybe she ain't that bad after all, I thought, but I reckoned, *she's being all kind and stuff 'cause she know she on death's door, and she don't wanna go 'foe her maker all mean and hateful.*

"Margaret, you'll be stayin' wid Marlene."

Turning toward Marlene, she licked her lips where a desert had grown and parted them enough to say, "Marlene, show Margaret where tuh put her things," then her lips' harsh dryness turned into the brightness of a smile.

"Join me when you've finished, and we'll get acquainted."

"Yessum," I said, then sprinted to follow Marlene.

We climbed the back staircase to the attic, and I placed my belongings in the corner of the room. It was spacious but it didn't come close in size to the parlor where we left Miss Ophelia.

"Whew! It be's mighty hot and stuffy up here," I said, which caused Marlene to cut her eyes at me right quick-like because children were to be seen and not heard. Yeah, I had said enough to make the wind gather up in her jaws, but she held her temper and didn't unleash a storm.

I scanned the room and admired its sparseness. Marlene had placed a brass bed up against the wall and dressed it with an elegant quilt that had intricate patterns. A nightstand, holding a vase stuffed full of flowers and a kerosene lamp, sat next to her shiny bed. A great big wardrobe stood opposite that, and a rocker had found a sunny spot right before the window. Marlene had one of those carpets that was similar to those downstairs. It splattered color on the floor in front of the bed.

Then, Marlene took me back to sit with Miss Ophelia, who seemed in better spirits. I thought I had caused her spirits to rise, but I still didn't know why she hankered to have me at the Big House. I mustered up my courage and asked,

"Miss Ophelia, why yuh wanna brang me here tuh be wid yuh?"

That first smile gon' be the last one I'm gonna get out of her, I thought, but she fooled me and smiled again.

"Unlike Mr. Hollis, I realized your deep friendship wid Candy. I 'pose having yuh here is like havin' a piece of Candy again."

"Why y'all sends her off tuh Uh'lanta then?"

Now, I knew better than that! Ain't 'posed to be talking to no grown folks like that. I could hear Mammy now: "If'n I done told'cha once, I done told'cha twice . . ."

"I see why Candy liked yuh so much," and then, leaning forward in her chair, she said, "Yuh're a smart one, you are." But her weakness forced her to shimmy back in between those wings, and with a sigh, she said, "Sendin' Candy there was Mr. Hollis's idea, not mine, child."

"Whut's the matter? Mr. Hollis, he don't like Candy?"

I did it again, flappin' my gums when I wasn't supposed to—it was my nature, and Mammy wouldn't have found enough willow switches to use if she suspected any hint of what she called "being sassy." But when I was ten, driving swarming bees through a snowstorm, with a switch, was easier than closing my trap.

"No, child. He adores her," she said. "That's what the Demmingses do for all their girls. They all attend boardin' schools when they're 'bout her age."

I pointed to the picture hanging above the fireplace and asked, "They send her, too?"

An abrupt no slammed that door.

After she asked me to sit down, we talked for a long time. Occasionally, I'd go to the kitchen, adding hot water to a bowl to moisten towels. They kept her forehead warm, and she liked that. Walking back and forth provided relief to me, too. All of her gum-beating wore on my brain. Miss Ophelia talked constantly, and eventually, I felt she pried too much. She wanted to know *everything*—she wanted to know how Mammy and Pappy met, those private and special things, and I thought that stuff was none of her business. She needed to be schooled by somebody with mother wit. They would've told her, "You ain't got no dawg in the fight and no horse in the race." Mammy had taught me better, and I thought Miss Ophelia needed better manners.

Hope I ain't got'tuh stay here long crawled up in my head when I got ready to climb into bed that night, but the image of the little white girl over the mantel fought its way above the chatter of my thoughts. I asked Marlene about her.

"Is she one of them secrets, Marlene?"

She rolled over, putting her back toward me.

"Marlene," I said in a loud whisper. She faced me and said, "That be's they first daughter. Her name Selma."

"Where her at?"

"Dead."

"When? How her die?" I asked, but that was one too many questions, and my violation of the "speak when spoken to" rule caused her to raise her voice to the pitch of anger.

"*Gal.* Go tuh sleep and stop *axin'* so many *questions!*"

Years would pass before the truth revealed itself.

⸺ ◦•◦ ⸺

One morning, about three weeks later, the house buzzed with activity. Mr. Hollis scampered around, talking about summoning Doc James because Miss Ophelia was in labor. He flew out of the house, leaving Marlene and me to tend to Miss Ophelia; however, Marlene banished me, saying, "Child, you underfoot; go on outside and watch for Doc James and Mister." But even from a distance, the sound of Miss Ophelia squealing unnerved me, reminding me of hogs at slaughtertime. I waited and waited for them to arrive, but her screams grew louder and to such a pitch that fear made me run to fetch Mammy.

Neddy and Lena's yelling announced my arrival before my feet hit the porch steps.

Mammy came running out of the house.

"Lawd have mercy, child. Whut's the matter?"

"Miss Ophelia," I said, panting. "Her screamin' sump'tem fierce."

"'Bout time for her tuh deliver. Did they send for the doctor?"

"Yeah, but he ain't come yet. She won't stop screamin'."

"Where Marlene at?"

"Marlene's there, but . . . do her know whut tuh do?"

"Yeah, Marlene know whut tuh do."

But back then, I thought Marlene was slow upstairs, and because she couldn't pour piss from a boot with the directions stamped on the heel, I insisted.

"Mammy, yuh gots tuh come."

By the time I pulled Mammy up to the Big House, Mister and Doc James approached. As Mammy entered behind Doc James, some of the colored field hands started singing soothing hymns under Miss Ophelia's window. But soon after, her moaning got louder, drowning out the peacefulness of "Deep River." Then, Miss Ophelia's moans turned into full-throated wails that made the hair on the scruff of my neck stand erect—just like at slaughter time.

Then the baby cried.

When I saw Miss Ophelia two days later, a rosiness flushed her cheeks, now that the baby breathed on her own. They named her Isabel, and I liked the sound of it, but it ain't suit her nary a bit. It pained me to think this, but she was uglier than a lard bucket full of armpits. Itty bitty eyes set right close together on a face that was small and pointy. The gal's head, bald as a jaybird, held no glow, and her complexion fared worse, resembling a newborn mouse or grapes left in the sun too long. Nah, her skin resembled molted snakeskin, all wrinkly from dryness. Yeah, she was as ugly as a snake in a dress.

Can you imagine that?

I stood ready that November morning to leave those crazy white folks behind. I yearned for home, but what could I do? As a child, I had no say. Moreover, I didn't understand my value. I failed to realize that once the Demmingses had me, it would be hard for them to release me. And sure enough, Miss Ophelia asked Mammy to let me stay a while longer so I could help look after her snake-in-a-dress.

FIVE

The Big House: Lawd, Them Men

Mr. Hollis didn't seem to care what happened to either Miss Ophelia or their snake-in-a-dress. During my time there, he never held the child, and I never saw him plant a kiss of affection on Miss Ophelia's forehead like Pappy did on Mammy's. His disaffection seemed even more meaningful when I noticed how he watched Marlene, fancying her like one of his prized fillies. The way Mr. Hollis latched his gaze onto her behind, I thought he would start sniffing 'cause he slobbered over her like a pig over slop. But one day, he went too far, and as Pappy would say, his shenanigans "sho' weren't in keepin' wid his redneck ways."

On leaving Miss Ophelia's room that day, I stopped on the landing at the top of the stairs just before I went downstairs to get some water. I viewed Mr. Hollis and Marlene from above as the two of 'em embraced. He had her squirming up against the wall with his hand down her dress, playing with her titties. She acted like he had slathered a glob of butter on a stack of wheat cakes. When his eyes drifted up to meet mine, he shimmied his hand from his stomping ground as if it belonged to a herd of turtles. He put his fingers under his nose and took a long sniff as he smiled brazenly at me.

Marlene, sweating like a Jezebel in an A.M.E church, glanced up at me before staring down at her feet. She looked like she was trying to back into the wall to disappear. I guess she was worried about me telling on her. But who was I gon' tell?

Besides, Mammy had already told me, "Whutever them folks does up yonder, ain't none of yo' business." Now those words I took to heart.

So, it didn't make me no nary a mind if Mr. Hollis smiled, parting his lips like he used a razor to cut loose the bees that had been making honey in his mouth. But after Mister's foolishness, I wondered if most white men sniffed after colored women. I had caught hints of that from Floyd, too, and had to contend with his shenanigans.

He was three years older than me, and it sho'nuf seemed Floyd had taken some cues from his daddy. He was full of smiles, followed me around, and always seemed to be ogling me. I tell y'all the truth: Before Floyd put a mouthful of food in his trap or fixed his mouth to say "Good morning" to his mammy, he'd throw me a sideways smile. His eyes chased after me, and when I bent down, I had a pair of peepers snooping up my dress. I learned to stoop when I scooped up something from the floor.

The boy was trifling, too; he didn't lift his hands to do nary a thing. He expected me to wait on him hand and foot. I tell you, he'd look up at me like I was a slice of his favorite pie and say,

"Margaret, brang me a glass of water." I guess he thought my name was Marlene and I had to wait on him like she did.

He was a spoiled no-count, and while he was slicker than snot on a doorknob, he was also a tall, handsome white boy.

***

Miss Ophelia fussed over her new youngin, but I spent plenty of time tending to her and that baby. When Miss Ophelia felt stronger, she spent pert' near all day sitting in the chair with the wings, reading. One day, curious, I asked,

"Whut'ja readin', Miss Ophelia?"

"Uncle Tom's Cabin," she said.

"Whut it about?"

Lawdy, that's when she started reading to me, and I was in high cotton, happy as I could be. I'd sit on the floor and listen to those stories. They fed the desire that God had stamped in me long ago; I loved words like a cat loves a cream jug. Yeah, I lapped it up, but I ain't 'preciate how that novel talked about colored folks. But I beared those parts in the same way I tolerated the mean and sneaky white folks living in these parts. New Harmony had plenty, and I wondered if Miss Ophelia hankered after "those kinds" of people and had a mind like theirs. Was that why she read the book? No matter. I loved to listen to the magic found in storytelling. Besides, being read to in that way reminded me of how White Candy read from her schoolbooks, but Miss Ophelia did more than that. She encouraged me to become lettered.

I took a shine to Miss Ophelia. The gossipers rumored her hateful, but if she was, she hid that from me. When she finished reading *Uncle Tom's Cabin*, I did what I ain't supposed to—I ran my mouth again. I asked,

"Miss Ophelia, why folks thank yuh so mean? Some of 'em is really scared of yuh—why is that?"

"By my design. Child, I haf tuh play my role. In the South, we haf tuh give folks what they expect. New Harmony is a stage, and my behavior becomes part of the show, my dear. Don't ever believe people are who they appear tuh be on the surface. Did yo' Mammy tell yuh not tuh judge a book by its cover?"

"Yessum."

"Well, life is full of contradictions. Do yuh understand that word?"

"Yessum. Somebody do one thang, but they believes sump'em different, sump'em else. They's wishy-washy. Is that right?"

"Exactly. I might look mean on the surface, but it dud'en mean that's who and what I am. My folks owned this plantation, and I remember plenty—I've lived long uh'nuf tuh understand the sins of the father. I do what I can tuh right some of the wrongs, but this is the South, Margaret. Colored and white folks haf tuh be careful." She took me by the hand, smiled, and said, "Let this be our little secret."

"Yessum."

"Most white folks are wolves in sheep's clothing, but I'd rather think I'm uh sheep in wolf's clothing. That's our secret, too."

"Yessum. But is Mr. Hollis a wolf or a sheep?"

"Cain't pigeonhole him . . . Child, how can yuh take hold and strangle the wind? It picks up and blows accordin' tuh its fancy. But don't worry 'bout him," she said.

At that moment, I felt she protected me from Mr. Hollis. He was a mystery—especially when I thought about what I *hadn't* seen between them—affection—and the way Mr. Hollis hated Negroes but played with Marlene's titties. That stumped me, and I wondered why somebody like her married a redneck like him. So I asked Marlene one day,

"Why Mr. Hollis hate colored folks so much? Us ain't done nuthin' tuh him."

"Gator," she whispered.

"Who he?" I asked, matching her whisper. I sensed this was a touchy subject and bordered on the forbidden.

Standing with one hand holding a rag (clean, but dingy from the cleaning it had seen), Marlene threw her finger up to her mouth with the other. Her eyes got right big, and she shook her head—slow, like the guts in the grandfather clock she stood beside. She marked this as something to whisper about.

"'Foe Gator he the salt of the earth, but after Gator done whut he done, sump'tem dies inside him."

"Whut Gator do?"

"Bet not say. When yuh's older, I tells you. When yuh's older."

She walked away.

Whatever Gator had done, it didn't seem to have infected Miss Ophelia, but if she had the disease, hating colored folks like Pappy talked about, she concealed it. And I was sure of one thing: she loved her children and was an excellent mother, even if Floyd didn't benefit from her caring.

Floyd walked and talked too much like his daddy, and I tried hard to stay away from him—to feed him and all those men (especially Kearns) with a long-handled spoon. However, every which way I turned, he was underfoot, smiling. Something didn't seem right about how he sniffed after me. And just when I thought I had adjusted to the situation, Floyd's flirtations inched toward aggression.

Marlene had sent me out to get the wash off the clothesline. As I gathered the clothes, a funny feeling came over me—like somebody was close by, watching. As I turned, I bumped into something.

The pile of clothes I carried shielded my eye, and a hand pushed them away from my face.

Floyd.

As I gazed into this good-looking white boy's face, he cocked his head and smiled. He whispered,

"Where yuh goin', Missy?"

I didn't notice that Kearns's ole sorry youngin, Timmy, had come up behind me. Before I could answer, he pushed me into Floyd, and I dropped the clothes. Floyd grabbed the back of my head and held my face in his chest. I couldn't breathe and wrestled to free myself, but his size and strength locked me there, and Timmy encouraged him with,

"Yuh's got the little pickaninny now!"

While Timmy mocked me, he pulled me by the shoulders and spun me around, doing what Floyd had done. Then Floyd took over. They shoved me back and forth like a sack of potatoes and I started to cry. Timmy kept saying, "Come here, little pickaninny," like he'd call a wayward chicken, and Floyd wheedled, "Come on, gal. Why don'tcha play nice?"

Marlene must have heard the commotion, because she rushed to the back door, and on seeing my predicament, she ran and got Miss Ophelia, who came flying up between us.

"What are yuh boys doin'? Leave this gal alone." Pushing them aside, she said, "She's only a child."

"Oh, Ma, we jest playing."

"She's not a plaything! What am I gon' do wid you boys?" Miss Ophelia said, grabbing me by the hand.

"Did'ja see the little yeller nigga squirm?" Timmy said, busting up laughing and poking Floyd in the ribs as Miss Ophelia pulled me into the house.

She dried my tears and got me to blow my nose. Miss Ophelia wouldn't even let Marlene touch me, and I appreciated how gentle she was with me. Afterward, I tried harder to avoid the men in the Big House.

I felt that Floyd's teasing was more like a game children resorted to when they didn't have the words to say, "I like you." I had seen enough boyish adoration to know the difference between what Floyd did and the downright nastiness of rednecks. I figured Floyd's playfulness had gone catawampus because of Timmy's presence. But that country-as-cornbread hick named

Timmy was another matter. As an adult, I thought he tried to cut his teeth on intimidation, but back then, he thought terror was a plaything. So, as a fledgling redneck, he was an unskilled country bumpkin and was as unsuccessful at intimidation as a one-legged duck swimming in circles in search of anything it could put in its beak. His sorry daddy, Kearns, had even failed to teach him the fine points of being an intimidating redneck.

Before I got into their bed that night, I knelt beside it and prayed God would keep me safe. And if something happened to Miss Ophelia, I vowed to leave the Big House as fast as I could.

Sunday, as a day of praise, also provided a respite from the Big House. Miss Ophelia encouraged me to go home so I could go to church with my family. We'd pile in the wagon, and off we'd go into town, passing deer and jackrabbits jumping across the fields and squirrels heading to the tops of trees.

I'd run into Miss Hillary, and her husband, Mr. Collins, almost every Sunday after services. She always wanted me to visit her, but I'd tell her, "I'm still helpin' Miss Ophelia, but soon as I's done, I'm gonna come." But I wasn't so sure about visiting after Joshua took-and-told me that Mr. Collins was an undertaker. I ran to Fannie and asked, "Whut'cha thank it be like livin' wid a man who fixes the dead for the grave? Could'ja kiss somebody like him?" Lawd, I couldn't 'magine him coming home and touching me with his 'I-just-rubbed-dead-folks' hands. So I decided to feed Mr. Collins with a long-handled spoon too.

As we headed to the wagon after services, we couldn't go a foot without someone saying, "Howdy do, Miss Lula." Everybody loved Mammy, and besides that, folks praised her as one of the best cooks on this side of Hampton County. Mammy's Sunday meals would make po' men whimper and rich men beg 'cause her food tasted so good. How good? Folks said, "If'n yuh put it on top of yo' head, yo' tongue would slap your brains out the way, tryin' to get to it." She'd fry up some chicken, and it would make you wanna holla! And don't say a word about her collard greens; she'd chop them right fine and cook them with ham hocks—served that with some

Southern-style potato salad and hot water cornbread. You had to wash it down with her lemonade, and then you'd have something too precious for rich folks. Never any store-bought bread or stuff like that. She made everything from scratch. And you hadn't had apple cobbler until you had a piece of Mammy's, and don't think you gonna eat only a slice, either. Wouldn't happen, as Pappy would testify, because he'd stuff himself every Sunday and would have to rest on the porch for a spell. Yeah, he'd be laid out, full as a tick on a coon hound. I hated when that happened 'cause it signaled my return to the Big House and folks who were as crooked as a po' dog's hind leg.

Mammy and Lena usually walked me back, and I'd see Marlene looking through the screen door; I'd hug Mammy before entering the Big House under the cloak of darkness. But one Sunday evening, when I returned alone, I found myself wrapped deep in the thoughts of an eleven-year-old. When I was halfway there, more confusion spun me around.

It was Floyd.

He stood smiling like a piece of sunshine had gotten trapped between his teeth. Kindness etched his face, and he appeared even more handsome to me and no longer the person I once considered pig snot.

I smiled.

We felt the heat of spring's night-shifting sky as it spread dryness across the meadow and found ill humor croaked up by tree frogs desperate for rain. I repeated what some old folks said—"Look like it wants tuh rain; tree frogs done gone tuh hollerin'—but talking about those frogs and the rain's absence didn't make the jitters leave my legs.

So, a slice of quiet wedged up alongside us, but I could sense he reeked of curiousness. And so, reinforced with the piece of sunshine he still held, curiosity found sufficient courage to fall into his arms and brush its interest against me, furtively. He spoke of the dreams held by a fourteen-year-old white boy, but for a eleven-year-old colored girl, it was like he jabbered about going to the moon. I didn't understand and I didn't want to know.

When we got near the back porch, he brushed his thumb against my cheek, which caused me to pull away. But it was Mr. Hollis who attacked from the darkness. He struck Floyd, saying, "Stay away from this nigga gal, boy."

Another whack sent Floyd to the ground, forcing him to listen real good to what his daddy had to say:

"She's a near-white nigga. Boy, yuh got'tuh be harder on them kind. Cain't have her 'round here thankin' she's like us. Cain't yuh remember that?"

Floyd leaped with youthful vigor but he lacked experience, which allowed his father to teach him the difference between being a man and a child. Mr. Hollis screamed, "She might be high in color, but she's still tar-brushed. You cain't be gettin' familiar wid no cream-colored niggas. It's ruinous to the others." With those words, Mr. Hollis expressed the nuances of the "do-what-I-say-but not-what-I-do" lesson.

"Yo' mother told me I needed tuh send you away, but I figured I need tuh reach down yo' throat and snatch this foolishness from the ruut." And that's what Mr. Hollis did until Floyd relinquished his belligerence.

Even at eleven, I had learned plenty from white folks, and Mr. Hollis's hateful words resembled ditch water poured in a porcelain vessel. I chucked it out. So, with my bowl emptied and cleansed, I went to Floyd. I had seen plenty of brutality before; it always made me sad, and I wondered if his daddy's fist had cracked Floyd's fragile vessel. Upon seeing his bruised and swollen face, I attempted to hold his scratched-up hands in mine. He jerked away and grabbed the fit he should have caught when his daddy smacked the sunshine from between his teeth. The beating had implanted his daddy's beliefs, and the word *nigga* rose in his throat and flew from his mouth like I've never witnessed before or since. Floyd's wind direction had sho'nuf changed, and it slapped me hard.

Anyway, I started understanding the differences between white folks and colored folks better. Miss Ophelia might have read to me, but she was white, and I was colored. She lived in the Big House, and I lived in the cabin. I liked her, and I thought she liked me—in the way she could feel about any colored gal. On top of that, I realized that I couldn't expect any semblance of respect from the men. Fortunately, Floyd no longer sniffed after me like I was in heat and he had the cure, but I never told Mammy or Pappy the things Floyd had done. I didn't want Pappy in any kind of trouble. Mr. Hollis still sniffed after Marlene, though, and I was always the one to witness his shenanigans.

One day, Miss Ophelia sent me to find something she needed in one of their sheds. I felt spring's presence at every turn and enjoyed being outdoors. As I ventured from the Big House, squirrels pranced all over the place. The smell of farm life laced the air. It shifted from Marlene's freshly baked biscuits to the scents of mooing cows and oinking pigs.

As I walked to do Miss Ophelia's bidding, an old stray dog that had taken to begging was underfoot.

"Shoo," I said, watching him move as slowly as a possum toward the barn. I felt sorry for that old raw-boned dog who wore the color of lye soap on his body and bleached cotton on his paws. He was as snaggletoothed as a broke-tooth comb raked through too many burr heads.

When I got into the shed, a hint of sound drew my attention. *Just a coon or maybe a 'possum. Hope it ain't no rat,* I said to myself. The mere thought of rats and coons made me tremble. So I snuck around to take a careful peep, and when my eyes adjusted to the light, I saw something that made me tremble worse than those critters. The pink soles of a woman's feet appeared as I tiptoed a little closer, and . . .

Lord, I had stepped into a pile of trouble. Old man Hollis straddled Marlene—he jumped up and down and kept kissing Marlene with his plump lips. He had his britches down near his ankles. But without his britches up around his waist, his hind parts, hairy and exposed, held the color of an Easter lily. I watched him in wonderment. His persistent stroking, the rise and fall of his flat, but determined behind, was a shocking sight. I had seen horses do it and had watched rabbits jump on and fall right off. The rooster in the yard would run up on the hens and fly past. But I had never seen folks do it.

They were grunting and sweating, so they were earless to my cautious intrusion. Old Mr. Hollis got to talking as if he was out of his head, and Marlene got to squirming like she couldn't control herself. I froze 'cause I didn't know what to do. If I spoke, trouble would be upon my head. If I moved, my feet would reveal more than footprints on the dusty floor. But when I understood they would realize my presence no matter what I did, both of 'em started screaming; he began thanking Jesus for something, and she yelled straight out. I thought: *What's the fuss?*

But all their fussing unanchored me.

He noticed me first and rolled off Marlene, jumping to his feet like a jackrabbit and snatching his britches up around his thighs. Marlene kept lying there with that "I-done-been-caught-but-don't-know-what-to-do" expression on her face. He didn't even pull up his underwear to hide his ding-a-ling but stood with a stallion's pride; he grabbed it and shook it at me. I couldn't describe it because astonishment bound my mouth shut, but fear anchored me to the floor. He cut loose laughter that seemed to transform into a full-throated howl that I hadn't heard before or since, and he said,

"Gal, yuh bet not tell, or I'm comin' for yuh!"

He yielded to the call of nature and aimed his ding-a-ling, directing its flood at me, but I jumped out of the way and took off running. He chuckled and called me a scaredy-cat as I scrambled for the door.

I thought Marlene should be ashamed 'cause I sho' didn't think favorably of her after that. Their shed story happened on a Monday, and I couldn't get away to tell Fannie or ask for advice, but I figured I needed to escape the Big House. Allst I knew to do was to pray. So I prayed and prayed, asking the Lord for some assistance. (I remembered that word from when I first met Miss Hillary.)

Seems like the next thing I knew, Marlene's belly had grown big enough that there was no doubt about what she had been doing. Everybody talked about her during the summer of 1916, and they speculated that Mr. Hollis had sired another youngin. None of the womenfolks, except for Mammy, would associate with her.

Marlene got bigger and bigger by the week. I thought she would have twins but she didn't. In January 1917, Marlene had a boy she named Burton. She should've called him Snowflake 'cause he was as white as snow. Other than a bald head, he resembled Mr. Hollis, but looking like his daddy didn't give him an advantage. Mr. Hollis didn't claim the boy. How could he?

About a month after Marlene's what-I-done-in-the-dark-sho'-come-to-light story revealed itself, Floyd's antics reminded me of Mr. Hollis's attempt to snatch Floyd's desire for me from the ruut. As I walked past the parlor doors that day, Floyd stood talking to Timmy like he displayed a peacock's train.

"She so fetching," he said. "Skin as sweet as heavy cream. Her hair—boy, the wind catches it like pieces of velvet ribbon. Boy, when she walks, plumes of black velvet flounce in the breeze. Ain't no white gal temptin' lac that. I don't care 'bout her being colored—she's the purtiest thang I ever done seen. Every time I see her, sump'em—"

"Damn, I thought yo' daddy kicked some sense in yo' head. He ain't gon' let yuh—"

"What's a beatin'? He ain't gonna kill me. 'Sides, he cain't say a word. He daddied what Marlene—"

Miss Ophelia interrupted him, yelling his name from the sitting room, and I shook my head as I continued my chores.

My long-handled spoon hadn't worked with that fool. Although Floyd kept his distance, he had found the piece of sunshine he had lost one Sunday evening when his daddy thrashed it from his smile. His expression brightened when he saw me, and his eyes flitted after my skirt tail, giving me more to study about. I guess he thought he was Mr. Hollis and my name was Marlene.

Exhausted from dealing with those men, I resorted to praying. I prayed hard to get out from under all their foolishness. About a week or two after Floyd's revelation, God answered my prayers in the strangest way, and I felt full of guilt—'cause I figured it was my doing. I shouldn't have prayed like I did. They found Miss Ophelia lying on that cold marble floor at the bottom of the stairs.

Dead.

Tripped, perhaps, on the steps and broke her neck on the way down. Seemed mighty strange to me, though.

Was it Mr. Hollis's doing?

Or Floyd's?

On March 6, 1917, nine days before my birthday, I fretted over losing Miss Ophelia. When I ran home and told Mammy about Miss Ophelia, she didn't believe me, but when it sank in, she dropped to the ground like all the air had come out of her. Mammy went with me to the Big House to gather my things, and while Miss Ophelia had been good to me, I didn't want anything to do with those men. When we left that day, I promised myself I would never return, but I didn't know then that the Big House and its masters would always frame my life somehow.

Oh, folks came from way yonder for Miss Ophelia's funeral, but they didn't dare to fall out in the aisle of the white folks' church. After her passing, Marlene stayed under Mr. Hollis like a secondhand heifer. She finally got the bull's full attention, and I suspected he always got what he wanted from her. In the end, Marlene became the wet nurse for Miss Ophelia's Isabel while she nursed Burton. That is, until Mr. Hollis hauled off and sent that gal to be raised by Miss Ophelia's sister in Atlanta. From then on, he kept the gal in the shadows.

A few weeks after Miss Ophelia's funeral, I was walking home from the spring, weary from the heat that felt more like August. From a distance, I saw my brothers and sisters marveling at someone's fancy car, one only a few people had back then. As I approached the yard, a white man placed papers in his satchel, nodding and backing up like folks do when they're trying to escape. When he got into his car, he pointed it toward Hampton, leaving us to part the flurry of the car's dust with our hands.

When we threw back the screen door to enter the cabin, Mammy sat at the table, glancing at the papers in her hands. Pappy stood over her, scratching his head while Mammy wept. She wasn't having one of those sad crying fits; she courted another kind.

"Whut the matter?" I asked.

Mammy pulled herself together and said, "Miss Ophelia done left us one thousand dollars, the twenty acres of land what us farms, and the cabin."

"A thousand dollars?" Neddy asked.

"Cain'tja hear?" Joshua said, but I nudged him to hush up.

"Who that white man?" Fannie asked.

"Miss Ophelia's lawyer," Mammy said. "After he done read whut her say in her will, he say everythang be legal."

"Seem like Miss Ophelia 'preciated all the thangs Mammy's family done did for her and her family . . . she sho' liked yuh a whole heap, Margaret, and thought yuh's smart," Pappy said.

"She left sump'em for yuh, too." Mammy pointed to the corner of the room.

"Books!" I squealed. I couldn't read a lick, but I had a pile of books.

"That's jest the first of 'em. Miss Ophelia wants tuh make sho' yuh learnt tuh read," Pappy said.

Thank you, Jesus! I said to myself.

"Whut's them papers, Mammy?" Neddy asked.

"The deed for the land and the check Miss Ophelia done left."

"Well, Lula. Reckon this our forty acres and a mule."

"Huh?" Lena asked, looking up at me.

I shrugged my shoulders.

"Whut us gon' do wid all this money?" Joshua asked.

"Us gonna thank the Lawd. That's whut," Mammy said.

———— ⋅•⋅ ————

In early April 1917, I was in high cotton, having turned twelve on March 15th, but I didn't know how important 1917 would be. It had been a hard winter, and we were eager to plant our vegetable garden. Mammy believed we needed to have plenty of rabbit food, and since she felt we required vegetables year-round, she did a lot of canning. She filled her jars with our harvest of string beans, corn, beets, okra, tomatoes, peas, all kinds of other beans, potatoes (both sweet and white), and all sorts of greens.

That day, Eastern bluebirds sang and butterflies flounced as Lena and I helped Mammy get the vegetable beds ready. As I stooped over and planted some lettuce seedlings, I felt the sweat dampen my back. I thought some trickled down the inside of my thighs, but the shock on Lena's face and her pointing caused me to look down at my legs. Something red streaked my legs, and my faded print dress was spotted with bright crimson. I suspected death sniffed at my coattails, and I ran, yelling,

"Mammy! Mammy!"

"Whut's the matter?" Mammy asked, as Fannie bolted from the house.

"I'm bleeding tuh death!"

Fannie took one look at me, and she busted out laughing, which made me raving mad. I started crying in earnest, demanding, "Where this blood coming from?"

Fannie bent over laughing, but Lena shook her head in confusion.

"Mammy, make her stop laughin' at me . . . whut's wrong wid you?"

Mammy hugged me and held me tight.

"Yuh ain't dyin', baby," she said with a smile. "Yuh always been special, but yuh's real special now. Yuh's a woman."

If tenderness could have flown up in my heart, it did when she kissed me, wiped my face dry, and told me she and Fannie did the same every month. But Fannie blew Mammy's gentleness away, messed it all up when she opened up her fast mouth.

"Now yuh gots the curse. Bet not let no boys mess wid yuh; don't let 'em touch yuh," she said. "Yuh don't wanna end up like Miss Marlene."

Mammy waved Fannie into silence as she told her to take care of me; she kissed my cheek, and that was how I became a woman.

SIX

Hints of Love

Initially, shifting into womanhood felt the same; however, the significance of my new status as a budding woman and its meaning demanded some schooling. For one thing, I didn't realize some women hated the bloating, fatigue, and pain of their monthly "gift" because I never ached. I always felt special and complete. Lately I've been thinking that I will miss her when she dries up and I become a pullet again, having only memories of what magic I once produced.

When Pappy learned the news, I felt he treated me like I was betwixt and between. But for both him and Mammy, some of my features and habits still lingered and marked me as a child. Any discussions about taking company with a boy made them furrow their brows, and they said, "Yuh too young." Besides, they had made Fannie wait until she turned sixteen in 1915, and they allowed Jeremiah, Fannie's first knucklehead, to come around 'cause his family attended Calvary every Sunday like devoted churchgoing folks. But Lena snickered when he showed up, and I understood why. He resembled one of those wart toads.

None of us children could grasp why she liked him. Perhaps Jeremiah courted Fannie because what he saw in Fannie was what he coveted most for himself. Her long hair coiled neatly into loose, silky curls and fell to her shoulders without the aid of either a hot comb or curlers. Her thick strands of hair never became gnarled like wire, forcing her comb to cry, "Lawd, have mercy," but Jeremiah had a tender head and a gap-tooth comb because he had raked it through his burr head too many times. But I believed anybody with hair that kinky needed to cut it clean off. No one hankered to see countless naps balled up as tight as fists. The boy wore his hair too long. But bless his heart, those knots, each strung out in their own little row, were why the boy hankered after Fannie's curls. He wanted to feel them brush against his face and experience beauty. I use'ta say, "Please, please, cut that stuff off yo' head, boy." But nah, not him. Too holy for God's eyes, I suspected.

Yeah, you should'ah seen him strolling down the road, coming to court Fannie, looking like a long drink of water dipped in pitch, but I had sniffed out his intentions.

Jeremiah yearned to touch Fannie's cream-colored skin with his bright pink palms and feel its softness. He desired her delicate face, one molded into a perfect shape and holding the dainty features sculptured by divine hands.

Jeremiah longed for the moisture glistening on her flawless lips and skin to soothe his own. 'Cause honey, his skin was so dry—ash covered his arms, went down his long skinny legs and right onto his whopping feet and between his flared toes.

He craved all her perfection for himself.

And in his visits, he paid barefooted homage—couldn't find any shoes to fit those feet, I suspect. Can you imagine courting somebody who didn't even wear shoes? Feet coated with dust—and toenails long, full of dirt, and sharp as razors.

Lawdy!

Visualize his bright pink soles coming to see a cream-colored girl with perfect feet. 'Spect he wanted to put 'em next to some skin that the sight of pinkness wouldn't startle.

Even so, he was tar-brushed, the blackest boy I'd ever seen.

How black?

Shiny black, blue-black!

So black you couldn't tell where his jet-black hair stopped and where his face started. His skin color made the sight of his teeth throw blindness in eight different directions when he parted his blue-black lips to smile. But his eyeballs were two oversized dingy marbles; they didn't resemble the pearls, holding topaz centers dotted with onyx that blinked their wonder to the world.

And to top it all off, Jeremiah had blue gums, which Southerners believed made a bite from him lethal. So of course, he fancied Fannie! Her smile was bright but not garish, and her gums didn't suggest they held a hint of venom. I would hate to see their children if they tied the knot.

Lawd, help 'em!

Joshua and Neddy teased her to no end, but she ignored them and me, and I'm so glad she did. What did I understand 'bout color and race as a child?

Thank God I learned better.

Jeremiah treated Fannie right nice, but he never captured Fannie's heart. I knew he wouldn't because I had spied on her one day and had caught her kissing Robert down by the spring. Mammy and Pappy didn't care that she loved him, though. They didn't care for his folks, the Gardners. "Trash," they said, which meant the boy "ain't good uh'nuf for Fannie." Of course, Fannie thought otherwise and kept flashing her topaz-colored eyes in that boy's handsome face. Robert's good looks meant nothing to Pappy, who criticized him worse than Lena did Jeremiah. Pappy was even suspicious of Robert's eyes.

"The nigga gots green eyes," he said. "Them hard-tuh-look-at eyes. How yuh gonna trust some nigga wid green eyes?"

I giggled when he told Mammy, "Yuh know that Gardner boy ain't worth a peg-legged man on ice skates. He gots too much of that cracker in him."

I couldn't fathom why he said that and neither could Mammy—'cause he and Mammy could've passed for whites. She shook her head and said,

"Jake, yuh jest talkin' foolishness."

Pappy grabbed Mammy tight around her waist and said,

"He needs them pretty brown eyes like yourn," before pecking her on the cheek. Sometimes, they acted like children.

Fannie drooled over Robert, which meant she treated Jeremiah kind of bad. I reckoned she hoped he'd get the hint and leave her alone. He didn't, and clung to her like a needy puppy. He just *loved* himself some Fannie, but she still met Robert on the sly. And since Robert had bewitched her, I figured she'd better take the advice she had given me. She told me, "Yuh bet not let no boy touch yuh!" when I became a woman. And wiser folks would've cautioned her, too, saying, "Gal, stop this sneakin' 'round and actin' like yuh blind in one eye and cain't see out the other."

Marlene should've heeded that advice because, during the fall of 1917, she had gotten herself a big belly again. Now everybody, and I mean everybody, caught wind of her situation, and folks used some pretty powerful words to describe her. 'Cause folks with mother wit said, "If yuh make a mistake the first time, yuh can chalk it up tuh experience. But if'n yuh does it again, then it sho' nuf ain't no mistake; yuh 'tended tuh do it." Pappy said, "Marlene done made her bed . . . now her got'tuh lay in it." When the baby came in the spring of 1918, Pappy announced it was "'nuther boy, lookin' jest like old man Demmings." I couldn't help but feel sorry for her, but the grown folks didn't appear to have even a spoonful of pity. They kept saying, "Her made her bed. Now her has'tuh lay in it." But back then, getting a big belly sho' didn't figure into what I wanted for myself.

Reading and writing were my dreams, and after Miss Ophelia's gift of books, Pappy let Lena and me go to school when Lena was eight and I was twelve. My heart swelled with gratitude. I've never been as thankful for anything in my life. Rain or shine, we walked the three miles into town to learn from Miss Hillary. Mammy said she had seen no one like me when it came to schooling.

Because so much book-learning stuffed Miss Hillary's head and fancy words filled her craw, some folks might have thought she would be stuck on herself. But humbleness graced everything she did. "She's a blessing," folks said, because a school for colored children didn't exist until her arrival. The white folks had burned it down over something that only they could rationalize. Mammy was thirteen when that happened. When I cared for Miss Ophelia in the Big House, I heard Kearns remind Mr. Hollis that Mr. Hollis's daddy wanted to make sure the Negroes stayed unlettered. So, anybody with any sense praised Miss Hillary and what she brought to New Harmony.

She and her husband spun a bunch of changes. A new crop of grown folks and their children arrived from different parts of Hampton

County, Charleston, and Columbia. By 1920, a right smart section of Negroes settled near the church and school. They sprang from the Low Country, where the sweet odors of myrtles and cedars laced the air. While Upcountry folks deserted the perfumed forests of oak, hickory, and pine, they wouldn't find wild pea vines growing high as a horse's back in our parts of the state. These new arrivals came from places like Devil's Woodyard, Possums' Corners, Ketch-all, Shuck Pen Eddy, Weeping Fountain, Pea Ridge, Pigeon Point, Bishop's Fishpond, and Buzzards' Roost. They left streets with names like Mulatto Alley, Tin Can Alley, The Cherokee Path, Zigzag Alley, Pork Chop Lane, Pinch 'Em Slyly, Boo Boo Lane, and Devil's Racetrack. They told stories about splashing and playing around in Swimming Pens Swamp, Jawfish Creek, Bellyache Creek, Dry Creek, and Alligator Creek (which had no alligators). These settings became the scenes of their tales where dark deeds of murder and mysteries took place.

Miss Bessie and her family came from Pea Ridge, a barren place where only peas could thrive, and she became one of Mammy's friends when she arrived in New Harmony. Her daughter, Zora Mae, became my best friend, and we were tighter than the bark on a tree.

◦•◦

Zora Mae had the prettiest chocolate skin and a pair of shiny brown eyes that made you think only goodness rested behind them. She hadn't yet received what Fannie called "the curse," but I informed her of Fannie's warning. I wanted her to be prepared and told her my coming-of-age story.

Despite Zora Mae's friendship, I didn't reveal I had fallen head over heels for a boy. I had known William Butler way before I started at Miss Hillary's school. Back then, he was just another knucklehead, but when I was fourteen, he stood handsome. Some folks nicknamed him "Skin" because his mammy cut all his hair off. Perhaps she believed it caused excessive envy. Years later, when he had his say and let his hair grow as long as he wanted, I came to understand that his mammy did the right thing because it laid too perfect on any boy's head, especially a colored boy's.

Pappy couldn't fault William's appearance. He didn't have green eyes like Robert's, but I wished he did; they were enticing. Lena and Joshua couldn't comment on his appearance because William looked more like them than like Jeremiah. He even had some peach fuzz growing above his faultless lips. I love to ogle William's sleekness, but one day, he caught me.

He asked, "Whut'ja lookin' at?" His voice had lost its boyishness and found some gravel.

I grinned, ashamed to be caught, but said, "Nuthin'."

After a while, I told Zora Mae about my feelings, but I shouldn't have 'cause she went and blabbed everything to William. I could've killed her because no matter where I turned, he beamed his grin in my direction, but I was too timid to respond. I figured I needed to ask somebody, somebody like Fannie, and since she was daring and outspoken, throwing her nose up at stuff so much, I took to calling her Fast Fannie. But while Fannie might grasp my situation, I thought it wiser to ask Miss Hillary.

I stayed after class one day to ask her the most important question of my life. But after she hemmed and hawed about how she courted Mr. Collins, confusion flooded me. I tried to understand what she'd talked about as I headed home, but I couldn't. So I said to myself, *Reckon I should'ah asked Fast Fannie in the first place.*

So one day I did, even though Mammy would have whipped my behind if she caught me asking Fannie about boys. But when I asked Fannie, she said, "Ask him if he wants tuh be yo' boyfriend."

"Jest lac *that?*"

"Jest lac that," she said.

After considering my options, I took Fast Fannie's advice. The next time we saw each other, William's face glowed like a bushel basket brimming with lightning bugs. I walked up to him, scared but determined, and asked,

"William, would'ja be my boyfriend?"

He took off running like a jackrabbit who scented a cougar.

I thought, *What be's wrong wid that boy?*

I didn't lay eyes on William for an entire week. Worry, fright, and sadness became my constant companions.

Maybe he don't like me.

I told Zora Mae, but she reminded me that William always smiled brighter when he saw me.

So whut be's the matter wid him then?

A bundle of emotions hounded me, but I had no time for feeling bad because I wanted William. I put all those feelings aside and walked to the Butler homestead. If Mammy had discovered I had gone unescorted, she would have skinned me alive. When I arrived, I gritted my teeth, knocked on the door, and pert' near fell over when William stood before me, but I had danced with the jitters long enough, so I said,

"I axed yuh a question, and yuh ain't never gives me no kinda answer. I comes tuh find out."

"Yeah," he said.

"Yeah, *whut?*"

He acted like a lost lamb.

"Yeah, Margaret, I always wanted tuh be yo' boyfriend."

"Why'ja run then?"

"Don't know," he said, but his confession forced his chin downward, causing him to mumble, "I was too 'shamed tuh come back tuh school." Then he found the courage to lift his head and correct his voice.

He smiled and said,

"Scared yuh thank I was crazy or sump'em."

"Yeah, I thought that. Yuh crazy, that is." We both laughed.

While I had only a paltry knowledge about being in love back then, I came to understand how Mammy felt about Pappy. His kindness incited love in her, and William did the same for me. I believed he would never be absent from my life.

———— ✦ ————

Since Fannie ran after Robert like a duck chasing a June bug, she had let that sweet-talking boy get her belly big.

"Lawd, Margaret. I ain't bled in three months."

"Oh, my."

"Gon' start showin' here de'reckly. Whut I gon' *do?*"

"Yuh gots tuh tell Mammy."

She spoke of fear but pleaded for secrecy, and I knew why.

Mammy gonna do one of two things: kill her right out or fuss so that after Mammy done finished preachin', Fannie gon' wish she dead. May as well get the shovel, dig a hole, and throw in the dirt 'cause Mammy sho' gon' preach that funeral. I can hear her now.

Glad it ain't me, I thought.

Mammy and Pappy believed in the Good Book, and Fannie had committed what the Good Book called fornication, but that seemed to apply only to women. (It was 1920, after all.)

Everybody gonna be talkin' 'bout her, callin' her baby that B-word, the one Pappy used for Burton after Marlene got a big belly.

I figured it didn't matter how much Fannie said, "I loves Robert." Fornicating was one of their no-nos, and I didn't believe they would approve of her marrying him, and I thought, *Pappy gon' give yuh some love when he finds out too.*

I'll never forget the day Mammy found out. Fannie and Mammy sat at the table, hulling peas. Mammy kept watching Fannie, eyeing Fannie's throat, that tiny part below her Adam's apple. Old folks use'ta say that spot beats funny when your belly is big. Then Mammy asked her, "Gal, yuh been foolin' 'round wid some boy?" It didn't sound like Mammy asked her a question; it sounded more like a fact.

"Nome." Fannie flat-out lied.

"Gal, don'tcha lie tuh me. I know y'all. I can spot lyin' miles away." Fannie tried to hide up in her silence, but Mammy raised her voice, spun Fannie around, and looked in Fannie's face.

"Gal, don't'ja stand there, lookin' me in the face and *lie* tuh me, lie tuh yo' mammy!" Fannie stood silent.

Then something happened I had never seen in our house. Mammy smacked Fannie hard across the face. I yelled, "*Mammy!*" and Lena began to cry. Fannie ran, but she dropped to her knees near the icebox. Overwhelmed and weeping like a woman caught between a rock and a hard place, she said,

"I'm sorry, Mammy."

Mammy took a sizable breath and reached down, took Fannie in her arms, and kissed her cheeks.

"Well, I need yo' forgiveness, too. And don't worry none; it's gon' be all right." She placed Fannie's head on her bosom and rocked Fannie like she was the baby of the family instead of Lena. I went over to them with

Lena, and we all hugged.

After a little while, Mammy said, "Yuh know us gonna haf tuh tell yo' pappy."

Fear flared up in Fannie again.

"Nah, Mammy. Yuh cain't tell Pappy. Please, Mammy, don't tell him." But Mammy held on; she kept on rocking.

"Us has tuh tell him, baby. It gonna be all right," she said, stroking Fannie's hair.

That evening, when Pappy entered the house with Neddy and Joshua tagging behind, the house was so silent you could have heard a hen dropping eggs in a feathered nest fifty paces away. Neddy and Joshua looked in our direction for clues, but Fannie's silence had infected us. Pappy surveyed the room with puzzlement and then focused on Mammy. She got up and grabbed his hand. She took him out into the evening air, where the crickets had begun their own mating song. She slid her arm through his, and when they got about ten steps from the porch, Pappy said, "Her *whut*!"

Lawd, I said to myself, *this gonna be bad, real bad.*

Pappy turned toward the house, but Mammy took a-holt of him. She didn't let go. She pleaded and pleaded hard. Pappy broke loose as Mammy tugged him toward the gate, but she managed to grab his arm, persuading him to walk a little farther, and near the gate, he stopped again. We couldn't hear what he said, but his face and gestures suggested that he fumed. Fannie bit her fingernails so far into the quick they began to bleed. Mammy and Pappy talked for a spell in the yard, and when Pappy closed the gate, Mammy turned toward the house just as us girls ran out to meet her. Joshua and Neddy hung in the doorway; they still suffered from the darkness of ignorance and hankered for a speck of light.

"Yo' pappy gwine on over tuh where that boy live at. Gonna talk tuh his folks."

Fannie's shoulders slumped with worry, and she didn't raise her head even when Mammy turned to her and asked, "Does yuh love that boy?"

Silence.

She grabbed Fannie by the shoulders and asked,

"Does yuh?"

"Yessum," blurted Fannie.

"Well, us gon' wait here 'til yo' pappy gits back. Then us gonna see."

When Pappy opened the door, the kerosene lantern lit his face at the threshold. We weren't aware that someone lurked behind him in the dark, but when Pappy stepped forward, Robert became visible.

"Uh-uh!" I said in my uneasiness.

He resembled a down-and-out prizefighter, beaten down and exhausted. Pappy looked at Fannie and said, "Gal, here yo' new husband."

Dat was dat.

'Nuf said.

SEVEN

Hitched Up B'foe Moonlight
and Rifles

Pappy arrranged for Fannie to marry that boy with them green eyes, and Mammy insisted that the wedding be simple.

"Ain't no reason tuh be makin' no fuss," Mammy said. "No need tuh go chunkin' mo' feed in folks' craw. They gots plenty tuh chew on already."

Pappy scheduled the preacher to perform the ceremony at our house the following Saturday. It was midafternoon, about two hours before dusk, when the Gardners's wagon appeared, all of them hanging off it like a gang of gypsies.

Here come Fannie's new in-laws, I said to myself.

They were a sight to behold—never seen such a raggedy bunch. Robert's mammy sat in that wagon with her patched-up print dress and hair tied up in a red turban. All their clothes resembled patchwork quilts. We used to struggle before Miss Ophelia blessed us, but these folks were way worse off, and I thought, *These are some real po' folks.*

Robert had seven brothers and sisters. His mammy, Miss Mildred, had the baby hitched to her waist, and the child's legs, heavy with baby fat, dangled on either side of her hip. His pappy, Mr. Winston, had one that was a little older on his hip. Two older girls stood giggling and whispering, pitching their flirtations toward Joshua and Neddy. Another one, about Lena's age, spotted Lena peeping from the window; Lena was hiding in the house, mad and crying, because Fannie was getting married and leaving her. Some younger ones scampered about like a bunch of mischief-seeking savages. But young or old, they all looked the same: pretty, pretty folks.

Yes, Lawd. I'll give 'em that.

Miss Mildred caught sight of Mammy, and over she came with that screaming youngin clutching her waist like a vise. "He teefing," she said, as she stuck her old nasty finger in the boy's mouth, past the youngin's two baby teeth, and massaged his pink, swollen gums. The boy stopped yelling and started sucking her finger. Even Mammy, known for her politeness and patience, found this spectacle too much. This flock of gypsies had brought chaos with them—youngins ran 'round like they didn't have an ounce of home training, and even our roosters got to chasing chickens through folks' legs. This was beyond the pale. Then there was Robert. His pacing and constant neck-rubbing suggested he had the jitters and was about ready to bolt. But Fast Fannie stood all doe-eyed 'cause she didn't have a grain of sense.

Mr. Winston tried to talk with Pappy, but talking wasn't high on Pappy's agenda since Pappy held only a speck of patience that day. His jaws held a fair amount of wind, and he appeared to be weighing either killing Robert or jerking him bald. Adding to the trouble, I noticed that all five hogs had somehow escaped from their pen. They headed toward the woods. Mammy yelled, "Lawd, Jake, them hogs done got loose. I told'cha yestiddy; they pen need fixin'."

Hogs are smart. Some, I reckon, are smarter than humans, especially when they don't want to be caught. Our only advantage was that they were about ready for slaughter and too plump for long-distance running. They were sly, though. You'd corner one, and it would dart the other way. Catch one, and it would slip through your muddy fingers. We ran and fell, sprinting and slipping as we wheedled and persuaded. We'd catch one and take off for the others. The youngins had a wonderful time, running, giggling, and yelling, "Sooey, Sooey," but we didn't think chasing hogs was fun at all. Mammy sprinted alongside Joshua, with Robert close on their heels, but—*uh-oh*—Mammy caught her foot on something and down she went, right into a puddle of mud. Robert, running fast behind, tripped. He flew over Mammy, landing flat out in another patch of mud. Mud oozed down Mammy's face to meet at her chin, but she took one look at Robert, covered in mud from head to toe, and busted out laughing. Then, Robert showed off for sho' and started slapping the muddy earth, acting all silly. Mud was just a-flying, and that piece of folly allowed Robert to lose his jitters.

While Mammy and Robert washed up, the preacher arrived as Joshua and Neddy caught the last of the hogs. After finding us covered in mud and sweating, Pastor Jones said, "Looks like that cloudburst yestiddy got y'all in a whole heap of trouble." Everybody fell out laughing.

We needed that.

The ceremony went lightning fast. Mammy held the broom while the preacher said those special words, and when he declared them husband and wife, Mammy threw down the broom. They jumped across it, and Fast Fannie became Mrs. Robert Gardner.

The boy was a sight even with his minstrel mask of mud wiped clean. The washcloth had freed the critical parts (eyes, nose, and lips), but vestiges of wet earth had settled in the curve of his nose and the dimple that set off his chin. Mud covered the sides of his face and matted his curly hair to his scalp. It flowed down his once freshly ironed white shirt and onto his black pants that had held razor-sharp pleats. Mud even covered his Sunday going-to-meeting shoes. He was still handsome, though, dirt and all.

Fannie gave him a quick peck.

Everybody shook hands, but Mammy brought us back to the seriousness of the moment when she said, "If'n yuh ever decides yuh don't loves her no mo', yuh sends her home. Her always gots a place tuh stay. Yuh hear me, boy?"

"Yessum, Miss Lula."

That was it.

As Fast Fannie climbed in the wagon with the rest of the Gardners and disappeared into the land of matrimony, Lena propped herself in the doorway with her arms folded, scowling in the wagon's direction. My eyes followed the drift of Lena's scowl, and I wondered what the newlyweds would do that night.

Where are they gonna sleep? Now it's eleven folks living under one roof, and the place ain't that big.

I didn't want anything like that and I made it clear to William. I reminded him of that whenever his nature flared. You know, I'd be with him sometimes, and he'd start beating his gums about being hot down in his britches. I'd tell him, with conviction all up in my voice, "You'd better gone down tuh the spring and douse plenty of cold water on that thang." He just laughed at me.

Sometimes, I wondered if boys thought about anything worth talking about at all. It seemed like their nature was always on their minds, but Fast Fannie and Marlene had taught me enough 'bout folks and their urges.

<hr>

Right after Fast Fannie jumped the broom, Marlene visited with Leroy and his brother, Burton. She visited for a good bit.

Mammy told her about Fannie's wedding, how the hogs escaped, and the mud puddles. We all laughed aplenty about that. Then, when Marlene composed herself, she said,

"Lawd Margaret, I wants tuh tell yuh—Miss Candy done come home."

I perked up then.

"How long she gon' be here?"

"Oh, 'bout a week or so."

"What she like now?"

"Lawd child, yuh ain't gonna recognize her not one nary bit. Her a lady now."

Marlene turned to Mammy and said, "Her done brung one of her friends with her. Calls herself Vivian."

"What's her like?" I asked.

"Well, I thanks her a 'Bama gal; her pappy gots a big ol' cotton plantation there. Her a nice-lookin' gal, but I'd stay away from her if'n I's you. Her not too friendly."

But I was so excited. It had been a long time since I had seen Candy. I asked Mammy if I could go to the Big House with Marlene to see Candy.

As we headed to the Big House, Leroy held Burton's hand as Burton held on to her dress tail. When we got closer, she stopped, turned toward me, and said, "I sees yuh wid the Butler boy."

My heart 'bout jumped out of my chest.

Then she said, "I ain't tells yo' mammy." She stopped, locked her eyes on me, and said, "Don'tcha be doin' nuthin'. You's fillin' out now." She had observed that my breast buds had already laid waste to the flat land-scape of my chest. She said, "Must'ta done got the curse if'n yo' titties showin'. Yuh gonna git a big belly and end up haulin' youngins 'round lac I does if'n yuh ain't careful." I had dropped my head, but she put her finger under my chin and lifted my face.

"Listen here," she said. "Yuh gots tuh stop this sneakin'. Yo' mammy 'bout the bestest one I ever done seen. Tells her how you's feelin'. Her gonna understand." I promised her I would tell Mammy, and we never spoke about it again.

As we neared the Big House, I saw a woman about Candy's age who I didn't know. She held court, surrounded by Floyd and some other white men that I didn't know either. The men buzzed 'round her like bees to honey and flies to buttermilk.

Marlene was right. Despite being only two years older, Candy easily passed for a grown woman. I looked like a youngin compared to her. I said, "Hey," and she said, "Hey," but she didn't act like she was glad to see me; her blue eyes held no twinkle. She flipped her blond hair behind her left ear like white women do.

"How yuh been, Candy?"

But before she could open her mouth, Vivian piped up, batting her eyelashes all in Floyd's face, and said, "Talkin' tuh niggas makes 'em think they're good as we are, Candy. My daddy told me tuh always keep the darkies in their place."

"Where's that, Miss Vivian?" Floyd asked.

"At my feet, of course," giggling before she leaned into Floyd a little to bat her eyes, twice. Floyd lapped it up and said, "Oh, Miss Vivian, you's uh gal after my heart." His behavior was in step with his daddy's and wasn't surprising, but I expected more from Candy. But like Marlene said, she had changed, and it showed when she looked right through me, using her silence to side with Vivian and Floyd.

Marlene just dropped her head.

They outnumbered me, but I knew who I was and didn't need

to acquire their taste or stoop to their level. Besides, the Great Spirits roamed Pleasant Bluff Plantation; they lifted my head and shepherded me to my folks.

As for Floyd, I suspected that after Mr. Hollis schooled him, Vivian's nightshade eyes had seduced him. I suppose the smell of lilac and the sounds of "Honey child" and "Bless yo' heart" were enough to flood him with desire. He had forgotten the velvet ribbons and the beauty bound in a colored gal.

The next time I caught a glimpse of White Candy was when she came home for her daddy's wedding. Mr. Hollis married that Vivian in the summer of 1921.

At twenty-one, Vivian was only three years older than White Candy, and it was like Mr. Hollis was marrying his daughter. Who'd figure someone as young as she would marry someone so old? Well, their marriage set folks' tongues to wagging.

Marlene was full of tears the morning of the wedding. After flopping into one of our kitchen chairs, she told Mammy the entire story.

"That Vivian jest done fell head over heels in love wid Hollis. First, her send him letters. Come tuh find out, he done been makin' regular trips tuh Uh'lanta tuh visit that gal. He ain't say one word 'bout none of this tuh nobody. He jest gits up, a few weeks ago, and tell everybody he gittin' hitched."

"Sho'nuf sent a shock through me," Mammy said.

"Vivian ain't even tell Candy. Now Candy gots a stepmammy 'bout her age."

"'Magine that."

"All Vivian's peoples, they done come tuh Pleasant Bluff a week ago. Her mammy, her pappy, and Vance, her older brother."

"Where Vivian at?" I asked.

"In town. Been in Hampton for a week . . . 'course her say 'tain't proper for her tuh stay at Pleasant Bluff and her not hitched tuh Hollis."

"Who them uh'ther folks I see up yonder?" Mammy asked, looking out the window toward the Big House.

"Her pappy done brung some of the coloreds from they plantation tuh work on that heifer's weddin'. Place swarmin' wid 'em," said Marlene.

"Whut they doin'?" Mammy asked, pulling her chair close.

"Miss Lula, yuh ortah see the place!" She dropped her head and whispered, "Her brung her wedding dress from Uh'lanta when her come."

"Whut it look like?" I asked.

Why did I ask? Tears flew straight out. She cried louder than before. Handing her a handkerchief, Mammy tried to comfort her.

"Whut'ja gon' do?"

"They is some hateful white folk, Miss Lula. They's worser than Kearns . . . they so nasty," she said, dabbing her eyes.

"Not surprisin', knowin' whut'cha told us 'bout the likes of Vivian," Mammy said.

"The one Vivian calls her maid, she warn me, and say beware. She call her a witch. Say Vivian ain't tuh be trusted 'cause hatred and evilness run in her family. She full of the devil."

"'Spect we gonna haf'tuh wait and see," Mammy said.

With her gaze fixed in the distance, she looked deflated. Crestfallen and weak-voiced, Marlene said,

"*Two!* I got two of his youngins, and us gots nowhere tuh go . . . ain't got no place but the Big House," and then she said, "God damn that Hollis!"

"Lawd always make a way," Mammy said as Marlene and Mr. Hollis's children started to leave, returning to slumber with her crazy white folks. But Mammy's confession confirmed what I suspected:

Mr. Hollis didn't have a heart, but what did Marlene expect? *She may have smooched and enjoyed his authority, but he made her colored just like us 'cause he didn't recognize Burton and Leroy as kin and married Vivian. Nuthin' but flat-out disrespect. Treated her like a piece of property, jest like he'd treat a slave.*

Years later when I read Daniel Defoe's *Moll Flanders,* I thought of how Moll reminded me of Vivian, the 'Bama gal, as Marlene called her. Moll's greed led her to crime, and people and relationships became simple business transactions. But unlike Moll, Vivian had no incentive to root after money. She had plenty. So, unlike Moll, Vivian couldn't use being poor as her excuse for having a hardened heart. But there was something else, another reason. I remembered how she behaved when she stood surrounded by men. In one sense, it was her coquettishness, her coal-black hair, her prissy nose, and the luminous nightshade eyes and eyelashes that she flounced. But perhaps it was her essence, "being Vivian," that overwhelmed and intoxicated every man who caught a whiff of her. In the final analysis, she shared the quality of her vanity with Moll Flanders; however, unlike Moll, Vivian didn't hold a trace of half-hearted repentance. She remained yoked that way until the end, even when we uncovered the truth.

———•❙•———

Later in the week, Mammy needed help at Miss Anna Bell Jackson's. I didn't want to go because I hankered to spend time with William, but since Lena was spending the day with Fannie and wasn't available, Mammy insisted. They required an extra pair of hands. Mammy and Miss Anna Bell went way back 'cause Mammy used to play with her children, and even when Miss Anna Bell's children moved away, Mammy made regular visits.

With the bushes scratching at my legs, we walked on the path for quite a spell. A canopy of oaks and sycamores arched over the worn path. Dogwoods, redbuds, tall pines, magnolias, and a few mulberry trees graced the forest floor as saplings. Others shot up like fortresses to shade ferns and low-growing moss. In a clearing, a dogwood, its trunk parted, split into two spiraling but gnarled limbs. Their branches fanned out into hundreds of tiny woody fingers that held petals, white as porcelain, at their tips. All stood bent but leaned forward enough to twist to heaven and shout, "Rejoice!"

Under that rejoicing, a heap of iron clamored.

"Whut's that, Mammy?"

"They say Mr. Ted's people did that right after the necktie party the white folks give 'em."

"Whut it mean?" I asked.

"Sump'em 'bout one of them African religions."

"Huh," I said, but it looked peculiar, all jumbled up next to the tree they said Christ had stunted in growth and commanded that its petals be fashioned into a cross with stained tips to remind folks of His great sacrifice and their salvation.

Miss Anna Bell's cabin stood smothered in the beauty of life. It was everywhere, underfoot and overhead. Birds chattered: first a mockingbird, then a finch, and then a sparrow twittered their melodious music. I thought that living alone in those woods would produce constant uneasiness and fright in me, but when I met Miss Anna Bell, I understood why she called it home.

She was a white-headed old lady whose age had bent her back into an arch. The hump she carried sloped to the small of her back, and she walked slow-footed with a cane. Every so often, she'd stop to brush hair from her face. She did that at a snail's pace, too, one strand at a time. Her hair, combed and brushed slick, spiraled into a ball and rested against her curved neck. Miss Anna Bell had little twinkling eyes that were as sharp as razors and clear as spring water but held the color of the bachelor buttons that grew next to her cabin. Her tiny, pointy nose rode the rifts of her valley-shaped face, and peach fuzz lay across the plain and above her top lip.

A smile came to her face as we emerged from the woods. She reminded me of Miss Ophelia, when she threw her arms around Mammy and said, "Lula, it's so good to lay my eyes on yuh." She turned to me.

"Is *this* Margaret? You sho' have grown!" She studied us both and invited us into the house.

No back door this time.

Her charming cabin held lots of her kinfolks' furnishings, paintings, clocks, rugs, chairs, and tables—antiques then, beyond a fortune now.

Once settled, she and Mammy recounted the tales of the sickly and recently married folks and those the Lord had snatched to His bosom. We had been at it for a long spell when Miss Anna Bell folded her hands across her lap, reflected a bit, and switched her attention to us.

"Been told Ophelia Demmings was extremely generous tuh y'all some time back."

Mammy smiled. "Yeah."

"And Hollis got mighty upset when the lawyer read her will, I heard."

"Been tryin' tuh take it 'way from us ever since."

"And?"

"Been raisin' sand 'bout it in the courthouse, sayin' Miss Ophelia out her mind."

"When will yuh hear the decision?"

"Soon, I suspect."

"How has he been treatin' y'all?"

"Been right sweet and had 'nuf gall tuh ask Jake tuh keep workin' the fields for him."

"That man got some kinda nerve," Miss Anna Bell said.

"Jake cried, bein' swamped—couldn't work for him no more."

"Oh, dear—more serious than I thought. He dud'en want tuh let y'all go either."

"Did'ja hear sump'tem, Anna Bell?"

"You know colored folks cain't refuse him—"

"Lawd, Anna Bell, that woman done been dead four years. She died in nineteen seventeen; Jake and the boys been workin' for Mr. Hollis right along."

"Now, don't be shocked, Lula. When a white woman gifts a Negro family such wealth and property, folks are bound tuh talk—particularly when the courthouse will not snatch it from 'em. That news reached me— even in my seclusion. Folks . . . well, they're fit tuh be tied over this.

"Y'all need tuh be very careful," she said, touching Mammy's shoulder. "Yuh remember what he did tuh Kearns?"

"Yeah," Mammy said. "Took the little land Kearns had and flung his wife and chilluns outdoors."

"Kept him close and waited twenty years, then he got even wid him. They were po' b'foe, but Hollis turned them in'tuh white trash. Didn't he?"

"That's for 'sho."

"Don't keep that money lying 'round yo' house, if yuh catch my drift . . . make sho' yuh keep it in the colored bank over in Hampton, Lula."

"Done that right off."

"Good. I ain't seen folks this upset in a long time. And uh'nuther thang." She leaned closer. "Tell Jake tuh keep that shotgun close by."

"Yessum."

"'Cause yuh know where you're living."

"Sho' do," Mammy said. "Sho' do."

"One mo' thing, and don't forgit this: Demmings *NEVER* forgets, and Demmings *NEVER* forgives." Her warning thundered like God had clapped his His hand and flashed lightning across a moonless night. It grabbed our attention like nothing else.

———————◆———————

A day or so later, Fast Fannie visited, toting her twins. She and Robert were doing well 'cause Robert was a hard-working boy. He worked at the sawmill long before she got a big belly, and since he eyed settling down, he squirreled away every penny he could. So when they got hitched, it wasn't as if they started with nothing. They lived with the Gardners for six months, and during that period, Robert and his pappy restored a run-down cabin for his new family. It was close to the Gardner's place. I was surprised that Fannie hadn't sniffed it out, and I didn't know how they had kept it a secret.

When she arrived with the twins, she beamed with excitement, recounting the story of her new home and the unexpected arrival of her babies.

She said, "Robert come talkin' 'bout he gots a surprise.

"But I tells him, 'I ain't gots no time for no foolishness, Robert Gardner. I gots my hands full wid this house and yo' mammy's chilluns.'

"Anyway, Robert kept on messin' wid me, and I gives in. 'Foe I could protest one lick mo', he done slapped uh old rag 'round my eyes. Well, I starts tuh gigglin', I said, 'Robert Gardner, whut'ja doin'?'

"Margaret, I could sense his joy when he said—full of the devil—'This be a surprise, 'member.'

"Off we goes. Pappy Gardner on one side of me, Robert on the other.

"Well, Margaret, I tells 'em, 'Don't y'all lemme fall out here.'

"'Us got'cha,' they said.

"When we gits there, Robert snatches the rag coverin' my eyes and say, 'This our new house.'

"Honey, I jumped up and down; threw my arms 'round Robert; nearly choked the life out'ah him. Well, it must've been too much excitement 'cause . . . when I walks in the cabin, my water broke on the spot!

"They talkin' 'bout they gon' take me back tuh the Gardner house. I told 'em, 'Nah, y'all *ain't*. I ain't gonna go *nowhere*. *My* babies comin' in the world right *here*, in my *own* house.'"

Robert fetched the womenfolks. Mammy and Mildred, Robert's mammy, brought them children into the world.

"Margaret, girl. Fourteen hours of labor. Fourteen! Ain't had nuthin' hurt like that in my *life*! Honey, if I'd been at the Big House, up in the attic where yuh stayed wid Marlene, I woud'dha hollered for somebody tuh open the wender so I could jump out."

Mammy and Lena came into the house, and Mammy picked up her first grandchild. She was so proud. When Pappy entered, Mammy said, "Look at that face and them litty-bitty fangernails! Who cain't fall in love wid y'all?"

Pappy grabbed the other baby out of Lena's lap. Mammy had one, Pappy had the other one, and they just walked back and forth, smiling and talking that baby talk. They couldn't help it. Those babies were as cute as a tow sack full of puppies.

Everyone started singing Robert's praises and commenting on the beautiful family he and Fannie had. He had turned twenty-four; she was twenty-two, and they had two babies. Life was full of surprises, and things seldom occurred the way we first imagined.

⸻ ⸰ ⸻

Folks never end up being what the gossipers rumored or the initial impression suggested. Miss Ophelia and Robert taught us that. Everybody was wrong about them and Robert's kin, too. So during the middle of 1921, I also wondered whether Mr. Hollis might change.

Maybe God will touch his heart one of these days, and maybe whatever Gator did, Mr. Hollis will forgive him so he can be fit for the human race again.

But when it came to Mr. Hollis, I didn't understand any of it. He hated Negroes so much, but he had two boys by Marlene. I reckoned he figured one thing had nothing to do with the other.

My changing circumstances, however, suggested that anything could happen. I had taken to heart what Marlene had told me, and as she suspected, Mammy understood. She allowed William to call on me, with her strict supervision, of course. She had changed her mind and confirmed that change was possible. So, when the judge said Miss Ophelia wasn't crazy and that her will was valid, even the courthouse and its decision suggested a shift in the law—when it came to colored folks' interests. At any rate, we got to keep what she had given us, but Miss Ophelia had said Mr. Hollis was like the wind, blowing according to his fancy. So, I thought, *What would courthouses and judges mean to such a man?*

————————

Right after Fannie left, Mammy handed me the letter containing the court's decision. Upon reading it, I realized it was a double-edged gift 'cause we were colored folks. It held both the gentle sweetness of generosity and the potential brutality of greed and violence. I could hear the old folks saying, "It be's good, but it be's bad." As I returned the letter to its envelope, Marlene and her boys entered the gate. They sat with us on the porch, and I watched Marlene push her fingers through the curls of Leroy's head. In recognizing the naturalness of her mothering, I realized I wanted to understand her life. I handed the envelope to Mammy; she gave it a gentle rub. She placed the envelope on the table next to her, and perhaps worried about what Miss Ophelia's kindness might mean for us, Mammy began telling a story about how her folks' struggled to raise a family during the time they called the Reconstruction.

After she finished, Marlene, encouraged by it, shared a story about her kinfolks. We only knew a thimbleful regarding her origin and nothing about her people. So I was all ears, sitting next to her that lazy afternoon, listening to her while mosquito hawks and June bugs danced in the soggy summer air.

Marlene said, "This happened way 'foe I sniffed a breath. I thank this took place jest 'bout a year 'foe 'mancipation. My granny, Ammeah Weatherby, and her youngins be slaves on a plantation in Jaw-ja, near Savannah. Granny had a son, Daniel, and six gals—my mammy, Abigail, and her sisters, Ella, Gloria, Jane, Carol, and Lucy. Abigail was jest a youngin then, 'bout nine, born 1855. They massa threw his tongue lac a real Jaw-ja cracker, an ornery devil if one ever lived, and Granny say he works them slaves pert' near tuh death. The overseer, he wan't no better. If anythang, he be worst."

"Why, Marlene?" I asked.

"If'n one of them slaves runs off, and he finds 'em, he don't brangs 'em back. He'd kill 'em on the spot. He scalp 'em, chop they ears off, and hangs they body from a tree. If they mens, he slashes they private parts and stick 'em in they mouth. Then he'd brang them scalps and ears back and hang 'em up in the slave street."

"Why?" I asked.

"A lesson, yuh know—same thang gon' be waitin' for the next nigga that fancied bein' a runaway. But it 'tweren't 'nuf tuh stop my kin and some others; they done settled on runnin' for the railroad, gon' cast they lot 'way from Jaw'ja. They done been plottin', but Granny say they waits 'til Christmastime tuh make they run.

"Everybody celebratin'. 'Sides, Christmas on a Sunday that year.

"They gits away fine, but when the overseer finds them gone, and he cain't finds 'em even wid the bloodhounds, he go crazy—done guzzled too much of that moonshine the night b'foe, and he be real ornery."

"What did he do?" Mammy asked.

"That mornin' he lines 'em up . . . all them grown slaves, he lines 'em up in one long row, and starts walkin' 'hind 'em . . . creepin' . . .

"He gots the gun in his hand," she said, as she stood and handed Leroy to Mammy.

"He'd walk a little ways."

She paused, glanced around, and in an ominous tone, she said, "The slaves could hear the gun—he cock the hammer and kept spinnin' the barrel in they ear. Nobody ain't gots no idea who he gonna shoot 'til somebody's wallowin' and whimperin' in the dirt." She leaned forward then and almost touched my forehead when she said, "They be drappin' lac flies 'til somebody tells him whut route they done took tuh the railroad."

She straightened herself.

"Did he kill 'em?" I asked.

"Nah, Margaret, he ain't kill 'em. He shoot 'em in they foot or they leg. When he finds out where they headed, he, wid some mo' men, high-tails it out after 'em. Ella, Gloria, Jane, and Carol git away, but they finds Daniel and Lucy and some of the others. They brung 'em back, and he hang the ringleaders in the slave street. The ones he don't hang, he shoot."

She closed her eyes and took a deep breath. She continued,

"The overseer shoot Daniel and Lucy dead. Daniel be first. Granny and Abigail grabs at his arm, beggin' him tuh spare Lucy. But he slaps 'em tuh the ground; Granny grabs Abigail jest 'foe he put a bullet in Lucy's head, but he hankerin' tuh kill Abigail, too. Oh, Granny say her cried and pleaded that day, as he reared back wid that shotgun's butt pointin' at Abigail's head," and I waited breathless as Marlene drew her arms way back; her hands laid tight around the invisible shotgun aimed at my head.

"And jest as he 'bout ready tuh smash Abigail's head in, the Mistress grab the shotgun.

"Granny said, her reckon the Lawd jest stepped right in and saved my mammy that day."

Marlene found her chair and sat back down.

"They left they body smack dab in the street," she said. "'Twas bloody when white folks celebrated New Year's Day—they kilt three mens and two womens that day. Yeah, I remember my granny saying the street was full of blood." When Marlene finished, the mosquito hawks and June bugs had vanished, and what remained was the heaviness around our hearts; it matched the heat and humidity always found in a South Carolina summer.

So that's part of her story. A white man killed her kin, and he would've killed her mother if he had his way 'bout it. *How could she stomach the sight of any white man, but particularly Mr. Hollis, who sired her two sons, didn't recognize his creation, and hitched himself to another woman's coattails?* She made no kinda sense. How did Marlene get to these parts, and what happened to her Mammy and Pappy? She's one mystery after another if you ask me.

That night, I got on my knees. I thanked the Lord for Fannie and Robert's twins and asked Him to help Marlene come to her senses: Stop wallowing in the nightmare created in the Big House and orchestrated by Mr. Hollis. I thanked God for Miss Ophelia's blessing but couldn't get the letter out of my head. What came next was only the beginning, but we didn't experience the full blow of her gift until years later.

———————◆◆◆———————

I got up early the following day, but my head was full of Marlene and her troubles, which reminded me again of Miss Anna Bell's warning. I got to praying, but the sense of doom became a nagging acquaintance. After breakfast, Pappy resumed repairing the cabin's siding and porch railings. After working for a while, he realized he needed provisions from the hardware store in town. As he prepared to leave, Mammy, remembering Miss Anna Bell's warning, reminded him to take the shotgun. He protested, but she raised so much sand that he relented and threw it in the wagon as Neddy and Joshua climbed in alongside him.

The sun stood a little beyond noontime when the sound of racing hooves filled the silence. Pappy's trail of dust, seemingly stretching for miles, ended in the yard. As he and Joshua jumped from the wagon, Neddy quickly mounted another horse and galloped toward the unknown. Joshua secured the horses and took his place beside Pappy just as Mammy reached the porch and said,

"Lawd, Jake! Whut's the matter?"

"Git the chilluns and git in the house."

"Jake, whut's the matter?"

"Woman, *don't* be axin' no questions. You git them youngins like I done told'cha!"

Mammy snatched me and Lena up. Pappy remained in the yard, gazing in the distance, but when Mammy reappeared, Pappy snapped,

"Lula. I done told'cha tuh git in the house, and yuh stay there!"

This wan't like Pappy at all. My heart raced.

About thirty minutes later, I heard galloping horses stop abruptly. Men's voices filled the yard. Joshua had come back, and Pappy led everyone into the cabin. Twenty or thirty colored men had come, including Fast Fannie's husband and his pappy, and all Mammy's and Pappy's brothers. It felt like every colored man in New Harmony was in our cabin with rifles, shotguns, and pistols. Pappy finally told us what had happened.

"When me and the boys goes down tuh the feed store tuh pick up some uh'ther provisions, I notices that the white folks, partic'ly the men, actin' mo' peculiar than usual. I walks by and hears one of 'em say, 'There's that nigga. Must'uh done had his way wid Miss Ophelia for her tuh leave his monkey ass all that money.' 'Nuther one say, 'Don't that boy know he ain't 'posed tuh be sparkin' wid no white woman?', and then one of 'em say, 'Seem lac the courthouse full of nigga lovers, too. Reckon we haf'tuh teach that nigga a lesson. Ain't got no business ownin' no land.'"

"I ignored it, kept walkin' back tuh the wagon where I waits for Neddy, but he walks by this old cracker . . . y'all 'quainted wid old man Spears?" Everybody nodded.

"Well, he took and grabs Neddy 'round the neck—Neddy squirmin' tuh cut the stranglehold. He bites Spears's hand and git loose, but Spears gits tuh chasin' him. I stands up in the wagon wid the shotgun. I tells this cracker, 'I'll see yuh in hell 'foe I let'cha harm a hair on his head.' I let my spit hit the sidewalk and said, 'Let him be. If'n yuh don't, I'll put buckshot in yuh 'till kingdom come.'

"Spears say, 'Nigga, yuh know who yuh talkin' to?'

"'Yessir,' I say, 'I sho' does, but he my flesh and blood, and I'd die 'foe I sees the likes of you harm him.' I tells Neddy tuh git in the wagon, and us hightails it back here."

Mammy had her arms around Neddy, but Pappy nostrils flared out like a charging bull's. Then somebody said, "Jake, don't worry. Us here now." A wave of colored heads bobbed agreement around the room.

Mammy prepared food, and everyone sat waiting for the white men to come, and expected a long night, but no one would leave until we felt safe. Everyone needed to remain vigilant throughout the evening and morning.

'Bout nine o'clock that evening, the sound of galloping horses broke the silence.

Necks stiffened heads to attention.

Some men jumped to their feet, scrambling to take a look into the yard. A bright, speckled full moon flooded the yard, illuminating tree trunks and fence posts.

Pappy and his companions ventured out and took up positions around the yard. One pressed up against the small curves of a tree trunk. Another tucked himself way back on the edge of the porch's roof, cheating the moonlight. Some sheltered in or perched atop the barn, and some clustered in the bushes. A few, sly like foxes, hid, cloaked by darkness, or concealed themselves behind other things. But others were bold, and stood unafraid in the moonlight. Some placed the butts of rifles in the dirt, positioning them like walking canes against their leg. Some held them like they nursed children against their chests, prepared to thrust their muzzles into the night and fire.

As the white men approached, the colored men stood at attention, which led to the curious sight of white men halting; then they turned and hightailed it, with that speckled moon lighting up their dusty trail.

They were gone, good and gone.

Some of the colored men jumped with elation, doing a victory dance, elated because few white men relinquished ground to Negroes. But Pappy was puzzled. "Not one shot," he mused as the others danced their jig, but was right in step with Mammy, who asked, "How come? Whut'ja thank they's up to?" But I remembered what Miss Anna Bell had said: "Demmings never forgets, and Demmings never forgives."

The next morning my head was full of Marlene's and our troubles. Miss Hillary had read poetry to us at school, and I got the idea that I would write some of my own. I found my writing tablet, and I went down by the spring. I wrote:

> *I's come here Lawd wid a heavy heart—*
> *   Bound up and feeling lac I's in de dark.*
> *Sometimes, it feels lac life is a-fallin'—*
> *Life's troubles be's vexin' and gallin'.*

> *Dis heart been thumpin' wid the suffering of the ages*
> *   'Cause folks ain't caught on to the wisdom of the sages.*
> *Lawd, when is dere ever gwine to be peace*
> *Oh Lawd, when will this sinfulness cease?*

My heart, Lawd, done seen too much fightin';
    And dese eyes done grown weary from cryin'—
Got me witherin' lac'uh flower in yo' sun.
When is dat cloud gon' come wid yo' son?

Last night, father, I seen they brother, dead—
    Evil took and tied a robe 'round his head.
Hung! Strung up lac ham in dat yonder barn.
Pray, that hate gwine cure wid yo' righteous dawn.

Yessir, folks fester wid too much hate,
    But I know this-here hate got's a date.
It's gonna die lac-uh tree stripped of its bark,
'Cause you gonna make it fly 'way lac a lark.

Den I's gonna shout, "Glory, Glory!"
Oh Lawd! Spread yo' wings of Glory!

Even in New Harmony, hope must thrive, and in the belly of condemnation and woundedness, hope seeds forgiveness. I prayed we'd all find some, as Mammy would say, "de'reckly," but in thinking back, it seemed that everything about my life created a tapestry for murder.

EIGHT

Crumbs

After all that commotion, Mammy's visits to Pleasant Ridge became more frequent. Sometimes, in the twilight of morning, she'd leave our dusty yard. On her way, she slipped around chickens who searched the broom-swept yard for any remaining morsels. She stepped over Lena's toys, leaving them up-turned and dust-covered. At the edge of our well-kept yard, she opened the squeaky, whitewashed gate, leaving it behind, unnoticed. She had grown accustomed to its squeaking parts.

When she passed the mailbox, its metallic flag standing at attention but chipped clean of red, she entered the woods. A twisted stretch of earth took Mammy past a pond packed so tight with lily pads that frogs could hop on a sea of green and reach the land on her left. On her right, a meadow of grass and wildflowers followed her up the road to Pleasant Ridge, which overlooked the valley below. From the Ridge's peak, the hills sloped to the river as gently as they pleased. The greenest grasses covered hillsides that held the tallest trees, standing like an army of sentinels protecting the earth.

In the evening, when the horizon blushed orange, pink, and purple, the magic spawned by clouds and sun was a sight to behold as flocks of birds turned their bellies to the sun's pallet and mirrored gold. Pleasant Ridge had become her haven, where she nurtured her inner being. So after the men departed—the white ones who came to harm us and the colored ones who came to protect us—Mammy visited Pleasant Ridge a lot.

One day, when Mammy had gone to Pleasant Ridge, Aunt Sarah and Uncle Luther visited us from Ridgeville, which was on the other side of Dorchester County. As they arrived in Uncle Luther's fancy car, a Packard Twin Six, I ran out to the gate, jumping up and down with excitement—I hadn't seen them in such a long spell.

"Gal! Is that you, Margaret?" Aunt Sarah asked, running up and giving me a hug.

"My, you done growed. Lookin' jest lac yo' mammy. You sho'nuf do. Don't her, Luther?"

"You done turned in'tuh a right fine-lookin' gal." With devilry in his voice and a mischievous grin, Uncle Luther said, "Now, you's ain't courtin', is you?"

I broke into a smile.

"Come on, 'fess up," Uncle Luther said.

"William. His name is William. Y'all gots tuh meet him."

"Look at her, Sarah. Ain't that the face of somebody in love?"

"Looks that way tuh me too, Daddy."

"Keep right on lookin' lac that, sugar, yuh hear me?"

"Yessir."

"Where Lula and the uh'ther folks?" Aunt Sarah asked.

"Pappy and the boys workin' at the mill, and Lena's in the house. Mammy's up on Pleasant Ridge."

"What her doin' up there?" Aunt Sarah asked.

"After those men, she visits the Ridge plenty."

Together, Aunt Sarah asked, "Who?" as Uncle Luther asked, "What?"

"We've had a lot of excitement 'round here. Mammy'll tell yuh. I'll go on up and fetch her. Y'all make yo'selves at home."

"Gon', honey."

She stretched and cut loose a yawn that revealed the back of her throat and the pendulum that swung there. After smacking her lips, she said,

"Gonna wait right on this-here porch. Ain't gon' move 'til yuh fetch Lula." Not energized by the first yawn, she unleashed another, followed by, "So glad tuh git out that car I don't know what tuh do.

"When they gonna fix y'all's road? Ain't *never* rode over so many rocks in *all* my life." She found the rocker and fell into it so hard I thought it would break into a hundred pieces. Aunt Sarah was no little woman.

After finding the handkerchief she had been fishing for, she got to wiping the sweat off her face before she set to fanning—just a-fanning, making waves with that white handkerchief, whooping the air while she rocked.

"Lawd, Luther, I tell yuh I'm plumb tuckered out. Wheeeeee!" She shooed me along, saying, "Run on, honey. Us gonna be fine."

Aunt Sarah was Mammy's oldest sister—twenty years older than Mammy, born in 1859. The hard years of slavery and Reconstruction were her childhood.

Since her hair had turned almost plumb white, I thought she was a living Great Spirit. The last time I laid eyes on her, her straight hair hung all down her back and loose around her fleshy face. Now, it was all tied up in a bun at her nape. I had forgotten her corded neck and how it almost concealed the Adam's apple that made her throaty-flute voice noticed above all others. She was the darkest of Mammy's people—the rest were much lighter than a brown paper bag.

I met up with Mammy on her way back to the house. I noticed her graceful glide first, but her headscarf startled me. She usually wore brighter colors, not a dull chocolate.

I approached her with excitement.

"Mammy, guess who done come tuh visit?"

"Too tuckered out tuh be guessin' today, baby. Ain't no riders, is it?"

"Nah, Aunt Sarah and Uncle Luther!"

"All the way from *Ridgeville*?"

"Yessum."

"Lawdy!" She took off running. I ran behind her but couldn't keep up.

When we reached the house and Aunt Sarah saw Mammy, she sprang from the rocker; they embraced, both of 'em crying.

Mammy spoke first. "Lawd, I misses yuh so. Ain't seen yuh since I had Lena." She kissed Aunt Sarah on the cheek.

Aunt Sarah said, "Lawd, child, lemme look at'cha. Lemme see yo' face." She placed both hands on Mammy's face; she studied it and said,

"Still as pretty as I 'members, and yuh look mo' lac us'es Mammy every day." That's when they sho'nuf hugged.

By then, Lena had joined us, asking, "Who dat?"

"Mammy's sister," I said as Aunt Sarah stooped down and placed a wet kiss on Lena, which caused Lena to turn the back of her cream-colored hand into a handkerchief.

When Pappy and the boys came through the gate, Aunt Sarah jumped to her feet.

"Boy, come here; plant one right here." She had her tongue poking in the side of her cheek. "Don't be takin' yo' time 'bout it, neither."

Pappy threw his arms around her, but before he laid a kiss on Aunt Sarah, he cut his eyes at Uncle Luther.

"You ain't gonna skin me now, is yuh, Luther?"

"Boy, yo' heart might not be strong 'nuf. That's a *whole* heap of woman yuh gots there."

Pappy kissed Aunt Sarah on the cheek, but he made a long, puckering sound that comes with pulling air right fast through gathered lips.

Everybody laughed.

"Always knowed you's uh devil," Aunt Sarah said. "Anybody kisses like that, they be too good for this world." She hooted one of her big, deep laughs. Everything about her was in that laugh.

On seeing the boys, she said, "Git over here, Joshua. You too, Neddy. Give yo' Aunt Sarah some sugar."

"You ain't changed one bit, Sarah," Pappy said, and from the corner of his mouth, he said, "Whut'ja been doin' tuh this woman, Luther? How yuh keeps her so young?"

Uncle Luther winked, and they laughed and ran off the porch to drool over the new Packard, which forced Aunt Sarah to say, "Don't you mens be gittin' in'tuh anythang out there. 'Cause I don't wanna haf'tuh come out yonder and whup y'all within an inch of y'alls' life."

"I loves you, too," Uncle Luther said, and with that, he and Pappy headed to the car. Neddy and Joshua sought shelter inside the cabin, leaving the porch to the womenfolks.

After taking a gander at the Packard, Pappy and Uncle Luther headed toward the barn. When they vanished into the barn, Aunt Sarah, gazing in that direction, said, "Luther ain't been doin' too good. I been wantin' tuh come way 'foe this, but too scared travelin' this far since he been feelin' so po'ly for so long. Won't say nary uh word 'bout it though, but I can tell

. . . us been tuh'gether goin' on fifty years. Knowed him since I's 'bout Margaret's age."

Mammy threw her arm around Aunt Sarah's shoulders.

"Well, us jest tickled yuh came." Mammy always knew what to say.

Aunt Sarah smiled again.

"Let's grab some chairs and take the weight off," Mammy said, eyeing the rocker, but Aunt Sarah grabbed that prize first and threw a grin in Mammy's direction.

"'Member Anna Bell—Anna Bell Jackson?" Mammy asked.

"Lawd! She ain't dead yet?"

"Nah, girl."

"She 'bout old as Methuselah then," Aunt Sarah said.

"I took Margaret down there. She still lives down in the bushes. Charmin' little place, but I'd be scared livin' in those woods, all by my lonesome."

"Always been a strange one," Aunt Sarah said.

"Yeah, Jake say she 'bout the onliest white person he ever done met ain't gots that disease."

"Whut disease?"

"The 'I-hates-dem-niggas disease'."

Aunt Sarah fell out, she laughed so hard.

"Where that boy come up wid that? Make sense, though. Ain't that funny? I-hates-dem-niggas disease. Wonder what the cure be?"

After some pondering, she said,

"'Spect the only cure be killin' all of us." She said it with enough gloom to make me wonder, but she returned to her senses with "They tried durin' them dark days, but us still here. Yuh hear me!" Then she stood up, bent over with her head almost touching the floor, put her hands on her knees, and started shaking her hind parts,

"I is still kickin', and I is still raisin' hell!"

"Oh, Sarah, you needs tuh stop! Jake's right; you ain't changed one bit!"

"Don't plan to."

Fast Fannie just like her. Just like her! I thought.

"Whut Anna Bell say to y'all?"

"Well, Ophelia Demmings done passed on."

"Yeah. Got wind of that. What that no-count, sorry-ass, backslidin', redneck, slave-drivin', nigga-hatin' husband of hers do when Ophelia left his sorry behin'?"

"Now, Sarah," Mammy said, with reprimand in her eyes.

I snickered, wondering, *How'd she come up with all that?*

"Well, it be the God's honest truth," Aunt Sarah said, snapping her handkerchief to the wind.

"After they done laid her to rest, her lawyer took and told us Miss Ophelia done left us some money and the land the cabin sets on."

"Nah! Well, *kiss—my—ass*, white boy!

"Ain't surprised, though. Ophelia had uh soft spot for us'es Mammy— and she ain't has much respect for that daddy of her'n."

"Really?"

"Yessiree, but I bet old Hollis 'bout shit in his drawers."

I fell out then. Lena threw her hands over her mouth.

"Sarah! The children!"

Aunt Sarah hit the air with that handkerchief again to punctuate her defiance, but her ears perked up when she heard about the colored men who stood their ground.

"What did the white men do?"

"They left without firin' a shot."

"Watch, they gonna be back."

"Lawd, I sho' hopes you wrong, Sarah."

"Always did lac yo' man, Jake—a fine, strong colored man, lac my Luther. Whut else done happen?"

"Well, Fannie married."

"Got caught, did her?"

"Yeah. Robert, he uh right friendly boy. Kinda 'minds me of Luther. Strong, hard-working, quiet."

Then Mammy told Aunt Sarah stuff I didn't even know, which caused Aunt Sarah to say,

"Us need tuh have a meetin', a family meetin'."

"What?" I asked.

"One of them shindigs where the old folks talk, and the young folks listen," she said with both hands on her hips. "Let us talk 'bout the olden days and tell y'all youngins where y'all come from—the stuff y'all needs tuh be right proud of. But us cain't has no shindig without no food! Mornin' us women folks gon' git them pots tuh rattlin'!"

"Mammy, can William come?" I asked.

"Yeah, he can come.

"Almos' forgot that piece of news, Sarah. Yuh gots tuh meet this boy," and Mammy whispered in Aunt Sarah's ear. They both got to giggling.

"That ain't right. What y'all laughing about?" I said.

"Whisperin' ain't polite," Lena said.

"What's wrong wid you gals? Y'all ain't 'posed tuh be correctin' or axin' grown folks 'bout they business." They laughed some more and chased me and Lena off the porch. Back then, I didn't rightly grasp what she stood for, nor could I have fathomed that the themes woven through her stories would one day become the seeds of hatred and murder.

—————•••—————

The next day was Saturday. I ran to William's. His mammy was in the yard hanging clothes.

"Hey, Miss Butler. How yuh doin'?"

"Fine, Margaret. How are you?" she asked as she reached in her pocket and pulled out another clothespin to hang another pair of men's drawers on the line.

"William ain't here, but he ortah be turnin' up in a little bit. You wanna wait?"

"Nome. I jest wanna let y'all know my aunt and uncle are here, and we're havin' a family shindig. We really wanna invite William . . . all of y'all tuh come."

"When Mr. Butler comes home, I'll ask him."

"Yessum. I hope y'all can come."

"Me too," she said, this time with a clothespin held between her perfect lips.

I thanked her and headed back to the house. Her face was still in my head as I spotted William sauntering down the road. What I held in memory had become flesh again, and it stopped me in my tracks. William took after his mammy, and because he had a smidgen of color, he landed on the high-yellow side. He had gotten his face and hair from his mammy but got his build from his pappy.

He grabbed me and gave me a hug and a peck on the cheek. We didn't have any business doing none of that, and Mammy would've had a conniption fit if she had seen us. Sixteen or not, she'd call me fast and him mannish.

"Been by yo' place lookin' for yuh."

"Whut for?"

"We're havin' a shindig. My aunt and uncle are here, and we want y'all tuh come."

"I sho'nuf would like to. Got'tuh see what daddy gon' say, though." I felt like my heart would break if he didn't come, and I must have looked that way too, because he touched my hair and said, "I'm gonna try my best tuh be there. Whut time y'all gonna start?"

"'Bout one." He gave me another brief peck and took off. I turned to watch him walk down the road, and thought: *He got a pretty behind, stickin' out and sittin' high. Wonder what it feels like.*

When I got to the cabin, the aroma 'bout knocked me to the floor. Mammy and Aunt Sarah were two cooking *fools*—pots and pans were *jumping*. They had sent Neddy up to the Gardners and to Fast Fannie's. They were cooking, too. Sister Jamison, Miss Bessie, Miss Annie, Sister Betty, and Miss Effie also fixed a mess of food. Pappy and Joshua had brought some fiddlers and some mouth-organ-playing men from town. They were getting out of the wagon and helping Pappy set up tables between the cabin and the barn. About that time, Marlene arrived with her boys; she brought chicken and dumplings. She made the best in the county. Miss Bessie's was a close second, though. Zora Mae helped her carry her things from their buggy.

Zora Mae and I ran off to be alone, leaving the old folks and their old-timey ways in the yard. We went to the spring, but I didn't want to lallygag because I wanted to greet William when he arrived.

"Mammy asked 'bout yuh yestiddy, wanted tuh know if yuh were all right, 'cause ain't nobody seen hide nor hair of yuh for the longest spell. How yuh been?"

Pride flared in her smile when she said,

"Guess whut?"

"Whut?"

"I can court now."

"Really!"

"'Bout time. I'm the last girl—everybody courtin' 'cept me. Yuh know why, though. Mama's so old-fashioned. She so scared I'm gonna git a big belly—she watches me lac'uh hawk. I gits so tired of her actin' like it's her pussy."

"Oh, Zora Mae! Yuh sound jest like Fast Fannie." I waited a tad and asked, "So, who? Is he bewitchin'?" I asked, gigglin' and goosin' her in her side. She ran a little ways to escape my playful thrusts.

"He ain't no ways as handsome as William, but he's right pleasin' tuh look at."

"Must be Wayland Lofton. He's sweet on you."

"Nah, he ain't."

My eyebrow arched with inquisitiveness but fell when I asked, "Well, is he a secret?"

"Okay. It's Willie Deke," she said.

"Bullock? From Hampton? The one they say is so B-A-D?"

"Oh, Margaret. Deke's a sweet boy."

"Sweet, my foot! He prob'bly wants tuh jump up and down on yuh. That's why he's sniffin'."

"Why yuh got'tuh spoil everythang'? I didn't say that when yuh told me 'bout William."

"William ain't like no Willie Deke. 'Sides, how old is that boy? Ain't he way older than Joshua?"

"Whut that got'tuh do wid anythang?"

"What Miss Bessie say? Does she know? Folks talk 'bout the way he treats cats and dawgs—he took two cats and tied their tails tuh'gether and threw 'em 'cross a clothesline. He kills things for sport! Folks have seen him in the woods shootin' birds out the trees, killin' thangs he ain't even gon' eat. Dud'en that bother you?"

She stood quiet, slapped her hands on her not-yet-full hips, and appraised me like I didn't have any sense.

I said, "It sho' bothers me. If somebody messes wid animals and treats 'em bad like that, yuh cain't expect 'em tuh treat people much better. He scares me, Zora Mae." I took her hand.

"Promise me yuh won't court him no more."

"Margaret, Deke ain't gonna hurt me."

"You sho' 'bout that? Lawd knows there are boys better than Willie Deke Bullock. Besides, yuh're beautiful and could have any boy yuh fancied." I touched her shoulder. "Please promise me."

She frowned the length of a fiddler's bow but promised.

I took a gander at the sun.

"We best be gittin' back."

When we arrived, the yard was full of people, but William wasn't there. I headed to the porch to help Mammy, but Aunt Sarah met me with a smile.

"Whut'ja lookin' all sad about? The most handsomest boy jest came through that gate."

I turned around.

"That William?" she asked.

"Yessum."

"Tell him tuh come here. Tell him Aunt Sarah wanna meet him."

I ran into the yard, grabbed William by the hand, and brought him onto the porch.

"Son," she said, "I done heard a right smart bout'cha. Come here and give Aunt Sarah a hug."

She grabbed him about the head and shoulders and pulled him into the middle of her titties. They were sizable ones, too! William tried to escape, but she held him right in there, tight. The poor boy fought for air; his face turned scarlet.

"Sarah! Whut'ja tryin' tuh do? Kill the po' child?" Aunt Sarah pushed him out from her and took a gander, head to toe, head to toe.

"You's uh right good-lookin' boy," she said. "Anybody tell yuh that?"

"Yessum," William said, eyes searching the porch floor.

Then she turned to me, "Baby girl, if'n I be about forty-six years younger, I whups yo' tail, and I'd take this little yellow nigga. If'n us 'tweren't kinfolk. Since we is, I jest wanna peck on the cheek."

William approached the target as if he'd rather do an about-face and run in the opposite direction, but he gave her a quick peck.

"Always been right partial tuh high-yellow niggas. Ain't marry one but I always lacs the way they be lookin'."

"William, don't pay her no mind. Been like this all her natural-born life, and she too old tuh change. So, we gonna haf'tuh keep her out'ah trouble," Mammy said.

"Yessum," he said.

"Y'all go on now," Aunt Sarah said.

William and I headed over to the tables to stake out a spot. I looked back and caught Mammy and Aunt Sarah staring at us. Mammy whispered in Aunt Sarah's ear again. They whispered some more, and Aunt Sarah's throaty voice screamed into a laugh that filled the yard.

It had been ages since so many people had visited our house, and they danced, slapped their knees in laughter, and were ready to feast. Down-home food covered every inch of those tables, and folks licked their chops and sucked their fingers. They gnawed and cracked bones, scooped out blood-rich marrow, and crunched tendons and sinew. They crunched on salads and smacked mashed potatoes to the roof of their mouths, washing it all down with tangy lemonade sweetened to perfection. After we finished eating, everybody was laid out, all fat and sassy. Aunt Sarah said, "Know what this 'minds me of? Them old carpet dances they use'ta have on the plantation."

"Carpet dances. What's that?" William asked.

"'Round Christmastime, the slaves take all the rugs and carpets off the floor. Mens decked out in they claw-hammer coats and womens in they frilly dresses. The whole family be cuttin' a rug and struttin' they stuff while the slave musicians playin'. White folks be eatin' some fine food—boned turkey, terrapin stew, stuffed and baked chickens, and plenty of jellies, creams, and pies. Us cook up doves wid orange peelings. Never could keep none of them slaves from the wenders; shinin' little black faces be pressed right up against the wenderpanes. Soon as the company done left the dinin' hall, the slave musicians go down tuh the street and carry on 'til the risin' of the sun."

"Oh, that sounds nice!" Lena said.

"Crumbs, baby. Crumbs," Aunt Sarah said. By then, everybody—old folks and youngins—had crowded around Aunt Sarah.

"Y'all 'members whut it be's lac. Don'tcha?" Heads bobbed up and down, along with the "uh-huh's" and "sho'nuf's" coming from the older folks all around.

She started again.

"Yuh 'members the story 'bout that boy. He 'bout five or six. He'd steal away and try tuh learn his ABCs every once in a while. One day, the old overseer ketches him in the barn down near where they store the corn. He drags the boy tuh the slave street. When he done summoned all the field hands, he say, 'I wants this tuh be a lesson tuh all y'all darkies. You ain't gots no right tuh learn tuh read.' Then he whups the boy. That whip rips at his back 'til his flesh be ruby red. He whups that boy 'til his po' back be cut open, and that whip be covered wid blood. But that wan't the worst of it, 'cause he beats the boy around his face and eyes so hard, the boy go blind."

She stopped then, stood up, scanned every one of those faces, but focused her gaze on Lena and said,

"Crumbs. See, baby, them few times when them white folks act lac they human beings, it be nuthin' but crumbs."

NINE

Aberrations and the Glow of Angels

I clutched the memories of our family shindig as tight as a jailer held a man waiting to be strung up. Not long after our gathering, White Candy came home for a visit. At one time, I thought we would be friends forever, but now she acted as if she was above my raising. She had become mighty biggety, and so uppity she'd drown in a rainstorm 'cause she held her nose so high in the air. Yes, indeed, she had gotten infected with the "creeping crud," that I-hates-dem-niggas disease, like her pappy. My friendship with her showed me that life can turn on a dime, and you can never be sure about what's gonna happen next. You never know when your friendships will dry up, and you'd be so desperate for friends that you'll end up acting like trees, bribing passing dogs to squirt their attention in your direction. You can't be sure if your nearest and dearest will support you after you had slogged uphill through molasses to support them. You can't foresee who will remain your friend when times get so hard you couldn't sell a hummingbird latched to a string for a nickel.

I had last seen White Candy just before her wedding but she didn't even say howdy-do. By then, White Candy thought the sun rose and set in Vivian, and when Candy got hitched in the fall of 1921, Vivian was her matron of honor. Candy had met her fiancé in Atlanta; he was part of the Southern aristocracy, too.

I hadn't laid eyes on Candy's husband, but Marlene said his name was Alexander and he was "mo' than a speckled pup in a red wagon"—

straight-up handsome, she thought. In that department, Vivian didn't fare better than White Candy. She had married old man Hollis when she was twenty-one. But he fared better than both of them, because when he was with Vivian, he sho' stepped livelier. I agreed with Fast Fannie, who said, "He ain't doing nuthin' but sappin' her dry wid his old dried-up tail."

I suppose Vivian didn't realize an old rooster had her, revived to prance with a peacock's stride by the spirit of a gal he suckled like a parasite. Perhaps before the wedding, she hadn't seen the flabby skin hidden under his tailored suits and starched, snappy shirts. Before the wedding, Vivian wasn't aware of the stiff and creaking joints of a decrepit body that forced his grunted moans after he'd sat too long in a chair. Before she married him, she hadn't witnessed his stiff morning shuffle.

Mr. Hollis sho' was a puzzle, given how he showered his affections on some and spewed his venom on others. I thought him a scoundrel, but Mammy possessed more wisdom than me. When she said, "Mr. Hollis be's one of the Lawd's chilluns, too," I held my tongue. But reflecting on his ways and listening to Aunt Sarah and Mammy, I wondered what life was like before I was born. You know, when more upcountry hillbillies and former slaves bumped shoulders. Pappy, having lived longer than me, said white folks only passed Jim Crow laws "so those po'-ass crackers didn't haf' tuh scratch around with Negroes tuh make ends meet." But Aunt Sarah swore po' white folks only got what they wanted by lynching colored folks, burning down their homes, and taking their land. According to her, they did whatever they needed so they could grin like a bunch of possums eating sweet potatoes.

Anyway, colored folks thought Mr. Hollis shared that thinking and figured he wore the Klan's hood, just like Fannie said. They believed he and his Klansmen had struck David Bechard Leakes, the man who ran the *Hampton Tribune*, the colored newspaper. The week before Mr. Leakes's kin found his body, he had published a story concerning Joseph Stewart, who the Klan had lynched.

"Murderers" filled most of the *Tribune's* front page, and white folks were fit to be tied. They weren't riled up because this colored Yankee from Baltimore had written about Joseph Stewart, the accused rapist and murderer of Rebecca Hays, a white schoolteacher. They didn't have wind in their jaws because Leakes had written that a mob had taken Stewart from the Hampton County Jail and pelted him with the deafening cries of "Hang him, burn him at the stake!" They didn't throw a fit because he stated the facts about Stewart's lynching: his charred body had been crammed in a sack, dragged behind an automobile to the courthouse, and hung from a telephone pole. They fumed because "this Yankee nigga" had the gumption to write: "These are the acts of demons and murderers." Leakes had the gall to say: "No God-fearing person would commit such acts on another human being." He dared to declare, "There is no justice in Hampton County, and we Negroes must defend ourselves and our families with whatever means necessary."

So, Mr. Hollis was somebody's child, but I didn't think he was the Lord's. After listening to all of Mammy's stories of Southern brutality, and by the time Mr. Hollis's sort-of folks had murdered those two men, I began to see colored folks as white folks' prey. But I was still a girl and not yet a mother, and I didn't realize that when I was blessed with a son, I wouldn't be able to protect him, and that his color wouldn't be the only thing that made white folks despise him.

—•—

Sometimes I wished Mr. Hollis and his cronies would have put the fear of God in Willie Deke. Maybe that would straighten him up, because I worried over Zora Mae. Just when I needed some guidance in that situation, Fast Fannie visited, and I spoke to her about my dilemma.

"Margaret, why her wanna mess wid him? Folks say he wild and mean, runnin' 'round here wid all these loose women, and—"

"Fannie. Whut should I do? Should I tell Miss Bessie?"

"You talk tuh Zora Mae 'bout this?"

"Yeah, and she promised she wan't gonna court him anymore."

"Well, if'n she don't, then ain't nuthin' tuh tell. Talk tuh her some mo' and figure out which way her head's a-leanin'."

I was about to ask her thoughts about Joshua's and Neddy's new girlfriends when Robert entered with the twins, and the sight of them prompted me to ask, "When y'all gonna have some more?"

105

"Oh, we has plenty," Robert said.

"Seem like it be 'bout yo' turn," Fast Fannie said.

Oh, I pushed from the table right quick, held my hand up, and shook my head with a long, "N-o-o-o! Don't think so." Fannie's face mirrored disbelief, so I added, "I'm too young tuh git married."

Fannie just shook her head and said, "Us gon' see 'bout that."

When they left, I took a walk to Pleasant Ridge. I thought I would take my book, *Portrait of the Artist as a Young Man*. Miss Hillary believed that at seventeen, I was ready for a writer as complicated as James Joyce.

The sky was two hours from twilight, and the weather had cooled. When I got near the Ridge, two people sat all hugged up together. My heart sank. It was Zora Mae and her no-count goldbrick, Willie Deke. She jumped up when I asked,

"Whut y'all doin' up here?"

"Oh, jest talkin'." Then, looking kinda sheepish at Willie Deke, who started inching himself to his feet, Zora Mae said,

"I'm sorry. Margaret, do yuh know Deke?"

He let silence do his talking, staring at me with those cold, root-hog-or-die eyes, the kind that looked right through you. His eyes never waffled; they gave me the willies.

I smiled, chunked his silent aggression over my shoulder, and said, "Nah, I don't think we've ever met." I extended my hand and said,

"Pleased tuh finally meet'cha."

He just stared at me, throwing his piercing and incredulous eyes up against me as if he divined everything about me but didn't like what he saw. Zora Mae caught that tension, and her eyes signaled a confusion that orchestrated the jitteriness of her movements.

His eyes released me.

Willie Deke pulled Zora Mae aside. They weren't in earshot, but the way he moved his head from side to side, bobbing it every which way, while he glanced at me occasionally, suggested he held a hefty dose of rage—but about what?

He was a smidgen lighter than tar, which made his hazel eyes intense and his gaze even more peculiar. I couldn't get over the strange way he looked at me, but I marveled at the beauty of his dark, shiny skin and the way it caught the light. He had a thick head of hair, a full nose, and strongly arched lips. They were luscious and made for kissing—a woman could easily find them in the dark. Willie Deke was a tall man with muscled shoulders, and the upper part of his body narrowed to a little waist, and his butt stuck out like William's. His bobbing head had allowed me to study every angle of his face, but after he finished his raging shindig, he turned and vanished. Before Zora Mae could catch her breath, I said,

"You promised you weren't gonna court him anymore."

Her chin hit her chest, but the confusion she had held in her eyes seemed to shift to her shoulders and cascaded into her arms and her hips 'cause she wiggled and shifted her stance when she said,

"I tried to . . . but he said he loves me, Margaret."

"Loves yuh? Why, you've known a stray cat longer. How can yuh believe such a thing, Zora Mae!"

She looked at me with a hint of smugness, and she arched one eyebrow as a warning, but these cues didn't stop me from saying,

"Have yuh told Miss Bessie?"

"I ain't tellin' her *nuthin',*" she said with her head thrown back like the devil was coming up behind her with reinforcements.

"Why not?" I demanded as I side-rolled my head for emphasis.

"I know whut she's gon'say," Zora Mae said. "She dud'en wants me tuh have *nuthin'* or *nobody.* I want sump'em I can call my own . . . somebody who's gonna love me jest the way I am."

"Zora Mae. He ain't the one. Sump'em 'bout that boy . . . I cain't put my finger on it, but sump'em ain't right 'bout him."

"You jest *jealous!*" she said and reared way back for emphasis, with a lot of head tossing, to say, "That's whut it is. *You . . . jest . . . jealous!* You are just like my mama."

"Oh, don't be silly. I'm yo' friend, and I'm always gonna be that."

"You ain't no friend. If'n yuh was, you'd help me, and you'd understand."

"Zora Mae. You's talkin' foolishness."

Her slow elevating head suggested the appearance of something new—defiance was its name—and it enabled her to enunciate each word with sure-fire authority. "*Don't—matter—none. Don't—matter—whut—you—*

or—Mama—thank—no—ways. Deke done *axed* me tuh marry him," was her final statement of sovereignty.

She had never inclined her nose in such a manner or sucked her teeth with such precision. In the wake of her assuredness, I floundered in a sea where even a dinghy couldn't rescue me, and in realizing that, I mounted only a shallow protest.

"Marry! Oh, no. You cain't!"

"Why not? I can do whutever I wanna do. Who gon' stop me?"

"Miss Bessie will. If yuh don't tell her, I will!"

She placed her hands on her wannabe-woman hips and moved close enough for me to feel her warm breath when she said, "If yuh tell my mama, yuh ain't no friend of mine, and I'll never speak tuh yuh as long as I can draw a breath."

"Guess that's whut it's got'tuh be then."

I turned and walked right to Miss Bessie's house. I crossed her broom-swept yard with hopes Miss Bessie could do something with Zora Mae, talk some sense into all that stubbornness.

———◦◦———

Pappy had been working up a storm. Before our dreams jarred us awake, he worked the crops as the morning chased the shadows from the fields. Joshua and Neddy toiled alongside him for most of the day, and then he'd join Robert and his pappy at the mill. I finally asked Mammy why Pappy was working so hard. Her silence broke open into a sigh, and she said,

"I 'spects it be time tuh tell y'all why Pappy gots tuh put mo' than one string on his bow. Us gon' have uh'nuther youngin."

"Mammy, ain't you excited?"

Another sigh, and she said,

"I'd hoped me and yo' pappy was gonna git time tuh'gether. This-here youngin gon' change everythang."

With the excitement of youth, I asked, "When, Mammy?"

"Sometime in October," she said. "Gon' haf tuh 'pend on yuh twice as much."

Being seventeen, I had been the knee-baby for a while, but Lena's position would shift with this new youngin. She would become a thirteen-year-old knee-baby.

Neddy and Joshua wouldn't be of any help. They had started sniffing after women, and Mammy was especially mad with Joshua because he had taken up with a woman named Constance. She had a sizable brood, but unlike the nursery rhyme, she wasn't that old and seemed quite capable. She was ten years older than Joshua, though. It wasn't apparent at first why he took up with her, but he sho'nuf hung to her coattail. I reckoned she was the first woman he jumped up and down on.

That messes up men's heads, you know.

Whether that was true or not, Constance was extra pretty, not high yellow, but she had a pleasing color, a cute shape, and long hair that she wore unpressed. She had a sweet voice like Miss Hillary, and I understood why Joshua took a liking to her.

Initially, nobody knew about Constance's origin or the mystery behind the children who bore no resemblance to her. Mammy and Pappy were beside themselves, and Mammy even declared it wasn't natural. "Her too old for Joshua," she said, but I figured Mammy opposed Constance because Joshua was Mammy's favorite and no woman would ever be suitable. But Pappy didn't like her because, he said, "Joshua ain't got no business takin' care of whut some uh'ther man done made."

We discovered Constance had adopted the children because their parents, friends of her family, had died suddenly. She moved to New Harmony because she thought it was beautiful, "a quaint village," and because she loved the South. Besides, her mammy had grown up in Hampton, and we learned of Constance's wealth; her pappy was well-to-do.

Imagine that!

Once Pappy learned of her roots, he said nothing else about her having all those children. Mammy still said, "Josuha ain't gots no business wid her. Her still too old."

Mammy may have fussed over Constance and Joshua, but she said little about Neddy's girlfriend, Hazel, who was about my age. If Jeremiah, Fast Fannie's old beau, had been female, Hazel and Jeremiah would've been twins. She was *ug-g-g-g-g-ly*! How ugly? She had to sneak up on a glass of water to take a drink. She was so ugly she looked like she fell from an ugly tree and hit every branch before hitting the ground. I mean, she could scare roaches away. Hazel would make blind children cry, and she'd make a freight train take to a dirt road. If she were a scarecrow, the corn would run away. She was a nappy-headed, lantern-jawed, big-foot, snuff-dipping woman with teeth so bucked she could eat corn through a picket fence. And on top of that, she was soot-faced. Jeremiah had a thick head of nappy hair that he should've cut off. So did Hazel. Her nappy kitchen would have screamed if a comb got close to it. Like Jeremiah, her only hope was a fresh start: *Cut it all off!* Neddy ignored what we thought or said, but Lena sho'nuf gave him a fit when she talked about Hazel.

With Pappy working and Joshua and Neddy gallivanting after women, the menfolk weren't any help. I had a lot of added responsibility, but I had to consider William's feelings. He wanted to marry me. Of course, I loved the boy, and if I were going to do it, I'd do it with him, but I wasn't ready to get married. Not yet. Not at seventeen.

By October, Mammy was enormous; sitting or rising required somebody's help. To make matters worse, she felt right poorly during most of the pregnancy. Because of her condition, Mammy sometimes struggled to get out of bed, or it claimed her completely. Fannie helped, but despite all the sand Mammy raised about Constance, Constance became one of her blessings. During those hard times, Constance was the first person to come around and the last to leave her side. Pappy did what he could, but his focus was putting food on the table and making ends meet. As Mammy got worse off, I needed to leave school. I didn't mind. Mammy came first, and I had learned to read. With that ability, my world grew beyond the limitations imposed on my status as a woman and a Negro.

My baby sister was born in the afternoon. It was Friday, October the 13th, 1922. A chill lingered in the air that fall morning as I prepared Lena for school and woke Mammy. I helped Mammy to the rocker, and she was more animated than usual. As we watched the fall colors, she spoke at length and brimmed with things to share, particularly about her mammy and pappy.

"My mammy lived on Pleasant Bluff Plantation way 'foe my pappy,

Rufus, come here tuh live; he come here from Mississippi.

"See, Massa Thornton of the Twelve Horse Plantation daddied him, and he be's one of the finest folks God ever let draw a breath. When Pappy born, Miss Angeline, the old missus of the plantation, hated him and his mammy, Ruth.

"Massa Thornton loved Grandmammy Ruth mo' than he loved Miss Angeline, who acted lac the devil done give her 'nuf poison tuh last her a lifetime. 'Cause of that, it be hard for 'em, but Massa Thornton protected them. But one day, he come down with a cold, and he gits powerful sick, so bad off he die.

"Yuh knows the first thang Miss Angeline do, don'tcha? That's right, her finds herself some nigga speculators. She splits 'em up and tell Ruth her bet not make one sound, bet not cry. If her do, her gon' git a whoopin' that's gon' cut her flesh 'til her cain't stand, and they gon' leave her so the buzzards can fill they bellies.

"Ruth's eyes fill up, so full her could hardly see through 'em, but her ain't open her mouth when they drags Rufus off.

"He grieved a long time, jest lac a whipped dawg, but Pappy ends up here, in Sowth Ca-linah."

"How did he git here?"

"The slave drivers brung 'em, and they worser than some of them over-seers. They drove 'em lac cattle, all chained up tuh'gether from Mississippi tuh Charleston. 'Twas 'bout forty or fifty slaves, all bound tuh'gether, suf-ferin' in the August heat. Ain't feed 'em much and ain't give 'em much water neither in all that heat and mis'ry.

"By the time Pappy gits here, he all raggedy and could hardly walk 'cause his feets all cut open. He say a young gal wid twinklin' eyes comes, washes and cleans him up. Her so moved by whut he done been through her reaches down and kisses his feets. He figured right then he gonna marry her, the gal wid the tender lips and healin' hands. That be yo' grandmammy, Emma."

"You always say Lena has hands like hers." I brushed away the tear that crawled down my cheek and asked, "How did they shoulder all that misery, Mammy?"

"Faith in the Lawd," Mammy said. The sound of the gate opening focused our attention.

"Oh, here comes Marlene," I said.

She took the chair to Mammy's right.

"Where the boys?" I asked.

"Left 'em up at the house playin'." She took a breath. "I is right winded today." She turned to Mammy and said, "You lookin' right good today, Miss Lula. 'Bout ready tuh end all this, I bet?"

"Any day now, I hopes. This youngin done gives me a fit. Never has no trouble wid the others, but this one, Lawd have mercy!"

"Guess I is blest. My two be right easy."

Mammy rocked a bit in the silence before she said, "Marlene, yuh told us 'bout how the overseer kilt some of yo' kin. Whut else yuh 'members 'bout the slave and Reconstruction days?"

"Lawd! Never wants tuh thank on it. Done seen . . . done come tuh know too many stories of them awful times, them weepin' times, the darkness . . . but Reconstruction wan't no better. I wanna stay in the light!"

With her eyes fixed in the distance, she was quiet for a while, and then she said, softly at first, "Y'all know I ain't lac talkin' 'bout this stuff."

"But the youngins, they need tuh hear," and Mammy gave her an encouraging pat.

"Granny use'ta say she'd never forgit their evilness, Massa Felix and that Pearson Hall. 'Cause he'd whup a po' slave so bad wid that cowhide, yuh could hear 'em pleadin' way in the next county: 'Massa! Oh, Massa, please have mercy, Massa!'

"He ain't care. Split a nigga's head wide open, chunk his body in the river. Say he ain't deserve no box; cain't be wastin' the wood.

"Granny say yuh could always tell his darkies when yuh seen 'em."

Marlene's eyes welled with tears, propelling her to her feet. She stood there briefly, then walked back and forth, like she stalked prey.

"See, my mammy and granny be pretty close. Ten years done passed after Daniel and Lucy done been kilt, and right after that done happened, the slaves be freed. Massa Felix still run the plantation like he done 'foe 'mancipation, but had them there after the war, sharecropping. During them years, life be's hard, but they gots each other. And a young buck from one of the plantations down the way started croppin' for Massa Felix. Mammy be's head over heels 'bout this fellow, named Cumberland, and he loves Mammy like nobody's business, and they jumps the broom, but it wan't meant tuh last. Massa Felix see tuh that.

"Never told this story tuh nobody 'foe today. Never *breathes* it tuh uh soul. Only Granny and the others know, but most of 'em dead and gone now."

Marlene took a deep breath.

"Granny say I was 'bout a week old when one day, durin' the summer of 1874, my mammy done sump'em that change everybody life on that place."

Marlene stopped pacing and found her chair again. Me and Mammy matched our breathing to Marlene's rhythm. She leaned back and started again.

"Granny say Massa ain't paid 'em in such a long time, it be's hard to make ends meet and everybody hungry. Food was sho'nuf scarce like hen's teeth. They starvin'. In the afternoon's heat, my mammy, weak from givin' me life, sneak out her cabin and steal a chicken from Massa's coop. After her go 'round back tuh pluck and clean the hen, her puts it on the fire, boilin', whilst Cumberland be's in the fields workin'. For some reason or the other, Massa Felix come down tuh her cabin. He seen the chicken boilin' on the fire; he leaves, but Massa ain't say nuthin'. He still treat'em like they's slaves, and who gon' stop him. So, when he come back, he carryin' his cowhide. He make her tote the pot outside, and he call all them darkies from the fields and they cabins. He told'em—says there's a penalty for stealin'. Granny pleaded wid Massa Felix—tellin' him 'bout me, tellin' him that Abigail done jest had me, was weak and starvin'—need sump'em tuh eat. So, Massa Felix tells her tuh eat that chicken scaldin' hot, and then he whup her. My daddy tries tuh save her, but Massa Felix shoot Cumberland. He hit the ground dead 'foe his left foot could meet the earth. Granny say he whup mammy sump'em awful—everybody on the street wept for her.

"He *kicked* her! And he *stomped* her! He kept kickin' her in the stom-ach—and she got'tuh bleedin' 'tween her legs. He waited 'til there wan't nary a sign of breathin', and as if none of that wan't uh'nuf, he cussed and spit on her. Left her there tuh waste away in that scorchin' summer heat. Wud'den let nary uh person tend tuh her; her die right there!

"Granny say Daniel and Lucy's killin' was hard, but Abigail's broke her heart, and her ain't never seen nuthin' tore up folks' hearts so."

Silence.

Marlene sprang to her feet and started walking, but then it was as if a haunting image grabbed her and jerked her toward us. Wide-eyed, she said,

"That night, they *kilt* Massa Felix. *Kilt* him dead."

"How, Marlene?" Mammy asked.

"There be this huge nigga by the name of Shane. He come up 'hind Massa Felix and slugs him so hard, he out this world. When he come tuh his wits, he be gagged and bound lac'uh Christmas turkey and fastened tuh uh whippin' post they fashioned in the woods. The mens took they turns, and they bloodied Massa Felix lac he lashed Abigail. When they cut him loose, they stomped him and whupped him wid every thang they could find, 'til he don't move no mo'.

She took to stomping at the porch hard, real hard, over and over again.

She stopped, and in almost a whisper, she said,

"He still breathin' though.

"Then they totes his sorry-ass body down tuh the riverbank, cinch-ties him, and chunks him in the river where he drowns. Next mornin', they finds him dead 'bout a mile or so downstream. He caught up wid some uh'ther trash."

She turned.

"Oh, Granny say they come—they badger 'em sump'em awful. Yeah, they acts lac they gon' kill all the niggas if'n they don't talk, but ain't nary a darkie open they mouths. The missus, her name Drucilla, fixed it so some of us ends up in Savannah, but some of the uh'ther folks start croppin' for uh'ther folks 'cause Drucilla had no heart for sharecroppin'. Folks got separated, but Granny reckoned there cain't be no situation or person worser than Massa Felix.

"That be's how I gits tuh these parts."

Marlene flopped in the chair.

A respectful and solemn silence fell over us.

She pulled out the handkerchief in her pocket, wiped her eyes, and blew her nose. She came to herself and said, "When yuh's a slave, a darkie, yuh is worser than any dawg—treated lac yuh ain't fit tuh even eat the crumbs from the Massa's table.

"I rather take a gun and blow my head clean off 'foe I lives lac they lived in them days. I got the stories of them times wrote down, wid some uh'ther thangs, but Massa Felix stole my folks from me—never got the chance tuh see 'em love each uh'ther lac yuh and Mr. Jake do.

"Lawd, I don't know how my Granny did whut she did!"

I understood Marlene better than I ever had before. All of us were in tears, and when Mammy lifted my chin, she said,

"Daughter, I wants you tuh keep these stories right there." She touched my chest, right where my heart drummed.

"You gots tuh promise me that when I passes on, you gon' tell these stories and keep these memories alive and fresh in the hearts of all the chilluns."

A knowing, ushered by the presence of the Sainted and described by old folks as the fingers of God moving from the unknown to the known, passed between us. With my hand in hers, the awareness took form and spoke. Its energy ruffled the marsh grasses and the moss that draped from trees, and its presence thumped and spoke of ancient drums to unify into a single beat in my chest. Mammy said,

"They's the Spirits of yo' people, daughter."

The touch of Mammy's hands and the sound of her voice lifted me that morning to their shoulders. So, in listening to their stories, I understood that courage sired me, and that courage would someday help me endure the loss of my son.

I hugged Mammy.

Marlene sat a spell before she climbed the hill and was swallowed by the Big House. I relished the peace of our cabin, and I stayed on the porch with Mammy, briefly listening to the sounds of farm life, before returning to my chores. Once inside, I pondered the stories that sifted through my mind, and I was in the shed sleeping room when a loud grunt snagged my ears. I ran to the porch, where I found Mammy all hunched over, her head nearly touching the floor.

Mammy held out her hand as if she were waiting for something. Fright struck me. I needed help, but those with knowledge—Marlene, Fannie, and Constance—were too far to fetch.

I grabbed Mammy, stood her up, and threw her arm around my shoulder. She was almost too heavy to handle alone, but I got her into the house before the water flooded her low-heeled shoes. I hankered for the jitters to leave my legs and for calmness to soothe my fingers.

"Mammy, whut are we gonna do?"

"Don't leave me. Youngin gon' be here 'foe yuh can fetch anybody. Us gon' be all right." She moaned, "Don'tcha fret now."

I struggled to hold on to her.

"I tells yuh whut tuh do. Git me on the bed," she said.

When I got her there, I propped her head up, and I wanted to be there, but I thought, *Something ain't right 'bout a child seeing their mammy's private parts,* but then, *Can't be wincing or flinching like that. Mammy needs me.*

She told me what to do.

After the shock that it was coming, Mammy assured me it wouldn't take long, but it seemed as though it was an eternity. We waited for "the bloody show," but Mammy's pushing was exhausting her. She arched her back, and when those awful cramps hit her, she gritted her teeth and didn't yield to the intense cramping that rushed through her. She repositioned her body when the pain fought for control, and I banished all thoughts of death and dying as she taught me what it meant to be a mother—a warrior of suffering through the gift of love. Mammy looked as if she wished it were finished, but she never screamed. Instead, she focused her breathing and directed her energy to giving birth. She sweated, and she struggled, and she thrashed through the agony of the crowning. I held on to her the best I could. Through it all, Mammy never yelled, not one time, but her face ached with pain. The baby's head was crowning, and when Mammy felt the head, determination etched her forehead. She coordinated her breathing with the crowning, and the head emerged. Mammy uttered a long moan. It was faint at first but grew louder until it filled the room. She had vanquished agony and hopelessness with the power of love.

It was a girl.

I placed her on Mammy's tummy; the afterbirth soon followed.

I cried.

I had never seen anything as beautiful in my life.

"Tie and cut the cord," Mammy said.

"Whut?"

"Use the string, tie it off . . .'bout right there, kinda close tuh the belly."

My hands shook. I feared that I would tie it off or cut it in the wrong spot.

I wrapped the baby in a blanket and placed her in Mammy's exhausted arms.

Pappy and the boys came home from the mill, and I met Pappy before he hit the gate. I told him what had happened, and he asked,

"How's Mammy? Old gal ain't whut her use'ta be," he said, smiling.

"She's sleepin', but she seems all right." Pappy kissed me on my forehead.

"Thank you," he said, and I'll remember that moment as long as I live. Tears crested.

He embraced me with a smile and said, "I is so proud of you." We went inside to check on Mammy. She had been sleeping but must've sensed somebody standing over her because she opened her eyes, glanced at Pappy, smiled, and drifted back to sleep.

Late that night—I don't recall what time it was—Mammy started groaning in her sleep and thrashing. I jumped up from the chair where I had fallen asleep and found her soaking wet. She was bleeding—blood had gotten on everything.

I woke Pappy, who had fallen asleep nearby.

"Mammy don't look too good."

"Whut's the matter?" he asked, half-awake.

"She's bleedin' mighty bad, and she's hot as a poker."

Pappy threw on clothes, a shirt inside out and mismatched socks. I knew he was in serious trouble when he tried frantically to put his right foot in his left shoe. Once that was resolved, he scurried out of the house, mounted the horse, tapped its hindquarters, and off they went to rouse the doctor.

By then, everybody was up, taking turns at the window.

Joshua mounted the other horse to fetch Constance, thinking she might be able to help, but Neddy seemed nailed to the floor with worry. I was glad Lena wasn't there. She had spent the night with Fannie.

When Joshua returned with Constance, who had insisted they also get Miss Hillary, Mammy looked worse.

"We have to stop the bleeding," Miss Hillary said.

"How we gonna do that?" I asked. "We aren't doctors!"

Constance held me by the shoulders and rocked me in her calm arms, and Miss Hillary started talking about something she had seen or done. I couldn't figure out what she ran on about. I did what she told me while Constance tended to the baby.

Pappy returned.

"Doc is drunk and talkin' 'bout he don't doctor on no niggas or animals."

Our hearts sank.

"Lord, when will somebody come who cares about us?" Miss Hillary pleaded.

Pappy paced the floor, but he finally pulled a chair next to Mammy and cradled her hands in his.

They spoke no words.

I had never seen my pappy cry, but he cried over Mammy that night, and none of us knew what to do. All we could do was wait.

Miss Hillary suggested Neddy get the preacher and Fannie.

I knew Pappy loved her, but I never realized how much. When the fulcrum of life shifted, love revealed itself in their eyes: their gaze reflected their first kiss and union, their first disappointment tempered by forgiveness, and their first child screaming at her first whiff of air.

The rolling boil of Mammy's breathing fell into a simmer and then collapsed into the flatness of still water. It felt like an indescribable emptiness had entered the room. It was the strangest sensation; it was nowhere but everywhere. Then there was that sound. It was like nothing I had heard before, but I imagined it as the last bit of her soul emptying from a dense vessel. With that silence, her lids parted, and her eyes glazed with awe as they followed the upward glide of something we could not see. In the course of their rise, only the white parts glistened. They vanished when her lids fluttered closed with the measured grace of God's right hand. A smile graced her face.

She was gone.

Everybody cried, calling after Mammy.

I had never experienced the death of a loved one, and I had never loved anyone that much. I studied her face, and I knew. I knew death. Peace was its name. Her face confirmed that there was no valley or mountain, dawn or sunset, river or ocean, or any earthly thing that revealed the anointed power and divine presence so clearly. She held majesty. She reflected love.

It must be true what folks said, "When you done lived a good life, an angel comes down from heaven, kisses yuh, and takes yuh right tuh the bosom of the Lord." But our pining was relentless and our grief unyielding. She was gone, had become one of His Great Spirits.

After the wailing diminished, Miss Hillary asked somebody to fetch Mr. Collins.

Neddy went for Mr. Collins. When Mr. Collins arrived, he waited, standing in quiet reverence, while Constance and Fannie prepared Mammy so he could take her body.

The cabin ached in silent solemnity.

It was late by the time they loaded Mammy into Mr. Collins's hearse—even later when we reached Miss Hillary's. I wanted to stay close to Mammy that night. Miss Hillary put me to bed, but I couldn't sleep. I was too busy thinking about Mammy and what Mr. Collins would do to her in his undertaker shop.

I couldn't stop crying.

The following day, when we returned to the cabin after sending for Aunt Sarah and Uncle Luther, it was like we were in somebody else's house.

All any of us could feel was bad.

Mr. Collins didn't get any sleep. He worked on Mammy all through Friday night and into the next morning. We had the wake at the cabin that Saturday afternoon. When he brought her home, she still had the glow of angels on her face. Everybody loved Mammy; it looked like every colored person in New Harmony came to pay their respects. Folks started streaming in early Saturday afternoon and kept coming late into Saturday night. We held the funeral on Sunday after the regular church services.

The funeral hung surreal and blurred. I remember our somber dress: womenfolk and menfolk were in black; Lena and the baby were in white. I couldn't wrap my head around it, entering the church with Mammy in a casket.

Fannie fell out; Robert and Neddy took her outside. I held the baby, who Mammy didn't have a chance to name. Pappy sat, head in his hands, hunched over. I couldn't fathom him living without her. Aunt Sarah and Uncle Luther sat stoop-shouldered from grief. Aunt Sarah was now the last of her mammy's children, and she said, "Even the baby girl done gone on 'foe me. 'Tain't right. I is 'posed to go 'foe Lula do—Lawd, 'tain't right. 'Tain't right," she cried.

When the funeral was over, everyone headed to the graveyard, but I couldn't watch them throw dirt into Mammy's face. I took the baby and waited in Mr. Collin's car.

We went home to a house full of folks and their food baskets. William was there, but his presence and concern only made me cry more tears.

He held me and rocked me from side to side.

"I'm so sorry," he said. "I love you, Margaret." He still wanted to marry, but with Mammy dying, I didn't think it was possible. *Pappy can't raise these children by himself,* I thought. Just then Miss Bessie pulled me from William's embrace and said, "I is gon' miss Lula sump'em awful. How you doin', baby?"

"Holdin' on, Miss Bessie. Where's Zora Mae?"

"Baby, Zora Mae done run off wid that Bullock boy. Ain't got no idea where she done run off to."

"When?"

"Been gone 'bout two weeks now. Us has a fallin' out, and her twisted out some mighty nasty thangs 'foe her leaves. Nobody ain't seen hide nor hair from her since."

"Gone off tuh marry him I 'spect."

"I reckon so. I axes the Lawd tuh keep her safe and don't let no harm come tuh her."

"Miss Bessie, if I learn anythang a'tall, I'll be sho' tuh tell yuh."

"I's sick wid worry, but this ain't the proper time for that. You need tuh take care of yo'self. Yuh hear?"

Marlene wasn't at the funeral—Vivian wouldn't let her attend—but she came to the house after we returned. She entered with her children, and silence gripped the room. I felt so sorry for her.

Nervousness walked along with her but left her side when she stood next to Pappy and said, "Miss Lula be a good woman, Mr. Jake, and I's *so* sorry God done called her on home. Her was the onliest breath of *decent* air 'round these parts." When Marlene said that last part, she said it kind of loud. Pappy took her hand and said,

"Thank you, Marlene. She thought right much of yuh, too."

"And I of her, Mr. Jake."

Marlene came over and stood next to me. She hugged me, kissed my cheek, and left as quickly as she had come.

I didn't think folks were ever going to forgive her. They treated her like she had leprosy or something worse. It didn't stop her from walking into a den of venomous snakes to pay her respects, though. Her courage had greater meaning than the sympathies of those pie-baking women and those head-nodding men. What price had they paid to be present? Besides, when they returned home, our cabin would shelter enough emptiness and grief to engulf the Big House.

I remembered something Marlene told me once. She said, "It's sump'em 'bout when mammies die that differ from when pappies die— there ain't a world big uh'nuf to hold the sorrow. Mammies give life; they the glue. They the ones who holds the family tuh'gether."

Her words weren't enough to capture the profound depth of a loss that stretched into the universe and beyond.

My life had changed forever.

TEN

Spun Into Cotton Candy

Pappy visited Mammy's grave often, but it took me some time before I could look toward the cemetery. Besides, anxiety always gripped me in graveyards. I didn't even like walking past them—too afraid haints would reach out from their abode and pull me into an airless chamber.

When I finally went, I jumped across graves as if pressured into an inspired game of hopscotch, thinking the slightest misstep was a sign of disrespect.

When I found Mammy's grave, I noticed our dry spring had caused only a green stubble to pockmark her plot of ground. Pappy had already kissed her headstone and said his words. The imprint of his right hand, palm and fingers spread wide, lay across the soft nut-brown earth about where Mammy's heart would be. Violets, their centers dotted with saffron, rested their bonnets against the plain white cross that identified her as "Beloved," held her name, and listed the dates of her beginning and passing.

I had picked some pink yarrow and Queen Anne's lace; I laid them next to Pappy's violets and knelt beside her. I started picking weeds from about where her neck would be, when a bundle of my thoughts broke loose into a web of remembrances.

"Mammy, I sho' miss you, but I know yuh're watchin' over us now.

"I fret 'bout Pappy, though. He's way mo' private and busies himself wid anythang that'll fill space or time . . . he can barely say yo' name.

"We named the baby Violet . . . yuh loved those flowers so, and she's as bright and cheerful as her name, growin' like there's no tomorrow.

"Fannie and Robert are doin' well, too. You ortah see the twins. They've grown so much. Cute as they can be . . . don't resemble our side, though. You'd be right proud of the way Fannie takes care of everybody. "Oh, let's see. Joshua and Constance are talkin' 'bout gittin' married. He still hasn't met her people; he's scared 'cause they're so rich and all. Yuh ortah hear him, Mammy. He said, 'I ain't got nuthin' tuh offer her.' I tried tuh tell him whut you would say, 'Boy! You got yo'self, and that's the most precious thang anybody can give tuh anyone.' That's whut you taught us . . .

"You'd be glad tuh know Neddy stopped seein' Hazel. Right after the wake, she snapped at him for cryin' over yo' passing, but when she followed that wid pursin' her lips and callin' him 'weak,' Neddy said she wan't for him. 'Cold-hearted and ain't show no kinda respect,' he said.

"And Lena, I'd find her cryin' herself tuh sleep, and I'd catch her sometimes in the wardrobe, holdin' on to one of yo' print dresses. She fretted so. But last month, she turned the corner.

"Of course, Marlene is still wid Mr. Hollis and Vivian, but Mammy, you ortah *see* her boys now. They've grown so, and they're as cute as they can be—spittin' image of Mr. Hollis. Marlene has 'em goin' tuh Miss Hillary's school.

"She misses yuh, Mammy. Pert' near every day, she says you were her only friend."

I bent over and kissed the cross after noticing that the sun had crawled as high as it could. "My Goodness, Lawd! I've been here for two hours or more." I jumped up.

"Got'tuh go, Mammy. Fast Fannie gon' kill me!"

When I reached the wrought-iron gate, a bit of weariness crept into my legs, but I turned and glimpsed her plot of ground one more time.

I smiled.

I couldn't believe I had parted Mammy's hair six months ago, scratched and blew dandruff from her scalp, and laid Violet in her arms. It had taken turning eighteen and a daily dose of burgeoning guilt before I knelt beside her again. Cheerfulness fluttered in my chest, and my head grew more buoyant as I drove the mare to pick up Violet at Fannie's.

"Thanks, Mammy," I whispered.

On my way to Fast Fannie's, clouds formed, and the sun disappeared.

First, a pewter-domed sky arched and touched the horizon. The grayness of those clouds turned into smoke-smudged cotton accented with slate and violet tones. The sky rumbled with thunder and sparked with lightning. I quickened the mare's steps, but the nightmare advanced, rendering the sky more sinister.

It's gon' be real bad, I thought as the wind stopped putting on airs and got right sassy.

When I reached Fannie's, I hugged her and started running off at the mouth. But all of a sudden, Fannie's face scowled as if she had seen a bunch of haints coming our way, irritated by the disrespect I probably afforded them earlier.

"Lawd, git the children!" she screamed.

"Whut?"

She spun me around, and I saw one of the blackest clouds I had ever seen heading toward us. It huffed, swirled, and snarled on the horizon, whooping the earth's tail and making a whole heap of dust.

We snatched up the children in our frantic scramble—Fannie had the twins and I had Violet.

"Yuh ain't got no cellar."

"The closet!" Fast Fannie hollered. "Git in the closet!"

As we shoved the children and their screams inside, a clap of thunder shot through the cabin like a cannon. We huddled in fear and darkness, hoping to brace ourselves against a wind that had plumb forgotten its home training. It sounded like a herd of stampeding wild horses, their hoofs striking lightning bolts across the darkened sky.

The house shook as the storm's fury battled against hard things in its path. The children screamed as eerie sopranos.

"Hush up!" Fannie scolded. "Hush up right now!"

They were too scared to silence themselves completely and took up whimpering like newborn pups. But when the wind picked up a butcher knife and pierced the closet door as if it had sliced through butter, the children hollered straight out. No more controlling them then.

The sound of battered doors intensified until the howling wind ripped them from their hinges; something shot through the windows, and the sounds of banging furniture, falling dishes, and breaking glass filled our hiding place.

Then, after all that fussing, there was silence.

"Better see," Fannie said.

I snatched her hand back.

"Don't open that door!"

She jerked away from me.

"Stop bein' a scaredy cat," she said as she turned the knob.

The house was a mess: flour, beans, rice, noodles, eggs, and every spice in the house splattered mosaics of color on the floor. On one side of the front room, the wind's collection of foreign debris had shattered windows. On the other side, remembrances and treasures remained untouched, but a closer inspection revealed the unimaginable: a straw angled itself through an unbroken windowpane. Furniture and broken knick-knacks sat in piles throughout the house. Even the black-padded seat of a red-framed tricycle rested upturned on another pile of debris, the tricycle's rubber wheels still spinning in the storm's direction.

If you only focused on the cloudless sky, it appeared as if nothing had happened elsewhere. The storm had spared the house, but on either side of the house, it looked like a gaint hand had gouged up the land, pried its fingers under other houses, scooped them from their foundations, and spun them into oblivion.

Robert approached, driving his mare toward us. He leaped from the wagon and ran up on the porch, grabbing Fannie and the children, kissing them all.

"Where Pappy at?" Fannie asked.

"Home," he said. "Boys, too; the twister skipped the mill."

I grabbed Violet and headed home to check on Lena. Our mare and the wagon had gone with that twister, so I borrowed Robert's.

As I drove the mare, the sight of the twister's fury astounded me—it had scarred the earth, uprooted trees, and plowed fields, creating new paths and drainage ditches. Cows, horses, mules, chickens, pigs, and sheep ran loose. A barn lay on its side, while scraps of fabric, keepsakes, large chunks of debris, and itsy-bitsy pieces of lumber littered the spots where stick-built houses once stood. Screen doors hung by one hinge; the limbs of a stripped tree snagged part of a fence, and brightly colored clothing (jackets, blouses, skirts, and pants) lent their colors to bushes stripped clean of leaves and blossoms; a chair hung in a nearby tree where the Griffin homestead once stood. And a spot where a forest once loomed now held tree trunks so gnarled and snapped that only splintered and jagged stumps remained for miles. Upon reaching the other side of the hill, I saw that our place didn't have a lick of damage. Pappy spotted us, and he ran to help us from the wagon.

"Thank the Lawd! Where y'all been at?"

"Fannie's. They're fine. House is in shambles, though."

"Where Lena at?"

"With Marlene—she got her this mornin'."

"Looks like they's all right up there," Pappy said.

When we arrived at the Big House, it looked deserted, but I spotted the shed and remembered the cellar's location. With Violet jiggling at my side, I ran toward it and stomped on the cellar door.

"Y'all in there?"

"Us down here," Marlene said. Pappy slung the door open.

Marlene, her boys, Lena, some colored hands, Vivian, Mr. Hollis, and Floyd all peered out from the darkness.

White folks and colored folks, men and women, were equal 'cause that twister forced equality—the wrath of storms didn't play favorites!

Pappy snatched up Lena. As we headed to Fannie's to drop off Lena and Violet, Pappy said, "Better head in'tuh town; they might need help if that twister hit 'em."

I accompanied Pappy.

The destruction unleashed on New Harmony shocked us—sadness gripped the town.

The twister had gobbled up one side of the courthouse, exposing its inner parts. Fortunately, the colored school still stood, but our church rested in another part of Hampton County. Nevertheless, our section of town escaped most of the twister's destruction. The white folks were in worse shape. Mr. Pete and his wife were killed when they were swept away along with their general store and all that penny candy and those ginger snaps. White children were in school when the twister came roaring through; all of the teachers and all but five of the children were killed—'bout sixty-some-odd folks in the schoolhouse when the twister came through. Mr. Henry, the blacksmith, wasn't hurt, but his business was gone, and Doc James, the one who said he didn't treat niggers and let Mammy die, well, he went on to meet his maker. The radio declared it the worst storm in Hampton County's history, and while no inferno had engulfed its hamlets and towns, hell seemed to erupt, and New Harmony stunk of evil. I hunted the crowd for William, and my heart flew in my throat when I snagged sight of him. He had been helping the other men. Dirt covered him. I took his hand, and to my surprise, Pappy said nothing. He surveyed us, and without flinching, he said, "'Spectin' y'all gon' wanna git hitched soon." He left us with a smile, turned, and walked toward all that death.

The following day, I woke early. I couldn't stop thinking about William and what Pappy had said. But Mammy's death had sparked uncertainty, and the twister made everything worse. At that moment, I didn't see the connection, but years later, after my son's murder and much reading, I began to view the twister as a metaphor for life. When I reflected on what happened to my baby, I saw how the murderer tore through our lives, snatching my Thad and leaving us with emptiness and loss. However, while I bathed Violet that morning, the cyclone of my thoughts spiraled and gravitated to what wasn't possible.

Just as I was about to dry Violet, William came by; he said he had something to ask me. We left, leaving Pappy and Lena to finish drying Violet. Mammy insisted on us being supervised, but Pappy trusted us a little more and let us walk without him. We arrived at the spring, and as I stood at its edge, William said,

"'Member when yuh asked me tuh be yo' boyfriend?"

I giggled.

"Now, I don't want yuh actin' lac'uh horse stung by a bumblebee when I axes yuh tuh be my wife."

I dropped my head and turned away but mumbled, "I cain't . . . not now."

He spun me around, cupped my face in his hands, smiled, and caressed my cheek. "Why not?"

"Mammy dead . . . and Pappy . . . well, whut he gon' do, raise Violet by himself?"

"My new pappy-in-law has given us his blessin'."

He smiled, reached up gentle-like and caught each of my tears with his finger. He waited for what he had told me to seep in, and then he said, "Think I'm gonna let'cha git away? I love you, Margaret Long, and I want you tuh be my wife, the mother of our children."

And he caressed me like I was a grown woman. I had crossed over, and with no desire to separate, I rested in his arms.

———————⋅⊙⋅———————

It was June 2, 1923, when I married my William. I asked Fast Fannie to stand with me, and William asked Robert. Since the colored church had gone with that twister, we got hitched in the churchyard. We didn't do a whole heap of planning. We were simple folk, and it made little sense to make a fuss. Besides, we wouldn't spend money on something that wasn't essential. Our love mattered most, and I didn't need a fancy dress—nothing like that. I needed his sturdy shoulders and the strength of his character.

Mammy had knitted me a lace shawl a long time ago; she had secured it in my hope chest, the cedar chest her pappy had given her. I wore the lace shawl across my head. So that was something old. Marlene put her talents to work and made me a simple white satin dress, which was something new. Before we left the house, Constance slipped me a gorgeous cameo that belonged to her grandmammy. She pinned it to the top of my dress, just below my throat. She said, "Now you have sump'em borrowed." Of course, not to be outdone, along came Fast Fannie. She pulled out a blue garter. I fell out laughing and asked,

"Where did'ja git that?"

"Now you's ready," she giggled. She was still my Fast Fannie.

I held a bouquet of violets, and I felt Mammy's presence.

Before getting in the wagon, I fussed with my appearance, but when Pappy approached and surveyed my dress and face, he said, "Yuh look lac all the sunshine in the world. You is beautiful—wish Lula could lay eyes on yuh. She'd be right proud of yuh. I know I is."

When we arrived in New Harmony, smiles in the crowd welcomed us. Some of the people I hadn't seen since Mammy's passing, and as Pappy and I walked toward the altar, the crowd opened like Moses parted the Red Sea. William gazed at me at the crowd's end, smiling as if I were the world's most beautiful woman.

Pappy let go, and William reached around and took my hand.

When the preacher asked William to repeat after him, William got stuck. He tried to speak, but something had stolen his voice. In his voiceless silence, he took my hand. The movement and grace of this gesture broke open recollections of how Mammy first glanced at Violet after I placed her in her arms—as she gazed with awe at what she had produced. It set me aflutter with anticipation of our first passionate kiss. It threw me into the joy of remembering childhood follies and triumphs. He held and kissed my hand like he had pressed his lips against the softness of cotton candy. I'll always cherish the affection of that moment. When he brushed my hand to his cheek, the tears moistening his face marked the joy and depth of the gratitude he unleashed upon becoming my husband, and with that display, I knew I would love him forever.

A solemn silence gripped the yard, and tears glistened on faces with eyes brightened by tenderness.

Pappy laid the broomstick down, and we joined hands. Before we jumped into the holy land of matrimony, I told William, "We got'tuh step high. The slaves use'ta say if'n yuh touch the broom, a spell would be cast on yuh. Whoever touches the broomstick first would be the first one tuh die." We both stepped high and then we kissed. Everybody came around hugging and kissing us, slapping William on the back.

⚬

I'd never been with a man, and anxiety and uncertainty showered me. Fannie briefed me on what to expect, and I loved William, but I wasn't sure if that was enough. When we arrived at the little place William's mammy and pappy had given us, he picked me up and carried me over the threshold. We stood there, unsure about what would come next but curious about the excitement that quivered below.

Honey, when we ended up in bed on those ironed sheets, and he was naked, and I was naked, he started kissing me, but gentleness ruled and directed his touch. He first kissed my forehead, then both my eyes. Before he flicked his tongue into my mouth, he ran it down my nose and across my lips. When he found my mouth, I ain't know what to do, so I started sucking on his tongue. He took me by the titties, and he began massaging them before he nursed like a baby. Nipples got real hard. I couldn't stay still and tried hard not to jump up and run.

I yielded to his desire, and he kissed me all over, in unfamiliar places.

I rubbed my nose along his damp skin to devour his scent. Hair, the texture a newborn baby would envy, blanketed the two perfect muscles that held me as I caressed his chest. I played in threads of silk that flowed as one thin line until it expanded, exploding to cover his belly. My tongue flicked against the firm contours of his body. I felt his shoulders, fingered the valleys and ridges of his muscled arms, and stroked the silky carpet that lay lightly on his forearms and hands.

Then he took his finger and began playing around down in my private parts. He rubbed its edges and started massaging. With my head arched and my back pert' near off the bed, I got to quivering. He didn't let up, and all I could do was stick out my tongue and wet my lips. I grabbed his head and held on, and he threw his tongue into my mouth. I shook like a leaf in the winds of that twister.

Then he stopped.

William's thing stood erect, the size of my wrist and the length of an extra-tall tumbler. When I was a child, I had seen Mr. Hollis's, but William's seemed mighty big to me, and I stood perplexed—was I to say, "Praise the Lawd!" or "Help me, Jesus!"?

When he put it in there, I squealed, "Help me, Jesus!" into a murmur, and as he jumped up and down, I began moaning, then I gritted my teeth and held on. His hands brushed across my breast and onto my arms; he whispered in my ear, telling me how much he loved me. Then, his adoration shifted into the muffled sound of "Margaret" to reinforce his desire and convey his passion for me. The tide turned as I threw my arms around him and held him tight. I dug my fingers into his back, but that didn't stop him none. A determined gaze took him over, and he pranced and grunted with each stroke. His brow glistened with the moisture that gathered into droplets that fell from his face and onto mine. But the sweat and the heat of the moment didn't dissuade his unrelenting thrusts or deter his lust for kissing. He whispered soft and sweet as his steamy breath blew his desire into me. I didn't sense anything quivering like before, but he rode me past the pain, past "Help me, Jesus!" and into "Praise the Lawd!"

His rhythms and pacing quickened, and he yelled, then grunted, "Oh! Oh! Lawd! Oh, Margaret! I'm coming." I knew where he was at and had felt it twice: once with his finger and now with "Praise the Lawd," but I didn't know "coming" was what you called it.

His body went limp right on top of me. He gazed at me as he had moistened cotton candy earlier at the wedding, then he rolled to my side and held me in his arms.

Well, that was that.

"Praise His holy name!"

I bled a little and walked around the entire week bowlegged, terribly sore down there—I told him he had to wait before we did it again.

But Fast Fannie had to put in her two cents the next day, and on seeing me walk, she said, grinning, "Whut's the matter, gal? Look lac'uh train done run yuh over," and fell out laughing.

The blush of a silly school gal flushed my face, but from my stance, you'd thought I fluttered like a peacock and had forgotten I was only a hen.

"Whut'ja thank 'bout it?" Fannie asked.

"Yuh left out the part 'bout the pain. Hurt like all get-out."

"Just wait," she said, "Mo' yuh does it"—grinding and swaying in the chair—"better it gon' feel."

"Oh, hush yo' mouth," but we both laughed.

"See, he done broke yuh in. Now, don't be waitin' too long 'foe yuh does it again. Believe yuh me, what yuh feelin' right now ain't nuthin'; wait til you has that baby."

"I don't want one then!"

"Soak in some Epson salts or some alum. Make yuh feel better—gon' git that old pussy nice and tight."

"*Stop* yo' old *nasty* talk! Women ain't 'posed tuh be talkin' like that."

"I does. 'Sides, who gon' hear? Ain't nobody here but us."

But William came, and I sneaked gleefulness in Fannie's direction.

She snickered.

Throughout the years that followed, I would remember the sweetness of cotton candy whenever William and I embraced.

ELEVEN

Conversion

Mammy used to say, "Yuh cain't finds the truth 'bout a peach jest in its fuzzy skin," and when she passed on, Aunt Sarah said, "Yuh cain't has no light wid'out no darkness." I figured that just as a sculptor transformed a rough slab of stone into a statue and the barren winter landscape thawed in the warmth of spring to yield meadows full of flowers, the forbidden could become the sanctioned, the despicable could transform into the reputable, and the sinful could emerge as the sainted. And that became clearer one morning when that gal called "change" showed out in Calvary Baptist Church.

Sometimes, when you're in church, you feel like the preacher is talking just to you, preaching to you alone. It happened to Marlene around Easter, when Pastor Jones preached about the adulteress.

He said, "Givin' in 'tuh temptation is a wicked thang. When yuh let yo' guard down and turn yo' face from the grace of Jesus, that's when seduction nibbles at yo' heels.

"We all done been there . . . oh, yuh know yuh have. Yeah, walkin' right wid the devil when yuh 'posed tuh be steppin' wid Jesus."

He grinned, and the Amen corner groaned, "Ahhh, tell the truth!"

"That's jest when Satan gets tuh workin' in yo' heart; he gets tuh whisperin', 'Go 'head. Who gon' know?' and that sounds so sweet."

Pastor Jones slapped the pulpit with the palm of his hand, moaned a preacher's groan, and said,

"Ohhh, Satan knows jest what tuh do tuh entice yuh 'way from Jesus!" which caused Miss Annie to shout "Amen!" to the ceiling rafters and for Deacon Samuel to jump to his feet and say, "Preach, boy!" as Pastor Jones danced his jig, and said,

"Where was she that she couldn't hear God's voice callin' out her name?

"Ohhhh, she was wrapped up wid the devil . . .

"Blind tuh Abraham . . .

"Blind tuh the face of Moses . . .

"Blind tuh John, the Baptist.

"There she was *lyin' up* wid him: a fornicator and adulterer. *Steeped* in sin! What are *they* tuh do wid her?"

Folks stood straight up and shouted, "Stone her! Stone her!" Pastor Jones shifted his gaze and softened his voice.

"But when they brought her tuh Jesus, He spoke: 'He that is without sin among you, let him first cast a stone at her.' And when Jesus lifted himself, he said, 'Woman, where are thine accusers?'"

Miss Bessie jumped to her feet, urging, "Preach, boy!"

Pastor Jones said, "She said, 'No man, Lord.' And Jesus proclaimed, 'Neither do I condemn thee: go, and sin no more.'"

Then, as loud as Gabriel's blast, Pastor Jones said, "Repent! Repent! And sin no more." Folks clapped their hands, saying Amen and Hallelujah, while Sister Alice's organ tweeted and moaned. The pastor shouted, "Repent, and ye shall be forgiven. 'I am the light of the world: he that followeth me shall not walk in darkness but shall have the light of life.'"

Then Pastor Jones said, right soft but as crisp as new money, "Let the light of Jesus shine in yo' heart this mornin'. Come tuh Jesus right now. He's waitin' for ya. Come tuh him right now. He'll wipe away yo' tears— every heartache and every sin. Come tuh Jesus. Let him be the light in the darkness of yo' despair. Come tuh the Christ. Every valley shall be filled, every mountain and hill shall be brought low, the crooked shall be made straight, and the rough ways shall be made smooth. And all flesh shall see the salvation of God."

Marlene sat alone in the church's rear. Only Pappy and us would sit near her; others considered her a no-good sinner. When Pastor Jones said, "All flesh shall see the salvation of God," she jerked herself to her feet and spoke in tongues. Nobody caught what she said, but folks figured the Holy Spirit filled her. She shouted along the aisle, her body rigid as a board. She clenched her fists and cinched them to her side; her eyes shut tight. When she slung her head, her hat fell off, and her hair stuck straight up.

The rhythm of Sister Alice's music changed, and Marlene moved as if her bones had become sinew and limber beyond her years, bending and flexing like sun-soaked rubber. She shortened and stiffened her gate along the aisle, paused, and oriented herself eastward. With her head arched to heaven, she threw up her hands, pressing them against the air three times, and said, "Selah." She danced some more but stopped again, facing north to talk and gesture as she had done.

She repeated "Selah" and performed her blessing twice more: once to the west and once to the south. Then, against Sister Alice's impassioned organ music, she collapsed at the altar, a puppet with its strings cut. You could have heard a mouse walking across a bale of cotton.

Everybody jumped to their feet, throwing their hands to the heavens, and in one massive voice, they shouted, "Praise the Lawd! Praise the Lawd! Hallelujah! Amen!"

It was the first time I had seen anyone else touching her except us. Deacon Samuel reached right down and helped her to her feet. Like Mammy used to say, "God—He be in places where yuh don't be expectin' sometimes."

The next Sunday, we walked Marlene and her two boys, Burton and Leroy, to the Ashley River, where Pastor Jones baptized them. She was born again, and from then on, she only wore white. Before her conversion, her eyes were dull and heavy, and her face wore sadness, but after her baptism, she had this glow about her. I rejoiced when she found the Lord and hoped He would stay with her for a long time, but I questioned if she could prevent Mr. Hollis from communing with the devil.

———— •••• ————

Marlene used to visit Mammy often, but when Mammy passed on and I no longer stayed in the cabin, our paths only crossed now and then. And when I lived there, I felt uneasy chatting with her. From my perspective as a child, her gray hair meant I had to hold my tongue—talk to her like a penny-pincher who reverenced the value of a dollar. I liked her, though, and when she arrived for a visit soon after her conversion, I tried my best to open my heart.

"Where the boys?

"Such a nice day, they been itchin' tuh play since it been so rainy and all . . . yuh know how them youngins is. I left 'em runnin' 'round up yonder."

"Well, let's sit out here and enjoy this weather . . . got some lemonade. Yuh want a glass?"

"Sho'." I handed her the glass as she rested herself in the rocker.

"How have yuh been?"

"Oh, I's holdin' on," and pressing against the rocker's back and taking a long look, she said, "Mo' I sees yuh, the mo' yuh looks jest lac yo' mammy."

"Marlene, that's a right nice compliment."

"Sump'tem ain't right 'bout her bein' gon' and all," she said and we both breathed a deep, long sigh.

"How's Mr. Jake? Got his hands full wid them two gals, ain't he?"

"Lena helps, but . . . he ain't said much 'bout Mammy."

"Gon' take a while, I reckon," smacking her lips from the tanginess of the lemons.

"Yeah, Pappy is better than most, but too many men either harness or squelch their feelings and—"

"Us women ain't no better," she said and took another sip of lemonade.

"How have yuh been makin' out wid Vivian?"

"Oh, child, don't make me choke on this-here lemonade," she said as she placed her glass on the table. "I knowed I done wrong and all 'foe I becomes a Christian woman, but that Vivian jest the devil." She raised her hand as if to testify and said, "I ain't 'posed tuh speak bad 'bout nobody, but Miss Ann be's Satan wid rouge in high heel shoes—jest lac her maid told me."

"Whut'cha mean?"

"I tells my boys they 'posed tuh stay in they room. They ain't tuh have nuthin' tuh do wid that woman, but that's useless. She thanks everythang in the world 'longs tuh her. Ain't uh'nuf tuh have Hollis tuh herself. Nah, her gots tuh own my chillins and me too, control us lac we is her slaves. Lawd, I prays a lot. And yuh cain't please her none either."

"How so?"

"Nuthin' ain't good 'nuf for her—walks through the house, and if she find one speck of dust, she havin' a fit. Gots tuh ride roughshod over everythang that breathes. Cain't cook right for her: seasoning ain't right—too much fat in this or that. Don't lac the way her underclothes be fixed. The iron gots tuh press 'em jest right. Pour a bath for her—the water be's too hot.

"Oh, she has'tuh have her hair brushed every day, and nobody can do it right 'cept me. I gots tuh do it, and when I does, her fussin' 'bout me bein' too heavy-handed."

She took a handkerchief from her pocket and tossed it on the table.

"See this-here? 'Bout as white and perfect as it can be, 'cause it done been washed and ironed just right. Well, everythang gots tuh be jest lac that, even if yuh gonna soil it wid snot. Woman sho' gon' bend my head tuh uh early grave!"

"My, my," I said and offered her more lemonade.

"Nah, thanks . . . Vivian done changed the whole house. Nuthin' lac it use'ta be."

Settlin' in and markin' territory, I thought, but I wondered, *I lac'uh clean house too, but I don't know what tuh make of folks who are too fussy. What are they tryin' tuh hide wid all that daintiness? Is she what she claims tuh be? If you ask me, she's a hard nut tuh crack—never understood why she married him in the first place.*

"And . . . does she know about the boys—'bout you and Mr. Hollis?" I asked. I couldn't believe those words came out of my mouth, but she didn't blink an eye.

"Yeah, her tries tuh act lac it don't bother her none, but I sees the way her be lookin' at 'em. She hate 'em 'cause her ain't been able tuh have none; reckon her hate me too 'cause I's done sump'em her ain't, and me bein' a nigga makes her failures even worse. Lac I said, that woman gots Satan's tail wrapped clean 'round her waist."

"Why do you think she keeps yuh? Seems like you and the children are nuthin' but a bunch of reminders."

"Who know whut tramps 'round in that head of hers. Did'ja know she done lost two babies?"

"Nah!"

"First time . . . her such a know-it-all. Knowin' her in the family way, she gots tuh keep ridin' that horse her done brung from Kentucky. Yeah, brung this racehorse all the way from Lexington."

"Don't say."

"Well, her done brung it here, and her ridin' the horse every day. She in the family way now, and us be tellin' her not tuh ride that horse. But nah, her ain't gon' listen tuh none of us, 'specially no niggas. Her hops on, not payin' us no 'tention, gits down in the meadow, and the horse, he throwed her down near the creek bed, where she lays for quite a spell 'foe somebody thank 'bout lookin' for her. Gits her back tuh the house and her out of this world for three days, and on top of that, her lost the baby."

"And the second one?"

"Second time ain't her fault. When her belly was all swollen that time, she even acted lac her uh decent human bein'. She 'bout seven, eight months along, and her starts havin' them pains—baby come early, but sump'em be the matter. The child ain't live through the night. First time hard, but the second time, they done seen the baby. Be's a boy, too. Well, that be's the worse'est time. I thought the pain was gonna kill her for sho', and I felt right sorry for her."

"Whut 'bout Mr. Hollis?"

"Oh, he nuthin' lac he was wid Miss Ophelia when she be livin'. Child, Hollis acts lac he could eat a mile of Miss Ann's doo-doo."

"Oh, Marlene!" I said. I couldn't help but try to conceal the laughter that had shimmied my belly.

"It be the truth. It be's the God's honest truth."

"Marlene, you's uh mess," I said. Then I got'tuh thinkin'. "But why is he different wid her? Is it because she's so much younger?"

"Maybe."

"Well, what about him and Miss Ophelia? Why was he so distant wid her?"

"Yo' mammy ain't never tell yuh 'bout whut happened?"

"Nah."

She closed her eyes and rocked from side to side, nursing the silence, coaxing it to break open. She said,

"Gator, po' soul. Never will forgit that boy. One of them stories, lac the one 'bout Massa Felix and Abigail, that I dud'en lacs talkin' 'bout. Gator sho'nuf changed everythang at Pleasant Bluff, though."

"Whut happened, Marlene?"

"'Member that picture of the gal in the parlor? The one over the fire-place . . . the gal you pecked me so much about when you was eleven or so?"

"Yeah. You said the picture was of their first daughter, Selma."

"You be too young then. It wan't right tuh tell yuh, but whut happened tuh little Selma and Miss Ophelia changed everythang. Nearly kilt Miss Ophelia, tore Floyd tuh pieces, and done turned Hollis in'tuh sump'em nobody ever thought he'd be."

"Whut did Gator do?"

"Little Selma . . . how Hollis babied that child, but her deserve every bit 'cause she be as satisfyin' as fudge filled wid caramel. And I ain't never seen no man love nuthin' lac Hollis loved that Selma. And he ain't never loved anythang that way since. That picture be painted when she 'bout five, but she don't live tuh see seven.

"Her born in nineteen hundred, Floyd born nineteen and two, Candy come 'long in nineteen and three, and you born in nineteen and five. Yeah, that's right. She died in nineteen hundred and six. Hard tuh 'member these-here dates, it be's so long and all."

Marlene was sho'nuf from the South. *We can't rush storytelling,* I thought.

"Well, I could tell right off Gator ain't lac white folks. I 'spect Gator be 'bout twenty when he come from Florida . . ."

She stopped, pondering as if she hankered to catch a gnat in mid-flight, before she asked,

"Now, whut they calls that place?"

I figured she'd do that. Yep, she's from the South all right. Got'tuh tell every detail and cain't be rushed tellin' a story.

"Tallahassee. Tallahassee, Florida," she blurted out. "That's the place.

Some white mens storm through there, and they kilt a mess of colored folks. Gator's mammy hides him, but he seen 'em. Kilt his whole family. He 'bout twelve then, and after that, he lived pillar tuh post, driftin' 'til he gits here."

"My word."

"Yeah, but I reckon Gator hid mo' than he tells. Anyways, when he come 'round here beggin' for work, the Demmings takes a shine tuh him. But after a spell, I notice how he be's lookin' at Miss Ophelia. First, I ain't pay much 'tention tuh it, but little by little I thank sump'em ain't right. And sometimes I'd catch him smilin' in Hollis's face, but when Hollis turn his back, Gator's sunken eyes gits tight and cold . . . then he gits tuh mumblin'. I figured he ain't let go what done happened down in Florida. I goes to Miss Ophelia, and I tells her not tuh trust that nigga, but she ain't listen.

"One day, Hollis take Floyd and Candy over tuh they grandpappy's tuh spend the day. I goes wid him tuh tend tuh the chillins. Miss Ophelia and Selma feeling po'ly, so they stays at Pleasant Bluff. It be's late when us gits back from Hampton, but as us gits closer tuh the Big House, I feels all nervous-lac inside, and the closer us gits, the worser I is. When we gits there, the door, it be's ajar.

"Hollis goes in, and he finds Miss Ophelia out on the floor lookin' lac her dead, bruised to high heaven, and clothes ripped asunder. He yells for me, and I scampers in there and tries tuh see whut I can do for her. Hollis runnin' all through the house lookin' for Selma, and her ain't no place tuh be found. He 'bout crazy when he finds Miss Ophelia, but Hollis really go out his head when he cain't find that gal.

"Hollis hightails it in'tuh town, and when he gits back, he brung the sheriff and the doctor, but Miss Ophelia, her still not woke. Lord, that woman was whupped so, but her must'uh put up one heck of a fight.

"Whilst Miss Ophelia out this world, the white men, and even the colored hands, lookin' for Selma. When her come to, her tell 'em whut done happen. Gator done almos' kilt her and snatched Selma."

"I bet they tore New Harmony to pieces," I said.

"Honey, they tears the *state of Sowth Ca-linah* all tuh pieces lookin' for that nigga Gator. Child, this was on everybody's lips—in every newspaper, even in Charleston. They finds Gator way off yonder someplace, and when they brung him back, the boy look lac he 'bout dead. They beats Gator sump'tem awful 'til he took 'em tuh where Selma be at—they finds her body all broke up, in the woods right 'hind y'all cabin.

"Hollis told me that Gator took and told him he done cursed him; say his spirit ain't gon' rest 'til Hollis die . . . he gon' be waitin' for Hollis in hell, and told him what he thank 'bout the blue-eyed devils. Said all that 'foe he spit in Hollis's face. He ain't make it tuh the jailhouse 'cause 'bout a hundred white mens took a-holt of Gator. Hollis shoot his private parts off 'foe they hangs him, and they leaves his body in the woods for the vultures tuh feed on. Since then, Hollis ain't never been the same 'bout colored men. One uh'ther thang: he ain't never forgive Miss Ophelia."

"Why?"

"Heartbroke I 'spect. Nuthin' wan't the same in that house after Gator kilt that gal."

Something doesn't seem right, I thought. *Being heartbroken don't seem to be enough reason for Mr. Hollis to hold Miss Ophelia responsible. Something don't seem right. Did Gator only beat Miss or did he do sump'tem else to her? And where was Selma durin' all that beatin'? Got to be more to this story.*

Instead, I said, "So, every colored man is Gator, the terror that made Mr. Hollis so cruel, and Miss Ophelia kept hopin' to rekindle sump'em in Mr. Hollis that died when Gator took his hands to Selma." I shook my head.

We had been quiet for a while when Marlene said, "Margaret, honey, speaking of po' souls. I seen Zora Mae the uh'ther day. Her wid that Bullock boy."

"Yeah. She ran off wid Willie Deke b'foe Mammy died. I haven't seen her since."

"She ain't livin' too far from here now."

"Where?"

"In the old Marcum place, tanglin' wid the devil. They fights all the time—he beats her mighty bad."

"Nah! 'Spect Miss Bessie didn't want me to know."

"Reckon so."

"I seen her in town the uh'ther day, and her face—yuh ortah seen it. Gal bruised up so bad her right eye 'bout shut closed. Whut a sight!"

"I tried to warn her."

"And I tries tuh speak tuh her, but she acted right skittish, lookin' lac her done been bullied tuh death: yuh know, cain't speak lessen he tells her.

"Few days after I seen 'em in town, I sees Bessie, and I tell her 'bout it. Reckon she might shake some sense in that gal's head, but Bessie say, her cain't do one thang. Willie Deke won't let the gal talk tuh her own Mammy. Bessie be beside herself."

"Lawd, Lawd."

"Willie Deke dranks all the time, barely work tuh keep vittles on the table; whups the gal for the least little thang, and on top of that, Bessie say he run 'round wid uh'ther womens."

"She wud'den listen, Marlene. She kept tellin' me she just wanted somebody to love her."

"Well, she done had one baby, a gal, and now her stuck out yonder again, fixin' tuh have uh'nuther one."

"Whut are we gonna do?"

"I 'pose us jest gonna haf tuh pray for her. Margaret, us gonna haf tuh pray."

Silence caught the air again, but Marlene broke it and asked, "How long you and William been hitched?"

"Lemme see. It'll be seven months on the second of January."

"Ain't tell y'all how glad I is. He's a right good man, and handsome, too. Miss Lula wu'dha been right proud."

"Yeah, she loved that boy. He was like uh'nuther son . . . Oh, Marlene, I forgot to ask 'bout Candy. Any news?"

"Honey, that be uh'nuther little monster. She still down in Uh'lanta."

"Still?"

"Yeah, 'bout tuh drive that po' man of hers crazy. Been listenin' tuh that wicked Vivian, and if she keeps on, I reckon she'll be comin' back here for good one of these days. Oh, they gots a youngin. That's uh'nuther thang that drive Vivian crazy—'cause Candy gots a youngin and she ain't. They calls her Christine. Honey, I prays for 'em every day."

Then, out of the blue, she asked me, "When yo' belly gon' be gittin' big?"

Marlene's talking must've put a curse on me. Lo and behold, I dried up down there. When I visited Fast Fannie's, I told her, and she said, "Here some clothes for you and the youngin. 'Gratulations!"

TWELVE

Nothing Stays the Same

After Fannie gave me her dresses, I danced around in them in front of the mirror, caressing the belly that would soon fill them. I prayed I would be as skillful with my children as my Mammy had been with us. In the excitement, I realized I required more clothes; the ones Fannie gave me would be fine when I got bigger. But I needed something for those earlier months. Marlene came to the rescue and agreed to make me something to wear almost immediately, so I went into town to buy what she needed.

I had gotten a ride that morning with old man Rae. His sons were friends of William. When we pulled up in the buggy on Market Street, Floyd strutted around, tipping his hat to the ladies and taking their hands into his. Mr. Hollis had cast his net far and near and held a lot of markers that remained uncollected, so his son benefitted as well. To top it all off (and I had to give the devil his due), Floyd was so handsome. Being both good-looking and rich made a powerful combination in Hampton County, and just like anywhere else, Floyd became a ladies' man who used every opportunity to blow his sweet-talk up a woman's skirt.

"'Bout as close as I can get," Mr. Rae said. "Don't wanna rile nobody, 'cause white folks don't want us colored takin' they spaces. You know how it is 'round here."

"Find a safe space and I'll find yuh. I won't be long," I said as I stepped from the buggy. I approached Wilson's Department Store, and as I reached for the knob, Floyd said, "Lemme git that for yuh."

"Thank you," I said.

Once entering the store, I looked for the right piece of material to flaunt what would soon become visible. After I had everything, I stood in line behind Wanda Lewis, a poor white who labored hard for respectability.

While the clerk, with fiery red hair and hateful eyes, waited on her, another white woman walked up behind me. It was Livia Coleman. Her family didn't live too far from Miss Lewis. They had been poor whites like the Lewises, but they had recently pulled ahead, having gotten rid of their outhouse the year before.

Floyd had taken to his perch in the corner, watching with a smirk on his face. He had cut his teeth on such scenes and waited for the inevitable script to play itself out.

I stepped forward, but the clerk snubbed me.

She caught Miss Coleman's attention, and her hateful eyes became considerate. Her lips cracked into a smile when she said, "Miss Coleman. So good to see yuh. Can I help you wid sump'em today?"

She flashed an "I-ain't-waitin'-on-this-nigga-so-you-can-come-on-ahead" smile at Miss Coleman. Miss Coleman, knowing her pearly skin and blondness made her better than me, caught that smile and stepped up to claim that other reward that came with getting rid of her outhouse the year before. Miss Coleman paid and gathered her things, but they kept on flapping their jaws. I waited for them to stop cackling so the clerk could wait on me.

"Did'ja hear whut happened tuh Jeannie Thomas?" the clerk asked.

"Nah," Miss Coleman said.

"Her husband fell out a tree and broke his arm."

"Mercy."

"Who gon' brang in the crop this year?"

"Haf tuh hire some workers, I 'spect."

"Niggas either lazy," she said, lookin' straight at me, "or they is so uppity yuh cain't 'pend on none of 'em for uh lick of work." Miss Coleman nodded and went on her way.

The clerk's hateful eyes mellowed, and her lips flashed another "I-ain't-waitin'-on-this-nigga-so-you-can-come-on-ahead" smile at someone behind me. I glanced back. *Here we go again,* I thought; it was Edna

Charles, after all. Her husband played second fiddle only to Mr. Hollis.

Sure enough, the clerk said, "Miss Charles, can I—" but before she could finish "help you," Floyd swooped to her side and said,

"Miss Edna, how have you been?" and pulled Miss Edna to one side. He turned to the clerk and said, "Beth Ann, could'ja help Margaret? I need Miss Edna's ear for a minute," and turning his charm on Miss Edna, he said, "Is that all right wid you, Miss Edna?" She nodded.

The clerk sucked her teeth, pursed her lips, and furrowed her brow. But when Floyd laid that sunshine of a grin on her, she grumbled, "Yeah, what does she want?" at him.

"'Scuse me one minute, Miss Edna," Floyd said. "Margaret, what would'ja like?"

"These things here and thread to match."

"She wants those things and some matchin' thread if yuh don't mind, Beth Ann. This is so kind of you. Did I tell yuh how lovely yuh look today?"

"Miss Edna," Floyd continued, "I want yuh tuh tell Mr. George that I'm still hankering tuh buy that prized filly."

"Lawd, son, yuh know how he is 'bout that horse."

"But I'm certain you can sweet-talk him for me," Floyd said. "Can yuh do that for me?"

"You such a devil," she giggled as the clerk scribbled out the slip, thrust it across the counter, folded her arms across her chest, and stared at me with rancor.

I went to hand her the money, but her hateful eyes directed me to place my money on the counter. She picked it up and tossed the change on the counter, flaunting nastiness with her pursed lips. I gathered up my feelings along with my change and sought higher ground. I looked her straight in the eyes, and with all the love my heart could muster, I said, "May the peace of Christ rest on you. Good day, Miss."

"Better learn yo' place, wench," the clerk said as I opened the door. I gently closed it to the sound of her snarling, "Uppity high-yellow nigga."

I had taken only a few steps when I felt Floyd's hand on my shoulder. I turned toward him.

"I thank you for what you did in there."

"Oh, I didn't do a thang."

"You did, and I'm much obliged."

"You're most welcome," he said, looking at me like he did when he was fourteen and I was eleven.

"I haf'tuh go. Mr. Rae is waiting for me, and I told him it wud'den take me long."

He stepped aside to let me pass, but before I took two steps, he said, "I understand it's Mrs. Butler now."

"Yes," I said.

"Pity," he said, leaving me mesmerized by the sound of his drawled-out "P-i-t-y" and the sight of his bowlegged gait as he slapped his soles against the sidewalk. My eyes followed him as he headed in the direction I had intended. He nodded to a few folks but stopped to talk with Miss Curtis, who walked with her two-year-old son. Floyd patted the boy's head, and as I approached, he threw me that twinkle he had in his eye. I stiffened my pace but nodded my head in uneasy politeness.

His treatment of me had never been proper, but I could do nothing to challenge him.

I kept trying to stay in the middle path.

Fannie sure told the truth. A month later, my belly started showing. When I told William we were going to have a baby, he grabbed me and pert' near choked the life out of me, hugging me too hard with what he fashioned as joy. Whenever he had an opportunity, he caressed my belly. If he sat in a chair and I waddled past, he'd grab me, and his lips would be right up on my belly, talking to the child I carried. We'd get in bed at night, and he'd pull up my nightgown and play rub-a-dub-dub. He'd have his lips fluttering against my belly, tickling me into laughter.

From the giddy-up, I had morning sickness. I tried to eat, but I threw up if I got a whiff of food. The nausea stopped as suddenly as it started, and then I consumed anything in sight. I relished food and ate the strangest combination of things: a meal of chitlins and applesauce would have me smacking my lips. But Fannie said the sight of me shoveling food into my mouth turned her stomach.

"Look nasty," she said. "That baby gonna be huge; gonna tear yo' pussy up. Yuh gon' be walkin' 'round here like yuh got sump'em stuck up the crack of yo' tail. You thank William's ding-a-ling had yuh walkin' bow-legged wid pain that first time? Wait 'til yuh has that pig yuh is feedin'."

I sucked my teeth at her. Who was she, a fortune teller? But I had forgotten Mammy's warning: "A hard head makes for a soft behind."

Pappy tried, too. Even Neddy and Joshua said I had become a trough. Lena thought a pinprick would make me pop like a balloon. They couldn't tell me anything, walking around with my swollen feet and looking all blown up. I was nineteen, married, and a woman. Miss Know-It-All!

My water broke as I ate a slice of apple pie.

When the first pain shot through me, I grabbed my belly and stiffened straight as an arrow. When the second one hit, I dropped my knees and arms to the floor and screamed right between the planks. Being pregnant, pride had convinced me I deserved the title "woman"; however, the third contraction cut like a knife and forced me to confess that I didn't deserve that title yet. I yelled, screamed, cried, groaned, scratched, and begged for my mammy! I prayed to Jesus, to the Christ, to the Nazarene, to the Lord, to Jehovah, to His mammy, and to the Holy Spirit! I promised I wouldn't do "it" anymore, and I clamored for Fast Fannie, Miss Bessie, Sister Jamison, Miss Effie, Marlene, Miss Annie, and *any* woman who knew *anything* about this rite of passage to help me. If I'd caught William, I would'ah hacked his thang off, right at the *root*.

The pain eased for a moment, and I stopped screaming long enough to hear a rooster crow 'way yonder, somewhere.

Then I screamed at the top of my lungs, but that didn't seem loud enough. I tried remembering what Mammy told me when I helped her with Violet, but it hurt too bad; I couldn't think straight.

The contractions eased again, and I took a deep breath and heard a car horn cry twice in the distance.

I rolled around on the floor, making circles with spit and sweat.

The door flung open.

"Lord! Thank you, Jesus!" It was Marlene.

"Child! How long yuh done been lac this?" she said. I couldn't talk, but I grunted something.

"Honey child, yuh gots tuh breathe," Marlene said. She kept saying, "Look. Look at me!"

I couldn't see her through all the sweat that stung my eyes.

It hurt so bad. I jerked away.

She yanked my head around, cupped my face in her hands, and blew.

"Like this. When yuh feels one of them pains, do lac this-here," Marlene said.

"Sweet Jesus, help me!"

William came running into the room. Seeing me lying there with Marlene crouched between my legs, he said, "Whut's the matter?" I rolled my eyes. *Ain't it obvious?* I thought. I didn't want him there; Marlene ordered him to the yard.

"You gonna haf tuh take a knife and kill me. I ain't gonna go nowhere."

He stayed right there, dropping down beside me so hard he had to have hurt himself. But he didn't hurt like me, that's for sure. He held me the whole time, and he cried when the baby came.

We named her Matilda.

When Marlene placed her in my arms, my thoughts turned to Mammy and how I had helped bring Violet into the world. The following day, when I went to scoop her up, it reminded me of discovering my first doll baby at Christmas. But she was no kind of plaything. She was full of life, full of giggles and smiles. I loved this beautiful child we called Tilda.

She was born on October 19, 1924.

Then I was pregnant again.

Neddy gave me a buggy ride into town to shop for household items, and on the way, I read the newspaper and learned that Monkey Trial had ended. To my surprise, the Tennessee jury found John Thomas Scopes guilty.

When I reached the market, I saw Floyd huddling with his cronies. There was no way to dodge him. I was four months pregnant.

"My word, Mrs. Butler, that boy got'cha big *again*? Girl, when you due?"

"December," I said.

He put on the gravest airs and said, "I'd stay away from them colored boys if I were you."

Puzzlement enveloped my face.

He stepped closer and whispered, "Why, yuh deserve rubies, my dear." His eyes twinkled, and he moistened his lips and whispered, "Pity," as he blinked his twinkle into a wink. I couldn't help but think that if our colors had been reversed, throwing his seductions to me as a white woman, he'd be dead by sundown.

A little later I ran into Miss Bessie, who updated me on Zora Mae's situation. By the time I returned home that evening, William was dancing with nervousness.

"Where you been at? I've been worried sick," he said.

"Got in town late and then ran in'tuh Miss Bessie; she got'tuh tellin' me about Zora Mae."

"She all right?"

"'Bout well as to be expected, given that husband of hers."

"When Fannie comin' back wid Tilda?"

"Ortah be here fairly soon. Said she had sump'em tuh show me."

"We're in for it then," William said.

"Whut'ja mean?"

"Saw Robert, and he said—"

Just then Fannie swung the door open. Robert held Tilda, and Fannie stepped in wearing a beige flapper dress that seemed to hold every piece of fringe and glitter on this side of Hampton County. She danced the Charleston—the latest craze to hit South Carolina.

"Whut'ja thank?" she asked as she twirled, showing off the dress she insisted Robert buy when they were in Charleston.

"Told Robert we had tuh git out that house and have some fun. Cain't be raisin' babies all the time."

Robert just smiled. He wasn't henpecked; he loved the ground she walked on, is all.

"Where y'all goin'?" William asked.

"Raleigh Marsh's place," Robert said.

"Way back yonder in those woods? Huh, y'all better watch out 'cause the pastor says that place is full of sin and sinners," I said.

She stopped dancing and threw her hands on her hips.

"Like he can talk."

"You shouldn't say that," I said.

"Every last one of 'em ain't nuthin' but a bunch of chicken eaters!"

"Fannie," Robert moaned.

"Don't hush me. All them chicken eaters be the same. They thumps they Bibles on Sunday and eats they fill of chicken and anythang else they can finds tuh fill they bellies. And I does means *everythang*! They jest a mess of hypocrites, like them Pharisees. They be talkin' 'bout bein' holy and sanctified, but that ain't whut they wants for themselves. Them chicken-eaters preach all that stuff, but they cain't practice whut they preach. Besides, him and Minnie Walker—"

"What about Minnie Walker?" I asked.

"Everybody know he layin' up wid her," Fannie said.

"Now, Fannie, you don't know that," Robert said.

"*I do so!* Rode by Minnie's the uh'ther night. Guess whut I sees?"

"Whut?" we all asked.

"Seen the pastor's buggy and horse there."

"So?" I asked.

"I pulls up and whispers in the horse's ear."

"And whut'ja axes the horse?" Robert asked.

"'Is he doin' *M-i-n-n-i-e* in there?' I axes. Know whut the horse took and told me?"

"Nah," we said, waiting for her to finish her tale.

"Horse nodded and said, 'And *J-e-n-n-i-e* too.'"

"Fannie, you ortah quit," I said, but we all slapped our legs and laughed straight out.

Robert and Fannie departed, granting us the serenity and space to contemplate the birth of a new child.

Helen was born December 17th, 1925. Afterward, I stopped going into town on Saturdays with William when he trimmed hair for some extra money. Instead I turned my attention to the children.

Pappy met this woman, Miss Lucille, at a church social the year before Tilda was born, and they married in April of 1925, around the time I was pregnant with Helen. Lena was sixteen, and Violet turned two that October. Joshua had moved to Hampton—his affection for Constance inspired his move. Neddy had dumped Hazel, and after their relationship ended, he desired privacy and swore he would never marry.

Pappy and Miss Lucille didn't tell anyone about their intentions. We only learned about it when he found a place in Hampton. I supposed Pappy felt he could do as he wished. He was 'bout forty-nine years old, and he needed help raising Lena and Violet. Lucille loved them, and I thought she'd be a right good mother, but I didn't like it that they didn't tell us. I didn't like it one little bit! "We're still his children!" I said to Neddy, but us children never said one word to Pappy or Miss Lucille about it, though.

When Pappy moved to Hampton, he gave me and William the homestead, the land, and the cabin. It was good enough for us, but I 'spect it wasn't sufficient for Miss Lucille. Of course, they visited, and I always treated Miss Lucille with kindness, but she wasn't my mammy and she never would be! Miss Lucille had plenty of book-learning crammed in her head, but she didn't have half the mother wit, the common sense Mammy had in her little finger. I didn't know what had happened to the bit Pappy had. How could he replace Mammy with *her*? The thought of him with another woman vexed me plenty, but Mammy's home-raising instructed me to keep my opinions to myself.

One day when Fannie visited, she learned that Pappy and Miss Lucille had gotten married, and she hit the roof. I told her, "You don't have any right to talk about Pappy and Lucille because yuh and William were the first ones to talk 'bout Pappy's good fortune, havin' a girlfriend. Y'all said they made such a fine couple, and Pappy deserved happiness, too. 'Oh, Pappy gots his nature.' 'Member?"

"Wash my face in it, why don't'ja."

"Somebody has'tuh."

"I ain't gots nuthin' 'gainst her, but Margaret, Pappy ortah told us. 'Sides, whut they gon' talk about? Lucille so highfalutin . . . gots so much education. Whut in the world her gon' talk tuh Pappy about? Whut they got in common? Yuh been tuh her house. You seen it. Now yuh tell me."

"Huh, 'spect she's gittin' whut she needs from Pappy."

"Well, I wish she was nasty, so I could be nasty right back. 'Foe yuh knows it, Pappy gon' have Lucille runnin' 'round here carryin' a youngin in her oven. My Lawd, Margaret, I don't want no half-nuthin', no brother or sister, to be fussin' over."

"Fannie, that ship has sailed."

She sucked her teeth and waved me away.

"Face it, it's long gone."

"Well, how old Lucille?" she asked.

"I think she's thirty-nine or forty."

"Margaret, he ain't gots no business wid nobody young like that."

"Fannie, yuh gonna haf'tuh let it go."

A car pulled Fannie's attention to the yard. Pappy and his new wife arrived, and he was driving one of those Packards, a wedding present from Miss Lucille.

When Miss Lucille entered the house, Fast Fannie's jaw stiffened slightly. She smiled, but when she gained her wits, she jumped up and said, "Lawd. I best git back to the house. Robert's watchin' the twins, and if I'm gone too long, I'll walk in'tuh a mess." She wasn't nasty when she did it, but Lucille wasn't a dead furrow.

Fannie tolerated Lucille, but it came to a head when Lucille committed the ultimate sin, an unfortunate blunder. She told Fannie, "You ought to—"

I held my breath, and Robert and William headed for the door, but Pappy braced himself, resting his forehead in the cup of his right hand as if to say, "Spare her, Lawd." Yeah, he prayed Fannie wouldn't harm his new wife and that God, in His grace, would allow Fannie to find something she had never shown before: tact.

Her wrath was short but decisive.

"Looka here," Fannie said. "Yuh *ain't* my mammy! Yuh got that?"

'Nuf said. Lucille got the message. She held her tongue from then on, but a polite and distinct wall grew up between us. That became even more pronounced when Fannie insisted that neither Lena nor Violet call Lucille Mama.

"Yo' mammy dead," she said to Violet. "Died brangin' you in this world, gal. Don't forgit her memory by callin' that woman yo' mammy."

Anyway, about seventeen months after getting hitched, Pappy and Lucille had a child, a little boy they named Isaiah. So, in September of 1926, Fannie got what she didn't want: a half brother who looked just like her.

———◆———

Ruth was born July 19th of 1927, and Isaiah wasn't a year old, but during that time, Pappy and Lucille visited every Sunday. I would cook a mess of food for dinner and watch my youngins play with little Isaiah, who had already begun pulling himself up on his bowlegs. Seemed like the boy didn't have a robust constitution, and at one point, he came down with a sore throat, couldn't rightly breathe, and his neck became swollen.

The doctor informed them that Isaiah had diphtheria, and the health authorities locked the entire family in the house. Eventually, the doctor cut his throat to insert a tube so the boy could breathe. Isaiah suffered for a considerable time with a weakened heart, and he passed on in the fall of twenty-nine, right before the stock market crashed. The strangest thing: Isaiah died on his birthday, September 20th.

After Isaiah passed, Lucille wasted away. She sat in the dark for weeks after they put the boy in the ground, and nobody could get her to move. Lucille wouldn't even talk to Pappy. 'Spect Lucille blamed herself, and she just sat and cried. She needed constant supervision, and Pappy hired a nurse to sit with her. Lucille suffered, and Pappy worried to no end.

She'd sit in the corner all day, mumbling and gazing in the distance. Other times, she'd rock in her chair for hours, patting her breast, holding and talking to little Isaiah, who she imagined nestled there. Sometimes, I'd drop in on Pappy and the girls to sit with her or brush her hair while she rocked and talked to herself or little Isaiah.

On November 20th, two months after Isaiah's death, Lucille was still pining, and knowing the nurse had the day off, I visited to give Pappy a break. When I got there, Pappy said, "When she got up this mornin', she was pert' near like she was 'foe Isaiah passed on, but—"

"What set her off?"

"She jest gits these-here spells; they seem tuh come over her like uh gully washer."

"Lemme see whut I can do."

When I entered Isaiah's room, Lucille was holding the teddy bear we had given Isaiah the previous Christmas.

"Lucille, how yuh doin' today?" I asked, but she stared out the window, stroking the teddy bear's face.

"Lemme comb yo' hair. When did'ja have it done last?"

Her hands fell and rested on the teddy bear's stomach. She stared up with a blank expression but nodded her head. I loosened the hairpins, letting her hair fall to her shoulders.

"My word, yo' hair sho' has grown—got so thick and pretty." She began stroking the teddy bear, and I told her about the new treasure I had found.

"Just finished uh'nuther book, Fitzgerald's *Great Gatsby*," I said. "Lemme tell yuh whut it's about. Well, I won't tell yuh everything; yuh might wanna read it.

"Gatsby could come from nuthin' tuh become sump'em, sump'em glamourous, but even after becomin' sump'em, it was all show, flashy. Underneath, Gatsby was still empty, and his aristocratic manner didn't mean one thing. Sort of like Mr. Hollis, I suspect. He has all that money and power, and I don't think he's happy 'cause everythin' he ever got probably came through shady dealings. That's what led to Black Thursday as sho' as yuh were born. Greed, nuthin' but greed."

She still rubbed the teddy's belly. After fixing her hair, I noticed the flowers in the vase on the dresser had wilted.

"Whut 'bout some fresh flowers?," I said. "They'll make yuh feel better." I called for Pappy to watch Lucille while I went to the side garden. I had only cut a few flowers when Pappy bolted onto the front porch, yelling, "Lucille!"

My eyes scanned the direction in which he ran, but everything got caught up in slow motion.

The milk truck couldn't brake in time; it pitched poor Lucille skyward.

Pappy stopped, frozen in disbelief and terror.

That truck killed her right on the spot.

The driver sat motionless. Pappy knelt beside Lucille and pulled her up into his arms. He whispered in her ear and rocked her. "I left jest tuh take the water from the fire . . . I was gone only a second . . . Why did'ja leave? . . . Why?" Pappy asked, his mouth resting on the crown of her head.

I stood over them, praying for Mammy to meet her and take her where she needed to go.

Rest in peace, Lucille.

THIRTEEN

Home Again

The stock market crash of 1929 and the years following were mighty hard. Some people lost everything they had when pert' near every bank in the country went belly-up. Folks jumped out of windows, and others had no job and nothing to eat. The roads were full of people tramping, and the well-to-do lived in constant anxiety, haunted by the constant fear of being targeted and robbed. Initially, these difficulties seemed insignificant, a little bump on life's highway. But many folks suffered for years, with most facing difficulties until the war in forty-one.

By then, I had four children. Henry Louis was born on June 23, 1930. Ruth would be three that July, Tilda would be six in October, and Helen five in December. With Henry's birth, William got the boy he had been yearning for. I read to them all the time. I read to the younger ones while William worked and Tilda attended school. And when Tilda returned from school and William from work, I continued reading. When Pappy visited, he would ask them about their books and tell them what their aunt Lena had accomplished, graduating from nursing school in Washington, D.C., and working in a big-city hospital. We yearned for our children to flourish and achieve their every wish.

By the time Tilda was nine and I was twenty-eight, I had five children. At each birth, William cradled me as they emerged and witnessed their first breaths. Henry was three when Thad was born (August 11, 1933), and after Thad's birth, I decided I'd rather jump off the roof before I had one more. I understood how Mammy felt when she got caught on the change with Violet.

What folks called the Great Depression gripped the country, and we had five children to raise. We made it because we still did a little farming, and everybody worked together. Lena sent whatever she could to help make ends meet until she married in January of 1936. Pappy and Fannie rode the Greyhound bus to Washington, D.C., to inspect this fellow named Charlie. When they returned, Fannie announced that he was a right friendly fellow, which meant he was a saint.

During those challenging years, we pooled everything and ensured nobody went hungry or lacked for clothing. William and I became the "bankers," and our house turned into the gathering and feeding place. Hard times didn't break us; they strengthened us and made us a better family.

The Demmingses didn't suffer—they had so much money they could buy and sell most folks three or four times. Despite all the misery caused by the Depression, Vivian still ran around like Miss Ann. But since she had her nose in everything, she found plenty of hornet's nests to agitate and brought trouble to everyone she knew. Marlene swore it took her so long to have a successful pregnancy because she had thrown such hatred toward Candy's sister, Isabel. Marlene said,

"Vivian fixed her mouth and tells Hollis the gal reminded her too much of Miss Ophelia. Pleasant Bluff need only one Missus—and that be's her."

I reckoned Isabel had too much of Miss Ophelia's golden light glowing on her face for Vivian to stomach. But in 1933, both Vivian and I were pregnant, and her Nathan arrived only thirty minutes earlier than my Thad.

About three weeks after their births, Marlene visited with her boys and Nathan. Vivian had placed Nathan in a fancy buggy, but when I looked inside, I jerked my hand back as if a coiled copperhead lurked there. The baby was clad in a pink dress, booties, and bonnet.

"Ain't he a boy?" I asked.

"Yeah, he uh boy, all right. I done changed 'nuf of his diapers tuh know."

"Then why the pink clothes?"

"Gonna give yuh only one guess," she said. "Vivian! The gal been walkin' 'round for months talkin' 'bout the baby gon' be a gal. Has her family and Hollis buy all these-here clothes, and not let nary one 'em give her one stitch in blue. Her want a gal so bad, and I guess her thank her gon' run roughshod over God, too. Well, God done fixed her!" Marlene said, rasping with laughter.

"Why dud'en she buy some blue clothes and give these pink ones tuh uh gal who needs 'em? Marlene, times are hard, but they have plenty of money."

"Chintzy. Nah, don't wanna be wrong, that's whut."

"You'd think Mr. Hollis would say sump'em, or one of the uh'ther men."

"Nah, everybody eats a mile of her doo-doo!" We both laughed.

"Marlene, you's uh mess."

From the very beginning, I sensed specialness in the boy. It was one of those powerful feelings you get, the ones stopping you dead in your tracks. I reached down and said,

"Let's see whut yuh look like." I picked him up and danced him around the room. "Well, yuh're a pretty boy." His face broke out into a smile. "Whut a good-natured child, Marlene."

"Believe Vivian his mammy? God done fixed her real good! This one gots a soul of an angel! Don'tcha, boy?"

Marlene took over and waltzed him around the floor to the sound of Thad cooing and smiling, but, still recovering from Thad's birth, I collapsed in a chair.

Constance walked into the midst of our merriment that day. I jumped up. "Lawd, I ain't seen yuh in a spell." We hugged while Ruth, Helen, Tilda, and Henry tugged at her skirt, yelling, "Aunt Connie!" at the top of their lungs.

"Marlene, you're acquainted wid Constance?"

"Oh, yeah. Ain't seen yuh in quite a spell. How yuh been?" Marlene asked.

"I'm well."

"God bless y'all, enjoy y'all's visit. I best be gittin' back. 'Bout time tuh feed them youngins. 'Sides, 'spect Vivian done tore up half the county lookin' for the boy."

With Henry and Ruth tagging along, I walked Marlene and Nathan to the gate. When I returned, Constance was rocking Thad in her arms. His agreeable temperament shone in his smile, which made him different from some other children, and sho'nuf different from Tilda, 'cause Lord, that gal drove me crazy.

—◦◦—

I tried to be the best mammy I could for all my children, but sometimes I felt I had failed with Tilda. I came to understand what some women had said about their relationships with their female children: "Oil and water don't mix." Something always came between us, and this persisted into her adulthood, but she and William were two peas in a pod. Truth be known, Tilda and her daddy were tighter than even Fannie's twins. I desired the same closeness with her, but I was also plumb jealous of anyone captivating William's attention. *How could any mother think that way toward her child?* Being resentful and jealous led to rumblings of guilt, and I prayed about it.

William cautioned me: "When yuh hold the reins too tight, yuh git nuthin' but struggle and resistance in the horse." But I chucked that over my shoulder and said, "Don't want her endin' up like Fast Fannie."

"Whut's wrong wid that? She has wonderful children, and Robert is the salt of the earth."

"She'll end up wid a big belly; that's whut's wrong wid that. 'Sides, yuh spoil Tilda rotten. I'm always the one who says no. She runs right tuh yuh, and yuh turn right 'round and give her whut she wants. She's spoiled rotten and yuh're tuh blame!"

"Margaret, whut's the matter?"

He stood up and came over, and held me tight. His hug was like seeing sunshine after days of rain. It reminded me of eating a warm bowl of stew with thick, crusty bread in the winter and the scent of honeysuckle lacing itself in the summer evening air. His hug appeared like a shooting star and a full moon in a pitch-black sky. It was akin to the warmth of cotton and the scent of familiar things. When I composed myself in his arms, I admitted I'd erred. I had to try harder.

I would ask myself why I worried so much about Tilda. Was fear the only reason for my worries? Did it have something to do with how Mr. Hollis treated Marlene? While I worried about such things, I also realized

Tilda had a different way about her. I learned a whole heap more one Saturday afternoon when I played possum.

Being plumb tuckered out didn't begin to describe my physical state on the last weekend before the school's summer vacation. I stretched out and drifted to sleep. In a state where wakefulness inched closer, I thought I heard a soulful lament. As the sound roused me from dreamland, the undulating crying morphed into a guitar playing the blues. When it imitated the pitch of a lone soprano, singing the last high note God ever imagined, I rubbed sleep from my eyes. The guitar faded into the background, and I heard some squeaky voices undercutting the guitar. Those squeaky voices belonged to Ruth and Helen, who listened as Tilda talked about me.

"Billie Rae—

"Tilda, Mama told'cha tuh call him Mr. Billie Rae," Helen said.

That's right, I mumbled to myself.

"Anyway, he put a jukebox in his store."

"Mama told'cha not tuh spend money listenin' tuh that music," Ruth said.

"Oh, she so old-fashioned. Do yuh think she got a tin ear?"

"Tilda, mama loves music. She just dud'en like swing. Ain't that right, Ruth?"

"That's right. Besides, why are yuh listenin' tuh the blues, anyway?"

"I wanna be a singer."

"Bet not tell Mama that," Helen said. "She'll have a fit."

Uh-huh, I said to myself.

"I wanna be a singer," Tilda said.

"You know whut she'd say," Helen said. "'Now Tilda, yuh gotta think 'bout the future—git a good education.'"

"'But Mama, school is borin','" Tilda said, imitating herself.

"'Tilda, how yuh gonna make a livin' singin'? I want yuh tuh do better than I was able tuh do for myself,'" Helen said, imitating me.

"'But Mama—'" Tilda said.

"'Gal, stop tryin' tuh grow up so fast—ain't nuthin' special 'bout bein' grown,'" Ruth said.

Giggles.

They'll understand when they get older, I thought. *When they have their own brood to worry over.*

Then Ruth started again. "'William, didn't I tell yuh so? I told'cha that gal wud'den do whut I told her to. I told her to go down yonder and come right back.'"

"'Margaret, don't fret. It's gon' be all right,'" Tilda said in a perfect William voice.

Giggles.

"You're daddy's little girl," Helen said, reverting to her own voice. "You were the firstborn, and yuh're daddy's heart, is all."

"And Thad is Mama's," Tilda said.

"Nah, Thad is everybody's," Ruth said in her correcting voice.

I dropped a book on the floor.

"Shhh," Tilda said. "Mama is up."

All their chatter confirmed what I'd thought: Tilda always felt I tried to control her life. I only wanted the best for her, but I couldn't convince her otherwise.

When Thad started school in 1939, Tilda was fifteen, and we couldn't keep her away from the jukebox and the radio. She couldn't resist listening to the blues and swing music and had even gotten Violet, who was seventeen, hooked on the blues. And Violet had Pappy rocking to the radio's blues beat, too. I reckoned they got that from Mammy, who loved the blues as much as I did, but Tilda's swing music irritated me to no end. She stood dreamy-eyed at the sound of any kind of music, but if I heard the Ink Spots sing "My Prayer" one more time, I thought I would scream. The Mills Brothers were popular then; Duke Ellington and Ella Fitzgerald, she believed, were the king and queen of jazz. She discovered Bessie Smith singing "Nobody Knows You When You're Down and Out," and she relished *Porgy and Bess*; "Summertime" became her theme song. But she fancied all the blues legends, including her idols Blind Lemon Jefferson, Ma Rainey, Alberta Hunter, and Mamie Smith. At fifteen, her feet got to itching, and she looked toward the big city, which consumed every conversation.

But how would she survive in the city's hustle and bustle? I fretted. Would she starve to death? And what about her education?

From the time she could crawl, I read to her and preached the importance of schooling, but when we got a letter from her teacher, I figured we had lost the battle. I stood in the doorway, waiting for her.

"Did'ja have a pleasant day at school?"

"Nuthin' changes there, Mama."

"Well, we got a letter from the teacher today, and Miss Ludlow is concerned 'bout yo' attendance. She asks if yuh're sick."

"I've decided I wanna quit school," she announced.

"Oh."

"Yes, ma'am."

"Whut do yuh think yuh wanna do?"

"I wanna sing, Mama."

"Sing whut?"

"The blues," she said.

"I see."

"Mama, when I sing the blues, it's like I can take everythin' that cuts at my heart and wrap it up in the music."

"I feel like that 'bout books, 'bout words, but—"

"Cain'tja understand, Mama?"

"I do, but we worry 'bout yuh bein' able tuh take care of yuh'self. Yuh cain't live here forever."

"Why should I stay in school when I hate it so much? I don't wanna be there."

"I thought yuh'd go tuh college, set the example for the uh'ther children, like yo' Aunt Lena. And Violet—she's doin' well at Howard."

"I don't wanna set the example. I wanna sing like Bessie Smith."

"Tilda, I want yuh tuh be yo' own person . . . be able tuh fend for yo'self."

"Daddy takes care of us."

"Yes, and yo' daddy does a fine job, but every man isn't like yo' daddy. Besides, yuh shouldn't haf tuh depend on a man."

"You have," she said.

"So I have, but I've been lucky. Look at Zora Mae and the mess she's in, gittin' beaten by Willie Deke whilst tryin' tuh tend tuh two youngins."

"Mama, I cain't stand uh'nuther minute of school," and through her tears, she added, "Why don't y'all believe me? Why don't y'all trust me? I cain't do it anymore."

When William came home, he told her, "Yuh haf'tuh stay in school."

"Times are hard," I said.

"Cain'tja see whut's happenin' all over the country?" William asked. "Why, some men cain't even provide for their families; they're trampin' 'round the countryside axin' for handouts."

"Honey, most colored folks don't even have jobs," I said.

Talking to her became pointless, and we tried everything, but she wouldn't listen. She had an adorable voice and sang at church, but what were her chances of making a living singing? She had gotten books about big cities from the library and spent hours daydreaming about Chicago, New York, Washington, D.C., Charleston, and Atlanta. She announced that she would leave before the end of the following year. We attempted to reason with her, but she still held a mouthful of foolishness. The realities of the war and the Depression didn't matter; we got nothing but "Y'all don't understand me" or "Y'all don't want me tuh be happy."

In December of 1941, not long after the beginning of the war and during the coldest winter we had had in several years, she vanished. One Saturday morning, just before Tom Rooster declared dawn, Helen and Ruth came running into the bedroom saying, "Tilda gone, Mama."

"What'cha mean, gone?" William asked.

"Her bed's made," Ruth said. "Her clothes—"

"Gone?" I asked, jumping from the bed and landing in her room. "Thad. Henry. Go search! Is she outside? In the barn? Go! Look for yo' sister."

"Did she say anythang tuh yuh, Helen?" William asked.

"Nossir."

"Lawd, William. Not even a note. Where is that gal?"

William went down to the train station, bus station, and everywhere else he could think of, but nobody had seen her. We sent word to Lena, thinking Tilda might have headed north, but Lena hadn't heard from her. Pappy sent word to Violet at Howard, but she had heard nothing.

I worried and I prayed. I never thought she'd run off like that. But she slipped away before I could convince her of a mother's love, one that never waned.

Worry hung around my neck until Marlene showed up one day with some news.

"I knows how yuh been frettin' 'bout Tilda," she said.

My heart stopped.

"Now, now. It's all right. Candy done seen her in Uh'lanta."

"What?"

"In one of them sangin' places."

"Workin'?"

"Yeah. Candy thought she seemed familiar—seen her someplace 'foe, and axes Tilda where her from. When Tilda say New Harmony—"

"Did she know who Candy was?"

"Don't thank so."

"Thank God for that. Otherwise, Tilda might've run off, and then what."

"'Least us know her all right."

"Where is this place?"

"She ain't say, but I'll axes her."

Almost a year later, in September 1942, to my surprise, Floyd appeared on my doorstep.

"Marlene all right?" I asked.

"I was headed in'tuh town and Marlene beg me tuh bring yuh this," he said, handing me a piece of fancy stationery.

"Whut's this?"

"Daddy got a letter from Candy; she included the address where Tilda sings. Marlene requested it a while ago," he said, as he peered inside and sniffed after what cooled on the kitchen table. "Is that sweet potato pie I smell?"

"Yes," I said, hoping I didn't need to be polite, but my Southern manners won and so I asked, "Would'ja lac'uh piece?

Where is Fannie when I need her? Thad played nearby, but I didn't trust Floyd and didn't want to be alone with him.

He entered, surveyed the place, and said, "Sweet little place yuh got here."

I sliced the pie, placed it before him, and asked, "Would'ja like some milk?"

"Thank you," he said with enough Southern delight to cause his "thank you" to drawl right into a "Thaaaaaaank yooouuuu" that almost made me chuckle.

"Hope yuh'll enjoy it," I said.

He took the first bite, smiled at me, and said, "Why don'tcha sit wid me?"

"You go 'head. I got so much tuh do 'foe the youngins git home."

"Would be mighty mannerly if yuh spared me the time," he said.

"All right," I said, hoping he'd eat that pie real fast.

He didn't. He fondled it, breaking off a small piece of the pie with his fork each time. Placing it delicately into his mouth, he gently mashed its sweetness around, swallowing it with a smile. He lusted after every bit, and the fork became the surrogate for his desire. His wet tongue drenched and licked it. He sucked its prongs into his mouth, up to the fork's neck. Then he surrendered it slowly through puckered lips, smiling at me the whole time.

"Mighty good. You ortah have a bite," he said, pushing the plate toward me. "I'm sure you'll feel the same."

"Oh, no thank you," I said, with much gaiety in my voice. But his voice was full of intimidation when he said, "I insist," and stared me down.

I sensed his menace and twisted my uneasiness into the chair, but then an angel said,

"Hey, whut'ja doin' down here?"

It was Nate.

"I ortah ask yuh whut yuh're doin' here," said Floyd, running over and scooping Nate into his arms. "Did'ja make us proud in school today?"

"Yes, sir."

"Don't stay long, 'cause yuh know how yo' mama is," he said, placing him next to Thad, to whom he didn't give a "Howdy do." He ambled to the door but turned to me.

"I sho' enjoyed that piece of pie." On reaching the door, he said, "Next time, we gonna haf tuh share a *big* piece . . . *tuh'gether.* I'll bring the milk."

After dinner, I brought out the pie that was missing a slice.

"Look like somebody couldn't wait," William said.

Thad looked at me, waiting for me to reveal the culprit—the man who had been in his daddy's kitchen.

"Floyd came by tuh drop sump'em off, and I couldn't git shed of him."

"He don't look right," Thad said.

"Whut?" I asked.

"He looks mean."

"Now, son," William said. He turned to me and asked, "Whut was it?"

"Tilda's address. 'Least where Tilda sings at."

"Whut'ja wanna do 'bout it?"

"I wanna know if she's all right."

"She might run."

"But . . ." Then my tears started.

William stood, pulled me to my feet, and embraced me. He said, "'Member how yuh use'ta say I spoiled her rotten?"

I nodded my head.

"I never admitted that yuh told the truth. She was my little girl, our first, and . . . whut wud'den I do for her?" he said.

"Yes, of course," I murmured, shaking my head as he rocked me in his arms.

"But she ain't a little girl anymore, and we gonna haf tuh remember what yuh use'ta say tuh all the children."

"Whut?"

All the children jumped from the table, surrounded us, and said as loud as they could:

"Everybody got'tuh know their own heart, Mama!"

The tears came for real then, but William and the children held me tight.

"Margaret, you were right, and now we haf tuh wait, secure in the love that we always gave her—"

"She gonna come home, for sure," Helen interrupted.

"I think so, too," Ruth said.

"And me too!" spouted Henry and Thad together. I seemed more solid surrounded by their faith. But she stayed gone for two more long years.

———————

I sat on the porch one spring morning in 1944, shelling peas and rehearsing plans to witness Violet graduating with honors from Howard University.

I felt proud of my little sister, and then I caught sight of a woman walking down the road with a suitcase. I squinted into the distance. With my awful eyesight, I couldn't see a thing unless it smacked me in the face or presented itself close to my nose. I needed to wear my glasses, but vanity made me too cute for those. I kept squinting, but I didn't recognize her until she loomed over me. It was my Tilda.

She wore a navy blue two-piece suit with matching earbobs. Her hat tilted to the left and dipped low, concealing her face; shades shielded her eyes. I stood up. Peas flew everywhere, and I didn't care. I hugged her like nobody's business. I kissed her and my tears away that day. When Thad and Henry overheard the commotion, they did somersaults. And when William came home, he 'bout dropped dead. He lost his voice for a minute like he did when we got married, but he wrapped the strength of a father's love around his baby. I didn't worry about 'em anymore. I wasn't jealous. Like in the biblical story, she was lost but found. We had no fatted calf, rings for her fingers, or fancy clothes for her to wear, but we rejoiced that day!

FOURTEEN

Revelation

Upon Tilda's return, Helen had just begun college. We were full of tears and pride when she left that August. Violet moved to New York and settled in as a high school English teacher. She and Helen were the first in the family to receive such extensive schooling. Ruth was a junior in high school and was eager to follow in their footsteps. The boys excelled in school, too, and Thad, at eleven, had a growth spurt and became nearly as tall as his fourteen-year-old brother, whose voice had deepened an octave. I believed with unwavering certainty that Mammy and the other Great Spirits protected them. I never suspected that, five years later, treachery would wait for Thad along New Harmony Road.

Tilda's spirit seemed heavy 'cause she sho' wasn't talking a gate off its hinges. When she was little, she'd talk the hide off of a cow about her dreams, but now that she was back, Tilda said much to nothing about Atlanta, her ambitions, or why she'd come home. She moped around the house and fretted over Zora Mae and her man. Her mood made me suspect that when she ran off to Atlanta, she thought she'd sit on the fence and birds would feed her. But I suspected Tilda had encountered something that resembled Zora Mae's hornet's nest instead. Yeah, she probably rubbed up against a man, thinking she'd reek from the scent of roses, but he ensnared her in the stench of his outhouse. I prayed Tilda hadn't met up with somebody comparable to Willie Deke because Zora Mae and her troubles sho' came to light one night.

It was well after bedtime, and we were off into our dreams, when Zora Mae came banging on our door. William jumped out of bed grumbling, "Who'cha reckon this is at this time of night? Folks ortah be sleeping."

He opened the door, and Zora Mae fell right at his feet.

Blood everywhere. It covered her.

I had never seen anybody, especially a woman, beaten like that. She tried to speak but only slobbered a mouthful of blood and spit. She had lost two teeth from the violent blows that had busted her lip open. Puffy bruises and cuts covered her body, and two fingers on her right hand seemed to be broken. Her bloodshot right eye seemed ready to fall out any minute; her left eye was swollen shut. From the way she clutched at her chest and by the footprint that marked her blue cotton dress, I guessed he had stomped her. The force of the attack to her head bloodied the scarf she wore, and deep gashes in her knees oozed blood along her shins. The ripped part of her dress that once hugged her neck exposed her bloody undershirt, and the bodice hung loosely from her skirt in the front.

Visions of us as giggling children thrashed in my head, but now my eyes held so much water I couldn't see beyond the color red. I had observed men fighting and seen the aftermaths, but beating her the way he did was beyond outrage; Willie Deke displayed the savage he was.

William put her on Helen's bed. I told him to get the doctor and thanked God that Doc James wasn't around anymore. We had a new doctor in town—this one from up north. His name was Isaac Rosen-something-the-other, and they said he was Jewish.

William set out for the doctor, and I tried to make her comfortable and stop the bleeding. Tilda and Ruth had spent the night with Fast Fannie, and I was glad they weren't home. I checked on Henry and Thad; heck, those boys could sleep through a tornado.

I kept pacing. I bet I peeped out that window fifty times but perceived nothing but pitch black each time.

Finally, William and the doctor arrived.

I had never seen Doc Isaac before. I had always taken the children to the colored clinic over in Hampton. He was a right nice-looking white boy, tall, with thick, jet-black curly hair. He wore a small piece of cloth on his head, secured by two hairpins. His hazel-green eyes conveyed gentleness and kindness; they twinkled when he looked at you. A pair of glasses rested on the bridge of his somewhat flared nose. Now that I consider that nose of his, it would've looked strange on somebody else's face, but it sat perfectly on his. He had lips not unlike a colored person's too, pink but thick. Hair sprang from his shirt and covered his arms and hands.

He examined her like a fragile antique, but when he went to move her, she began yelling. He'd poke; she'd yell. He apologized but poked some more, and it became a duet with a familiar refrain where everyone responded with perfect pitch. He asked us to step onto the porch with him, and he explained she had some serious injuries. There were broken fingers and ribs like I thought, but Doc Isaac also expressed concerns about possible internal bleeding. He requested to stay overnight to monitor her condition, which we willingly obliged. Doc Isaac would transfer her to his clinic in New Harmony if she survived 'til morning. I couldn't believe how kind he had been, 'cause that was rare among white folks in New Harmony, South Carolina, and that said everything you needed to know about Doc Isaac.

Zora Mae did make it through the night, so the next morning we loaded Zora Mae and Doc Isaac into the wagon. She stayed hidden in Doc Isaac's clinic for three weeks before she could walk alone. I snuck in occasionally to check on her. But once she healed, Zora Mae went back to Willie Deke.

A woman with a gnat's worth of sense, I thought.

Weeks later, Pappy and I were in town one Saturday afternoon, and we met them on Market Street. Willie Deke peered right through me, and Zora Mae dropped her head and didn't speak. She didn't dare with him there, I imagined. A few days later, while I was weeding in the garden, a small, timid voice called my name.

"Zora Mae?" I said in my surprise.

She stood before me, holding the pink fabric of her cotton dress balled up in her right hand. "I'm so sorry 'bout the uh'ther day. I was too scared to speak 'cause Deke was wid me. I didn't want him actin' up in the street, but I wanna thank yuh again for whut yuh and William done for me. I 'preciated it."

"Why does he—"

"Deke dranks sump'em awful now. He hates for me tuh open my mouth. If I say hello, he thinks I done gone 'hind his back. He done accused me of sleepin' wid every man on this side of Hampton County. My eye is all messed up 'cause he said I was sleepin' wid Mr. Collins."

"Miss Hillary's husband? Ahhhh, that's foolishness. He'd be the last man in Hampton County tuh fool around."

"My world turns on a dime when he's drankin'. Margaret, I'm scared tuh walk 'cross the floor wid'out his say-so. Fearful that the children ain't dressed right tuh his satisfaction; afraid they gonna make too much fuss; terrified tuh cook, 'cause when I do, it's not whut he wants tuh eat. I git beat for that. Even brangs his women and flounces them right in my face. I walk like I'm on eggshells all the time. If'n somebody say sump'em tuh me, I 'bout ready tuh jump and run."

"That's no kinda life," I said, taking a deep breath. "Zora Mae, you deserve better than tuh be wid somebody who wipes their feet on yuh."

She dropped her head, but I raised it and asked, "Cain't Miss Bessie help?"

"Ma's too old, cain't do much, and ain't got the room. Where are me and two children gonna go, Margaret? Pappy dead and I ain't got no kinfolk tuh speak of but Ma. And—"

She stepped backward as if to retreat but then took a deep breath and whimpered, "He said he'd kill me *and* the children if I left."

I held her, and I took her inside so she could pull herself together. She didn't stay long because she had to return home before Willie Deke found her missing.

Within a month of Zora Mae's visit, the death bell rang.

A colored man caught Willie Deke fooling around with his wife in the very bed they shared. The husband restored respect to his household by shooting Willie Deke dead. When I learned what had happened, I visited Zora Mae to pay my respects. I'm sure she felt like a free woman, but she displayed the proper amount of grief and numbness. On my way out of her house, I bumped into Wayland Lofton. He fancied her when we were in school, and I had hoped they would get hitched. *Well,* I said to myself,

Zora Mae's free. I was glad we planted Willie Deke that Saturday afternoon and not her. After the burial, Zora Mae moved to town. She wanted to leave the house where Willie Deke had committed tremendous violence and left too many imprints of anger on the walls and floors.

Lord, may Willie Deke rest in peace!

———•◦•———

Unlike Zora Mae, Tilda didn't carry any scars, but her mind was somewhere way off. She fretted for months. I'd catch her gazing in the mirror for a long time, and if I didn't give her another task, she'd spend the entire day tending to one pot on the cookstove. Tilda would do anything I asked her, but she acted like the walking dead.

One night, while others slept, I heard her weeping. I got up quietly so I wouldn't wake William. She sat at the kitchen table with her head in her hands. I placed my hand on her shoulder, and the floodgates opened. Heard a lot of crying in my day, but she cried like her very soul was broke in two. Holding her, I asked,

"Whut's the matter? You can tell yo' mammy, cain't yuh?"

"Nah, Mama. Not this."

I held her face. "Tilda, you were my first. I was only nineteen when I had yuh. I had little knowledge back then and made plenty of mistakes, but one thang is certain: yuh're my daughter; I'd give my life for yuh."

"Mama, but—"

"Ain't no buts. Thought I was gonna die the day I had yuh. I've seen a lot of thangs that caused folks a bunch of hurts, and I wanted—I wished I could'ah protected yuh from 'em."

"I know, Mama, but—"

"I thought I'd die when yuh left like yuh did, but yuh're home now. Tell me whut's wrong so I can share this wid yuh, baby."

"The things I've done." She dropped her head. "You aren't gon' want me as yo' daughter when yuh learn whut I've done."

"Gal, see that floor? I laid right there and gave life to yuh."

I told her the story about Marlene popping in when she did, how William cradled me, and how we were the first ones to hold her.

"That's whut we will always do. Now, take this and wipe those tears; yuh gon' always have a family who gonna love yuh."

Then she started her story.

When she arrived in Atlanta in December of 1941, she ended up in the colored section of town, but everyone was color-struck.

"I had little money, so I wandered 'round lookin' for work. Folks said, 'Whut's that white woman doin' over here?'"

Since everybody thought she was white, she decided to look for work on that side of town.

"I found a job workin' at a diner. It was so excitin' tuh be in Atlanta, but I missed y'all so much."

Experience had taught her that when you're as attractive as she, every no-count hound could sniff you out.

"I had uh'nuf sense never tuh take money from none of 'em. I remembered whut you said, 'Nothin' like yo' own.'"

One day, a fellow named Fred asked her out. He took her to this little colored juke joint where folks sang the blues. When she got there, colored and white folks mingled together, but the number of white folks surprised her. Colored folks didn't seem to mind. Folks drank liquor, ate, smoked cigarettes, and danced to the music.

"The music got in my bones, and I sang," she said, and upon hearing her, Fred pushed her to the front of the room.

"Y'all haf tuh hear this woman sing," he said. Everybody started clapping and whistling.

"I started timid-like, and when my confidence broke loose in my throat, I sang full out. Mama, my sweet voice filled the air, and when I had 'em in my hands, I was in heaven."

When she finished, everybody was on their feet, clapping.

"B'foe I left, the joint's owner offered me a job singin' every Friday and Saturday night. I was such a proper, well-raised girl, Mama, until . . ."

She lowered her head and said, "I was good until he walked in late one Saturday night, wid his olive skin buffed clean and his dark hair combed perfect."

She smiled and brought her eyes level with mine. "He was so tall, taller

than daddy. He had a jaw that was kinda like daddy's . . . square. His face
. . . well, the kind any Roman god would envy. Mama, he was so handsome, right down to his spit-shined wing-tipped shoes."

With her eyes closed, she said, "He was the handsomest white man I
had ever seen. Steel-gray eyes wid just enough blue to make 'em sparkle."

When she opened her eyes, she studied me to discern if I held a hint
of outrage. I didn't say one word and didn't bat an eye. Acted like I didn't
care, like it didn't matter none. It did, but this was *her* story.

"He came up at the end of a set and offered tuh buy me a drink. I told
him I didn't drink, thanked him, and walked away."

She was polite and everything, but it didn't feel right talking to him,
even if he thought she was white. But he wouldn't leave her alone—he
came to the joint often to hear her sing.

"Mama, I'd come tuh work sometimes, and I'd find beautiful red roses
waitin' for me. One night, I found a box tied wid a lovely white bow. When
I opened it, the fragrance of gardenia blossoms filled the air. When I dug
deeper, I discovered a box of chocolates—all the way from Paris, France."

"Whut's his name, baby?"

"Alexander," she said. "Mama, I was so confused, but I told him I
couldn't take anything from him. Of course, he wondered why. I confessed
that I was colored."

"Whut did he say?"

"Oh, he didn't care. He said he couldn't eat or sleep and thought about
me constantly. He begged me tuh spend time wid him."

She cleared her throat and said, "Mama, plenty of men wanted me, but
they weren't whut I wanted. I figured Alexander had tuh be 'bout Daddy's
age, and folks would say he was too old for me, but somethin' 'bout him
touched me. All those times when I said I didn't want him . . . every time
I said no, I lied to myself. So, I stopped foolin' myself, and when he asked
me again, I said yes. It happened mid-May of forty-two. We explored the
countryside and had a picnic; we talked for hours. His father owned a
plantation, and I told him what I knew 'bout those times—told him some
of your slave stories. He said he spent a lot of time in the North when he
was younger and that altered his ideas 'bout bein' white, life, and agin'. His
daddy still runs the place, but Alexander is a lawyer. He's rich, Mama."

"I see. 'Spect yuh had tuh go all in, as Mammy would say, 'whole hawg' . . . livin' lac'uh white person."

"Yessum. I passed, Mama."

Right then, she held a basketful of shame, and the tears came, but I didn't open my mouth. Thoughts of Mammy's life, of the Great Spirits, flooded me, and she dared throw their struggles away on a white man. Didn't I teach her anything? That's how I felt, but I didn't say one word. It wasn't what she needed to hear.

"I can imagine how yuh must be feelin', Mama, but I—"

"Don't worry 'bout me and my feelings."

She took a deep breath.

"I met him 'bout five months after I got'tuh Atlanta, and I'd say I was head over heels within three months.

"What was I thinkin'? Guess I thought I had it all, but then he told me."

"That he was married," I said.

"Yes, ma'am," she said with more shame. "He insisted she didn't love him, that she didn't understand him, and that she was impossible. He wanted me, but I never felt such betrayal.

"Mama, my heart broke that day. But that wan't the worst of it."

Then the floodgates opened again, but this time she sobbed quiet-like.

"I guess his wife started gittin' suspicious, and then it happened.

"One night at the club, his wife approached me in the middle of a song—cain't remember what it was now—and she slapped me. Spun my head right 'round she walloped me so hard. Smacked me in front of everyone, called me a whore and a nigga bitch."

Nah. Nah, this cain't be . . . Lawd, don't let it . . . Atlanta's a big place; 'sides, plenty of men named Alexander in the world.

"She must've seen me b'foe and knew he had been comin'. Mama, she even knew who I was! She knew all about me, about you and Daddy.

"Told me if she had her way, she'd have me pulled out wid a rope 'round my neck and have my black ass strung up and left tuh rot like they did nigga men back in South Carolina and rural Georgia.

"She spat in my face, and I went for her lac'uh pig goes for slop. We fought like men in there, and I snatched her by the hair and dragged her 'round that room. Several men separated us, and one of 'em, a friend of mine, got me out of there b'foe the police came. But I hadn't—I just couldn't—"

"Whut, Tilda?"

"Mama, I didn't tell Alexander that . . . that I was gonna have his baby."

She cried some more.

"Whut happened tuh the baby, Tilda?"

"I thought I'd go tuh one of those women who took care of those kinda thangs, but I couldn't kill my baby. I told my best friend, Della, who was my roommate. Alexander sent me letters, but I wud'den open 'em. He'd come tuh the house, and I had Della tell him I wan't there."

She waited a little to finish.

"I got pregnant in August of forty-two, and he was born May of forty-three. Della promised tuh take care of him 'til I figured out what I was gonna do. Couldn't bring him home, out of the blue, like that."

"It's White Candy's husband, isn't it?"

"Yessum," she said, with no surprise I knew that piece.

She cried right good then.

"Let it out, baby. The Lawd gonna make it all right. He always does. 'Sides, don'tcha know?" Holding her face, I said, "We learn life best when troubles tear the world apart. Yuh're home now."

Tilda and I talked way past midnight. I vowed not to breathe a word, but not telling William would be difficult because I never kept anything from him. Still, my promise bound me, and her revelation united us in ways we had never been before. I asked about her plans for the baby, but she needed to decide the right moment to inform the family. Given how she handled everything, I figured this would take a lifetime.

Tilda told me that before she left Atlanta, she and Della had the baby's picture taken. She retrieved it from her hiding place, and when she joined me at the kitchen table, she held it to her breast and offered her sacred gift like bread and wine brought to the altar of the Baptist church on the first Sunday of every month.

"Oh, he looks like an angel," I said. The boy looked like he didn't have a drop of colored in him. And while Pappy use'ta say, "Crackers always been under colored folks' bed," I worried about raising *this* colored boy right under Hollis and Candy's noses. What would it mean for our family?

The following day, my head buzzed when I thought about her affair, about Hollis, and about White Candy standing in that joint with her head thrown back, puking her venom. I assumed she had countless reasons to be enraged, but to spit in my baby's face, to spew her dreadful words, and to endorse the lynching of colored men—well, no words could express the depth of my outrage. What possessed that gal? Vivian had taught her well.

FIFTEEN

The Bastard

Tilda's leaving and returning happened right slap dab in the middle of the war, and even before Helen went off to Howard, hard times seemed as plentiful as crabgrass. Rationing made everything scarce during those years, but because we lived in the country, we were better off than city folks. We grew vegetables and managed to get some pork or beef when somebody slaughtered, and we raised plenty of chickens and roosters, but sugar and flour were difficult to come by.

I was nine when the first war started and thirty-six when the Japanese bombed Pearl Harbor. The attack made white folks mad as vipers, and some colored men considered joining the fight. It felt absurd: Negroes hankering to join an army where they couldn't serve alongside white soldiers. But Robert's younger brother, Toby, had joined the Army, and William ran around talking about how he would enlist. Seldom did I take a stand, but that was one. I told him right away, "Over my dead body! Go to war and git killed, whut will me and these children do?" Joshua and Neddy's age saved them from the draft. I was thankful for that.

Every morning when I got Henry and Thad ready for school, adjusting their shirts and brushing any imagined harm from their brow, I thanked God they were too young to go off to war. I kissed their cheeks, knowing the only wars they would wage would be with their sisters. Those campaigns of playful jabs and taunts unfolded on the fields of decency and gentleness established by me and William. But we didn't escape the horrors of war. In

183

1943, they brought Toby home in a box. He was twenty when the telegram came, and we were full of grief when the colored soldiers dropped that box in the church cemetery. Oh, they played taps and handed the family the flag they had draped on top of that box, but we all knew we'd never hug him or kiss his cheek again.

———— ◦•◦ ————

While white folks talked about honor, sacrifice, and protecting their democracy, Tilda got a letter from Della saying she couldn't keep the baby any longer because times were so hard. Like Mammy always said, "Whutever yuh does in the dark sho'nuf gon' come tuh the light." Tilda's chickens had come home to roost.

When she gave the letter to me, she stood trembling and fainthearted. After we had an extended talk, she realized the moment had arrived. She packed her bag, and I pulled together a bunch of food for Della. It was the least we could do for her. I sent Henry to fetch Robert, the only one in the family who possessed a car—an old black Ford he had gotten from somewhere—and we put Tilda on the bus for Atlanta. I told her I would explain everything to William and the rest of the family. She was in tears. I kissed her and said, "Bring my grandbaby home."

When I returned from town, I asked Henry to take Robert fishing so neither he nor Robert could blab to William before I informed him. Thad was playing with Nate at the Big House and Ruth was spending the weekend with Pappy, so I stood over the wood cookstove in silence, finishing supper and sweating something fierce when William came home.

"Mighty hot in here," he said.

"Yeah, hot uh'nuf tuh kill a horse today."

He came over and kissed me like he always did.

"Where is everybody?"

I took the food from the fire and grabbed him like Mammy did Pappy when Fast Fannie had a big belly.

"I feel like walkin'," I said. When we got past the fence, he said, "Must be bad news."

We sat under a tree, and I let Tilda's drama rush out like it had been hindered by a logjam. He didn't say a word. He listened, but when I told him about White Candy and her husband, he jumped up and started pacing, just like Pappy did when he got excited. But as always, he remained calm and composed, and when he pulled me from the ground, he asked,

"Whut are we gonna do?" I threw myself into his arms and said, "Whut we always do: love her."

◆◈◆

Tilda had been gone for a few days when we received a telegram saying she would arrive Saturday morning. The whole family, even Pappy, went to the bus station in Hampton to welcome her and the baby. We stood outside the door marked "Colored" and waited for the shiny white-and-red bus to appear. Once it arrived, white men with loosened ties and suit jackets slung over their shoulders descended along with white women clad in their Sunday-going-to-meeting best. After all the white folks got off the bus, the colored folks stepped from the bus and shook the hands and slapped the backs of waiting friends and family members whose bright smiles took away the inhumanity of having to sit in the rear.

At first we didn't see Tilda or the baby, but we heard a faint whimper. I felt the dread of a mother who wishes she could remove her child's struggles. But if they did, a lesson wouldn't be learned. We waited for Tilda to move along the aisle and reach the steps. She paused in the door and studied our faces, and then she walked to William and gave him the baby, saying, "Daddy, this is William Alexander. I call him Alex."

With careful grace, Tilda transferred her son to his grandfather's left arm. William Alexander's head, back, and bottom pressed against William's long arched arm, from bicep to forearm. He rested in the cradle of William's affection, and with a smile, William celebrated and conferred the sameness of power, lineage, and bond onto his grandson. He handed the boy to Pappy, who greeted his great-grandson with a kiss. The rest of the family pert' near knocked Pappy and the boy to the ground with our embrace as the concluding rite. It was another occasion when we rejoiced. "Blood always thicker than water," just like Mammy said.

185

—◦—

Tilda found a job in Hampton, and I babysat William Alexander during the daytime. When Thad came home from school, the first thing he did was to sniff out William Alexander, and William Alexander would start cooing as soon as Thad's voice became audible. Thad would grab him and put him on the floor, and they would play like nobody's business. Everything seemed to be going well, but we soon realized that evil lurked nearby.

In this case, it wore a dress and came from the Big House.

I had put William Alexander down for his nap, and William Faulkner's *Light in August* lay waiting for me on the kitchen table. I stood over the cookstove fixing up herbs for tea when White Candy "*throwed* my front door wide open," as Mammy would say.

There she was. So scalding hot, she was ready to argue with a fence post. She was something else, decked out in her tailor-made finery, standing with her hands on her hips. Lo and behold, Vivian was with her.

I almost dropped the teapot, but I raised my voice and blew my wind in her direction and said,

"Is that the way yuh come tuh somebody's house? Showin' out like yuh ain't got no home trainin'. Miss Ophelia taught'cha better."

Candy slung her head back and swooped strands of hair behind her right ear. She held her nose so high she would've drowned in a rainstorm, like the one that rumbled in the distance. Raising her voice, she asked,

"Where's that nigga bastard?" and then tilted her head to say, "Yo' daughter's a whore."

"A tramp," Vivian added, hanging in the doorway, which emboldened White Candy to dash toward the crib, but I reached it first.

My blood boiled.

"Now, I've seen many a mean and hateful thang you and Mr. Hollis have done. I've never said a word to yuh, couldn't have raised my finger tuh stop yuh, but if'n yuh touch one hair on his head, I'll scrub this floor wid yuh. Don't care whut'ja do tuh me, but yuh ain't gon' harm him!"

"Don't let this nigga talk tuh yuh like *that*," Vivian said. White Candy reached for the crib, but I grabbed her hand. Our eyes met, and I said,

"When we were children, I loved yuh. You were my friend. I wu'dah done *anythang* in the world for yuh!"

She jerked away.

"Felt sorry for yuh when Mr. Hollis beat'cha 'cause yuh read yo' books tuh me. Cried when yuh went off tuh Atlanta tuh that school, and I even rejoiced when yuh got married. Hoped you'd be happy."

She backed up, inching for the door and Vivian as I walked forward.

"Now, yuh're a hateful woman who dud'en recall when she was sweet and kind. You don't even remember yo' own mammy and how decent she was. Candy Demmings, you have turned into an evil, malicious person. Now, I want you and Vivian tuh never, as long as y'all are white, white as a slice of store-bought bread, step yo' feet in my doorway again!"

Tears pooled in my eyes, and I balled up my fists. I was willing to sling 'em like cats if I had to. Oh, White Candy's face was as pink as an evening sky, but I didn't care not one nary bit. I couldn't do much to defend myself or the boy. If a colored woman hit a white woman, she'd be a piece of low-hangin' fruit before the hoot owl could say *whooo*. Well, maybe God touched both of 'em, because they left, headed back to that cauldron they tended and called the Big House.

I grabbed William Alexander from his crib and soothed my nerves with the warmth of his smooth skin and his silky hair against my damp cheek. As I stepped on the front porch to catch some air, our old dog Duke, with an arthritic gate, limped toward the porch steps.

"'Least yuh cu'dha warned me of the two old copperheads. Where yuh been at, dawg?"

He dropped his head.

"Running 'round here chasin' that bitch wid the hangin' tits?"

He peered at me with sad eyes. He didn't know that inside of six months, God would call him home to shore up the pack where the good dogs go.

I climbed into my rocking chair, where William and Tilda found me, humming mournful but spirited hymns of praise and gratitude; the impending storm never materialized. William took one look at me and asked, "Whut's the matter?"

After I recounted the story, Tilda dashed into the house, and we followed.

"Whut are yuh up to?" I asked.

"Got'tuh pack. Mama, you know how they are. I'm takin' the baby and goin'—"

"Where?"

"Anywhere. Away from them . . . from her."

I walked over to her and pulled her around to face me. "Stop this," I said.

"Mama, I got'tuh—"

"Stop this. Whut do I haf'tuh do tuh make yuh understand? Yuh *cain't* run away from everythin'."

"No mo' runnin'," William said.

"That's right. The best place tuh stand is here, wid the family," I said. She calmed down.

⸻ ❖ ⸻

As I played peekaboo with William Alexander the following day, I heard a knock on the screen door. It was Marlene.

"Look lac feathers almos' did some flyin' yestiddy," she said as she took a seat at the kitchen table.

"She been talkin'?"

"Margaret, that's all that gal's been doin' since that husband of hers went over yonder tuh fight that war. She ain't never gon' forgive him. I feels sorry for that po' child. . . . that anger and hate. . . . it gon' kill her sho' as I is sittin' here."

"Whut did she say, Marlene?"

"She told Hollis 'bout the baby and whut Tilda done did."

"And whut did he say?"

"Whut he gon' say? He gots two and had one of 'em whilst his first wife be livin'. For him tuh say anythang . . . well, be lac the pot callin' the kettle black. 'Least Tilda carin' for the boy. She done mo' already than he ever done for my boys or or his uh'ther gal. Chucked that Isabel to Miss Ophelia's sister, and 'cause of Vivian's meddlin', her still there."

"Sho' is the truth, but they might do sump'em—jest for spite."

"Nah. Her gonna head back tuh Atlanta in a day or two. Thangs gon' calm down de'reckly. I keeps uh eye out, and I'll tell y'all."

"I sho'nuf would rest easier if yuh did that."

Before she left, she checked on William Alexander and said, "That boy gots the prettiest eyes I done ever seen. Come here, boy. Lemme look at them eyes," as she kissed him on both cheeks. "Lookin' mo' lac yo' daddy every day."

Somehow, Alexander learned that Tilda had returned to New Harmony.

I was near the mailbox when the postman brought a letter addressed to Matilda Butler, New Harmony, South Carolina. I waited until she was alone to give her the wrinkled envelope. She looked at it for a spell. I figured it held the hopes of a young colored girl's fancy, and I could sense a flood of memories emerging as she rubbed her thumb over the faded overseas postmark.

"He's yo' baby's daddy, honey," I said.

She opened the letter. She said he apologized for everything; he was saddened that Tilda left Atlanta and delighted he had a son, but wished Tilda had told him. He wanted a picture of them both. His unit was heading into the heart of Germany, but he believed that the war would end soon and hoped for their reunion afterward. He told her how much he missed and loved her and begged her to write to him.

"Mama, he signed it 'With love, Alex.'"

"Well, now you know how he feels," I said.

White Candy must've told him about the baby. How else would he have known? I supposed Alexander figured the postman knew everyone in a small town like New Harmony, and posting the envelope with just her name was plenty. Tilda decided she'd do the right thing and send him the picture he requested. From then on, one of those wrinkled letters arrived almost every week, but during the winter of 1944, without warning, there was silence from the front.

Tilda visited the mailbox daily for two weeks, but in the third week, she stopped and thought him dead like other men who had been lost in

Europe. In June of that year, many soldiers had died on the Normandy coast, and a whole heap of families received one of those tragic telegrams. Alexander's abrupt silence that winter conjured what other women feared.

SIXTEEN

Innocence and Deceit

William Alexander was such a well-behaved baby. He reminded me of my boys, Henry and Thad, who were always good, but my Thad was unique that way. The few times I raised my voice, Thad acted as if I ripped his heart into shreds. He was about the most soft-hearted boy I had ever seen, and he stayed near my dress tail; he didn't want to stray far from his mammy. Thad loved his daddy, too, but we were mighty close. I used to say he had such a gentle spirit—an angel on earth, but I suppose most mothers feel that way about their sons. At least, I hope so.

I could take him anywhere. I'd say, "Stay here, wait 'til I come back. You be quiet now. Yuh hear?" He'd sit as quiet as you please. He'd be right happy in Doctor Rosenthal's office, the store, any place, playing with his toy. Unlike Tilda, who had been the wild one, he was obedient and didn't fuss, but none of the other children were like him.

I remember the first time Thad's little wee-wee let loose, and it rained right in William's face as William changed his diaper. And I remember the times when I fed him and how he pushed carrots, pears, and chicken (all the consistency of pudding) across his plate and onto his high chair. Food went everywhere, including his hair, his clothes, and the floor. Then I bathed him, to his and my delight. I remembered how he smelled after a bath when I put talcum powder on his little bitty bottom.

I can smell him now. He's as fresh as a breeze on a springtime morning; he fills my nostrils like it was yesterday, but that only adds to my grief.

I remember the first time he stood unsupported and wobbled to the middle of the room, grinning. He wore no shirt, had a head full of curls, and his diaper sagged near his knees. His fat little bowlegs slapped against each other as he tore across the floor so he could throw his arms around my dress-skirted legs. He sat like an adult for his first haircut until the clippers appeared, and then he cried like there was no tomorrow. Couldn't do anything to appease him. He cried and he cried.

I read to him when he was little, and he had my passion for books and school. But when I sent him to school for the first time, his teacher sent him home because she thought he wasn't old enough. Thad and Nate had become close friends long before starting school, though. Nate pestered Marlene to bring him to visit Thad all the time, and Marlene said she couldn't get any work done until she brought him to play. And each day after he finished classes at the white children's school, Nate would hightail it right down the road and wait until Thad came from the colored school-house. Their friendship seemed as natural as the earth being stroked by wind and rain. It stayed that way until the end.

Nate would pull his chair to our kitchen table like he was home. He was, and we loved him like our son despite Vivian and Mr. Hollis. Unlike his parents, Nate was always kind and soft-hearted, but I worried they would send him off somewhere and he'd come back like White Candy—all evil and bitter. *Hateful!*

Colored children always played in our yard, running around with Thad and Nate. They hunted for snakes and lizards in the woods and caught butterflies and lightning bugs with their bare hands. I don't remember Nate having any white friends, and when the white children found him and Thad together, they'd call Nate "the nigga lover." One day, while I hung clothes on the line, my heart jumped up in my throat when I caught sight of Thad and Nate running and crying. A bunch of white children threw rocks at them as they chased them toward the house. When they saw me, they called me a nigga too, but they ran off after I yelled, and Henry ran after them.

Blood ran down both their necks, and that's when they called them-selves blood brothers. Those white children were something awful. They behaved like little monsters in the making, and Thad would tell me how they bullied Nate: they said he'd be swinging from the trees like a monkey if he kept eating our food. They mocked his lips, saying they were "nigga lips," way too full for a white boy. However, the size of his lips wasn't unusual for the men in his family and reminded me of Floyd's. Nate's head full of curls didn't help his situation either. The taunts didn't dampen his spirit; he knew what he wanted and cared little about other people's opinions—not even his kinfolk. Nothing turned him away from us or his Thad.

One day, as I sat at the kitchen table, smiling and listening to William and Henry slap their knees over a funny story William had remembered, up popped Nate. He was almost eleven.

"Do you hate me?" he asked while tears pooled in his eyes and his face stretched down to his knuckles.

"Hate yuh? Now, why would I hate yuh?"

"Cause I'm white, and the way white folks treat colored folks. They're jest plain mean tuh colored people."

"Well, not every white person," I said.

"Yes, they do! Mr. Kearns got mad yesterday, pushed Mr. Brown's face in'tuh a barrel, and held it underwater. Mr. Brown almost drowned. Then Mr. Kearns called him a no-count sorry nigga. That ain't right."

I pulled him right close and said,

"You know Doc Rosenthal, don'tcha?"

"Yes, ma'am."

"Why, when my friend Zora Mae got hurt real bad, Doc Rosenthal was the only doctor 'round these parts who'd help her."

"That's right," William said. "I fetched him in the dead of night."

"He even set up a clinic for Negroes in town. 'Foe that, we had tuh travel all the way tuh Hampton," I said.

"I remember that," Henry said.

"Don't forgit Miss Ophelia," William said.

"Yo' daddy's first wife," I said. "When she died, she left my family this house and land."

"And money, too," William said. "And Miss Anna Bell—when those colored children lost their mammy and pappy in a fire and their house burned tuh the ground, Miss Anna Bell took 'em in."

"See, everybody ain't like Kearns. Nate, folks like Miss Anna Bell and Doc Rosenthal do the right things."

I kissed him.

"Just like you," I said. He kissed me and ran off to play with Thad.

His kind and open heart took my breath away! Took it right away. That was Nate. He had always been like that.

———————

Marlene, our news carrier, brought frequent updates from the Big House; this time, she couldn't wait to share the news.

"Where the chilluns at?" She started looking around the house. "Gots tuh make sho' they ain't here. Don't wants 'em tuh hear none of this. Where William at?"

"Oh, he's gone," I said.

Marlene flopped into the chair and wiped her face. She was covered with sweat but bounced with excitement.

"Been a *mess* today. Big old ruckus at the Big House this mornin'. Never guess whut done happen." She was right giddy.

"Miss Vivian . . . Miss Ann . . . Miss White Woman . . ." Then she busted out laughing. "I ain't 'posed tuh rejoice in uh'ther folk's troubles and mis'ry, *but* . . ." Her laughter all but crippled her.

"You should'ah seen it!" she said, laughing with her hands over her mouth and her head between her legs.

"Marlene! What?"

Her eyes got all big.

"Child, Hollis done ketched her."

"Caught who?"

"Hollis on his way tuh Uh'lanta tuh see 'bout Candy. She ain't doin' so hot. I guess he done been out the house 'bout forty minutes, but up he comes again. I be's in the kitchen cleanin' when he come thru' the back door, and I axes him whut done happen. He say he forgits sump'em Candy wants him tuh brang, sump'em her wants of Miss Ophelia's. He say it be in his bedroom.

"'Members how Floyd use'ta cut up when he be 'round Vivian?"

"Yeah, I remember. He buzzed 'round her lac'uh bee 'round honey."

"Well, Hollis ketches 'em . . . . Floyd be jumpin' up and down on Vivian, and she uh-screamin' and yellin' for Jesus when Hollis walked in the bedroom."

"Nah!"

"Yes in-dee-deedy! Right in the middle of his bed . . . wid his wife. *His own son!*"

"Nah. Lawdy, Lawdy. *Ain't* that a mess." I clicked my tongue and shook my head.

"What did Mr. Hollis do?"

"Plenty of cussin' and yellin'. I runs upstairs, and when I gits there, I knowed what done happened. Vivian, her nekkid as a jaybird sittin' on the edge of the bed, touchin' the corner of the sheet to her eyes, actin' lac her cryin'. Floyd, he tryin' to pick his clothes up off the floor."

"Was he—

"Yeah, he buck nekkid, too. Hollis callin' both of 'em low-life trash and yellin' lac there ain't no tomorrow. He wrapped his mouth 'round some words I ain't never heard nobody call nobody. All kinds of sons-of-bitches and muthafuckas. Child, even my face done turned red. Yeah, he cussed them quiet 'till Vivian caught a whiff of me and started in on me. She gits right brazen. Calls me a no-good nigga bitch and tell Hollis he ain't shit cause he done fucked me and got some nappy-headed niggas, jigaboos, runnin' 'round *her* house."

"Oh, Marlene!"

"Sho' did, or no hawgs ruut in Sowth Ca-linah. Yeah, tell him he cain't say *shit* tuh her cause he ain't nuthin' but a no-good nigga-lovin' son-of-a-bitch hisself."

"Oh, my."

"Yeah, she nekkid as a jaybird and say that. Her done said all that after he ketches her in his bed wid his son."

"Naked."

She gave a slow but deliberate and emphatic nod, and said, "Titties jest a hangin', sweat runnin' down her body from that ride old Floyd done give her. I'd say a right good ride judgin' from the size of his pecker. Hollis called her a strumpet and worse than any nigga he done been with.

"Nigga or strumpet—don't seem lac much of no honor, no shape or form. Anyway, he say, 'Git out my house, and never come back.' He tells Floyd the same thang. Floyd still standin' in front of his daddy wid his private parts danglin'—all shriveled up from 'barrassment, but I must say he gots quite a bit hangin' even after it shrunk in'tuh the shyness of its hood."

Must've been impressed. She said that twice.

"Floyd walked toward Hollis, and Hollis hauled off and slugged him. He topples right on top of Vivian. Hollis tell 'em they deserve each other, and he leave the room. Honey, it was a mess!"

"Lawd, Marlene."

"Yeah, but there's more. Hollis go through the house, pullin' belongings off the walls, out closets, and everywhere else. All us colored folks jumpin' out'ah the way. Other folks wonderin' what done happened. As he finds 'em, he take her stuff and start chunkin' 'em out'ah the wenders and the back door. Whut he cain't carry he tell colored Ben tuh. Hollis cussin' lac a sailor whilst he do it, too.

"They takes this-here stuff and piles it in the backyard. Hollis tells colored Ben tuh git the coal oil; he pours it on that stuff and sets it a-blazin'. Y'all ain't see it this mornin'?"

"Nah!"

We went to the porch; smoke still lingered.

"Lawd, how much stuff did he burn?"

"Pert' near everythang she had and more."

"Then what? Where did she and Floyd go?

"Oh, wait. 'Foe Miss Ann leaves, her stands on the staircase and tell Hollis tuh kiss her ass. Hollis start toward her; she throws her head back, tell him he bet not put his muthafuckin' hands on her."

"Oh, Marlene, we thought she was so prim and proper. Where did that gutter talk come from? She sounds like one of those low-down, raunchy, loose women—a back-alley woman. My God, where did she learn tuh talk like that; she sounds lac'uh strumpet."

"Now us has the truth. Tells Hollis her hates him, and primes her mouth and say her lost them babies 'cause his seed be too old; it wan't her fault. Tells Hollis he be too old for her . . . her wants a mo' younger man.

Somebody who can love her lac her 'posed tuh be. Floyd twice the man he be. Then her tell him, the last thang her gon' do, 'foe her leave the Big House—her gon' take Nathan wid her."

"Oh, no!"

"Hollis grab her up by the throat and push her tuh the wall; had her danglin' off the floor. He tell her he sooner see her dead 'foe he let her strangle the goodness out'ah Nathan. Should'ah seen her strugglin' and kickin' her feets, lac her doin' the jig at the end of a rope, turnin' all red in the face and her eyes poppin' out, full of water.

"He let her go, and her grab at her throat and runs out the house, tellin' him her hope his old ass burn in hell. By then, Floyd, he done drove up, and they takes on off."

"Whut 'bout Mr. Hollis?"

"Know how evil he can be, but I feels for him. He in the parlor, hunched over in a chair. I touch him, first time since I don't know when. He turned and planted his face in my belly and cried lac uh baby."

"When did this happen?"

"'Bout nine o'clock this morning."

"Well, 'least Nate wan't home for all that ugliness. Whut y'all gonna tell him when he comes from school? Cain't tell the boy the truth. It'll break his po' little heart. He's as soft-hearted as Thad."

"Don't know whut Hollis gon' tell the boy. One time, they aimed tuh send Nate away tuh school. Don't thank that's gonna be happenin'. Hollis gon' keep him close, I reckon."

"Thank God! Breakin' him and Thad up would be . . . well, I cain't imagine it."

I must admit, I held enough rejoicing in my heart to stretch right out into my feet and all my toes. Floyd had become Vivian's problem; from where I sat, it couldn't have happened to a more deserving person. After Vivian's departure, White Candy returned to the Big House, Christmas of forty-four. 'Spect she planned on staying a while since she brought her little girl, Christine, with her. Marlene said Candy had changed. She was stranger than before 'cause, at forty-one, she covered herself in black from head to toe. The black dresses she wore seemed to frame and mirror her inner darkness. It didn't seem she would ever get over Alexander, who had committed the ultimate sin—shamed her.

During that time, Mr. Hollis hired one of them Johns boys to work up at the Big House. We used to call him Lee, but by the time he became a handyman for the Demmings, he insisted on being called Harvey Lee. I remembered the boy's mammy and pappy, and as a boy, he always held a mouthful of manure when he talked, lacking respect for everyone, even his parents. He wasn't much better as an adult, but Marlene appreciated the help.

SEVENTEEN

Some Mo' Chickens Done Come Home to Roost

William Alexander was growing like a weed, and the boy possessed jaw-dropping good looks. You could tell he was gifted 'cause the boy had quite a vocabulary by the time he was two. While I didn't see one bit of color in his skin, his steel-gray eyes, thick eyebrows, jet-black hair, sculptured lips, and perfect nose would break your heart. I was making my way back home after flapping my gums at Fannie's, and my thoughts turned to his half-sister, Christine, who lived up at the Big House. I considered their relationship and pondered the likelihood of their meeting. The gravel kicked up by an approaching car alerted me to step out of the roadbed, and I stood alongside, waiting for the automobile to pass. Christine and White Candy sat in the back of Hollis's Cadillac. I lingered for a spell, watching that car long after it disappeared in its created dust. Perhaps Christine and William Alexander's meeting might be as accidental as that encounter. I never imagined their meeting was right around the bend.

The war in Europe ended on William Alexander's second birthday, the 8th of May, 1945. When the news spread that day, there was a ruckus! Initially, we didn't realize why. I couldn't even listen to *The Guiding Light* on the radio with the racket from church bells and car horns. They interrupted programming to tell everyone that the war had ended and to announce the celebration in the square. I decided to take William Alexander.

When William Alexander and I reached New Harmony, a mess of townsfolks rambled in the square, and at the same time, a band played Fourth of July music. Everybody hugged and kissed, knowing their loved ones would be home soon. Nate and Thad ran around blowing toy trumpets with the other children released from school. Henry snuck up from behind and laid a kiss on my cheek while Ruth strolled with some of her classmates, showing them the letter she'd showed me earlier. She had been accepted to Fisk University in the fall. White Candy and little Christine nudged their way through the knot of folks, and from a distance, you could see William Alexander's resemblance to Christine; they took after their pappy.

William Alexander stood waving a flag someone had stuck in his hand. Given my appearance and the sight of me holding his other hand, I suspected folks assumed I was his wet nurse or a "caretaker," like during the slave days, and not his grandmammy, because the white ladies sho'nuf fell all over him. They didn't know he wasn't like them—he was only near-white.

Somehow, Christine had gotten separated from White Candy. Through the jostling crowd, she made her way to where William Alexander stood, holding on to me and his flag. I don't remember who started it first, but they began talking. My uneasiness held me captive, paralyzing me with indecision. Should I distance us from her? If we stayed, White Candy might cause trouble if she caught them talking to each other. As certainty itched at my feet and I turned to pull William Alexander away, I looked right into White Candy's face. She still wore a black dress and had her hair pulled tight into a bun. We momentarily locked eyes, but she recovered, reached down to grab Christine's hand, and saw William Alexander for the first time since he was a baby. He said, "Oh. She yo' mama?" But when he smiled and added, "She so pretty," I think William Alexander's innocence grabbed at White Candy's heart and anchored her feet to the concrete. When she came to herself, she snatched Christine and took off. She walked so fast that she almost dragged the poor child. 'Spect looking at William Alexander reminded her too much of Alexander's and Tilda's sin and her humiliation.

The celebrations lasted for days, and during that period, we learned the other side of Hitler's war. He killed millions of Hebrews. I could barely look Doctor Rosenthal in his face, and my heart felt for him and his people. The world had gone insane! In the end, I was glad our colored men joined the fight. Without their help, Hitler might have won the war. If he had, as sure as white folks believed in Jim Crow, they'd add colored folks to the list of undesirables that fed the Third Reich's concentration camps.

When the Japanese surrendered on September 2nd of 1945, I went to church. I prayed for people from every nation, both allies and foes, but especially for America, who created *that* bomb and *used* it on the Japanese. But it was Fannie who made me think even more when she said, "That loud-talkin' cracker only dropped it on them Japs 'cause they skin is yellow. Truman's mammy ain't come from no Japan, and her name sho' ain't Hiroko."

Henry was fifteen when the war ended, and Thad turned twelve on August 11th. Where had the time gone? They had grown up so fast.

Around the time Tilda reasoned that Alexander was a casualty of war and put him behind her, White Candy decided she no longer wanted to be his wife. With divorce papers in her hand, Candy packed her belongings and returned to Atlanta. Mr. Hollis decided to get shed of Vivian as well. He divorced her and started spending more time in Atlanta with his other daughter, Isabel. He refurbished and redecorated the Big House, replacing things he had burned when he banished Vivian. The last anyone knew, she and Floyd had moved to Alabama, Vivian's Yellowhammer State. I attempted to determine Nate's relationship to any future child Floyd and Vivian might have. When I did, I shook my head and said, "Whoever heard of such nonsense?" Nothing unusual for the Big House, though.

William and William Alexander spent a whole heap of time together that summer and fall of 1947. When you saw William, William Alexander wasn't too far behind. They fished a lot, and one morning, when they headed off to the pond close to where Fast Fannie and Robert lived, I walked to the Ridge. Miss Hillary had lent me Richard Wright's *Native Son*. As I nestled into the spot where I could view the entire river valley, I intended to relax and read the book she proclaimed as "one of the most outstanding books ever written on the idea of social protest." I had settled into reading for quite a spell when I felt an uneasiness that had my insides all tied up. The reason for my anxiety appeared in the corner of my eye. At first, it was just two young folks running in the distance, enjoying themselves. I thought nothing of it, but then I recognized the voices. When they got closer, I saw Tilda with that old Johns boy. My heart fell.

"Mama, whut'ja doing up here?"

I cut my eyes at him, and she blurted, "Mama, you remember Harvey Lee?"

"Harvey Lee, how yuh been doin', boy? Workin' for Mr. Hollis, are yuh?"

"Yessum. For a right good spell now."

"Now, y'all children be careful. I'm goin' home; been sittin' here too long, startin' tuh git stiff."

I left agitated, and I prayed this flirtation wasn't serious. Given Tilda's headstrong nature, I couldn't say anything because any opposition from me would drive her into his arms.

When I reached the porch, William Alexander sat beside William with a box of Lucky Strike candy cigarettes sticking out from his shirt pocket. One of the slender, red-tipped sugar sticks dangled from his lips. I threw him a smile.

"Better be careful wid those cigarettes; they'll stunt yo' growth."

He giggled.

William had caught a mess of catfish and perch, and William Alexander hadn't done too bad either.

"Look, Grandma!" holding up his string of fish, mostly perch.

"You've turned in'tuh a right smart fisherman. It's gittin' late; you run on inside and git cleaned up. I need tuh talk tuh yo' grandpappy 'bout sump'em," I said, but the sight of the gate opening caught his attention; he started waving and said, "Grandma, here comes Aunt Fannie," before he entered the house and closed the screen door behind him.

With Fannie standing by my side, I turned to William.

He already knew.

"Saw Tilda wid that Johns boy, did'ja?"

"Oh, Lawd," Fannie said.

"How long have yuh known, William?" I asked.

"'Bout two months now. I figured it wan't none of our business. She's grown now, and there ain't nothin' we can do 'bout it."

"But—"

"He from Slop Jar Alley," Fannie said.

"So?"

"William, c'mon! They uh bunch of po' folks. Even they dawgs are pitiful. And they're a bunch of raw-boned dawgs movin' as slow as 'possums, scroungin' for food 'cause scraps of meat 'round there 'bout as scarce as rabbits sproutin' horns durin' matin' season."

I chuckled. "Fannie's right."

"Here comes Marlene, axe her," Fannie said.

"Whut?" Marlene asked.

"'Bout them folks from the Slop Jar," Fannie said.

"Them folks ain't gots nuthin' tuh eat but cornbread, corn pone, hush puppies, and cornmeal hash. Maybe if'n they scrimps, they gits a smidgen of molasses tuh douse on top of it," Marlene said.

"But they gits plenty of fatback grease and meat skins to top it off, I bet'cha," Fannie said. "They ain't never wrapped they mouth 'round no biscuits or store-bought bread wid thick chunks of side meat. If they did, they'd drop dead."

"Oh Fannie, why you got'tuh overdo everything?" William said.

"William, if a piece of meat fell on they plate, they wud'den know what tuh *do* wid it. Bunch of po'-ass niggas eatin' too much poke salad and drankin' nuthin' but pot liquor."

"William, that's the God's honest truth," I said. "Tilda ain't got no business messin' 'round wid the lacs of him."

"Yeah, that's right," Fannie said. "Folks from the Slop Jar be the kinda colored folks who'd pee down yo' back and then try tuh 'suade yuh that it wan't nuthin' but rain."

Marlene chuckled. "Fannie, you ortah hush yo' mouth."

"It's the truth!

"And if'n I 'members right, wan't Tilda and that boy in the same grade? Ain't that right, Margaret?"

"William, you remember. The boy use'ta torment that gal sump'em terrible. He'd chase her home, pullin' at her pigtails . . ."

"Slop Jar then, and Slop Jar now," Fannie said.

"Pestered her so—you had tuh go and talk wid his pappy. Remember?"

"Yeah, but—"

"Didn't do one lick of good. May as well been talkin' tuh our beagle, old Biscuit."

"Don't forgit Miss Annie's granddaughter," Fannie said. "Remember her?"

"Oh, that's right. Stuck Miss Annie's granddaughter wid a big belly and left her high and dry."

"Mammy's flippin' in her grave, and Pappy? I don't even wants tuh hear what he gon' say," Fannie said.

"Margaret, you and Fannie gonna haf'tuh stay out of this. Tilda's a grown woman."

Fannie threw up her hands before placing them on her hips and throwing, "Folks from the Slop Jar ain't *like* regular folks," straight between William's eyes. "Everyone knows that even a blind pig finds an acorn sometimes if it stays wid the Lawd—everybody *'cept* them folks from Slop Jar Alley."

"She's grown, Fannie," William said again.

"William, sometimes . . . oh, lemme git out'ah here. Margaret, try tuh talk some sense in his head 'foe it be too late. Bye, Marlene."

"We gonna haf'tuh let it be," William said to Fannie's back before turning to me. "Look whut happened the last time. She ran away and returned wid a child but no husband."

"But—"

"Ain't no buts. Tilda's a grown woman, and she has tuh learn tuh live and clean up her own messes. That's whut yuh use'ta tell me, right?"

"Yeah, but . . . he ain't no good, William."

"Margaret, yuh know whut us old folks say: yuh can take a horse tuh water, but yuh sho' cain't make him drank," Marlene said.

"That's right," William said, putting his arms around me. "She has tuh find it out for herself."

I turned to Marlene. "I wish Tilda found one of yo' boys interestin'. They're attractive, and they're sho'nuf better than Harvey Lee."

"Well—"

"I bet Burton must be workin' like the dickens at Meharry. Got'tuh be a lot harder than being at Fisk . . . how's Leroy?"

"Well, he's been kinda busy, too," she said.

William chuckled and said, "Whut are yuh two hens hatchin'?"

"We ain't doin' nothin' a'tall," I said. "Now, jest mind yo' business." I tagged him on the shoulder. "Go 'head, Marlene."

"Well, I's right proud of 'em. Don't know if I gots one thang tuh do wid it or no. Both of 'em did right good in school, and Miss Hillary, her pushed 'em and tell 'em 'bout different places where they can go on tuh school.

"You know how they is. Right under each uh'ther all the time. If one of 'em do sump'em, tuh'ther one gots tuh do the same thang. But when it come time for Leroy, he say he ain't gon' follow 'hind Burton this time. He go on tuh Morehouse. I thanks both 'em too young, but Miss Hillary, her right there, and her say I gots tuh let 'em go. Leroy, crackin' them law books at Howard in Washington. Last I heard, Leroy talkin' 'bout gittin' hitched tuh some gal. I ain't seen nary one of 'em in a spell. I misses 'em lac nobody's business. . . . Wish they comes home."

"Marlene, will they come back to New Harmony when they finish?" I asked.

"I hopes, but yuh know youngins."

"How'ja do it?" William asked.

"Miss Ophelia."

"Whut?" I said.

"Yeah. Miss Ophelia left money in her will. She wanna make sho' Burton git some schoolin'. 'Spect her believe it be Hollis's duty, but her know Hollis ain't gon' do nuthin' for him—Burton ain't ask tuh be brung in the world, and I 'spect Miss Ophelia knowed I couldn't do nuthin' much for him. She die 'foe Leroy be born, but her left 'nuf money for both of 'em. Her lawyer took care of everythang."

"Yes, Lawd. The woman was a saint," I said. "Bless her heart, and I thank her every day for whut she did for us."

"Yeah. I 'members."

"You never can say where yo' blessings stem from," I said. "Anyway, it's too bad Burton and Leroy aren't here. They sho'nuf a sight better than Harvey Lee."

"Harvey Lee might surprise us," William said.

Me and Marlene said "I sho' hope so" at the same time.

Yeah, I tried hard not to pass too much judgment on the boy, but as hard as I tried to dislodge it, the thought of Harvey Lee didn't sit right in my craw. I felt it when he was little and when he stood grown in the Demmings's backyard.

Yeah, the boy was trouble and reminded me too much of Willie Deke, whose eyes cannibalized every woman he encountered. He made my flesh crawl, too.

Every time I turned around, Harvey Lee was underfoot with Tilda: sitting at my table, eating my food as if he had earned it. I knew he wasn't up to no good. His eyes revealed everything but a smidgen of love. They held the lust that tore at your flesh, never leaving you the same once it took you over. I didn't think he knew how to cherish a woman or appreciate a woman's love for him.

He and Tilda could get hitched if they wanted, but William Alexander would stay with us. Let her go off, let him run her down and dog her like Willie Deke dogged Zora Mae.

I told her, too.

"If you and Harvey Lee wanna run off tuh'gether, that's fine, but William Alexander is gonna stay *right* where he *is*."

"He's my child and—"

"If he's so important to yuh, then why yuh wanna marry Harvey Lee? The man's poison. Gal, it's as plain as the nose on yo' face. He's sneaky, and he's mean."

"You wrong, Mama."

"Honey, I—"

"You don't want me tuh be happy. Do yuh?"

I threw up my hands.

"Whut 'bout yo' singing? Have yuh forgotten 'bout that?"

"Ancient history," she said.

"And Alexander?"

"Mama. Where is he? *Vanished* . . . been gone for so long I stopped countin' the months, the years. How am I 'posed to live? Walk 'round in mournin', like Candy?"

"But do yuh love Harvey Lee the way yuh loved Alexander?"

She turned away and looked in the direction of Hampton.

I threw up my hands.

"Well, I'm puttin' it in the Lawd's hands, but William Alexander is stayin' wid us. Now *you* can put that in yo' pipe and smoke it."

She huffed on out of the room.

———— ••• ————

Two months later, in November of 1947, we sat around the kitchen table a few days before Thanksgiving. When they arrived, Harvey Lee was bright-eyed and bushy-tailed, grinning with teeth gleaming like a strand of freshwater pearls dipped in whipped cream.

"We got married today," Tilda said, acting as if she was Princess Elizabeth and had just married Lieutenant Philip Mountbatten at Westminster Abbey. I dropped my fork and cornbread and walked out the door.

In a little while, she joined me.

"Be happy for me, Mama. Please be happy for me," she said, choking back tears.

"I wanna be happy for yuh, baby, but I don't want yuh tuh throw yo' life away. Whut can he give yuh?"

"He's a good man, Mama."

"Let's pray tuh God that's true."

They found a place down the road, and initially, I thought I would have to eat every negative word I uttered about Harvey Lee. For one thing, when he got paid, he brought his earnings to Tilda. He planted them right in her lap, and he even started taking classes at the colored trade school over in Hampton, "hankering for some white man's work," he said. However, we were in for a shock.

———— ••• ————

In 1948, when Henry graduated high school, he attended the trade school in Hampton for plumbing. At the end of the summer, Ruth, having taken summer classes each summer, graduated early from Fisk, and Henry and William insisted on a celebration. We all gathered at the house. My brothers and sisters, along with their children and mine, hugged Ruth, and everyone told Thad he would be the next to wear a cap and gown. He had set his sights on Morehouse. Throughout the day, men formed tight groups to tell tales and slap their thighs while the women gathered to speculate about Tilda's situation.

Helen, spotting Tilda across the room, said, "Now, would somebody please tell me 'bout Tilda and this Harvey Lee?"

"My question, too. Why did Tilda marry him?" Violet asked.

"Rebound," Fannie said.

"Yeah, from William Alexander's father," I said.

"Well, that marriage is gonna last 'bout as long as a fart in a whirlwind," Lena said.

Helen and Violet snickered.

"She cain't love him. The man cain't even hold a decent conversation," Violet said.

"I'm wid Violet on that. What do they talk about, anyway?" Helen asked.

"But when a man looks like him, I wud'den worry 'bout what comes out his mouth. It's his uh'ther attribute that raises its head and speaks *volumes* for him," Lena said, winking at Fast Fannie.

"Yessiree! Honey, look at that *butt* and them *thighs*! Lawd, have mercy! Glad I is a married woman!" Fannie smacked her lips and threw Lena a nod.

I had to snicker.

"Fannie, you's uh mess," I said. "But, have yuh forgotten? He's from the Slop Jar."

"Oh, Margaret! I's talkin' 'bout his *body*, girl! Not his character."

The celebration for Ruth was a milestone, but it was nothing compared to what happened a few months later. Another one of Tilda's chickens came home to roost.

I was up bright and early that fall Sunday morning. Before breakfast and church time, a black Cadillac Coupe de Ville pulled up in the yard. It looked brand new from the dealership, and so spit-shined and fancy you needed shades to protect your eyes when the sun hit it. When he stepped from the back seat, he saw William Alexander first; seeing his reaction, I sensed he found part of what he sought. He walked with a cane, and as he came closer, I noticed he limped a little.

Before he could open his mouth, I said, "You're Alexander, aren't you?"

"Yes, Ma'am," he said. "Is this William Alexander?"

William Alexander was five but still shy around the edges. He hid behind me, holding on to the lilacs covering my dress while he peeped his curly head around my hips.

"Yessir. This is yo' boy." William Alexander looked up at me and said, "He's my daddy?" His face lit up, and he wasn't shy anymore; he ran and jumped into Alexander's arms. They hugged and hugged. Alexander cried, and it pained me to see anyone cry, but when I saw him crying, it warmed my heart. That man held William Alexander . . . well, ain't no words to describe it but love.

When we entered the house, William was drinking coffee while reading the Sunday paper at the kitchen table.

With his daddy in tow, William Alexander said, "Granddaddy! Granddaddy! My daddy came! My daddy came!"

William 'bout scalded himself to death with his coffee.

It took William a while, but he got his wits together and stumbled over to shake Alexander's hand and wave him to a seat.

"So pleased to meet y'all. I thought today would never happen," Alexander said, holding William Alexander in his lap. They kept looking at each other. William's nervous eyes first flitted to his coffee cup and then up at me. Thank God it was one of those mornings when Marlene visited.

"Miss Marlene, this is my daddy!"

She glanced at me, at William, and then at the two of them.

"Whut done happen? Everybody thank yuh dead. Where yuh come from? Where yuh been at?"

"I returned Stateside in January but spent the last year of the war in POW camps in Germany and Poland," Alexander said.

"What's POW?" asked William Alexander.

"Prisoner of war, son," he said, looking at William Alexander, and then to the grown folks, he said, "When the Allies found us, I spent more than a year recuperating in the army hospital in Frankfurt, Germany."

"Bet that wan't no way tuh spend the war," William said.

"No, it wasn't. When I got back to the States, I had surgery at Walter Reed Hospital and then spent several more months mending in the hospital back home before I could travel. I was hoping to talk with Tilda. How is she?"

But Fast Fannie's voice broke through as her feet hit the front porch.

"Margaret, whose Cadillac is that?"

She came busting in as usual, loud and full of cheer, but this time, the sight of this white man holding William Alexander on his lap stopped her cold. She wasn't dumb.

"Oh, it's *you!*" she said.

"Fannie, please," I said, but I knew how she felt about Tilda, and she said,

"Don't shush me! After he done made this *mess*! Where yuh been? Jest lac'uh man. Yuh gots some kinda *nerve* brangin' yo' white ass 'round here after all yuh done caused. Wan't uh'nuf for yuh tuh leave yo' wife and yo' daughter, mess up they lives, but now yuh gots tuh come here and finish makin' a mess of Tilda's and the boy's." She walked closer and got in his face.

"Lucky for *you*, I ain't no man. I'd take yuh to the woods and *hang yuh* by yo'—"

"Fannie, not in front of the boy," William whispered as he pulled her by the arm and moved her toward the door, but she intended to cut Alexander to the quick. She didn't take her eyes off him, either. She kept rolling them, throwing daggers all over the place. Before reaching the door, she snatched her arm from William's hand.

"Margaret's too nice. She's too kind, but she *knows* it's the truth. You's trouble, and all us gon' haf tuh pay for it 'foe it done with. *Yuh mark my words!*"

"Daddy, Daddy, whut's the matter?" William Alexander said, burrowing his head into Alexander's chest.

"It's all right, sport. Come here," William said, but William Alexander resisted until his daddy said,

"I'm not leaving. I'll be here." Alexander turned toward us and said, "I didn't come to cause trouble. I really didn't. I hope y'all believe that. All this happened when—"

"The world was upside down," I said.

"Exactly. I want to make sure my son has everything he needs. That much I can do for him."

"Well, it seems you and Tilda have a lot tuh discuss, but it might be wise for yuh tuh leave. Tell me where yuh're stayin'."

"At the Drake Hotel in Hampton."

"I'll tell her yuh came by. Yuh go on now. Don't worry. We'll be here when yuh return."

When he reached the yard, William Alexander was all over him again—never seen him come alive so.

By the time William placed his arms around my shoulders, Fannie was nowhere to be seen. The weight of Fannie's hateful words still hung all around as we waved our goodbyes to Alexander as he pulled away in his shiny black Cadillac. The tires of this rich, white man's car spun up dust, as fine as stone-ground cornmeal, to consume his car and drift back onto us.

"Whut now?" William asked.

"Tell Tilda," I said.

EIGHTEEN

At Right Angles

It was a curious fall.

The honeysuckle still scented the evening air, and the insects stood confused, being seduced by plants that had lost all reference to their proper season. Summer's lingering presence rendered the seasons out of kilter, but I loved the continued spectacle of cape jasmines, hydrangeas, hollyhocks, and black-eyed Susans that this curiousness provided. At first, I thought Alexander's arrival had sparked enough heat to blaze summer into this peculiar fall, but I remembered Marlene whispering that Floyd and Vivian had also returned. Well, between the three of 'em, I figured they could stir up sufficient turmoil to spin the earth backward, forcing us to swelter in December and on into Christmastime as if it were June. During the fall of 1948, no one imagined how much misery their presence would create.

After Alexander's visit, I sat on the porch, watching an orange and purple evening sky, but when Tilda entered the gate, the sun's reddish-orange disk hung low on the horizon.

Twilight was a-coming, and the darkness would follow.

"Mama, whut'ja doin' out here? I can hardly breathe; the air is so heavy, and yuh're full of sweat."

I looked up and fixed my eyes on her belly, and I still wavered over her being pregnant with Harvey Lee's baby. The impending birth added an element to an already curious autumn.

"I relish this weather. It seems like I'm mo' in tune wid the earth."

Thad came running onto the porch.

"Tilda, I thought I heard yuh out here."

"Boy, every time I see you, yuh've grown uh'nuther inch. Look at those feet. B'foe long, Mama ain't gonna be able tuh find shoes tuh fit those ant killers."

"Oh, Tilda," he said with a grin that would turn hostility into a smile.

"Thad, you run on now. I need tuh talk tuh yo' sister 'bout sump'em," I said.

"Yessum." He came over and gave us both a peck on the cheek.

"When yuh gonna visit me?" Tilda asked.

He turned and smiled. "I'm comin' over the day after tomorrow."

"Okay, make sure you do that now. I'll be waitin' for yuh, and tell Nate tuh come, too."

Then she turned to me. "What's wrong, Mama?"

"Let's walk a bit." Tilda helped me out of the rocker, and Prince, our new mutt, stretched his legs and followed us out into the yard and down the road a piece.

"Must be serious if we're headin' to Pleasant Ridge," Tilda said.

"Maybe. Maybe not. . . . We had a visitor this mornin'."

"Who?"

I looked at her, and she threw her hands to her mouth with the shock of recognition.

"Alexander?"

"Yeah, he's alive, baby, and he came lookin' for you and William Alexander."

"When? How he—"

"Came 'bout eight thirty this mornin'. We didn't even go tuh church. Yuh should'ah seen William Alexander's face when he met him.

"Had his man drive him up from Atlanta . . . he's stayin' over at the Drake Hotel." I walked up and put my hand on her shoulder. "He wants tuh talk to yuh, baby."

"For *what*? Ain't heard from him . . . he disappeared, and now he comes *waltzin'* back here like he gots *rights* and *privileges*. Why?"

"'Cause he's yo' son's daddy."

"Guess he wants to take him away from me, too. Mama, where has he been? Why didn't he write to me? And don't tell me he was shell-shocked."

I dried her tears and hugged her, but she pulled away and wailed, "Mama, I'm so scared!"

"You haf'tuh face him, baby. It ain't gonna be easy, but yo' pappy and me . . . long as we both draw breaths, we'll be right here." I took the handkerchief from the pocket of my print dress and dabbed at her eyes.

"Yuh cain't settle anythang tonight, but I think yuh need tuh meet him. Don'tcha think so?"

She moved her head into a cautious nod.

"At some point, yuh haf'tuh decide who yuh're gon' love and whut kinda life yuh wanna have. He says he still loves yuh."

"Mama, I'm married now. What does he want? Wish he had died over there."

"Now, yuh don't mean that. Yuh jest scared . . . takes a long time for yo' first love tuh leave yo' heart."

I cupped her face with one hand and then, touching her chest with the other, I said, "Baby, he's still gnawin' there.

"Sit here for a spell. I come here when my troubles weigh heavy on my shoulders. Let the valley clear yo' head." I kissed her on the crown, the way my pappy calmed us when we were little.

"Come home when yuh've composed yo'self."

As I approached the house, Harvey Lee neared the gate, and he waited there to open it for me. He stood fresh and handsome before me, and at that moment, I wasn't sure which man was worse: Harvey Lee with his fitful ways or the white boy, Alexander, with his sparkling eyes and spit-shined, wing-tipped shoes. Neither would be of my choosing.

"Where Tilda at, Miss Margaret?"

"Oh, we walked up tuh Pleasant Ridge, and she wanted tuh stay a while."

"Mighty hot, and it's gittin' dark. Will she be okay up there?"

"Oh, she'll be fine. She'll be down de'reckly. Come on in the house and git sump'em tuh eat . . . it's the Sabbath, and we got a mess of food in there."

The cheerfulness in my voice evaporated when William Alexander ran toward us, brimming with excitement, and said,

"Harvey Lee, guess who came here this mornin'?" Harvey Lee reached down and grabbed William Alexander under the armpits and hoisted him high into the air and on up into his arms. William Alexander threw his legs around Harvey Lee's waist.

"Who, Curly Top?"

"My daddy came. He came all the way from Atlanta . . . tuh see me!"

William Alexander's face beamed at Harvey Lee as bright as the first hint of sunshine when it burned away the morning fog. But the rays of William Alexander's joy only stoked uneasiness in Harvey Lee, and his eyes registered darkness. His nostrils flared and the veins in his neck pulsed straight out. Harvey Lee's jaw tightened, but he turned to me, relaxed enough to ask, "Did he?"

"Yeah, Alexander came by this morning."

I watched whatever goodness Harvey Lee possessed drain from him like the sand in an hourglass, and a haunting, gloomy silence shrouded him. He put the boy down, took a deep breath, and walked away. He ascended the steps and sat on the porch to watch for the first signs of Tilda's heather-blue dress.

A pensive silence consumed me, and neither the birds tweeting nor leaves brushing against tree limbs distracted me. But while Harvey Lee brooded, nervousness crept into my body as I waited for Tilda near the gate. When she entered, I whispered,

"Careful. William Alexander told him."

"Lawd." That's all she said.

When she reached the middle of the yard, between the house and the gate, Harvey Lee was up in her face, grabbing her by the shoulders and shaking her.

"Whut'ja gon' do now?"

He became more aggressive, and I tried to intervene, but he shoved me to the ground. When I looked up, William, Henry, and Joshua ran toward Harvey Lee, surging forward like a pack of wild dogs craving the same bone.

"Take yo' hands off her!" Joshua said.

"You want some of me? Better git out my face 'foe I snatch out yo' innards and tie a knot 'round yo' yellow ass."

"Cain't you hear? Take yo' hands *off* her," Henry said. The three men locked eyes with Harvey Lee like bulls lost in the lust of rutting season.

William helped me to my feet. "You all right, Margaret?"

"I'm fine," I said, with most of my hair hanging out of my headscarf.

William got in between the boys and Harvey Lee. "Stop this! Right now. *I mean it.* Joshua, Henry, take Tilda in the house." They inched toward the porch and left Harvey Lee to fume, glowing like a potbelly stove that had devoured too much kindling and kerosene. Oh, he was *hot*, hotter than a scalded lizard.

"Harvey Lee, no man in this family has done this one thing: lay their hands on their womenfolk. I 'spect this is hard for yuh, but yuh haf'tuh take control of whut yuh're feelin' right now. Whut the gal needs is yo' love and yo' strength, boy, not yo' weakness and fear. Yuh understand whut I'm tellin' yuh, son?"

"Yessir," he said.

"I want yuh tuh go on home and calm down. I don't want yuh 'round here 'til yuh cucumber-cool. Hear whut I'm tellin' yuh, son?"

Harvey Lee left the yard with his tail between his legs, got in the clunker of a car he picked up from somewhere, and disappeared.

"Oh, William," I said. "I'm afraid Fast Fannie might be right."

———— •••• ————

Harvey Lee was nowhere to be seen for a week. Folks said he was three sheets to the wind, stumbling drunk from guzzling moonshine. The sheriff locked him up after he got into a fight with Ike Johnson. He was from the Slop Jar, too.

William got Harvey Lee out of jail and brought him to the cabin.

When Harvey Lee got out of the car, Prince ran toward him, wagging his tail in delight, but he stiffened and recoiled with the first sniff. I wondered if that was the reason Harvey Lee walked like a motherless child, slouching as if his shoulders ached from carrying a heavy load. Bruises and cuts covered him. He stood sober as a deacon, though, but I suspect he suffered from a guzzler's hangover.

I felt sorry for the boy.

"Sit down here, Harvey Lee, and git some food in yo' belly. When did'ja eat last?"

"Been a while, Miss Margaret. Been a while."

He inhaled the food but stopped shoveling long enough to ask, "Where Tilda at?"

"She wanted tuh spend some time wid Fannie and the twins." I didn't tell him that Tilda had seen Alexander the day before. That would've set him off on another bing.

I placed my hand on his shoulder.

"Have yuh got this out yo' system?"

"Yessum," he said, and I patted his shoulder and nodded to say,

"There's mo' here tuh study on than jest yo' feelings."

"Yessum."

"Why don'tcha stay here tonight? Tilda's comin' back tomorrow and you can see her and talk 'foe y'all go home," I said. Then I caught a whiff of stale rotgut and tobacco, and I said, "I want yuh tuh take a bath. Even old Prince acted offended, and Prince loves everybody."

Like I said, unbeknownst to Harvey Lee, William and I accompanied Tilda to Hampton the day before Harvey Lee's release from jail. We didn't want her traveling alone.

The Drake Hotel took up the entire block across the square from the courthouse. Its lobby walls and floors were of marble imported from Europe. Oh, it was a beautiful building. I wished I could have seen its interior close up, but the only Negroes who graced its threshold were those who worked there. William pulled aside one of those colored men who wore that I's-so-glad-to-meet'cha smile and asked him to fetch Alexander Bouchard. While we waited, a crowd of high-stepping white folks, decked out in their Sunday best when it wasn't Sunday and there was no church to go to, wandered in and out.

Tilda exited the car, but when she saw Alexander leaving the hotel lobby and approaching us, I feared she might faint.

Oh, he was handsome.

Yes, sir. Flawless! I thought. *I have to give the white boy that.*

He greeted us but took his time looking deep and long in her eyes. He got lost in a river of brown. When he reached to take her hand, I remembered my wedding day when William kissed my hand. The thought of cotton candy consumed me.

Goodbye, Harvey Lee. Boy, you ain't got a chance. This-here is the real thang.

We attempted to enter, but the bellhops barred us at the door. We couldn't enter even with a rich white man to serve as chaperone. To add insult to injury, the doorman said, "Folks, you gots tuh move y'all's car."

We piled into the car, and William remembered the colored diner on Auburn Street. We left Tilda and Alexander there, and William and I visited Pappy. He lived alone now. My two baby sisters, Lena and Violet, were long gone and grown, and we tried to get together with Pappy as often as possible. He had a little rheumatism but strutted as straight and lively as William. White-headed or not, nobody would guess he was seventy-two, confirming what Mammy use'ta say: "Colored folk jest don't break like white folks do."

Every morning, Pappy woke at dawn and sat at the kitchen table with his coffee and the colored newspaper. When he moved to Hampton and married Lucille, he decided it was time to learn to read and write. He went to school, and he had been a reading and writing fool ever since.

Pappy pecked me on my cheeks, and he and William shook hands as if they were in a wrestling match.

"Gittin' mighty weak, young fellow," Pappy said, smiling as he hit William on the back. We stayed a while, and then it was time to fetch Tilda. When we approached the diner, we saw Tilda and Alexander perched at a table close to the window.

He held her hand, and she nodded as he talked.

I hated interrupting, but William Alexander would be done with school soon. I didn't want him home alone. We couldn't depend on Thad; he was probably off somewhere with Nate.

We went on in.

Alexander jumped to his feet.

"Is it time already?"

"'Fraid so," William said.

"Why don't y'all sit. What about a cup of coffee? A piece of cake? Pie?" He looked so pitiful.

Far off, a car horn blared a warning while colored folks lollygagged by the window.

"Please don't go. Not yet," he said.

"Y'all folks stayin'?" the waitress asked, as if some nastiness had hocked up in her throat. I wondered if Alexander's lily-white presence offended her.

"Two coffees, please," William said.

We sat, looking at each other, when some glass broke, and somebody said, "Shit." We smiled but fidgeted in our seats to dodge the silence.

Alexander broke the silence.

"How is your father?" Alexander asked.

"Oh, yeah, how's granddaddy?" Tilda asked like the hiccups had cut loose in her throat.

"'Scuse me," the waitress said, scowling, sliding fresh-brewed coffee in front of us. When she returned to the others behind the counter, she mouthed, "Whut's that cracker doing in here?"

"Pappy's fine." I turned to Alexander. "Y'all have a productive talk?" They exchanged glances and nodded.

Alexander said he still loved Tilda, and that would never change. I wanted to stuff my fingers in my ears, but he kept right on gabbing.

"For our son's sake, I hope you'll get to know me. Please believe me when I say I don't want to cause any trouble."

"Accordin' to Fannie, you did that when yuh showed up," I said. William grabbed my hand.

"We brought Tilda here because we want whut's best for William Alexander," William said.

"Y'all are grown," I said, "and have made y'all's bed. It's up tuh y'all tuh decide whut y'all wanna do 'bout yo' feelings, but we don't want William Alexander to be hurt by either of yuh. Be in love. It dud'en bother us, but don't hurt the baby.

"When Tilda married Harvey Lee, I told her it was a mistake. Baby, I don't wanna wash yo' face in it, but Harvey Lee has proven he ain't the one, and yuh didn't have any business marryin' him. But yuh're his wife now, so yuh haf'tuh decide which of these men yuh want. I think I know the answer tuh that question, but yuh're the one who'll haf'tuh decide."

I stood up. Pointing to William, I said, "See this man right here. I love him like nuthin' else in this world. I'm proud of him, and I'd stand in the middle of the road and scream it tuh the hilltop. If y'all decide yuh cain't live wid'out each other, y'all haf'tuh find someplace a sight better than South Carolina. Yuh might haf'tuh leave this country. And this is the part that hurts; the part y'all cain't do nuthin 'bout."

I looked at Tilda.

"He's a white man, and you, my daughter, are colored. If yuh stay here, both of y'all will end up dead. Whutever yuh plan tuh do, yuh need tuh do soon." William took my hand again.

"Margaret's right. Yuh need tuh think carefully 'bout whut y'all playin' wid. People could git hurt, killed if y'all aren't careful." He turned to Tilda. "We need tuh say this because we love you. Whutever y'all decide, we're gonna stand wid yuh, no matter whut."

Only the rumbling tires and the whistling of wind accompanied us back to New Harmony that afternoon. Tilda sat in the rear with her head out the window. The wind tossed her hair into strands to dance and glisten in the sunlight as she looked to the horizon. But the sun, big and perfect in the sky, wasn't enough to hold my attention. I adjusted myself in my uneasiness and listened to the rocks and pebbles kicked up by the tires, but the trail of dust that billowed behind set me to wondering.

NINETEEN

The Darkness

Darkness is a funny thing. Twilight comes early in the winter. Night arrives too soon to swallow shadows, quick and deep. Daylight appears too late to devour the slumbering night. As aging creeps upon us and tramples youth and we understand the evenness of fall and the ensuing slumber of winter, we realize those pieces of creation we neglected to see. When I was a child, I didn't consider such things; the seasons didn't matter. I failed to appreciate the splendor of green leaves bowing to another part of their essence, allowing the rusts, yellows, golds, and reds to shine through. By only mourning fall as death, I ignored fall's beauty, and so I didn't comprehend how fall and winter figured into the nature of being. But as an adult, I visited Pleasant Ridge to witness life's ebb and flow. I observed the valley beyond the river's edge, and on the Ridge, the wind caressed my face and whispered God's promise. I visited Pleasant Ridge in all the seasons and at different times of the day to sense God's presence in the air, the changing light, and the shifting clouds.

While I rested there that early fall Sunday in October of 1949, I remembered how Marian Anderson awakened me by singing "My Lord, What a Morning." I recalled stumbling toward the kitchen as she ended with "When the sky begins to fall." Thad picked up the song, and the depth of his voice halted me. His resonant baritone voice held a story and gift. My baby sang like the rock of ages sat on his shoulders, and I wondered when he had wrestled with the kind of pain that fostered redemption and salvation. On that morning, my baby no longer belonged to me. God had surrounded my son and anointed him because each note Thad sang offered another piece of grace to mortals who hoped to gain what he had realized.

The next day, as I sat on Pleasant Ridge observing the squirrels scurrying around, I believed I was the luckiest woman in the world. The critters' steady attention caused me to pause, though. Our warm weather seemed incongruous with their frantic activity. Their fussing suggested a hard winter because they sho'nuf ran around looking for whatever they could find to put into their cache. I wondered what it all meant.

My thoughts turned to Alexander. It was hard to believe that a year had passed since he showed up in the fall of forty-eight. He had only stayed a month that time, but it had been tense. I was sorry to hear about his mammy's sudden illness, but his departure that November gave us some breathing room. In his absence, I had prayed he wouldn't write Tilda, and thank God he didn't. During his absence, we had some peace; Harvey Lee was, as William would say, "cucumber cool" by that December. When Christmas came, I felt like I could breathe, but William Alexander did more than just breathe. He did some downright rejoicing that Christmas—Alexander had sent the boy enough Christmas presents to last three or four years. Then there was Tilda's New Year surprise: she announced she was pregnant—the baby would be born in October.

Lawd, does everything in my life happen in October?

Alexander's visits complicated everything. I didn't believe Tilda had come to grips with her feelings about either man, and I wavered over her being pregnant with Harvey Lee's baby. How would Alexander figure into all of this? To me, it was a head-scratcher. But Alexander didn't seem shocked or disturbed when he showed up that spring and saw that Tilda's condition was as plain as the nose on your face. I figured his love for her was so deep that nothing she did would sway his affections one bit. He only stayed for a few weeks but told William Alexander he would return in August. He wanted to be there when William Alexander started the first grade and told me he had missed too much of the boy's life. When Alexander returned in August, he said he intended to be present for as many milestones as possible—he would stay indefinitely. I wondered if he had even considered what Fast Fannie told him when she went head-to-head with him the year before. Well, I couldn't get it out of my head. At first, Fannie's warning was more like a bell ringing, but when he announced he would stay *indefinitely*, it was more like a siren wailing—one he didn't seem to hear.

So, he arrived in New Harmony two months ago, and each of his visits had stoked more concern. I figured there would be a heavy price to pay if he wanted to ensure that Tilda and William Alexander had everything he felt they needed. *Lawd, where did that man think he was? Did Alexander consider Candy and Hollis's feelings—how they might react?* Harvey Lee had hit the roof when he caught wind of it—the brazenness of Alexander. Things got so heated that Tilda stayed with Fast Fannie and Robert, which worsened things. Harvey Lee started drinking and acting like a fool again, but he settled down about a week ago and returned home. The boy said he had his head on straight, but Tilda still refused to return home. She said he needed to prove himself; she didn't believe he was stable enough to be trusted. So, when I left the Ridge that day, my mind buzzed with worry.

On my way home, I met Marlene, who had ventured to take a stroll. She hadn't been too well. Burton learned from Doc Rosenthal that she had a heart condition, and both he and Leroy checked on her almost every day. Hollis had hired Eleanor Simms, a woman Marlene knew from church, and a bunch of other folks to watch after Nate and do the chores around the house 'cause he wanted her to rest. I shook my head, amazed by the strange relationship between this man and woman. Burton pressured Marlene to live with him, but she flat-out refused.

"The boy gots his life, and I ain't gon' be no burden," she said. "'Sides, the Big House the onliest home I knows. But 'nuf 'bout me. How yuh been doin', gal?"

"Things have been all torn up wid Alexander bein' in Hampton."

"Is he stayin'?"

"Seems like it . . . been here for quite a spell . . . since August.

"Well, is he gon' do some lawyerin'?"

"He told me he was gonna take the exam tuh practice law here, but it isn't necessary—finishin' law school and bein' a white man are uh'nuf in

South Carolina. I don't relish axin' Tilda much about the situation, but I'm worried to death."

"'Cause of Harvey Lee?"

"Yeah."

"Well, 'God moves in mysterious ways . . . His wonder to perform.' So, ain't no need tuh worry . . . Everythang gon' be revealed in God's sweet time."

"Indeed." She had her arm around my waist. I pulled away and asked, "How are the boys?"

"I ain't use'ta all this fussin': Mama this and Mama that. Child, they 'bout tuh drive me tuh the crazy house wid all they carin'."

"But yuh know yuh like it when they visit. You know yuh do."

She giggled. "Yeah, I loves tuh see 'em; I jest love 'em tuh death."

She shivered a little.

"Oh, I thank I's gittin' a chill. 'Spect I best be gittin' back tuh the house. I prays for yuh every night."

"Thank you, Marlene. Take care of yo'self and come visit as soon as yuh can."

"Oh, I will."

Sister Jamison, one of Mammy's quilting bee ladies, had been feeling poorly, too, so I stopped by her place on my way home. When I arrived, only her head and bonnet peered from under the covers; I reckoned her condition sprouted from all the crazy weather that descended on us that October. She sounded awful. I told her to send for Doc Rosenthal, but she rebuffed the idea with a frown and an upturned eyebrow.

"I ruuts 'round in the woods and finds some of them remedies old folks use'ta use when I's a child. They cuts the mis'ry better than anythang some of them doctors can give yuh," she said, adding, "I gots my castor oil, and it's gwine cut this-here cold."

Not that, I thought.

The mere mention of castor oil or black draught was enough to make me shiver. Old folks believed those were the remedies for all ailments, from fever blisters and boils to the common cold. Both were terrible; even a pinched nose and orange juice couldn't conceal their vile taste. They cramped and gnawed at your stomach. You'd strain and sweat before laxatives ran out the other end. Think I'd rather die before I took another dose of either.

"Have yuh been able tuh fix anythin' tuh eat?" I asked.

"Nah, been layin' up in this-here bed."

"Now, that bed gon' sap yo' strength. You need tuh move 'round; don't wanna catch pneumonia.

"I made a pot of chicken soup, and I'll have Thad bring yuh some."

"That's mighty kind of yuh, Margaret . . . yuh reminds me of Lula every time I see yuh. Honey, I'm glad'ja took the time tuh check on me. I really 'preciates it."

"Now, yuh're welcomed."

"You take care of yo'self, yuh hear. Give all the family a hug; will yuh do that for me, sugar?"

"Yes, ma'am. I sho' will." She was a sweet old soul.

Tilda's mess still buzzed around in my head, and when I remembered that Doc Rosenthal expected the baby's arrival in two or three weeks, it set loose more worries. All those troubles shifted when I looked down the road a piece and saw Thad and Nate laughing. They were so good together. I told Thad I needed him to carry something to Sister Jamison.

"Whut time?" he asked.

"'Round seven. Come home soon."

He yelled, "Yes, ma'am," back at me before the darkness swallowed them up.

When I returned, I found William and William Alexander cooking.

"Grandma, look what I did today!" He ran to his book bag and showed me his spelling test; it had 100 written in large print.

"Oh, my goodness! Gimme a hug. Did'ja show granddaddy?"

"Yes, ma'am."

"Looks like we have us uh'nuther George Washington Carver or uh'nuther W. E. B. DuBois," William said.

"It sho' does. Whut y'all fixin' up?" I asked.

"I've got a chicken fryin', and I'm warmin' up some vegetables from yesterday."

"Wonderful. I stopped by Sister Jamison on the way home. She's flat on her back; she sounds sump'em awful. Chest full of cold. I told her Thad would bring her some soup."

"He'll be flyin' through the door de'reckly."

"Speak of the devil," I said as Thad came in. "We're gonna be eatin' in 'bout an hour, but b'foe we sit down, I want yuh tuh take some soup tuh Sister Jamison."

"Mama, do I have time tuh finish sump'em first?"

"Oh, sure. Her place isn't that far . . . shouldn't take long, but we wanna eat supper 'bout seven thirty, so figure in uh'nuf time tuh wash up b'foe dinner," I said. Then the sound of footsteps shifted our attention to the opened door, causing William to announce,

"Henry Louis, whut a surprise."

"Thought I'd come by and rub this old knucklehead," he said, pushing Thad's head into his writing tablet.

"Okay, you two."

Looking at the clock, I said, "Thad, it's 'bout time for yuh tuh go tuh Sister Jamison."

"Yes, ma'am." He closed his books, put 'em away, tore a sheet from his writing tablet, and put it in his shirt pocket. Then he grabbed the soup pot and out the door he went.

I turned to Henry, pulled his cheek, and said, "Son, you were here earlier this morning. What brangs yuh back?"

"Knowed it was 'bout dinnertime," William said, smiling.

"Nah. Sump'em told me tuh drop by."

A car backfired.

"Wow, somebody needs tuh work on their car," Henry said, and we all laughed.

Within minutes, the full-throated peal of a bell sounded in my ears. A light breeze passed through my body, and his scent washed over me, filling the air, but I thought nothing of it. What was I thinking? Old folks had taught me the signs, but I didn't connect the dots.

"It's seven thirty. Where's that boy?"

"Ran in'tuh Nate, I reckon," William said.

Seven forty-five came around, and still no Thad. I got worried.

"This ain't like him. Henry, see whut's takin' yo' brother so long. Should'ah been back here by now."

———————•••———————

Oh, it was like no other time. Not even my mammy's dying came close to that pain. *This* was incomparable, unlike any other time. Truly, no other time. I kept praying, "Be merciful unto me, O God; be merciful unto me."

TWENTY

At Calvary's Door

It was the third Monday in October 1949, October 17 to be exact, when somebody murdered my baby.

William bore Thad's body with a solemnity matched only by the grief that walked alongside. He placed him on our bed, the same bed where I lay sixteen years ago and wrestled him out of my body. This time, a pale pink chenille bedspread was tucked over and under pillows that cradled his head. A folded crazy quilt, resting under his feet, supported one dusty, soup-speckled black Oxford shoe. The other rested in that ditch, blown away like his chest. His peacock-blue stocking foot stood frozen.

His bier, the same bed where Mammy wasted away, laid up against the wall opposite the oak five-panel door that gave the room privacy. A brass-trimmed and porcelain-painted kerosene ceiling lamp cast shadows across his face. The night before, William had admired the room's romance and intimacy; the lamp glowed "Just uh'nuf light to see the beauty in yo' eyes," he said. But in this gloom, I grabbed William by the arm, and we rocked in disbelief while I listened to William ask,

"Why?"

I reached for a lamp so I could see my baby's face, but upon catching the sight of William's face in our wedding picture on the nightstand, I cried all the more.

'Cause I could hear my baby say, as he had done so many times before, "Mama, I look jest like Daddy, don't I?"

Then another voice whispered, "He's passed on, Margaret," but I wanted to scream my objection 'cause "passing on" is what old folks do after they've lived a full life.

My insides screamed, "*He's DEAD!*"

William left me. He slumped in the rocker and squeezed tears in the slop jar at his feet. He stood and asked,

"Who?"

I looked over to where Henry stood; he leaned into and balanced his grief up against the wardrobe, banging his head, mumbling,

"Oh God."

William stood beside me again, and I felt his palm trembling his sadness across my back.

"Who done this, Margaret? Who done this?"

I didn't speak but bent over to pick the leaves from my baby's hair. I caught the smell of urine. Whoever did this thing peed in my baby's face and wetted his hair enough for it to lie close to his scalp.

I choked back my tears and asked Thad, as sweet and as gentle as I could, whispering,

"Baby, who did this?"

We stood hushed, waiting.

I asked him again,

"Baby, who did this awful thang to you?"

In the gloom at the edge of the bed, I pulled my chair close and took his hand.

I kissed it and rocked it in my breast.

I brushed his forehead and followed the arch of his eyebrow with my finger.

I caressed his cheeks and kissed his lips. My unblessed hands fondled his neck where his red plaid shirt opened, and I lamented each ounce of blood that seeped into cotton threads and streaked its way to his Levi's jeans.

William Alexander's tears soaked Thad's peacock-blue sock while his cries of "Don't leave me, I love you so much!" filled the room. Then, from behind me, I heard a timid voice say, "Miss Margaret," as if it sought to inquire. But when Nate saw the sight of death lying quietly before him, he wailed, and it lifted me, forcing me to face him.

Our sobs paled and grew silent, and we paid respects to the white boy's anguish. No words captured the grief set loose in Nate. I had never seen anyone scream so. The stillness of death pierced his heart, and if misery and tears could've resurrected Thad, Nate's lament would have. He put on no airs and suckled grief. He fell at Thad's bedside, pulled at his shirt, grabbed at his hand, nudged at his thigh, and with his face now streaked with my baby's blood, he cried a "Nooooo" that stretched out into the starry night, heard by the hoot owl who asked, "Whooo?" and ricocheted off the barn and into a forest of trees and darkness. Nobody could ease that poor boy's grief and heartache.

Marlene had accompanied Nate, and she held on to the grace and wisdom found in repeating, "Lawd, have mercy. Lawd, have mercy," as she reached down and took Nate in her arms. She helped him to the corner, but he never stopped crying.

Fast Fannie brought Tilda, and before long, the room filled with mourners. Tilda attempted to comfort William Alexander, but he wouldn't leave Thad's side. He threw himself across Thad's legs, calling Thad's name and pulling at his trousers. Fannie tried to console me, but she could hardly stand the pain herself. Robert and William held on to Henry. Joshua had Constance. Neddy came and put his hands on my shoulders.

Somebody muttered, "Who done this awful thang? Who done this?"

Neddy fetched Mr. Collins, who had a helper then. They stood silent in their dark suits and ties made more perfect by the starched white shirts they wore and the black homburgs they held, and then they carried my baby into the night, where colored folks filled the yard. Women covered their mouths with their hands, and they wailed when the blood-soaked sheet covering his body reached the porch. As they slow-walked their way to the hearse, men dropped their heads and bit their lips in disbelief; no, in anger. I had seen nothing spread through New Harmony faster than Thad's killing, but how these folks learned the news was a mystery.

When they closed the hearse's door, Nate carried on so that Marlene took hold of him, and through her tears, she asked him, "Did'ja love him?"

"Yes. Yes, Marlene."

"Yuh haf'tuh hold on tuh that, boy. Remember that. 'Cause he sho'nuf loved you."

Somebody must've called the sheriff. He came through the gate with a lackadaisical stride and fake empathy. William pulled him aside, and they talked for a spell. He proceeded to the ditch where we discovered Thad, surveyed the spot, and then was gone.

When the hearse carried another piece of promise away, women hugged their sympathies around my neck. The men met William to share their silent outrage. The women cried, but the men didn't. Neither stayed long, but the family stayed up late into the evening trying to comprehend what had happened. There were no more tears that night—even sorrow finds a way to silence weeping.

———◦◦———

The following day, Alexander brought Pappy out to us. When I saw Pappy, the well, now sufficiently primed, allowed my weeping to spring forth again. I fell into his arms the way I did when Mammy died, and he threw his head back before he rested it on top of mine.

Finally, Alexander said, "Is Tilda here, Miss Margaret?"

"Yeah," I muttered.

Nobody had seen Harvey Lee, and I was pleased about that. I said to myself, *Can't handle 'em meeting right now. Glad Fast Fannie isn't here either. We have plenty to fret over besides her going off on Alexander. Not now, I can't.*

Alexander left Pappy and me in the yard and knocked on the screen door.

"How yuh holdin' up, daughter?"

"This is harder than anythang I've ever done. I can comprehend the joy and beauty of givin' birth tuh him, but for the life of me, I cain't fathom none of this." He threw his arms around me and said,

"In time. Durin' the proper season, yuh will."

"Pappy, it's hard not tuh shove my fist in God's face. Why did He do this tuh me?" I buried my face in his chest, but he pushed me from him and stood me out at arm's length; he looked into my eyes.

"We raised yuh better than that. Yuh knows better 'cause we taught'cha better. So, yuh jest hush up wid this foolishness." Then he said real soft,

"Why you? Yuh ain't no better than nobody else. I could ask, 'Why me?' I lost yo' mammy, who I loved mo' than this earth, but I never asked Him why. Whut piece of her will that brang back?"

He cupped my face in his hands. "Now dry yo' tears, daughter. There's gon' be plenty of time for mo' of them—if'n yuh keeps on livin'."

"Yessir." We walked on in the house, where Alexander stood holding Tilda in his arms. He was so gentle with her.

"Is there any way I can help?" he asked.

"Alexander, I would appreciate it if yuh notified Thad's sisters, Helen and Ruth, and my sisters, Lena and Violet."

"Be glad to. Where are they?"

"Tilda, honey, give Alexander their addresses. Look over in the book there." She found it and held it up.

"Yeah, that's it. All of them are in Washington, D.C., 'cept for Violet. She's in New York City."

"I'll send them telegrams when I return to town."

Both he and Pappy stayed a while, with Pappy chatting with folks who he hadn't seen for a spell and Alexander attempting to ease William Alexander's sadness. Before Alexander left, he kissed Tilda on the cheek, telling her how sorry he was. It made me feel right uneasy, this white man having his hands all over her, since she was still married.

Almost ten minutes after they left, Harvey Lee came running up on the porch.

"I seen Miss Marlene; she took and told me Thad done been kilt." Tilda didn't spare him a glance. He came closer and kneeled beside me.

"Miss Margaret. I'm powerfully sorry, and I know that pain. They kilt my brother when he was way younger than Thad. They run up on him one morning on his way tuh school. Took him in the woods and used him for target practice. That was years 'foe I comes here tuh live. Don't thank I'll ever git over it, and I thank that's whut destroyed my family. Broke Mama's heart, and Daddy's, too. I've seen plenty of pain, Miss Margaret."

"Thank yuh, son. I appreciate it."

"What can I do for y'all?"

"Nuthin' right now."

"I'd like tuh be wid y'all at the church." By then, Tilda approached.

"I think yuh should. Thad liked yuh a lot," Tilda said.

"I liked him, too." Then the tears came, and I thought, *This boy is full of one surprise after another. What's next?*

————•••————

It looked as if every colored woman in New Harmony brought food to eat, and every friend I had or imagined I had was in my house. They stood undifferentiated in black, except for their bright, aprons of cherry red and pearl gray, moss green with specks of ocher, and apricot with ivory ruffles. They swarmed and fussed about with their smiles and eager hands. Their apron pockets were stuffed with crisp, spotless white handkerchiefs, suggesting they came prepared for any eventuality.

They said, "Miss Margaret, you sit right there and don'tcha move. We're here now, and we're gonna tend tuh everythang." I smiled, but I knew they couldn't. All they could do was sweep the floor, wash the dishes, wash the clothes, and cook the food. They could do a surface cleaning; they couldn't scrub where the trouble was. I had to do that. While they hovered in the kitchen fixing this or that, I sought refuge by the spring. Deep in thought, I sat earless to the approaching footsteps. A gentle touch and a familiar, soothing voice roused me.

"I'm sorry I've been gone so long," she said. "But I'm glad I'm here now tuh share this time wid yuh," and she followed it with the long, comforting sounds of "Shhhhhh, shhhhhh, don't cry," in the way that women have always consoled their wounded. She knelt and wrapped me in arms that had become stronger from her remarriage—this time to Wayland Lofton, the boy I had hoped for her long ago when we were children.

"You helped mend me when I needed someone the most," she said. "Margaret, you saved my life that night when Deke almos' killed me." She pulled me even closer and said, "It's all right. I'm familiar wid whut pain is; my arms are strong uh'nuf tuh help yuh shoulder yourn."

She rocked me with the soothing sound of "It's all right" until my screams fell into whimpers, my sighs fell into a whisper, and my cascading waterfall fell into a pool of still water.

"I love you, Margaret."

"Oh, Zora Mae. I've missed you."

William got up early that Wednesday morning and rooted around in Thad's room.

"Whut'ja lookin' for?" I asked.

"Tryin' tuh find—" He collapsed on the edge of the bed.

I kissed him.

"You want me tuh help yuh find clothes for him?"

He nodded.

I reached into my dress pocket and pulled out a handkerchief, and he wiped his eyes. We found Thad's dark blue suit, the new silk tie Violet had sent from New York City for his birthday, and a starched and pressed white shirt.

"What 'bout his underclothes?" William asked.

"Here," I said, but it prompted William to remind me of his—

"Socks?"

Before pulling them to my nose, the thought of Tilda saying "Mama ain't gonna be able tuh find shoes tuh fit those ant killers" reminded me of Thad's giggle.

I handed the socks to William and smiled.

William placed them in a brown paper sack.

"Want me tuh go wid yuh?"

"Nah, baby. I need tuh do this alone. It's the last thang I'll ever do for the boy."

After Robert came to drive William into town, I sat in my rocking chair, surveying the room that had sheltered mourners. The glow of the kerosene lamp and the flickering shadows it had cast across his face and arms didn't soothe me, but I didn't want to forget how the bed cradled him in pink chenille. It held the memory Mammy's death and his.

I breathed a sigh that pushed the weight of my body into the rocker. I rubbed its arms and mourned with its creaking sounds, asking who had done this awful thing, and when it seesawed to a stop, I demanded, "God, find us some justice!" And then I reached out and touched the cherry wardrobe lined with cedar. It hid a secret—the woolen sweater I'd knitted Thad for his birthday. Now he would never wear it. The thought of it being "brand-new," unworn by him, made me raise my face to the heavens. Then I saw his face in the pictures on the top of the wardrobe. Pictures of him at one, six, twelve, and sixteen—just two months ago—filled me with love and loss. The phone rang, jolting me out of the rocker and away from the gravity of my loss.

Lena.

Upon hearing my voice, she screamed through the sobs and said, "I got Helen and Ruth. They're wid me now. We're leavin' as soon as I git off this phone. We should arrive in New Harmony late tonight."

"Are the children comin'?"

"Nah, they're stayin' wid their grandparents. It'll be a car full of grown folks.

"Margaret, I'm so sorry. We're gonna be in New Harmony as soon as we can. Hold on 'til we git there."

Lena had called Violet and learned that Violet would arrive Thursday morning by bus.

When the colored newspaper came that Wednesday, Thad's picture and his story dominated the front page. The Obituary section listed other folks: Oralie Rae Reed, Nancy Turner, Daniel Wilson, and Hattie Mae Brown, but they were 83, 94, 69, and 76, respectively—grandparents all.

I felt incoherent, beyond wretchedness.

I was beyond sorrow.

Children weren't supposed to rest in the arms of Jesus before old folks, before their mammies and pappies. It wasn't the natural order, but in New Harmony, perversion prevailed where "good was bad, and bad was good." I noticed Sheriff Hadley and his deputy at the ditch. They poked around but didn't venture to share their thoughts. They didn't because they were familiar with the state of things. If my Thad had been a white boy, no stone would be left unturned to find his killer. But he was a colored boy.

———— •‖• ————

We had prepared the front room for the wake. By the time Mr. Collins arrived early Thursday morning, folks had gathered in the yard. Only the family members followed the casket into the house. Mr. Collins opened the coffin and pulled back the overlay, and God pushed a button deep inside my soul. I threw my hands across my mouth; I had never seen Thad look so handsome. I remembered when Sister Betty put him in my arms right after he was born. He was beautiful then, but this rendered me speechless. When I composed myself, I touched his face; I fixed his necktie and smoothed his starched white shirt a little. It snapped back as if to say, "This is where they hurt me, Mama." I had no anger, only love and loss.

I turned to Mr. Collins and said, "Thank you for all you've done." He dampened his eyes.

"Margaret. God bless you. Hillary will visit soon. She has been ill, but I wanted to assure you that you are in our hearts and prayers. If you need anything, please call us." Turning to William, he said,

"I'll arrive at 10:30 on Saturday, then we'll head to the church."

"We'll be ready."

Mr. Collins left, and we crowded around the casket as Marlene and Nate entered the room. The children grieved so; I thought they would climb into the casket with their brother. Nate approached—his riveted grip anchored him to the casket. Marlene had to go get him. Folks waiting in the yard filed in after Harvey Lee opened the door. Some people brought flowers, but others had them delivered by the colored florists in New Harmony and Hampton. Wreaths draped with colored ribbons and tiny envelopes holding sympathy cards overflowed the room, and we started putting them on the porch.

Late into Thursday night and all day Friday, folks came to pay their respects, and even strangers were among them. By Friday noon, I'd grown tired, and I wanted them to go home. I needed to be alone with my family and to watch Thad's face in peace, 'cause once they closed his casket in church, I wouldn't see my handsome boy again.

Some family members lodged at the Raven's Nest, a colored hotel in Hampton, and some stayed with Fast Fannie or other family members. Everyone gathered back at the house by ten o'clock that Saturday morning. We had decided the male members of the family—William, Henry, Neddy,

Joshua, and Robert—plus Nate, whom we considered family—would carry Thad to his final resting place. Pappy suggested that we shouldn't use Mr. Collins's hearse. Instead, we should use a wagon pulled by a mule for his journey to the church. We had come a long way, but we remembered our roots.

By ten thirty, we were ready.

We lined up.

The wagons loaded with flowers were in front, followed by the wagon that carried Thad. Family members, others who wanted to walk, and folks riding in vehicles joined the procession.

We headed west on New Harmony Road.

The white Easter lilies Alexander had shipped from God knows where covered the coffin; their trumpets blasted their purity and their hope for the resurrection to the sky. Fallen leaves rested alongside; their dried skins crunched under our feet against the dirt and pebbles lining the roadbed. Trees with their trunks and limbs in shades of birch, charcoal, smoke gray, stone, and black, stretched their mournful hues right to the tips of their woody fingers. A turkey buzzard flew part of the way overhead. "He's not for you," I said while a red-shouldered hawk spotted and captured some rodents in Mr. Pritchard's recently plowed field. The stunted and snapped growth left in the twister's wake of 1923 no longer marred the earth, but I saw the tree trunk where William had carved "Margaret" inside a heart. Thad would never again climb that tree, find safety in its branches like he once did, or celebrate living beneath it. My baby no longer knew life, but the river we passed, flowing with fish and the freshly washed sins of the newly baptized, did. The faces of little Negro children, running to the margins of their yards, where they dared not cross, did. The folks who traveled along the twists, turns, hills, and dips of New Harmony Road, and the paths and roads that crossed it, did. The Holloways, the Conroys, the Hacketts, and the Evans, secluded in the backwoods, did. They were mullers of history, cultivators of the present, and visionaries of the future who framed existence. All stood the same but him.

When we reached town, even white folks came to their doors. Folks got out of their cars and off their wagons. White men removed their hats and dropped their heads. Floyd was among their number, buffed and spit-shined from head to toe, with his hat in his hand. As we neared the church, the bells in the steeple pealed to announce our approach to the slopes of Calvary. When we halted at its steps, the men pulled Thad's coffin from the wagon, and we followed behind them while the bells tolled, and our shuffling feet kicked up dirt and twisted on pebbles and stones all the way to Calvary's door.

PART TWO

TWENTY-ONE

Demons as Challenges

When we returned home, the yard was full of folks fluttering around, setting up tables. It looked like a reunion feast or a church harvest gathering. Women, in their aprons, fussed over food. They mouthed or smiled their condolences, but I wanted to banish them, having had my fill of grief-watchers and condolence-huggers. Those brighter-side smiles, the ones they called "sympathy," failed to meet my challenge. I wanted to scream, "Cain'tcha see yuh barkin' up the wrong tree, 'cause lookin' on the sunny side jest don't make no kinda sense to me." I just needed to crawl up somewhere like a wounded critter, lick my wounds, suck my fingers, and push the world away. So, yes. Those colored women barked up the wrong tree, but decorum and etiquette demanded I act like I had a proper raising.

"How yuh doing, baby?"

I patted William's hand, and after taking a proper breath, I said, "I've been better," as I turned and gazed into his eyes and asked, "How are *yuh* farin'?"

"Feel like I got hit by a team of horses. We expected trouble wid Tilda and Alexander. Never thought—"

"I know. I know," and patted William's hand again. Robert pulled William to the side and whispered something in his ear. Zora Mae threw me a smile from across the yard, but Fast Fannie's voice forced my attention to the porch where she talked with Lena and Violet. Even from where

I stood, I sensed her hissy fit but knew she poked a hornet's nest when I caught "Bouchard" at the tail end of her sentence.

"He didn't come tuh the funeral, Fannie," Violet said.

"Violet, he's jest a fox wid devilish eyes. Sly and shifty, sittin' out in his car, watchin'. Did yuh see him, Lena?"

But Lena turned to me and asked,

"Margaret. Whut do yuh think 'bout Tilda and this white man?"

"Tilda's a grown woman, and she needs tuh do whutever her heart tells her."

"Now Margaret, that's not whut I asked yuh. Honey, whut'ja think 'bout the man?"

"I think he's—"

"Oh, stop beatin' 'round the bush. When yuh gon' have the gumption tuh say whut's in yo' *heart,* Margaret Butler? Think of it . . . that child havin' relations wid one of *them.*"

"Fannie, I want her tuh be happy."

"We all desire that, but he will bring her only heartache," Violet said.

"'Sides, he too old for her anyway. Whut she want? Uh daddy?"

"Fannie's right 'bout that," Lena said.

I closed my eyes, sniffled, and said, "I cain't think 'bout that now."

Lena placed her arm around my shoulder, but Fast Fannie snapped,

"If yuh ask me, it's that cracker's fault.

"Whut Bouchard thank? He can come 'round here, rub his shit in Hollis's baby gal's face, and not have somebody pay for it?"

"Fannie," Lena whispered, shaking her head and mouthing, "*Not now.*"

"Fannie, white people never need a reason tuh kill us," Violet said.

"Whut did Thad ever do tuh anybody? Besides, why would Hollis kill his son's best friend?" Lena asked.

"Somebody kilt the boy," Fannie said, casting her eyes toward the Big House, "and if Tilda and that Bouchard ain't careful, they gon' end up gittin' kilt, too. It's *one* thang tuh brang William Alexander back here when she ain't *even* married. It's uh'nuther thang altogether for Bouchard tuh come here lookin' for her wid his hairy knuckles, his flat ass, and his highfalutin' ways. And he gots the nerve tuh claim the boy! 'Sides, Hollis always figure he ruled our family's life. 'Sides, he white, and he ain't got'tuh have a reason to kill one of us."

Fannie placed her hands on her hips and tilted her head in opposition to Lena's insistent frown; she continued,

"Just like uh cracker—thank he can have whutever he wants whenever he wants it."

"C'mon, Fannie," Lena said.

"It be's the truth, and y'all need tuh—"

"Well, if this was New York—" Violet said,

"Y'all needs tuh stop actin' like y'all wants 'em tuh git hitched," Fannie said. "I needs tuh remind y'all; she gots a husband—"

"Who *ain't* shit," Lena said.

"But who *is* colored. Everybody forgits 'bout Harvey Lee. He ain't never caught a break—had a leg up; he ain't been valued by nobody. I hates the idea of Bouchard slitherin' his way in'tuh our lives. That's jest like white folks. They wanna gobble up everythang and then shit it out."

"That's uh'nuf," I said. "We're family, and we ortah support whutever Tilda takes a notion tuh do. Now hush up. Here come Aunt Sarah and the children."

I stood surrounded by my children, a piece of Thad in each one. I smiled with that in my heart.

"Fannie, yuh ain't causin' no 'strubance out here, is yuh?" Aunt Sarah said.

"Somebody gots tuh."

"'Spect so," Aunt Sarah said. "How y'all holdin' up?"

We let our dropped heads and silence speak for us.

Folks stayed late that night, nitpicking the trivial, and helping with the cleaning, and their kindness humbled me. The following day, everybody scattered to their respective places. Helen, Ruth, and Lena returned to Washington, and Violet took the bus to New York City. Aunt Sarah was alone now—Uncle Luther had died two years earlier—and so Neddy drove her home to Ridgeville. Tilda and Harvey Lee returned to their house, and while this tragedy created a space for peace, Alexander's presence jeopardized the relationship's stability. The situation with Alexander troubled me, but Nate's refusal to return home to the Big House and his adamant insistence on living with us concerned me just as much. He felt he'd be closer to Thad if he stayed with us. Of course, old man Demmings threw a conniption fit. Marlene convinced him that leaving the Big House was out of the question, but even with that resolved, something other than Thad's death bothered Nate. I sensed he wanted to discuss it, but somebody or something always stopped him from telling me.

Not long after we laid my baby to rest, Miss Hillary brought me books of poetry by Phillis Wheatley, James Weldon Johnson, Langston Hughes, and Paul Laurence Dunbar. She accompanied me to Pleasant Ridge, and I rested in the serenity of the landscape while she read some of the poems aloud. One was James Weldon Johnson's "Sence You Went Away." When she read it, my tears overflowed and waterlogged my print dress. And Langston Hughes's "Mother to Son" spoke of what I knew:

> *Life for me ain't been no crystal stair.*
> *It's had tacks in it,*
> *And splinters,*
> *And boards torn up,*
> *And places with no carpet on the floor—*
> *Bare.*
> *But all the time*
> *I'se been a-climbin' on . . .*

I loved the sound of Miss Hillary's voice. As she read to me that day, I remembered our first meeting and how perfect she looked sitting in the wagon, like she had been hit by a spring breeze. I loved the time we spent together, and she provided even more comfort after s omeone murdered Thad.

A few days after the burial, Marlene visited. She and Miss Hillary both comforted me during that time. She didn't come often because of her heart trouble. Walking required effort, and it took her a while, but when she arrived, she was mighty mad. I don't think I've ever seen her so worked up. She struggled to get the words out.

"Oh, I could chew nails and spit 'em in his eyes, don't know whut done got in'tuh that man . . . he gon'—"

"Whut's the matter? You haf'tuh calm down. You got a weak heart." She kept pacing the floor while muttering,

"Gon' send Nate away."

"Where?"

"Wanna send that boy away tuh some kinda private school . . . it gonna kill him. Ain't the best time, but cain't convince Hollis, he gon' send the boy way over yonder tuh grieve by hisself. Tell me. Whut kinda daddin' is that?"

"Oh, Marlene. Whut's Nate sayin' 'bout this?"

"He made a fuss all right. Done learnt how tuh do that, learnt that from that Vivian.

"Boy tell Hollis he hates him . . . Hollis wan't no kinda father. Nate say I done been mo' of a parent than Hollis or Vivian, and the Butlers done been mo' of a family tuh him."

"I bet his daddy didn't like that."

"Oh, he done jumped high as this house. Went in'tuh hissy fits, actin' lac his feets on fire and his hind parts ketchin' the flames. Said he know all 'bout Nate and his ways. He start jabberin' 'bout Nate ain't nuthin' but a nigga lover. Hollis say he was sick of Nate hangin' 'round wid that no-good nigga, Thad Butler."

"And Nate?"

"He gits such a cat fit he storm out the parlor and slam the door. Hollis blood-red, yellin', tellin' Nate his nigga-loving ass best be ready in the mornin' cause he sho' gwine tuh Charleston. Tells the boy he can go wid'out a fuss or he'd lash his nigga-lovin' ass tuh the car. It up tuh Nate."

"Have yuh talked tuh Nate?"

"He hides in his room and stare out that wender, mumblin' that he wish somebody kill Hollis."

"That won't do. Lemme go. Maybe I can git him tuh listen."

"You can try."

We headed to the Big House, and Marlene got Nate. He still steamed; his mouth still pushed out.

"Nate, baby. Talk tuh me."

"I'm so tired, Miss Margaret, and it hurts so bad . . . nobody is gonna understand how I'm feelin'."

"You can talk tuh me."

"No . . . no, I cain't."

I hugged him and said, "You're sufferin' now, son, but it will pass. Why, sufferin' is part of bein' human. We haf'tuh understand that darkness, but when we do, we realize that compassion springs from there.

"My mammy use'ta say 'Yo' weakest moment is yo' strongest hour.' It's hard tuh understand that right now, but try as best yuh can." I held him out from me a little ways, and I asked, "Whut'ja wanna do?"

"Miss Margaret, I don't wanna go to Charleston. I wanna stay here. Daddy needs to give me more time. I need time tuh think."

"But yo' daddy isn't gonna give yuh that. You haf'tuh do whut'ja need tuh do in Charleston. You're sixteen, but 'foe yuh know it, yuh'll be old uh'nuf tuh do whut'ja wanna do."

"But Miss Margaret—"

"Baby, I want yuh tuh remember this: yuh cain't celebrate anythang in this world if yuh haven't stood the test. Like Mammy said, 'Cain't be a witness wid'out no trial,' and wid'out a trial yuh cain't lift yo' soul tuh that place it needs tuh be—right there in the light of all there is."

"Yes, ma'am."

He looked at me, and with his eyes full of water, he said, "But I loved Thad; I miss him." He cried, and me and Marlene cradled him.

"Think yuh can go tuh Charleston now?"

"Yes, ma'am."

"And whut'ja gon' do when yuh git there?"

"Study hard."

"And remember this: every dawg has his day, but a good dawg has two." He smiled.

As I walked home, I saw Harvey Lee's V-8 Ford speeding toward our cabin like an enraged madman. The boy nearly hit me, he drove so wild, and when he brought the car to a screeching stop, Tilda jumped out.

"You all right, Mama?" she asked. Then, sneering in Harvey Lee's direction, she said, "Sometimes I cain't figure out if he knows whut it takes tuh be a man."

She grabbed my hand when she yelled for Harvey Lee to go on home.

"Me and Mama gonna walk tuh the house. I'll git daddy tuh bring me home." He raced on, the wheels kicking up dirt he left so fast.

"Whut's wrong wid him?" I asked.

"Foolish . . . touched in the head. *Crazy*."

"Yes, but whut triggered it this time?"

"I went in'tuh town this mornin' to do some shoppin', and Alexander was there. He offered his sympathies and asked if he could do anything, but Harvey Lee saw us talkin', and he—"

"Had a fit."

"Right on Market Street. Oh, he was so ugly, Mama, callin' Alexander all kinds of names."

"Whut did Alexander do?"

"He tried to walk away, but you know Harvey Lee—he got in his face. Alexander didn't say one word, but Harvey Lee's yellin' and screamin' coaxed some white men tuh see whut the ruckus was about. Finally, Eugene Whiteaway told Harvey Lee he'd better git his darkie ass off the street before he gets cut down a peg or two—git a taste of Southern justice.

"Harvey Lee grabbed me and pulled me down the street yellin' tuh Alexander: 'Stay 'way from my wife!' I have never been so embarrassed."

"Well, yuh cain't fault Harvey Lee. Baby, yuh cain't burn both ends of the candle."

"Mama!"

"It's the truth. Yuh gonna haf tuh face it."

"Tomorrow. Lemme face it tomorrow."

"I want yuh tuh remember whut me and yo' pappy told'cha."

"Mama, I remember, but I jest need mo' time." She shook her head, grief clouded her gaze, and we both began to cry. We stood embracing until she said, "Let's go home."

I kissed her cheek.

In a voice that reminded me of when she was little and tormented by the boogeyman, she said, "Can I stay wid you and Daddy tonight?" I dabbed at her eyes and took a deep breath that collapsed into,

"Sure. That'll be nice."

"Mama, did the sheriff find anything?"

"He ain't said much of nuthin'. We're goin' tuh the jailhouse first thang tomorrow."

"You'd think they'd do sump'em."

"This is South Carolina, honey."

When we visited the sheriff and his deputy, Cliff Hanson, at the courthouse the following day, Sheriff Hadley sat behind his desk with pompous authority. It was apparent that our presence inconvenienced him. But we pleaded with him to look for Thad's killer, but he said, "Ain't got no clues tuh speak of."

"Whut 'bout tire tracks or sump'em like that?" I asked.

"Nuthin'," he said.

"Did'ja find footprints, anythang a-tall down there?" William asked.

"No footprints, no nuthin'—"

"'Ceptin' a blown-off shoe that laid up in the ditch," the deputy said.

"Y'all done tromped 'round down there, nuthin' but flat dirt when me and the deputy got there," the sheriff said.

"Did'ja find the shell casings?" William asked.

"Nah, they done got up and disappeared, too."

"Did'ja talk tuh any folks 'round town? Maybe they heard sump'em," William asked.

"Everybody say it's a pity, but they ain't givin' up no rain, boy; we sho' ain't gon' git no kinda gully washers out'ah these-here folks."

"'Sides, yuh ortah know that, boy," the deputy said.

I grabbed William's hand and held him steady.

"Whut 'bout talkin' tuh Mr. Hollis? He knows everythin' that happens 'round here," I said. "My boy and his were best of friends."

"Cain't do that." The sheriff smiled. "Cain't go trublin' folks, 'ticularly folks like Mr. Demmings, over sump'em lac this."

"Well, cain't yuh do sump'em?" William asked.

"Folks, ain't nuthin' else tuh do. Y'all gonna haf tuh 'cept it, and thank the Lawd y'all gots some mo' youngins," the Sheriff said.

William persisted, "Do yuh think the Klan did this?"

"Don't worry 'bout them. Klan ain't been restless in these parts since, ohh . . . how long that been, Cliff?" he asked, turning to his deputy.

"Ain't heard 'bout no lynchin', stuff like that since I's a boy," the deputy said. "But how come y'all thank white folks done it? Could'ah been some drunk-out-his-head niggas who done this."

My eyes lit up like a lightning bug, but I held my tongue. William asked, "Why would *colored* folks kill my boy?"

"Maybe they thank y'all some uppity niggas. Might be tryin' tuh tell yuh y'all ain't white, or could be tryin' tuh tell yuh y'all ortah be careful. 'Lessen y'all a bunch of fools or jest plain ig'rant," the deputy said.

"'Scuse me?!" William said. I grabbed his arm before he could step any closer.

"Ain't nuthin' else I can tell y'all 'cept I's real busy right now," the sheriff said. He looked up and smiled. "Don't lemme haf tuh turn the dawgs loose on y'all."

And with those words, we took our rage back to New Harmony Road, passed the ditch that had held him, and wallowed in the bed that had been his bier.

———————

We had just shaken off the sheriff's insults when Mr. Hollis's driver brought Nate down to say goodbye before going to Charleston. He appeared lighter and assured me he'd be fine. After hugging me, he got into the car and leaned out the window to wave as it drove off.

I yelled, "Call us!"

He was a handsome boy, but somehow it had escaped me until now. His curly brown hair was growing long, but his blue eyes lit up his high-cheekboned face. White folks always talked about noses and lips. By their standards, his were too big, too full, but they were perfect in my eyes. Thad was six feet two when the invisible hand of death snatched him up. Nate stood a little shorter. But with his departure, I felt like I had lost another piece of Thad.

After Nate left for school, we had a break in the weather, and autumn appeared ready to settle in and stay for a while. It didn't last, though, because the morning after Harvey Lee almost killed me with his car, it was hot as the blazes again. I awoke early that Saturday, made a pot of coffee, and cut on the radio. Harvey Lee came, and he and William went to the barn to do some work. I paid little mind to *The Guiding Light* on the radio—too busy watching Tilda from the front room window. She awakened early; the seasons' rhythms and the day's sounds had attuned her to morning's light, and she fancied a walk in the garden. While she could no longer bend to work the garden's soil, she admired her prior efforts—marveling at what she had accomplished before succumbing to the heaviness she bore. Harvey Lee watched from the barn but summoned enough courage to approach her. He stood humble and sorry, like a beggar praying for forgiveness. Afterward, he headed back to the barn and she to the porch.

Later that hot Indian summer day and in the heat of midday, when the air was sopping with moisture and folks wondered what this strange weather foretold, Tilda's labor started. She grabbed for the porch railing and struggled to put one hand on my old rocker. From there, she yelled, "Mama!" with a tone in her voice somewhere between panic and exhaustion.

I left *The Guiding Light* and the radio behind as I rushed out the door.

Panting, she pushed out another "Mama."

As I got to the porch, her water broke. It ran down her legs and onto the extra-wide, low-heeled shoes she had borrowed from Fannie.

"Lawd, child! It's time."

I screamed, "Harvey Lee!" He ran from the barn, startled by my pitch. "Go on yonder and fetch Sister Betty. The youngin is comin'." The weight of my voice whetted his resolve and he high-tailed down the path to Sister Betty's. Just as Harvey Lee turned the corner, the sound of Henry's Ford pickup truck grabbed our attention. Before he could say good morning, I yelled, "Henry, fetch Fannie!" I helped Tilda to the same bed where I brought all my children into the world and where I had mourned for my dead Thad.

Without the comfort of an electric fan, it was a hot and sticky October day. I grabbed a church fan with CALVARY BAPTIST CHURCH printed on one side and a picture of a white Jesus, with his hands pressed in prayer, on the other. I measured my strokes, gliding the fan back and forth, revealing first Calvary and then Jesus in a slow-moving arc. Many births and ample practice made me wise. I figured I'd be there for quite a spell and didn't want to tucker myself out. So, I sat with my hair tied up in a scarf and my glasses pulled down a little ways on my nose as if certainty were my name.

The sweat pooled on Tilda's skin, dampening her cotton print dress. I remembered that dress: little bitty red flowers all over a white background, with fancy buttons, short sleeves, a scoop neck, and a white bow. It was one of the old dresses I used when I was pregnant with Thad, and its faded color and fraying collar provided another reminder of loss. Tilda's moans and Fannie's arrival finally forced me from my chair. Fannie took over cooling Tilda's brow, and I went to the door, watching for Sister Betty, but became amazed by Harvey Lee instead.

Even though he "didn't have a pot to piss in or a window to throw it out of," as the old folks said, Harvey Lee swaggered like a peacock and boasted like a bantam rooster who ran up on a sashaying hen when he turned to Henry and said,

"Everybody say its gon' be a boy." Then, with his chest stuck out far enough to reach Hampton, he said, "A full-blooded colored boy, not some kinda highfalutin' half-breed. A boy tuh carry the name of Johns."

Henry looked in my direction, and I shook my head in dismay.

Harvey Lee cast his sights down the road, saying, "That old nag of a mule better hurry up 'foe Tilda done had that youngin," but on seeing me behind the screen door, he ran toward the porch. As he reached for the doorknob, Tilda screamed, and he froze. Couldn't move. Couldn't bear Tilda's pain, but he sure caused her plenty.

"Miss Margaret, Sister Betty on her way if'n that old nag of hers don't drap dead in this damn heat."

I hated it when he used cuss words, and Harvey Lee knew that, but he was too accustomed to the ways of Slop Jar Alley, as Fannie would say.

A few minutes later, I saw Sister Betty straddling her old mule, Gertrude. As she made her way toward us, a few corn-rowed plaits stuck straight up on her head, and the willow twig she had used to clean her teeth still dangled from her mouth. She was barely five feet tall—bright-eyed and impossible to ignore, but size didn't determine her power or deeds. Her speech sought holiness, her lips always curled up into a smile, and her eyes never judged but sparkled with clarity and knowing. She used her weathered hands for healing, catching youngins, and doing God's work. Because of that, they were perfect. But she couldn't perform her magic without Gertrude, her ancient mule, who carried her before I was a pullet, when I was too young to appreciate Sister Betty's significance and gifts. Now, Gertrude was long in the tooth. Although the hair around her mouth held the color of bleached cotton, she still lumbered along because Gertrude had the blessings of the Almighty too. Sister Betty hopped down and stroked Gertrude with thankfulness.

She chucked that willow twig in the bushes and looked in Harvey Lee's direction.

"Harvey Lee, could'ja give old Gertrude a drank of water for me, please?"

"Yessum."

"Thank you, son." She stopped and asked,

"How yuh been, Harvey Lee?"

"I'm gon' be much better when Tilda has this baby."

Sister Betty just looked at him, fanning herself with the red bandanna she swung in her right hand before she wiped her brow and entered the house with her bag—the one that held her secrets and could cut all kinds of pain.

Her voice was full of sweetness when she said, "Wants tuh tell yuh again how sorry I feels 'bout yo' loss. I prays for Thad every day."

"Thank you," I said.

"How yuh holdin' up?" she asked.

"The Lawd always makes uh' way."

"Ain't that the truth," Sister Betty said.

"And Fannie, how yuh?"

"Pretty good."

"How's our gal doing here?"

"The pains, they gittin' pretty close now," Fannie said.

Sister Betty scanned the room and said, "Gon' need mo' water and towels. Us gonna be needin' 'em de'reckly."

"Yessum," I said.

Sister Betty told Tilda, "Yeah, yuh looks lac yuh done had a time of it all right. Gal, how yuh doin', sweetheart?"

"Doin' my best."

"Well, you jest rest now. Best yuh can, rest yo'self."

Sister Betty placed her hands on Tilda's belly and eased the pain. No one knew how she came by her healing gifts, but they made some folks question the source. A few insisted her blessings weren't natural. Folks claimed they saw her in the woods, all hunched over, scraping and picking herbs, roots, and secret things. Some youngins reported seeing her late at night in her yard, throwing stuff in the cauldron, making what they called her witch's brew. Some said she was a conjurer, but others declared she came from healers.

Tilda's thrashing eased with Sister Betty in the room, but it took pert' near ten hours of labor before she had that youngin. With the crowning and the final push for the "ring of fire," Tilda cried for Jesus, her body glistened with sweat, and dried cakes of spit collected in the corners of her mouth. But then all erupted into cries of joy.

The baby emerged covered with the veil.

"Git it off his face," I yelled. I feared he might not get enough air, and we would haf'tuh bury uh'nuther boy. Sister Betty peeled it from his face—she was familiar with the old ways, knew the caul's special meaning—and placed it on a sheet of paper. She handed it to me for safekeeping.

Excitement filled the room. "Mama, does he have everythin'? Fingers? Toes? Does he look all right?" Tilda asked.

Sister Betty said, "Yeah, Miss Tilda, yuh gots a right fine-lookin' baby. Looks jest lac yuh." She planted a hefty kiss on Tilda's forehead, and Fannie yelled, "Harvey Lee! You gots a son!"

As Tilda whispered thanks to the Lord, the overwhelming fragrance of honeysuckle drifted across the bed. I imagined catching its sweetness in the blanket as I bathed and clothed the boy. I placed him in Tilda's arms, and I'll never forget the tenderness in her eyes when she said, "Oh, my little Bubba."

Yeah, that pain evaporates when you lay eyes on and touch your youngin after wrestling him or her into life.

Tilda named the baby Thaddeus after my Thad. I wasn't surprised. The boy was the spitting image of his dead uncle when he was brand new. I considered it a sign; Southern folks held plenty of superstition, myths, lore, and a whole heap of color during the 1940s. But I had to escape—I couldn't bear another second of her miracle and my misfortune. As I prepared to bolt, Harvey Lee entered as if he paid homage to the baby Jesus. Baby Thad was the only youngin I had ever seen him truly cherish. As he lifted the boy into his arms, he cradled Thaddeus with an affection that rivaled Tilda's.

"My son. Yeah, my boy," Harvey Lee said, turning the boy to face us like they spun on a merry-go-round. "Ain't he fine-lookin'?"

He spoke the truth, but I wondered why the birth of a male child made the worst man surrender. 'Spect that's why he looked and smiled like a rat with a shiny golden tooth.

"Yuh gots a right fine boy there," Sister Betty said, touching the well of Harvey Lee's back. "Now yuh takes care of Tilda and the boy."

"Yessum."

Sister Betty patted him on the shoulder, saying, "God bless yuh, son." But I felt overwhelmed—only twelve days had passed since I held my Thad's hand and rocked with death. The misfortune of my loss broke loose and fluttered in my chest.

I had to leave that room.

Harvey Lee stood in my path, but he was oblivious. He didn't have enough love to understand an old woman's grief and a young woman's miracle. Harvey Lee had even forgotten the sympathy he had displayed when he bent on one knee before me and shared the loss of his brother. Neither the death of his brother nor that of my son—buried only the week before—scratched at his heart. Celebrating Thaddeus's birth stuffed him with pride, and he acted like the sun came up just to hear him crow. As I walked toward the door, Harvey Lee mumbled, "Thank God she ain't have no gal. I is sick tuh death of these goddamn split-tails. Women ain't good for a muthafuckin' thang, 'cept havin' youngins."

Fannie was right; he never left Slop Jar Alley.

Baby Thad resembled my own too much, and he forced me to consider whether colored boys and men could ever live in New Harmony. The loss and anger over my boy's murder were no longer seedlings—rage anchored its taproot deep, and grief made it valid. I felt I was hemorrhaging in my loss. The caste of my birth—my color, my sex—forced me to stew, to burn, to seethe in hatred, and to jump down nobody's throat but my own.

Friends said the Lord, as the ultimate healer, made everything new and straightened crooked paths, but I yearned for the times when grief didn't overwhelm me. I rejoiced when He had mended me enough so only the cracks showed, but it would be years before He mended me completely.

Baby Thad, little Bubba, was a sweet-looking thing, and he and Tilda stayed with us for a few days until she felt stronger. Harvey Lee visited every day, but Alexander kept his distance. He seemed happy and called to check on her and the baby. About a week later, she returned home, and then it happened. It was late when persistent knocking jolted us awake.

The frantic banging rattled loose recollections of Zora Mae showing up bleeding and broken. William confirmed my fears when he said,

"Oh, my God!"

I jumped out of bed, and Tilda stood in the doorway, two-week-old Bubba in her arms, with her eyes swollen and her lip split open. Her hair stood up all over her head, and her knees were scratched and bleeding. Thank God he hadn't harmed the baby, and Tilda seemed to have fared better than Zora Mae did after the pounding she received from Willie Deke.

William paced, pounding the floorboards until he reached for his shotgun.

"I'm gonna kill him! I'm gonna *kill him dead!* That no-count, sorry dawg! Beat my baby!"

He headed for the door; I pulled him back. I begged, "I've lost my baby, and I don't wanna lose yuh, too. Please put it down. Yuh cain't do this. Please, William. What if sump'em happened tuh yuh?"

The sight of protruding veins that stuck out from his neck and the one in the center of his forehead didn't righteously telegraph this anger— revealing the full extent of his rage. I talked for a long time to settle William before we could tend to Tilda and the baby. I figured Thad's murder was twisted up in William's outrage at Tilda's beating, and while William's race held him powerless in getting justice for Thad's murder because Thad was a colored boy, Harvey Lee's assault was another matter. The sameness of color and gender made justice possible.

William had never harmed a soul, but since Harvey Lee's behavior hadn't benefited from his gentle warning before and had escalated into battery, I figured retribution would be harsh. Knowing how William felt about his womenfolk and having been married to him for twenty-six years, I knew the hand of the Lord's wrath lay in wait for Harvey Lee. And with the certainty that the sun would rise in the East, William told Henry, Robert, and my brothers, Joshua and Neddy. Harvey Lee had been warned before, but since he didn't take heed, they were going to fix Harvey Lee's little red wagon, as the children use'ta say. It would come to pass, as inevitable as the old folks saying, "Sho'nuf."

Tilda's injuries were not severe, and she recovered fast enough. We were more concerned that she distanced herself—just stayed away—from Harvey Lee. Bubba was doing well, and William Alexander loved his baby brother. As soon as school let out, William Alexander ran home to check on Bubba. In mid-November, when the weather had turned frosty, Joshua, Neddy, Henry, and William were working in the barn when Harvey Lee showed up. What was that boy thinking? After abusing Tilda, he should have known not to come close. But two weeks after abusing her, Tilda, me, and the babies were in the house when Joshua's yelling unmoored us.

Well, Joshua had seen him approaching the porch. He never liked Harvey Lee, but he had always been "mannerable" out of respect for Tilda. Everything changed when Harvey Lee beat Tilda.

"Whut'ja doin' back here?" Joshua demanded.

"She's my wife! This ain't none of yo' business."

"Nigga, Tilda don't want yuh here. Yuh needs tuh *git*!"

"I ain't goin' no goddamn where! Who yuh thank yuh is? Yuh ain't *shit*! Nary one of yuhs. All y'all light-skinned muthafuckers thank y'all better . . . thank y'all *WHITE*. Well, yuh ain't white! You's uh nigga jest like I is, yuh's jest uh'nuther *black* son-of-a-bitch."

That was it. Joshua had heard plenty.

Joshua tackled Harvey Lee, throwing him off the porch. They rolled around on the ground until Joshua stood him up, and then they slugged it out like prizefighters. Harvey Lee didn't realize reinforcements were only yards away, heading over from the barn. William, Henry, and Neddy surrounded him, passing him between them as if he were their punching bag. When Harvey Lee hit the dirt, Neddy picked him up and knocked him to the ground again. They kept doing that, and pretty soon Harvey Lee hugged the ground and played possum. The boy was no fighter, no matter what he thought.

William and Henry approached the porch while Joshua and Neddy turned toward the barn. Harvey Lee slithered on the ground before stumbling to his feet, and then he pulled a knife, sneaking like a fox to attack Joshua and Neddy. A hunch prompted Henry to turn around, and when he saw Harvey Lee and the knife, Henry attacked from the rear. Oh, they beat that boy something awful, and finally, in their exhaustion, they told him if he ventured near Tilda again he'd pay the ultimate price. They threw Harvey Lee in the back of Henry's truck, drove him to downtown New Harmony, and kicked him out. They left him there.

It was horrendous.

In the spring of 1950, Harvey Lee took up with Ike Johnson again and ran around raising hell. I thought the boy had gone crazy for sure, drinking moonshine and picking fights. But later that year, the jailhouse became his home. He and Ike broke into Mr. Young's filling station, not knowing that since burglaries occurred so often, Mr. Young had begun sleeping there. When Ike and Harvey Lee broke in, Mr. Young woke up and shot Ike dead, but Harvey Lee shot Mr. Young before he could get off another round. Old man Young didn't die immediately, but he was bad off and wasting. The sheriff, along with some other white folks, hunted after Harvey Lee for days before they found him hiding in the woods, and it surprised me that the white folks didn't string him up right there. Folks said Sheriff Hadley held firm: "The boy needs to stand trial."

I asked Tilda to ask Alexander to help Harvey Lee because he couldn't afford a lawyer. But Harvey Lee told Alexander he'd sooner rot on the end of a rope before he let Alexander do anything for him. Well, that's what happened. Mr. Young died, and the moment the white folks caught wind of Mr. Young's passing, a lynch mob drug Harvey Lee out of the jailhouse and lynched him in the town square. Henry was in town that day, and he said Harvey Lee became quite the sassy nigga. Henry reported that before they strung Harvey Lee up, he told those white folks that they could kiss his black ass. He spat on them, too.

I felt right sorry for the boy, but he never recognized his demons as challenges and chances to better himself. His demons always took over and consumed him. He had just turned twenty-six when they hanged him, but he never learned that he didn't need to handle his affairs like he did when he was twelve.

TWENTY-TWO

Next Time

I hadn't seen Mr. Hollis in a month of Sundays. Then one day he showed up on my porch. I saw his driver waiting in the shiny car. Other than the absence of his beard, he had changed little. Marlene told me he had taken to shaving, and now you could see his firm-lined lips sitting on top of his rounded chin, which had a dimple large enough to hold the tip of your little finger. Salt-and-pepper hair covered his scalp, and he had the bluest eyes, but they were icy blue. Even in his seventies, Hollis Demmings stood dashing. He had nary a crow's-foot or a laugh line. Mr. Hollis was no gap-toothed, liver-spotted, prune-faced white man with hair sprouting out of his ears and nose. Honey, he'd put Cary Grant to shame, but he was an evil snake that should've been trapped long ago. I had no idea why he was here, but I went onto the porch thinking, *I'm glad William Alexander is in school.*

"Good day, Mr. Hollis. Whut can I do for yuh?"

"Understand Alexander Bouchard is still in town."

"Yessir."

"Been comin' 'round here quite a bit, I hear."

"A bit."

"Been seein' right much of Tilda, I've been told."

"Somewhat."

But then, with a slight tilt of his head, he latched hold of me with his icy-blue eyes and said, "They strung Harvey Lee up for shootin' old man Young. Didn't they?"

"Yessir."

And while his icy-blue eyes still had a-holt of me, he arched an eyebrow, but I didn't quiver like a captive, which caused him to lean closer. He clenched his jaw but loosened the grip enough to moisten his lips to say,

"Would be a shame if the boy—now, whut's his name? Oh, yes— William Alexander, yes that's right, William Alexander—if William Alexander had tuh lose his daddy . . . or you, yo' daughter. Wud'den it?"

"Yessir."

He shifted his stance, crafted a lopsided smile, and stuck the cigar he held between his thick fingers into his mouth. He chewed on it a bit, then flicked it to the other corner. His icy-blue stare still hadn't released me. When he placed his left hand on my shoulder and inched me closer, I detected a frankincense cologne mixed with the cigar's sweet, leathery aroma. He flared his nostrils and said,

"Tell Tilda she'd best be careful 'bout whut she decides tuh do. Folks 'round here ain't gonna be so happy 'bout no Negress takin' up wid no white man . . . particularly *that* one."

He dug his fingernail into my shoulder like a dagger, but I shot back with a razor to cut him to the quick.

"Like you and Marlene when Miss Ophelia was livin'?"

His eyes tightened and his face turned beet red, but the robust smile he crafted didn't match his quivering chin. But a quick breath allowed his Adam's apple to bob and produce tones different from what his face suggested. He unleashed a voice that meandered into a whimsical but haunting Southern lilting, suggesting the terror that bore low-hanging fruit. He said,

"Remember when the men came that night? A supermoon lit the sky."

Puzzlement shifted my eyes to his frozen stare, and Fannie's theory linking Thad's murder with Alexander's doings flashed through my mind. He pulled some air up through his nose as if to sniffle and said,

"Right after Ophelia died. Bless her sweet soul. Left y'all a heap of money, and land, too." He softened his stare, sweetening his smile. He said, "Those riders didn't harm the family. Did they?"

I honed my gaze and he continued,

"I never forgit, and *I* decide the payment, Margaret. *I* choose the timing."

I jerked away from his smile, but Miss Anna Bell's warning blasted in my ears.

"Maybe we need to make a few adjustments; talk tuh yo' husband, perhaps. I can arrange that, but I wud'den want nothin' happenin' tuh none of y'all. Not tuh some righteous colored folks like y'all . . . not after y'all suffered such uh *shameful* loss."

Tilting his head toward me, he said,

"It's no need tuh change our relationship. Have a pleasant day, yuh hear?"

With that, he twisted out another half-hearted, wooden smile and tipped his hat like any Southern gentleman would 'cause politeness and civility were intricately woven into the fabric of intimidation and cruelty. Off he went—practically as old as dirt, without a worthwhile bone in his body. He turned when he reached the gate.

"Tell the family I came by . . . don't forgit, girl."

He stuck his cigar in his mouth and disappeared behind the tinted rear windows of his car. His driver drove off in the direction of Hampton.

My heart raced.

Was Fannie right? Nah, he wud'den—couldn't—kill his son's best friend. Still, Miss Anna Bell's warning echoed in my head: "Demmings never forgets, and Demmings never forgives."

I had no business smart-mouthing him as I did. Such a slip could ensnare William Alexander and Tilda in Hollis's web of violence. Being sassy could cost us our home and all we had worked for. Besides, our house was more than what William and I had scratched together. It held the sacrifices of our kinfolk who had faced the lash. They nursed broken backs so we could have a future. This place held the blood, pain, tears, and sweat of five generations.

———— •◦• ————

I pondered Mr. Hollis's visit, but splitting hairs or quibbling over our family's involvement with him only reminded me of what Mammy said: "Don't wear a pair of boots that squeeze too tight, 'cause you'll end up with corns as sure as flies lay maggots on tainted meat." So, I took his visit to heart, believing that as long as Tilda and Alexander kept fooling around, they jeopardized everyone. By the time William arrived, the jitteriness set loose by Hollis shifted from my legs and trembled into my hands, and caused William to ask,

"What done happened?"

"Hollis came by. He ain't happy 'bout Alexander bein' here and seein' Tilda and William Alexander, and I'm—"

"Where William Alexander and them at?"

"I don't know. That boy should'ah been here by now."

My fretting vanished when Tilda, with William Alexander and his daddy in tow, entered.

Tilda knew me too well.

"Whut now?" Tilda asked.

"Hollis came down, but he wan't happy. He—"

"When will it end?" Tilda said.

"Would it be wise to take Tilda and the children to Hampton? They could stay at the Raven's Nest for a while," Alexander said.

"Cain't you and Tilda understand? It won't git any better than this! It won't be *for a while*. This is how it's gonna always be for y'all in New Harmony."

"Daddy, do yuh think we really need tuh worry 'bout this tonight?"

"Yeah, I do. I'm calling the men. Alexander, looks like you're stayin' here tonight."

"What can I do?" he asked.

"Better git them guns and load 'em up."

Soon after, we had a house full of men.

"Henry and the rest of you men," William said, "start fillin' up any-thang that will hold water and soak plenty of rags. When yuh finish, put them where we can git tuh 'em, jest in case they try tuh burn us out."

I cooked dinner as fast as possible because I didn't want any lights on when it got dark. Otherwise, we'd be like sitting ducks easily picked off after sunset. We ate leaning against the walls close to the windows, and while several men pondered what to expect, others studied Alexander on the sly. I suspected they wanted to divine if he would try to take over or whether he held a sliver of something they could hang their hats on. They desired a hint of connection. Perhaps sensing the men's thoughts, Alexander began telling war stories and then shifted the topic to how shameful this was. Before the evening ended, the colored men talked as if they had known him their entire lives. After those exchanges, I'd wager those men would've trusted their mammies to Alexander.

Late in the night, while William Alexander and Bubba lay sleeping, the sounds of twigs snapping or branches scratching their leaves across the window perked up my ears. Growing louder, it erupted into a symphony of light and sounds, and the entire yard seemed to ketch fire all at once. Amazed at first by its intensity, I came to myself and screamed,

"They're burnin' a cross in the yard!"

Then, a voice pierced the darkness.

"Alexander Bouchard. Come out here."

A familiar voice, but its owner, I couldn't place.

We had inched our heads to the window, staring at a shrouded figure wrapped in a sheet standing close to a flaming cross.

It spoke again.

"Alexander Bouchard. Come out here."

Tilda raced to Alexander's side and pleaded,

"Don't . . . you cain't."

"I have to."

"We ain't gonna hurt yuh. We jest wanna talk tuh yuh for a spell."

Silence.

"Now, patience ain't part of our callin' card! Don't make us haf tuh knock down the door tuh git'cha."

Alexander started creeping toward the door to enter the yard.

He stopped a couple of feet from that voice and talked to 'em briefly before they took their bedsheets and hightailed off into the fullness of darkness. After a few minutes, Alexander turned toward us, letting the burning cross light his path, and when he returned, he stood dazed.

"I have to go," he said.

"Whut did he say?" William asked.

He waited a minute and said,

"His voice was eerie, but it was also one of those gentle, sweet, Southern-sounding voices. But his eyes . . . they were something else. I've seen eyes similar to those on the faces of murderers. But that voice . . ."

He composed himself and said,

"He threatened Tilda and William Alexander. If I'm not out of the county by tomorrow evening, his men won't stop at a cross burning. Next time, there'll be blood. I must go."

I'd hoped he'd take his tail on up north, but I suspected he wouldn't. He'd stay around here, and we'd end up getting strung up. How could he leave? He never had to run for his life, and I figured when his pride started leaping up and having fits, he'd forget about trying to save us misery. When his self-importance lapped at his heels, defiance would consume him, and he'd say, "Who do these low-life hicks think they are? I'm rich, and they cain't tell me what to do." That's what I thought he'd say to himself tomorrow, but tonight he muttered,

"I need to gather my belongings from the hotel. May I borrow a gun? I'll return it tomorrow."

He nodded his goodbyes, kissed Tilda and William Alexander, and sped away, vanishing in the dust and darkness. I turned to William and said,

"William, I want y'all to git that thing out my yard. Don't want the babies seein' that when they wake up. I'm tuckered out; I'm goin' tuh bed."

———◦│◦———

Nervousness and exhaustion overwhelmed me, and I succumbed to sleepiness. When I woke up the next morning, everyone had left. I cleaned up a bit and fixed myself a cup of coffee when the sound of Alexander's car turned my attention to the yard. By the time he handed me the gun and had pulled a chair up to the kitchen table, Fast Fannie slung the door open, just about taking it off its hinges.

"It ain't the Klan," she said, as she threw a nasty glance at Alexander, and with not even a "Howdy do" on her lips, she said,

"You all right, Margaret?"

I nodded as Alexander rose, saying he'd be back as Fannie's ire followed him out the door. Fannie hated his guts. She had made that clear to everyone, but I told her not to treat people like dirt in my house.

"'Scuse me! I guess I'll keep my black ass home when I knows that cracker gon' be here."

"Let it go, Fannie."

"It be's wrong, Margaret, and yuh know it!"

"Fannie."

"Don't *Fannie* me. Bad 'nuf he done knocked her up and William Alexander runnin' 'round here lookin' like he *white*. And now this cracker wants tuh father a colored boy; he ain't had *nuthin'* tuh do wid his creation!

"Whut he know 'bout bein' colored and livin' like we haf tuh live? Whut he know 'bout whut it takes tuh raise a colored boy in'tuh a man so he won't git lynched or broke down 'foe he becomes a man? That white man ain't even been schooled 'bout slaves runnin', hidin', and beggin' for they freedom. He don't know nuthin' 'bout the *scars* and the *pain* caused by slave ships, overseers, massas, and the law! I bet'cha nobody ain't ever turned they nose up at him. So, whut he know 'bout seein' uh'ther folk enjoyin' they freedom, but knowin' yuh ain't gon' ever be free? Whut he know 'bout bein' *spit* on? Or seein' noses turned up at yuh 'cause yo' mammy and yo' pappy come from Africa? He don't know nuthin' 'bout how tuh keep on believin' you're somebody God loves when yuh're called niggas, spooks, coons, or jigaboos! Whut he know 'bout bein' called *boy* or *gal* when you's older than they is? Whut he know 'bout bein' treated lac'uh child?

"Margaret, the one thang he know is he can walk right now in'tuh any store in New Harmony or Hampton, and they're gonna say, 'Yessir,' and they're gonna say, 'Nossir.' So, don't'ja *Fannie* me!"

"Yes, but we don't haf tuh stoop tuh their level."

"That's whut wrong wid us colored folks now. Us always haf tuh take the high road. They ain't the one's callin' on Jesus so they'll do the right thang. Us the ones that always haf tuh pray, the ones that always haf tuh beg they sorry white asses for sump'tem that God done give tuh us jest like He done give it tuh them. How they gon' *give* me freedom or tell me tuh wait for it or when and how I's 'posed tuh git it? I was *born* wid that! They so puffed up! They so full of theyselves! I hates 'em. Always have. I 'members them stories Mammy told us, but I ain't hear in 'em what yuh heard. Yeah, I heard the pain and the sufferin' of my peoples, but I always knows whose fault it was."

"But we 'posed tuh love one uh'nuther, Fannie."

"Love? Love my ass! That's whut's wrong now. Us been tryin' tuh love sump'tem that cain't love back. How white folks gon' love sump'tem they feels ain't even like them? Margaret, this ain't our problem 'cause us ain't the ones that gots the disease. Baby sister, the sooner colored folk learn that, the better off us gon' be. Ain't no sense in tryin' tuh prod and teach somebody tuh love yuh. Huh, they can kiss my ass, 'cause I ain't care 'bout they sorry asses or care if they love me or not. I want me and mines tuh learn tuh love each other. White folks' *burden* is that they don't thank anybody or anythang else is in the world 'cept them, and they thank they're better than even the earth. They don't even hold that sacred. They cain't 'preciate all the comforts they has that come from the sweat of somebody who ain't white. If'n you ask me, ain't nothin' worst in the sight of God than a soul who preys on uh'nuther who done been made out to be weaker. Only puffed-up demons do that. I hope tuh *God* Tilda won't marry him. I hope tuh *God* she won't."

"Fannie, that ship has sailed; if it hasn't, we're powerless."

"You cain't trust no cracker! Now, yuh mark my words, Margaret Butler, and this gon' be true long past when they chunk dirt in my face and the worms done ate my black ass: white folks gonna always thank they better than us. I don't care who they is or where they comes from. They gon' always thank they better. Yuh can snuggle up tuh this copperhead if'n yuh a mind tuh, but that snake is gon' turn 'round and bite y'all one of these days—'cause that's its nature!"

"For William Alexander's sake, I hope yuh're wrong."

She reached for the screen door, but she turned to me and said, "Yuh know what the funny thang is? I hope I's wrong, too. I wanna believe in this love thang, and I wanna believe he a decent man." Tears pooled, and with that, she ran to the car Robert had given her and headed home.

It was midmorning when Fast Fannie stormed in and out of the door, leaving her whirlwind spinning around in my head. Yes, Fannie said a mouthful, but I buried it like a good little girl and sipped my coffee and waited for William Alexander to return from school as I read *Cosmopolitan* magazine's serialization of Hemingway's *Across the River and Into the Trees*.

I had finished the first chapter when Marlene, looking troubled, knocked on the door. I jumped up from my seat like a scalded haint.

"Whut's the matter?"

"Y'all all right down here?"

"Some of Hollis's friends paid us a visit last night."

"Well, it wan't Hollis this time. Us got word from Charleston. Nate in the hospital, he done tried tuh kill hisself."

"Oh, no!" I pulled out the chair for her to sit at the kitchen table. "Marlene, I just got a letter sayin' he'd be home soon. What's Mr. Hollis sayin' 'bout this?"

"Now, he reckons puttin' the boy in that private school be a mistake, and he faults hisself. I tells him it too late for that. I axes him tuh please brang the boy home so us can look after him."

"Whut happened? How is Nate?"

"He crawled up in a tub of hot water and laid his wrists wide open. One of the uh'ther boys finds him."

"Po' boy. When are they gittin' back?"

"Not a word yet. But Hollis calls that hateful Vivian tuh tell her whut done happened. She gon' meet Hollis in Charleston. Lawd child, evil be fixin' tuh wag her head."

"Marlene, I thought they weren't talkin' tuh each other."

"Lawd, who knows."

"Well, it's kinda curious—her goin' tuh see 'bout Nate after vanishin' from his life. Anyway, we have uh'nuther mess."

"Least he ain't die, but they talkin' 'bout puttin' him in one of them crazy houses."

"Now, that sounds like Vivian's meddlin'."

"Maybe, but I jus' hopes they finds some help for the boy," Marlene said.

"Po' Nate. Perhaps this'll bring 'em back tuh'gether. Nate ortah have some kinda relation wid his mama. Whut'ja think?"

"If'n yuh ask me, her and Floyd nuthin' but trouble—cain't trust nary one of 'em," Marlene said, stretching out the kinks as she righted herself. "Well, I need tuh head back. Reckon I needs tuh sit by the telephone lac I done most of the mornin'."

"If yuh hear from Nate, tell him I'm prayin' for him."

"I sho' will."

As soon as Marlene left, Fannie drove up again.

"Whut's the matter? Yuh forgit sump'em?"

"I jest wanted tuh say I'm sorry 'bout flappin' my gums like I did. This thang got me balled up in knots."

"I understand better than yuh think."

"Was that Marlene I seen leavin'?"

"Yeah, Nate tried tuh kill himself, a white boy grievin' sump'em awful over somebody colored."

"I ain't never understood that, neither. They *too* close, if'n yuh ask me."

"Been like that all their lives. Maybe 'cause there's only a thirty-minute difference in their ages. Born on the same day."

"I ain't know that. How Nate doin'?"

"They found him in time. Hollis even sent for Vivian."

"Oh, Lawd," Fannie moaned.

"Yeah, she's back—been livin' over in Hampton."

"Mo' trouble."

"Never been able tuh figure how Vivian was his mammy."

"Ain't that the truth," Fannie said.

"Whut'ja gonna do today?"

"Nuthin' much. Whut'ja got in mind?"

"Tilda is gonna pick up William Alexander from school. 'Spect Alexander gon' wanna see 'em 'foe he hightails it out'ah town. Why don't we check on Pappy?"

Visiting Pappy, we laughed so much we forgot about the time.

"Lawd, y'all, I got'tuh git. William gonna be comin' home soon."

"Oh, Margaret. Sit down; he won't die if'n yuh ain't there, girl."

"Nah, Fannie, I haf'tuh go right now!"

We were almost home when these two vehicles caught our attention. The one in front of us, a bright red Ford pickup, kept running into the back of the Cadillac in front of it.

"Slow up, Fannie! Don't git too close."

The pickup slammed into the Cadillac, pushing it into the ditch, and sped away. I screamed, "Oh, Lawd, Fannie, *stop the car!* It's the children!"

We scrambled from our car and rushed to rescue them, but the pickup spotted us and spun around.

"Lawd, here they come," I said.

"Okay, everybody in the woods," Fannie said.

Alexander grabbed Bubba, and Tilda had William Alexander. We hit the woods, running as fast as we could. Fannie fell. Alexander helped her to her feet. We ran a far piece before we found a safe place to catch our breath. We rested a while, but the sound of a loud boom and the sight of billowing smoke in the distance stood us erect.

"Let's git out'ah here," Fannie said.

We took off. We had a considerable distance to travel through the woods, but Fannie reassured us and said, "Don't worry none; we almos' there. I trample these woods all my life."

When we arrived, William jumped from his perch on the porch and peppered us with questions. After calling Robert and Joshua, who came with Neddy and Henry, William gave Alexander the shotgun to take care of the womenfolks so William and Neddy could retrieve the cars. When they returned, Neddy said,

"They tore the cars apart . . . ruint."

"Alexander, they firebombed your car," Robert said.

"They put this on it after the car stopped smolderin'," William said, handing a note to Alexander.

"'You're next, nigga lover,'" Alexander read aloud. He turned to me and asked, "What's wrong with these people?"

I touched his chin and said, "Look at me. Wish I could make this easy for yuh, but some folks live by a unique set of rules. When yuh came here lookin' after Tilda, I knew yuh loved her and William Alexander. But sump'tem is missin', and it's sump'tem yuh must accept. Yuh must understand this: colored folks are conjured as uh'nuther species in the South.

"I understand yuh didn't figure there was any difference, but yuh cain't bring yo'self tuh accept how deep hatred can go and how it destroys. Yuh don't realize good intentions and righteous livin' aren't uh'nuf sometimes. That's what Fannie tried tuh git me tuh see, all of us tuh see. Sometimes it dud'en matter how much yuh love, hope, dream, and pray 'bout a thang. Sometimes thangs are gonna be the way they're gonna be, or it may mean yuh haf'tuh have faith, so when yuh take that leap, sump'em will be waitin' tuh ketch yuh or yuh know yuh're gonna sprout wings and fly."

Alexander turned to Tilda. "I have to leave, but I'm not leaving without you and the children."

"Where would we go?"

"Doesn't matter. Marry me," he said. "We can't marry here, but there are alternatives . . . New York or Paris. It doesn't matter. Marry me, Tilda, and let me make a home for you and the children."

She ran into the house, which forced Fast Fannie to suck her teeth and say, "Goodness gracious, how come folks gots tuh carry on, actin' like everythang ain't nuthin' but trouble lookin' for a place to happen?"

"Fannie, sometimes folks need to lick the red off their apple," I said as I chased after Tilda.

She sat at the kitchen table, crying.

"Tilda. Do yuh love this man?"

"Mama, I—"

"Baby, yuh haf'tuh take a stand one of these days. Now, do yuh love this man?"

"Yes."

"Yuh know whut yuh haf'tuh do. It's gonna be hard, but y'alls strength will be in each other. Hold on tuh that." I left her to ponder.

When she came outside, she carried suitcases. Alexander hugged us. Fannie even hugged Alexander, and he gave Fannie a peck on the cheek.

"Watch it, white boy. You gots tuh prove yo'self first."

Robert rode shotgun as William drove to Lena's in Washington, D.C. I watched them pull away and disappear into the dust of New Harmony Road. From Washington, they traveled to New York; they married there. My sister, Violet, stood with them. I knew little about New York, but it had to be a better place for them than New Harmony, South Carolina—'least that's what Violet said about them coming to New York City. They moved to Paris, France, during the summer of 1950. Once they settled, I received a remorseful letter from Tilda. Perhaps this was the first time in her life that she had the comfort and safety to reflect on her mistakes—the decisions she had made that placed the family in so much jeopardy. She asked for my forgiveness and thanked us for the sacrifices we had made for her. But she said the South primed her for the decisions she made, and she expressed little hope for America and vowed never to live here again; the Negro faced too many hardships here. Alexander wanted their babies to have every opportunity, and she didn't want her sons murdered like Thad. I thought about how I would miss Baby Thad and William Alexander, little "Curly Top" (Harvey Lee had given him that nickname, and it stuck).

<hr>

By the time Tilda and her family settled in Paris, Nate had finished his treatment in Charleston and came home during the summer. Oh, he had grown so much—the boy shot up overnight.

He came to see me one day, and I took his hands.

His depression had left both his wrists scarred, and I could sense that his inner wounds still festered when I pulled him close and patted his back.

"You all right now?" I asked.

"I'm not fully back, but I'm much better," he said, released from my embrace.

"Ain't gonna do anythang else foolish, are yuh?"

"No, ma'am. While I was in the hospital, a cellist visited us one day and performed. The richness of its sound consumed me so much that my doctor encouraged me tuh take lessons, and Daddy bought me a cello. It's a difficult instrument, but I love it, and I think I've found something that really helps me. Miss Margaret, I was able tuh visit Thad's grave this morning. I knelt there for a while, reminiscing the old days. Wished I knew what happened that night."

"Well, maybe one day we'll discover the truth and put this grief behind us, but grief takes its own sweet time, and I'm glad tuh hear yuh've taken a liken tuh music—it can be healin'."

"I've found my callin'. By the way, how's Curly Top?"

"Speakin' French lac'uh Frenchman. Bubba too. They're talkin' 'bout comin' home for Christmastime."

"Speakin' French—isn't that sump'em," he said.

"So, whut 'bout you? Whut are yuh gonna do?"

"Oh, I'm goin' back tuh Charleston in the fall, and I'll study cello seriously."

"Hope we gonna see a lot of yuh 'foe then."

He smiled.

"By the way," I said. "Hadn't seen Marlene for a spell. How's she doin'?"

"I worried a lot about her while I was away. I saw her when I got back, and she didn't seem well. She just turned seventy-six, and her health is . . . well, I'm concerned. When I git back tuh the house, I'm callin' Burton and Leroy. They need tuh convince her tuh see the doctor."

"Tell her I'm comin' tuh visit her tomorrow."

He headed to the Big House. As I watched him, he reminded me of my Thad, the way he carried his upper body, the way he slung his arms and moved those feet, those ant killers.

TWENTY-THREE

Innocence's Death

Floyd and Vivian returned to South Carolina during the late spring of forty-nine, just about five or six months before somebody murdered my baby. At first, they lived in Hampton, but they purchased a home on Ashley Road in New Harmony shortly before Nate's release from the hospital. Their mansion, nestled in a dignified spot in the old part of town, was eye-catching. The rear of their property stretched to the edge of the bluff that overlooked the Ashley River, and all kinds of birds and other critters thrived on their grounds. Their land had one of the prettiest azalea and camellia gardens of any place in South Carolina. A roadside plaque identified the house as a historic spot, claiming that George Washington once stayed there. I hadn't been inside, but their colored help said it was grander than the Big House. Vivian's daddy left her a whole heap of money when he died, so I figured she wanted to outdo Mr. Hollis. And people rumored Floyd lived off her—his father had cut his purse strings.

The town had exploded with gossip over what had happened between Vivian and Mr. Hollis, and according to Marlene, folks had no intentions of giving Miss Vivian "the sweat 'tween they toes." Vivian wanted to be invited to the rich folks' fancy parties and stuff, but they snubbed her like nobody's business. White Candy had fixed that. When Vivian walked down the street, the women threw up their heads and turned their faces. They whispered, "There's that Jezebel" and gossiped behind her back. While Vivian wasn't the socialite she once was, her race still gave her certain advantages. Most colored folks didn't want to associate with her, but somehow, she had persuaded Zora Mae to be her housekeeper.

Zora Mae's new job and two extra children left her with little time to socialize. I missed her so much, and when I ran into her downtown on Market Street one day, I convinced her and her husband, Wayland, to visit. I had made peach cobbler and had the coffee brewing when their car tires dug into the loose gravel and stopped that Saturday afternoon. Wayland had darkened somewhat over the years, but "Pinky," the nickname conferred on him at birth, remained. He and William went to the barn, and Zora Mae and I chatted at the kitchen table.

"Honey, I'm sorry I ain't seen that much of yuh," Zora Mae said. "I've been busy wid the children. And, of course, there's Pinky. He may as well be my uh'ther child. That man cain't find *one* thing. Dud'en matter whut it is. It could be in front of him, and he goes, 'Zora Mae, where's my so-and-so?' I haf'tuh stop whut I'm doin', walk tuh t'other side of the house, and it's sitting right in front of his face. If it had been a snake, it wu'dah bit him." She lightened her coffee with some milk and blew it cool.

"I've got one too. I know exactly whut'ja mean," I said. "Now, don't fret none 'bout not havin' seen me. I'm grateful that yuh visited when yuh did."

"Been some time since the funeral . . . how yuh doin' now?"

"Oh, better, but still angry."

"Did the sheriff do anythang?"

"Not uh'nuf tuh uh'mount tuh a thimbleful. Came out here twice, looked around. We pleaded wid him and that deputy, Cliff Hanson, tuh do sump'em, but we should'ah known that gittin' help from them was like placin' a milk bucket under a bull. All's we got was a mouthful of insults."

"Plenty painful, but colored folks have always had tuh wear pairs of shoes that's so tight yuh couldn't walk two steps in 'em," Zora Mae said.

"Ain't heard a whimper out'ah them since."

"Yeah. Whut's the life of a colored boy worth?" she said.

"Zora Mae, sometimes Thad'll pop in'tuh my head, and sometimes I feel like I can sense him—yuh know, when he's tangled up in a whiff of wind, or I smell him when I enter the room. Girl, ain't uh'nuf Kleenex tuh wipe the tears. Jest the uh'ther day, I scratched 'round in the chest of drawers for sump'em. Oh, I don't remember whut I was lookin' for, but I found his obituary. I dropped tuh my knees, cried lac'uh baby."

"I cain't begin tuh imagine the pain, but me and Pinky been keepin' y'all in our prayers," she said as she took my hand.

"How's William?" she asked.

"Holdin' a man's anger."

"Uh-huh. Yeah." She nodded with recognition.

"Did'ja hear 'bout the uh'ther mess?"

"Folks still talkin' 'bout that, too. Yeah, chewin' their cud on that 'til sump'tem else sticks in their craw or scratches 'em behin' the ears."

"Zora Mae, you sho' said a mouthful."

She took a bite of cobbler. Huge smile.

Silence.

"So, yuh're workin' for Vivian and Floyd."

"I was out my mind when I gave her the nod. Well, I felt so sorry for her. But I didn't realize she was such a wench . . . a strumpet, too." A sip of coffee washed down more cobbler.

"Girl, yuh ortah hush yo' mouth."

"Honey, I should'ah talked tuh yuh. Why didn't I? Well, she was po'-mouthin' so."

"Whut's it like workin' for her?"

Zora Mae laughed so much I thought she would fall out of the chair. She hooted, but when she came to herself, she said,

"I haf tuh laugh," she said. "She's lac'uh little bitty child wid her nose in everythang. Cain't do *nuthin'* right for her. Oh, it takes a whole heap of prayin' tuh work for that woman. Every time I goes tuh quit, sump'em happens tuh her, and I git tuh feelin' sorry for her all over again. Pinky told me I needed tuh go on and quit."

"Whut about Floyd?"

"A devil walkin'. That's whut I think. He ain't got no kinda respect for nobody. Well, I'll take that back. I believe he respects Vivian, but uh'ther than her, not a soul. Walks 'round the house all day long drankin', cussin', and fussin' 'bout this or that nigga."

She stopped.

"Why in the world am I workin' for these folks? They're awful!

"Uh'nuther thang. Sometimes, I believe the man has gone crazy. I walk in the room, and he's talkin' tuh somebody under his breath—real quiet-like, and there's this scent in the air. I cain't describe it, but there's a curious smell in the room where he sits. He'd say, 'If yuh don't leave me alone, I'll fix her and him for once and for all.' He'd cuss, and then he'd say, 'Nigga, I ain't scared of yuh.' When he sees me watchin' him, he says, 'Ain't nuthin' but that nigga again. I'm gon' fix his black ass, though.' I cain't figure out what in the Sam Hill he's talkin' 'bout or who he thanks he's talkin' to."

"Well, I stopped tryin' tuh figure out those crazy folks a long time ago."

"Oh, then he gits to mutterin' about his daddy. I ain't never met Mr. Demmings, but folks say he ain't worth a mess of hawgs rootin' 'round in a pigpen wid no kinda trough."

"That's the God's honest truth."

"Floyd claims his daddy took all the money that should'ah come tuh him when his mama died. I tell yuh, when he gits tuh mutterin' 'bout his daddy, he gits this strange look in his eyes and gits right quiet. It's uh'nuf tuh give me the willies and set my teeth on edge. Honey, I leave the room when I sense that, don't wanna be nowheres near that; but when he talks 'bout his mama, he gits a twinkle in his eyes. When did she die, Margaret?"

"In seventeen or eighteen. I cain't remember. It was 'foe Mammy died in twenty-two.

"Mo' coffee?" I asked.

"Please," she said, handing me the cup. "Margaret, on the night y'all had the trouble, I believe he was one of 'em."

"I told William the voice was familiar. Kept sayin', 'I recognize that voice.' So Floyd was the one who gave Alexander his marchin' orders."

"Ain't take him long tuh git that hood back on his head, did it?"

"Sho' didn't. But when we talked tuh the sheriff and his deputy 'bout Thad, Cliff Hanson had the gumption tuh say the Klan had'en been restless since he was a boy."

"Where he been at?"

"Must've had monkey paws over his eyes the past twenty years," I said.

"Or he one of 'em," she said, shifting her weight to stand before saying, "Well, I got'tuh git Pinky and git on home and tuh the children. I'll let'cha know 'bout the folks on Ashley Road."

"You do that now," I said, giving her a hug. "Want some peach cobbler tuh take wid yuh?"

"Margaret, I ain't never been able tuh refuse yo' peach cobbler."

"All right, and let's wrestle the menfolk from the barn."

"Y'all hens through gossipin'?" Wayland asked.

"Look at 'em," Zora Mae said. "Guess y'all been talkin' about baseball, huh?"

"Ketchin' up wid old Skin," Wayland said.

"I'd forgotten 'bout that nickname . . . been years since anybody call'cha Skin. Well, William, yuh gots a head full of hair now," Zora Mae said.

"Yeah, Mama use'ta keep it clean as a crystal ball."

We walked them to the gate, and William said, "Y'all got'tuh come again."

As they got in their car and drove away, I turned to William. "Guess who that was in the yard that night, tellin' Alexander tuh git out'ah town?"

"Who?"

"Floyd Demmings."

"Not surprisin'."

"Zora Mae figured he was one of 'em. I told'cha that voice belonged tuh somebody I knew."

"At least we know where one of those snakes hides."

"One on the hill," I said, "and the uh'ther one in its woodpile on Ashley Road."

"Ain't that the truth . . . but who's driving that fancy car?"

A Lincoln Continental, brand spanking new, black, buffed, and polished, with chrome parts shining like new money and whitewall tires gleaming pearly white, pulled up right in front of us without a speck of dust from New Harmony Road.

"Burton . . . Burton, is that you?"

"Yes, Miss Margaret. It's me."

"Boy, when did'ja git home?"

"Last night. I came tuh check on Mama."

"I ain't seen yuh in a spell. Is Marlene bad off?"

"Well, Isaac thinks she needs lots of bed rest. I want tuh take her tuh Meharry and meet with a cardiologist, but she will not hear of it."

"You know yo' mama. Are yuh plannin' on stayin' this time?"

"Isaac asked me tuh join him at the clinic, and I thought I never would, but given Mama's health, I'm stayin'."

"A colored doctor of our own. I cain't believe it. When Doc Rosenthal first came, the white folk 'bout ran him out'ah here," I said.

"I'm excited about workin' with Isaac, and it'll be good to spend more time with Mama and Nate."

"Bet Marlene is bustin' wid pride," I said.

"She'll never admit it, but I think she is. Well, I should be goin'."

But he shifted his weight, and then, with a somberness one would gleam from someone twice his age, he said, "Miss Margaret and Mr. William, I was so sorry tuh hear 'bout Thad. I'm sorry I couldn't attend the funeral, but I hope you realize how much Leroy and I care about y'all and the family."

I pushed back the tears. William cleared his throat. "Thank yuh, son."

Before he headed his shiny Lincoln in the Big House's direction, I said, "Marlene is gonna be thrilled."

He was so handsome with his broad shoulders and curly hair; I bet that's what Hollis looked like at that age.

As I turned, Nate approached.

"Boy. Speak of the devil. We were jest talkin' 'bout you," William said.

"Mr. William. How are yuh doin'? I missed seein' yuh the uh'ther day."

"Doin' pretty good. You stayin' out'ah trouble?"

"Yes, sir."

"See that yuh do.

"Margaret, I'm goin' inside. I'm petered out." He kissed my cheek. When William neared the house, Nate asked, "Does he always do that?"

"Do whut?"

"Kiss yuh like that."

"For twenty-seven years."

"Was that Burton?"

"Yeah."

"I can say goodbye tuh him, too."

"Where yuh off tuh now?"

"I'm leavin' tomorrow. Daddy is gonna lemme spend the rest of the summer in Europe. I'll be in Paris, studyin' wid the French cellist Paul Tortelier."

"Oh, my word."

"Should I take somethin' for Tilda?"

"Nah. Jest give all of 'em hugs and kisses for us. When yuh comin' back?"

"August fifteenth. Want me tuh bring yuh anything?"

"You. Yuh jest come back safe and sound. Take plenty of pictures. Now, come inside and lemme give yuh her address and everything . . . remember to kiss the little ones for me."

When he left that sultry summer, he didn't realize it was his last summer of innocence and that within five years, everything would change—and we would be tied in unimaginable ways.

TWENTY-FOUR

No Safe Place

After spending part of the summer in France and returning in August of 1950, Nate decided he would make Paris his home when he finished college. He only stayed in New Harmony for a week. Then he left for Charleston, declining to return home for Thanksgiving or Christmas. We wouldn't see him again until the beginning of summer, 1951.

In New Harmony, our conditions remained the same. Segregation and Jim Crow still reigned supreme. We sat in the back of buses, couldn't eat at the lunch counter at the Five and Ten over in Hampton, our children went to segregated schools, and the word "colored" determined where you drank water or peed. The Negro section of town stood separate, "on t'other side of the tracks." Most of all, a constant smoldering fear, persistent in its seething, enveloped us. As a mother, I felt like a lioness, trying to protect my cubs and my mate from predators who held a sense of privilege and killed out of hatred.

Fortunately, Vivian, Floyd, and the other Demmingses lay low, and thank God Marlene still held on. She had her seventy-seventh birthday just before Nate finished high school. When he arrived home from Charleston, he received his draft papers, and after boot camp and advanced training, they sent him to Korea. When he departed to fight for God and country at the end of the summer, saplings of worry sprouted, and they persisted until his safe return.

He took part in the war's most intense battles. I sensed immense suffering in some of his letters, but he endured and grew from it. He served two years in the army, returning home in fifty-three, near the war's end. I almost didn't recognize him when he walked on the porch, with his barrel-like chest, broad, strong shoulders, and muscled arms.

"Lawd, boy, look at'cha," I said, examining him from head to toe. "And my word, you got a chest full of medals, too—you's uh *handsome* devil. Well, you always were, but my goodness, look at'cha now. When did'ja git back?"

"Just now. I wanted to thank yuh for all the letters."

"Oh, that was nuthin'. How'yuh doin'?"

"I'm dawg tired, been travelin' for a week."

"C'mon, let's sit a spell," I said, pulling him inside.

"The first people I met when I came back to town were Mother and Floyd. He slapped my back and told me how fine I looked, while Mother was . . . well, Mother is Mother, if you know what I mean."

I nodded.

"Floyd invited me to shoot targets with him when I got settled. He wanted me to try out some pistols he had purchased when he and Mother had visited Alabama. I was shocked at his kindness and the joy he expressed when he saw me."

He lowered his head a bit.

"Not sure if Daddy will be happy tuh see me, though."

"Marlene sho' will."

"How is she?"

"Holdin' on; she's tough as nails. Want sump'em tuh eat? Some coffee? Got peach cobbler."

"Now, that's bein' back home. I've dreamed of yo' peach cobbler and the food I use'ta eat when . . ."

He dropped his head.

"When Thad was alive," I said as I opened the pie safe. "It's hard tuh believe three and a half years have passed."

"I think of him every day, Miss Margaret."

"Me too. When it first happened, I couldn't believe he was gone. My mammy was the first person I loved who died, but when Thad died, that was a different sorrow. William wud'den even talk about it, but I knew a man-sized ache curdled inside him. Seemed like darkness appeared at every turn—the mess wid Harvey Lee and Tilda, then her and Alexander gittin' married and movin' tuh Paris, and you and yo' troubles . . .

"I blamed myself for Thad's death. Believin' if I hadn't sent him down tuh take that pot of soup tuh Sister Jamison, he'd be alive. I seethed wid her, too. Why did she haf tuh git sick? I was mad 'cause there's no justice for colored folks. Furious 'cause nobody raised one finger tuh find my boy's killer. Angry 'cause nobody cared 'bout him but us. Livid 'cause nobody will remember him but us. Mad 'cause God didn't protect him.

"It took me pert' near two years tuh feel whole . . . but the weight and ache have vanished; I can visit his grave after church now."

I grabbed his hand. "How yuh doin' wid it now?"

"I'm slowly makin' my way tuh daylight," he said but stopped there.

Another man, I thought, so I didn't press but cut him a slice of cobbler.

"I'm elated to be back in the States, and I missed home so much," and then, spotting a book resting on the table, he asked, "What are you reading now?"

"Just finished *The Catcher in the Rye.* Now, you'd like that. Oh, yuh haf tuh read *Invisible Man* by Ralph Ellison and *Dust Tracks on a Road* by Hurston. I've started readin' James Joyce's *Ulysses,* too. It's a struggle." I handed him the book. "Whut'ja gonna do now that yuh're back?" I asked after placing the cobbler in front of him.

He took the book, flipped through its pages, chewed his cud a moment, prepared himself for the cobbler, and said,

"I miss my cello, and I wanna start practicin' again. Once things settle down, I'll be off to college or a conservatory to study music. I love the cello and want tuh become really proficient."

"Do yuh wanna become a performer or cello teacher?"

"Teachin' would be wonderful. I think I might be good at it."

"You have the care and patience tuh teach. That's for sure," I said as he took a forkful of the cobbler, smiled, and fell back in his chair.

"Oh, that's heaven. I'm glad I lived through the war tuh have uh'nuther taste of this."

"You go 'head and enjoy it."

Between bites, he asked me about Tilda and her family, and I told him they still lived in France. Both boys were well, and everyone seemed quite happy. Tilda worried about what might happen if they returned to the States. Most of all, life in New Harmony remained unchanged since I wrote to him last.

"Truman changed a lot of things when he integrated the army. I believe we've just seen the beginnin'."

"If that's true, we're in for some rough days ahead," I said.

He finished his pie and stretched his long legs. Looking at his feet, I once again remembered "ant killers."

He smiled, stood up, and took a proper stretch.

"I better git up there."

I watched him make his way to the Big House, and I said my prayer out loud. "Lawd, please give Hollis the wisdom tuh leave the boy alone. That's allst I pray for."

When Nate left, I got to thinking about some of the books I had suggested. Reading had always schooled and comforted me, and after Thad's murder, I consumed books like the twister that had ravished New Harmony in 1923. After his killing, the writings of my favorite colored authors helped me recover from what I thought impossible. In reading Margaret Walker's poem "For My People," I began to understand the Negro experience more deeply, especially when I read the verse that goes:

> *For my people standing staring trying to fashion a better way,*
> *from confusion, from hypocrisy and misunderstanding,*
> *trying to fashion a world that will hold all the people,*
> *all the faces, all the adams and eves and their countless*
> *generations.*

That verse spoke to the suffering of my loss but hinted at the resilience that nurtures hope for a better tomorrow. But there was more to my boy's murder. I struggled to understand not only the "why" of his murder but also the darkness surrounding color and negritude. Who was responsible for his death? Was it the person who pulled the trigger, or was it every person who spewed their dark and hopeless thoughts about white or colored folks? Zora Neale Hurston's *Their Eyes Were Watching God* opened my eyes to the world that color had built. Hurston makes Janie's hair one of the book's most essential images; her hair represents her power, identity, and freedom, and I had never thought about hair that way. I had never thought that assaults on kinky hair were subtle ways to kill everyone's spirit. Then there was the question of dark skin, as in Chester Himes's *If He Hollers Let Him Go*, where the light-skinned Alice Harrison felt embarrassed and fretted over being seen in white society with a man whose skin color was much darker than hers. My Thad was high in color, but the darkness of negritude rendered him worthless—unfit to breathe, some white folks believed. So, Himes and Hurston's work, along with James Baldwin's *Go Tell It on the Mountain*, Ellison's *Invisible Man*, and Oliver Killens's *Youngblood*, helped me to see that slavery took more than our freedom—it bred and normalized negativity. Hatred struck my boy dead because white and colored folks contorted beauty. Reading helped me to reflect on my thoughts about colored folks' appearances, as I once did with Jeremiah and Hazel. In reflecting on how I once thought, I now see how it allowed somebody to render my son grotesque, deciding he was unfit to live. I pray that I'll never speak ill of another soul.

TWENTY-FIVE

Wisdom Becomes a Butterfly

One Sunday afternoon in October, after we had come from church, Marlene visited. She walked with a cane then and moved rather slowly, but she was like that old tortoise: she inched along, but she got there. When she reached the porch, she flopped into the rocker like she was in her last state of exhaustion.

God had blown all the clouds away that sunny fall day. Under a clear blue sky, the oak tree next to the house cast its shadow deep, making it chilly in the shade, so we sat in the sun. Red, purple, green, yellow, and pink bounced off geraniums, verbena, wandering Jew, and ferns, and begonias in white and blue lard cans that hung from the porch roof. Flocks of ducks and geese flapped and honked, showing their bellies on their way to the river and to points farther south. Butterflies, large and small, flounced on the gate posts, moved to bushes, flowers, eaves, the roof, and then vanished.

A stillness hung in the air that I only found on Sunday mornings after church, when the spirit filled my core.

Marlene leaned back in the chair. "Been lookin' for y'all," she said.

"I went by tuh visit Thad's grave. Hard tuh believe somebody killed him five years ago today."

"Did'ja have a pleasant visit?" she asked.

"Yeah, always do. How yuh been?"

"I is mighty worried, Margaret."

"'Bout whut?"

"'Bout seein' Jesus when I dies."

"Marlene, you're gonna outlive us all. You know that, don'tcha?"

"Wish that be so. I has a dream; it been preyin' on my mind."

"Whut kinda dream?"

"I be's in bed, watchin' myself sleepin'. A man come in, and I sensed him hoverin'. I wakes up. The finest-lookin' man I ever did see done bent down over me. He gits tuh kissin' me on the mouth, and I ain't never felt no kiss lac that. Not that kind of passion from no man before. He kisses me, and then he gits tuh gnawin' on my neck. First, it feel right good, but then it ain't seem right. So I pushes him away. When I forces him away, I seen his face turn in'tuh . . . that's when I—" She sat quiet, and locked those recollections away.

"Marlene. Who was it?"

She still said nothing.

"Who was it, Marlene?"

She gasped, "Devil. It be's the devil," she said.

Butterflies hovered, sky-danced, and then scattered in frantic fright.

"Whut did'ja do?" I asked.

"Lifts my feets; gives him a hard kick, and he went up in thin air. Gone jest lac dat. Oh, I screams. That be's when I wakes up." Her eyes shut out the fear she felt, but it was her "Margaret, it be's so real" that made me realize how deep the devil had struck.

"I wu'dah been terrified tuh death. Could'ja go back tuh sleep?"

"Ain't sleep a lick the rest of the night."

"Whut do yuh think it meant?" I asked.

"I thank the devil gon' be's comin' tuh git me soon."

"Oh, Marlene, you're washed in the blood; Christ has forgiven yuh for everythang that happened in the past."

"But Margaret, that dream *shook* me so."

"Yuh have a beautiful heart, Marlene. Yuh were like that even 'foe yuh were born."

"I done been prayin' a lot, preparin' for my journey home, 'cause it ain't gon' be long."

"Well, I pray it's gonna be quite a spell 'foe yuh leave us. Whut are we gon' do wid'out yuh? Huh?" I patted her on her leg.

A butterfly came and perched on the porch rail.

"Want some coffee?"

"Thank I will."

I entered the house, but I continued talking while I fussed about in the kitchen, and when I reached the door, I said,

"Marlene, how is Burton?"

But as I stepped onto the porch, I nearly tripped on her fallen cane.

She had that glow, the glow of angels. Her head touched her chest, just to the right of her chest bone, and a gentle breeze caught strands of her hair. One or two pieces blew ever so slightly in the fall breeze.

The butterflies are gone.

I walked to the kitchen, placed the cup on the table, locked my hands on a chair, and took a deep breath.

I called Burton and Fast Fannie. She arrived before Burton, and we couldn't believe Marlene was gone. Marlene had been like my second mammy and had been more of a mother to Nate than Vivian. When I phoned him, it seemed the boy was in my yard before I hung up. He ran toward the porch but stopped cold at the bottom step. Then, he walked with reverence onto the porch, paying homage to something beyond life. He pushed the hair back from her forehead, and he kissed her like God first kissed the world.

Burton had called Mr. Collins before he left town, and they arrived at the same time. Oh, that boy cried something awful that day; his eyes were scarlet. But I'm not sure who sobbed more after Marlene: Burton or Nate. There they were: half brothers, one white and one black, crying over a colored woman who was born during Reconstruction time.

She died on October 17, 1954.

Since Leroy couldn't get to New Harmony until later, Burton started making funeral arrangements. Mr. Hollis offered to help, but Burton refused. He had promised himself that after his mama died, he would never set foot in the Big House again. Nate and I went with Burton to prepare for Marlene's funeral and burial. Later in the day, as we completed plans, we walked near the square and ran into Vivian.

The way she carried her body and the way her hips swayed suggested she had a bunion, a pebble, or something precious in her shoes. Or was it a mild flirtation held below the waist and centered on her hips? Oh, she was full of cheer and sweet venom.

She didn't cut her eyes at me or Burton, but she was all up in Nate's face, saying, "Lord, Nate, whut are yuh doin' in town? Come in town and don't visit. That ain't no way tuh treat yo' mother."

"Marlene died yesterday, and we needed to—"

"Why don'tcha come wid me? I'm goin' down tuh the department store tuh—"

"Mother, I said Marlene died yesterday!"

"I heard'cha. You don't haf'tuh yell. I ain't deaf, Nathan."

"Don't'ja feel the least bit—?"

"Haven't yuh learnt anythang?"

"Learned what, Mother?"

"They're jest dark—"

Before she could finish spewing the "i-e-s" and attach it to "dark," Nate slapped her right across the face. Oh, he turned her head clean around.

"Nathan!"

Her mouth slammed shut from the shock of his hand imprinting red across her face.

"If you wanna continue havin' a relationship wid me, don't you *ever* use that word again in my presence as long as yuh live."

His voice began to break.

"Marlene was more like my mother than you were."

"Hollis is right. These niggas and that war have jest . . . boy, I really think yuh're touched in the head. I am yo' mother!"

Nate bolted.

"Ain't no nigga bitch ever give birth tuh yuh, boy!" Vivian continued shrieking. "*I DID THAT!*"

Nate didn't look back; he kept walking, with us running on up behind him.

She yelled, "Yuh hear me, boy?"

As Nate walked on, she stopped to stomp her foot, but kept yelling,

"Yuh hear me? Ain't no nigga bitch ever give birth tuh yuh!"

He walked so fast I had to say, "*Nate*. Please slow up. Have mercy on this old woman."

He stopped and looked down the street, where she still stood, stomping and yelling, "I did that!"

"People like her are the problem," Nate said. "Burton, I'm sorry yuh had tuh witness that."

"I hate tuh say this, knowin' Vivian is yo' mother, but considerin' the source, I'm not the least bit offended," Burton said. "Her prejudice has never wavered. She's just like Hollis; she'll never change."

"Our father is—"

"No need tuh explain. But why did Mama stay in that place with him for all those years?" He turned to me and asked, "Do you know, Miss Margaret?"

"Nah. I thought 'bout that the uh'ther day, and I don't understand it one bit either. Whutever it was, she guarded well, as they say, the western gate, and took it tuh her grave."

———————— ◦◦◦ ————————

For the rest of the week, a cloud hung over New Harmony, and everything seemed to move in slow motion. When Leroy came, he stayed with Burton, and they agreed to have the wake that Friday. Hollis offered to have the vigil at the Big House, but they refused and held it at Calvary.

The hearse pulled up to Calvary at about ten o'clock that morning, and they laid Marlene out in the church. I didn't have any idea so many people loved her. William and I joined the boys that evening around seven o'clock, and several folks were there. Some of 'em sat quiet, caught up in their silence, but others muttered to the person accompanying them. Miss Effie was living then—oh, she must've been way in her nineties. While gazing at Marlene, she turned to Miss Bessie, who was well into her eighties, and said, "Looka here. Mr. Collins sho' done a wonderful job wid Sister Marlene. She looks so peaceful lyin' there."

"Yeah, he sho' did. Don't thank I've ever seen her look so peaceful. Whut color is that dress they has on her, Effie?"

"Ivory . . . naw, chantilly lace." She sighed a bit. "They sho' put her away nice. Didn't they, Bessie?"

"They sho' did."

I had never seen two women who loved funerals so much. They would have sat with the family on the front pew if possible.

Burton, Leroy, and Nate sat near the casket, talking to folks who came to offer their condolences, and other murmurings filled the church until the doors opened and there stood Hollis.

The church folks fell dead silent. I bet, in all his seventy-some-odd years, he had never been inside a colored church. We sat in amazement at Hollis Demmings coming to view this woman, born to recently freed slaves, to a people he seemed to despise. I suspected the bond they shared allowed him to pierce the protective sacredness of Calvary—a place that had sheltered colored folks from people like him.

He didn't look at a soul.

He entered with his head high, but his face stood expressionless. The boldness of each step toward her casket left us stung in Calvary's dimmed lights. His eyes didn't veer from their target, and he walked straight until he stopped, touching the casket's edge.

He looked down.

Pulling the netting back from the coffin, he peered at her face.

The whispers of his voice echoed through Calvary and into the evening's silence.

People shifted in their seats, mumbling to themselves or the person next to them.

"Whut is he doin' here?" someone said.

"Whut he doin' up there?" Deacon Paul asked.

"He ortah be 'shame of hisself comin' here," Sister Jamison said.

But Hollis lingered, never shifting his body or bending more than his neck until he reached into his inside suit pocket. He placed something next to Marlene's face. Folks really started jabbering, and we all wondered what he had put beside her.

He turned toward the boys.

One resembled him, but the other two, darkened by Africa, remained unacknowledged. After surveying his piece of white bread and two cinnamon sticks, he walked out of the church with the same boldness that brought him through its doors and down its death-silent aisle.

In the casket, Burton found a dried, flattened red rosebud and an envelope. We found a lock of braided hair, a feather, and a wedding ring inside the envelope. What did it mean? We looked at each other and shook our heads.

———————

The following Saturday, Hollis watched from his car as folks came to say farewell to Marlene. Even after Nate begged him, he refused to attend but stayed in his shiny Cadillac with his driver. Burton and Leroy sat in the front pew with Nate beside them while Fast Fannie and the rest of our family sat right behind.

Five of Nate's cello-playing friends sat near the pulpit, and when Nate joined them, they set the mood by playing Casals's "Song of the Birds." It was somber but inspiring and allowed Pastor Jones to say,

"Marlene Rhodes was a mother, a friend, and our sister in faith. We will miss her. We will miss the warmth and the beauty of her spirit."

A mournful "Uh-huh, yesss" came from Sister Bessie's Amen corner.

"She stood alone for so long. She witnessed the horrors and the pain of the Reconstruction. Durin' the Negro's darkest times, an angry and godless overseer snatched Marlene's mother and kin's lives. However, a lovin' grandmother and a benevolent God shepherded her."

"Amen," Sister Jamison said.

Pastor Jones reminded folks of Marlene's suffering but rejoiced in how she laid the curse of sin behind and picked up the cross of Jesus.

"Sister Marlene, like the woman comin' tuh the house of one of the Pharisees, sought Jesus. She was a sinner, but she knelt at Jesus's feet, weeping, washin' his feet wid her tears; she wiped them wid her hair and anointed them wid ointment from her alabaster box."

"Ahhh, go 'head boy," Miss Effie said.

"When the Pharisee, knowin' that she was a sinner, protested, Jesus said to him, 'Thou gavest me no water for my feet: but she hath washed my feet wid tears, and wiped them wid the hairs of her head. Thou gavest me no kiss, but this woman since the time I came in hath not ceased to kiss my feet. My head wid oil thou didst not anoint: but this woman hath anointed my feet wid ointment.'"

"Oh, sweet Jesus!"

Then he slapped the pulpit.

"Jesus said, 'Wherefore I say unto thee, her sins, which are many, are forgiven; for she loved much.'"

"Preach! Tell it lac the Lawd told'cha, boy," Miss Bessie said.

"Yes! Sister Marlene loved much. Look what she leaves us today! Two fine sons. One's a doctor, and the other one's a lawyer. Yeah, she was a mighty warrior leanin' on the cross of Jesus. Sleep, Sister Marlene. Sleep in the arms of Jesus."

Pastor Jones hummed, subdued at first, then he got louder. It was Marlene's favorite hymn, "Amazing Grace." He started softly, and then, from the choir loft, a lone woman picked up that song. I can't remember her name, but I'd seen her in church and around town. She sang that song with low notes and high notes. The woman sang it with "uh-huhs" and "oh yeahs." She sang it with Amens and Hallelujahs, and she sang everything in between. That woman wove that song like a master weaver weaved a basket. She wove Marlene's pain and beauty into that song . . . Carrie. Yeah, Carrie, that was the singer's name. Carrie sang it like a sad song, but she sang it like a song full of hope, too. You sensed brokenness but found healing in it. We floundered in grief but became redeemed by it. When she finished, there wasn't a dry eye in the church.

TWENTY-SIX

Got a Knife?

The fall of 1955 blasted in on the heels of a curious summer. When I arose that October morning, knowing Nate would meet me later, I prepared for Robert's arrival. I planned to shop, oblivious to what lay in store. As I dressed, I remembered Marlene died a year ago, and I made a note to visit her grave when I visited Thad's. She and Thad died on October 17, with Marlene dying five years after Thad.

As Robert approached, I opened the mailbox, and lo and behold, Tilda had written. I was about to open the letter, but Robert rushed to a stop. He urged me to get in because he was running late for a meeting. I jumped in and put the letter in my pocketbook, planning to read it as we traveled to town. But on the way, Robert, filled with stories about the new grandbaby Fannie helped to deliver the day before, diverted my thoughts about Tilda and the children until we neared Market Street. As I stepped out of the car, he asked,

"Want me to pick yuh up later?"

"Nah, Nate's here somewhere, and we're gonna meet up later and visit Thad's grave. He'll give me a ride."

"Don't forgit yo' letter."

"Oh, I had plum forgot. Thanks."

By the time I turned onto Main, I was busting at the seams to give Tilda's letter a careful read. As I headed toward Wilson's, now a department store, I strolled, reading while I listened to the taps of heels and the slaps of soles. Oh, the family was fine, and they would come home soon.

As I walked along, the fresh-baked bread from Olsen's Bakery and hand-dipped chocolate from Miss Neale's new candy store filled the street with their scents, which reminded me of my youth and spring. However, the cut flowers at Saunder's flower shop confirmed it was autumn. As I approached Wade's Shoe Repair, I put the letter in my pocketbook and looked up. I noticed Floyd nearing.

He quickened his pace toward me.

I tried to duck into Lulu's, a women's clothing store, but it was too late. He was too fast. And before I could utter a hint of resistance, he forced me into the alleyway. He settled his glossy blue eyes on my bosom and pushed away the pocketbook that protected them. Floyd moistened his lip.

"Margaret. Whut'ja doin', girl? Out here all by yo'self."

He leaned closer, sniffed at his quarry, sounded a long, breathy "Ahhhh," all upside my face, and licked his lips.

"Oh, cat got'cha tongue?"

The stench of his breath showered me; he was full of liquor and reeked of stale tobacco.

I attempted to scoot from under him, but he seized my arms and pinned me to the building, and the roughness of bricks and concrete tore at my back.

"Whut's wrong, Margaret? I remember how yuh use'ta watch me."

I pushed against him; he was too big.

He squeezed his thighs into me and whispered, "Don't you fight, now."

As he nestled into me, he tried to unbutton the top of my dress. I grabbed his hand, but he jerked it away and pressed my back against the wall.

My pocketbook hit the dusty alleyway.

"Whut's wrong? Yuh don't like me no mo'?" he asked, sounding like a real sad sack.

He trapped my hands behind me, and he stuck out his long pink tongue and licked me from the bottom of my neck and up across my face.

The sound of his panting grew heavy, but his steamy breath landed frigid up against my soiled, wet skin when he pressed closer, jiggled his hips, and rubbed, "Don't that feel good?" up against my ear. Marlene was right; he was huge down there. He rubbed *"fear"* against my leg.

I opened my mouth to scream, but he freed one hand and slapped me hard across the face. He threw his hand across my mouth real quick and said, "Don't do that. If you scream, I'm gonna cut yo' throat right here. Yuh hear what I'm telling you, gal?"

He never spoke above a whisper. Throughout this, he never spoke over a whisper.

Grinding "*fear*" against me, he whispered into my neck and down into my breast,

"Yuh bet not move. A white man killin' a nigga bitch? Shit, girl—it don't mean nuthin' tuh nobody 'round here who matters. You know that."

He peppered me with his lips and licked some more, but he was right. White folks saw my dilemma as they crossed the alleyway, but no one raised a finger.

Emboldened, he yanked up my dress.

My eyes stretched full; white parts turned to heaven while I scrunched my body into the wall, hoping to disappear, as he sniffed at my breast and tried to bury his face there, murmuring,

"Yuh want me tuh give yuh some of this? Don'tcha? I bet yuh do."

And then, looking down at me, he grinned and licked his lips to say, "Ohhhhh, I can tell."

I wanted to bite his hand, but I couldn't. I couldn't move.

Panic wailed, and I tried to scream. Only my panties screamed their protest, but he tugged at them more, and they fell silent around my ankles.

My eyes stretched wide; I wailed, and then pleaded: "Floyd, please. Please don't do this awful thing," but lust had struck him deaf and dumb.

His whispering voice said, "Margaret, I told him what I was gonna do tuh yuh if he kept on wid his foolishness."

What was he talking about? He yammered like a crazy man for sho', so I prayed. *Oh, Lord, come to my assistance. Lord, make haste to help me.*

I prayed over and over, but he cut me off.

"Vivian . . . she's such a *bitch*! She won't give me even a sniff of her precious white pussy."

Then he hit me with another slow grind and whispered, "Oh, that's so *good*," in my ear. "Bet yo' nigga pussy is even better," and slammed "*fear*" hard against my leg.

He licked me across the face again.

"Don't struggle none," he whispered, but then he raised his voice. "I told'cha: don't make no fuss!" Then his voice fell into a whisper, saying, "It ain't gon' hurt yuh none. Girl, yuh got that enormous buck at home.

"Shhh. Hush now. Whut'ja cryin' for? Ain't no sense in that."

He pushed me farther down the alleyway with his hand around my throat. If I didn't get loose soon, I was a goner. He parted his lips, wetted them with a tongue dance, and said, "Lemme catch them tears for yuh."

Floyd puckered his lips.

"Does he kiss them lips like this?"

His wetness marked my forehead.

"Does he bang that pussy, or does he take his fat black nigga dick and tickle it 'foe he bangs it in?"

He slammed up against me, smiled, and licked me up again before he sighed "I'm gittin' so *wet*, Margaret," in my face and whispered, "I want yo' pussy, right now," all down my neck and into my breast.

I shut my eyes in darkness but flooded them with weeping.

"Yeah, whimper for me like yuh do for yo' buck. Will yuh do that? For me?"

His zipper's rush incited panic against my legs, and his hardness brushed against me when he gripped the top of my dress, but something grabbed him. When it pulled him away, the top of my dress ripped, screaming its objections.

I opened my eyes.

It was Nate.

He said nothing to Floyd but spun him around and hit him with enough force to burst Floyd's lip. His blood splattered on my face as he fell to the ground. Nate pulled him up, saying, "I've wanted tuh do this all my life." Floyd crumpled and fell in the dirt, but Nate picked him up, yelling, "You're a sorry son-of-a-bitch!" before he slugged him again.

Floyd landed on the ground.

Nate kicked him.

"I ortah kill yuh, yuh no-good sorry bastard." Nate kicked Floyd until his breath grew short while Floyd's tools hung out of his britches. It wasn't hard anymore!

Nate gathered my things and cradled me in his arms like I used to do to him when he was little. I was never happier to see someone.

Floyd hugged the ground, whimpering, "I love yuh, Margaret. Always have."

I sheltered myself in Nate's arms, shivering from the thought.

Nate put me in his car, and I told him to drive to Fast Fannie's. William couldn't see me like this; he'd take that shotgun, go to Ashley Road, and kill Floyd. Besides, I wasn't hurt.

When we arrived at Fannie's, thank God Robert wasn't there.

Fannie said, "Now, I know William ain't touched you. Who done this?"

"Floyd."

"Floyd Demmings? My God, he worse than his no-count daddy."

I looked at Nate.

"Hell, Nate ain't no cracker. Why, Nate's blacker than most colored people I knows," which was Fannie's highest compliment.

"Margaret, girl, did he hurt yuh?"

"Fannie, I'm all right."

"Look at yo' dress."

"I think she's all right," Nate said. "Just a little shaken up."

"You ortah call the law on his no-good cracker ass," Fannie said.

I trembled and said, "No!" and then covered my face, sniffling into my palms. "Fannie, I cain't do that. Whut that gon' do? They gonna say I egged him on, and then . . ."

"Oh, honey. It's gon' be all right," Fast Fannie said, looking at Nate.

"Are yuh sure, Miss Margaret?"

"I'm fine, but I need a dress. Cain't go home lookin' like this. William would shoot Floyd dead. I cain't lose my William over sump'em like this. Y'all got'tuh promise not tuh tell him. Y'all swear?"

They both promised.

"Come on in the house. Here, take this and wipe yo' eyes and blow yo' nose."

"Whut did he do?" Fannie asked.

"I was this close to being raped."

"Raped! I wished I'd been there. I wu'dah cut his pecker clean off. He'd be pissin' through his goddamn navel or his asshole when I got through wid his sorry ass."

Nate snickered.

"That's right," Fannie said. "This is whut I wu'dah told his sorry cracker ass. I wu'dah said, 'I wants yuh tuh feel real-good. Lemme taste it for yuh.' Then I wu'dah bite that son-of-a-bitch slam off, and I wu'dah pulled them balls of his clean from the ruut. He'd be singin' lac'uh goddamn soprano when I got done wid his sorry ass. Crackers ain't worth a damn no ways."

When we stopped laughing, I said, "Nate came jest in time, and yuh should'ah seen the boy fight, Fannie."

"Should'ah took a knife to that pecker."

Then I remembered.

"You know whut he told me in the alleyway? Floyd said he told this man that if that man didn't leave him alone, Floyd was gonna git me. Told me tuh stop the man. Whut'ja think he means?"

"He's a crazy-ass cracker," Fast Fannie said. "Don't try tuh make no kinda sense out'ah what he's talkin' about. They ortah strang him up by his balls, but he's a cracker, and they's two-faced when it comes to justice."

We talked for a while, and then Nate drove me home.

"Are yuh sure yuh're all right?" he asked.

"I'm fine."

But I was nowhere near being fine. I felt like someone had thrown me on top of a manure pile. It took weeks before I left the house by myself, and sometimes, when William came up behind me, I'd jump to high heavens.

"Whut's the matter?" he'd ask.

"I'm so nervous . . . cain't reckon whut's that about." I threw it off like that. But in bed, I had to remind myself it was William, not Floyd, who caressed me.

When I saw Nate again, he asked, "How are yuh doin', Miss Margaret?"

"I'm fine, boy," I said—but I was lying and I prayed every moment to keep the jitters at bay.

I required time and lots of long talks with Fast Fannie before I could get over the assault, and we grew even closer as sisters. I love Fannie . . . and her hot temper.

⋆

Not long after Floyd's assault, a tap on the front door interrupted my reading.

Hollis.

"I had a visitor the uh'ther day," he said.

He didn't look at me.

"My visitor tells me Nate beat up her husband, and it seems like they accused yuh of causin' it."

With his head turned toward the Big House, he said,

"When they told me this story, it didn't sound like anythang Margaret Butler wu'dah done. Does it?"

"Nossir!"

"That's what I thought, too. Good day, Margaret."

Then he was gone, just like that.

I hated Floyd Demmings. I thought I was getting better, and here his daddy comes, bringing it up again. My mind raced toward what Floyd had told me. He said I had to stop him. What did he mean?

Zora Mae's rushed visit the next day amplified my worries.

"I promised tuh tell yuh if I heard anythang that y'all might need tuh know," she said. "Now Margaret, we goes way back, and honey, if yuh—"

"It's all right. We can talk 'bout this. I wanna talk 'bout it."

I told her the story.

"Oh honey, I'm so sorry. All the mo' reason I needs tuh tell yuh this then."

"Whut is Floyd up tuh, now?"

"A triflin' no-account, like that wife of his. Margaret, you 'member Kearns?"

"Oh God, yes! Use'ta work for Mr. Hollis, 'foe Mr. Hollis settled score wid him."

"Well, they done hired him."

"Kearns?"

"Yep. Takes care of the garden."

"My Lawd, why in the world—"

"They're schemin' 'bout sump'em, but they won't lemme hear whut it is. They mouths close as tight as a terrapin when I enter."

"Wonder whut they're up tuh? Well, it sho' looks like Mr. Hollis's enemies have pulled up in one place."

"There's uh'nuther thang. The scent, it's stronger now. It's throughout the house. 'Foe this, it was jest where Floyd sat. Every time the wind blows, Floyd looks like he sees sump'em, and he mutters tuh himself all the time now."

"Whut is he sayin', Zora Mae?"

"Best I can make out he's tellin' this man tuh leave him alone. He's warnin' the man. If the man don't stop, Floyd gonna git both of 'em. Seems like he's 'bout ready tuh snap, if'n yuh axes me, lookin' all wild-eyed and crazy, full of booze and stinkin' of cigars."

She looked up at the kitchen clock. "Well, I got'tuh git home and see 'bout Pinky and the children. Take care of yo'self, and if there's anythang I can do, call me."

"I sho' will."

"God bless and be strong."

The dust hadn't settled on New Harmony Road from Zora Mae's departure when the phone rang.

"Butler residence."

"Margaret."

I recognized the voice.

"Guess who?" he said, but I stayed silent.

"You gonna end up like that boy of yourn if you ain't careful, Margaret. Whut was his name . . . the one they found dead on New Harmony Road?"

"I know yuh're there. I know yuh can hear me."

He laughed, but then, using the same whisper voice he used in the alleyway, he said,

"I know who killed him, Margaret. I seen it," and then he chuckled.

The phone went dead. I still held it when William entered, and I shook so.

"My God, woman! Whut's the matter?"

"It was . . . it was . . ."

"Who?"

"Floyd."

"Whut in the world is he doin' callin' *here*?"

"He said I'm gonna end up jest like Thad if I wan't careful."

"Whut?"

"Said he knew who killed Thad. He saw it."

William took the phone from my hand, and I cried, sinking to the floor. William knelt beside me, asking,

"Whut in the world's the matter, Margaret? Whut's this uh'bout?"

I told him the whole story.

He didn't say one word; he just held and rocked me. "I love yuh mo' than life itself," he said. "Whut'ja need me tuh do for yuh?"

Lord, I married a good man.

"Jest hold me. Jest hold me."

He did that for a long time.

"Think we need tuh tell Nate?" I asked. "Floyd's so crazy. He's liable tuh do sump'em."

"'Spect that might be wise . . . so he can be on guard."

When I called, Eleanor, Hollis's new housekeeper, said Nate had gone to Hampton. I asked her to make sure Nate called me when he returned the next day.

The phone started ringing early that morning, and I let it. It kept ringing and ringing, so I put my fingers in my ears and ran onto the porch to escape.

Late in the afternoon, Nate was on my doorstep.

"Miss Margaret, what's the matter?" I told him what Floyd had said, and he exploded from the porch like water poured in a frying pan full of sizzling fatback grease.

The phone started ringing again, and it kept on ringing until about four o'clock. I was sitting on the porch when a haze of dust clouded the road as Fast Fannie raced up.

"Lawd, been tryin' to call yuh all day—been worried sick. Where yuh been at?"

"Here, but Floyd—"

"That cracker botherin' yuh again?"

"Fannie, he said he knew who killed Thad."

"Hush yo' mouth."

"He said he saw it."

"If yuh ain't gon' go tuh the law, 'least tell William."

"I told him last night."

"Whut he say?"

"He asked me whut I needed."

"That ain't gon' git shed of Floyd. Somebody haf tuh shoot his face off."

"Lawd, Fannie. Why yuh so mean?"

"Mean, hell! That no-good, sorry-ass cracker was fixin' tuh rape yuh, and now he's talkin' 'bout *killin'* ya. Margaret, honey, are yuh touched in the head? Yuh needs tuh git *mad*, girl."

"Stop it! I'm worried sick. Nate has gone over there, and there's no tellin' whut might happen between 'em."

"Well, if yuh ask me, this one of them times when William needs tuh call the menfolks."

"Fannie, I'm scared all the time."

She stayed with me until William came home from work. When Fannie got home, she told Robert, who found William in the yard. When they finished talking, Robert took off, and William came in the house and announced, "Yuh're goin' over tuh yo' pappy's house. Best call him and tell him yuh're on yo' way."

TWENTY-SEVEN

Good Riddance

Before that October evening, I had never noticed how the road to Hampton twisted every which way, making the car illuminate the forest with its headlamps. Sheets of rain poured for a while but yielded to itty-bitty drops that sprinkled themselves over the Ford's slick windshield.

It was late when Pappy's front porch light greeted us.

"Aren't yuh comin' in?" I asked William.

"Nah, I got'tuh meet Robert. We got sump'tem tuh take care of . . ."

I looked at him.

"Don't'ja worry, things gon' turn 'round." He bent toward me and pecked me on the cheek.

"I'm gon' come by tomorrow tuh check on yuh." Then he smiled, and I ran to the door, trying to duck between raindrops. William waited for Pappy to appear at the door, then drove off.

"Where he gwine' tuh?"

"He and Robert got sump'em they need doin'."

"Y'all all right?"

Through the tears, I stammered, "Everythang's fine."

He grabbed me by the shoulders and pulled me into the house.

"Then why yuh cryin'?"

I buried my face in his arms, muffling my voice into his chest.

"Whut? Now, yuh got'tuh stop this mumblin'."

I lifted my head from his chest and said, "Floyd 'bout raped me . . .

then he called the house. He said he was there . . . he saw Thad murdered."

His face grew strained.

"Wish I was a younger man. I'd cut his privates off and shove 'em down his throat!"

Still sniffling, I said, "I'm so tired, Pappy."

Fatigue nestled in; it had been creeping toward me all day.

"Hush now. I got'cha bed made up. Yuh go on and rest; we gon' talk 'bout this in the mornin'. Everythang'll seem brighter. Yuh'll see."

Pappy put me in Violet's room, which he hadn't touched since she left for college. Violet had decorated it right nice. Lace curtains hung from the windows, and the sage-green paint adorning the walls made the room look homey. The old pine plank floors shined like glass, and a little square hook rug stamped out a spot next to the bed. Violet had stuck every kind of doll in every place imaginable. I crawled in between sheets that hid beneath a pink chenille bedspread, and one of Mammy's quilts rested at my feet. I pulled its Jacob's Ladder pattern (pieces of silk, wool, cotton, and gabardine) up to cover my shoulders, and before the first sheep lifted its legs to prance over that fence, I was asleep.

The next morning, I rattled around and crept into the kitchen—I didn't want to wake Pappy. I stretched and reached for the radio.

"Good to the last drop," it announced.

"Where's the coffee?" I mumbled.

Found it.

"Still g'tting' it from the A&P, I see."

When I opened the bag, the ground coffee's aroma pushed me back to the olden days when I was a child. Pappy would hold my hand at the A&P as we waited for the clerk to dump our beans into the sparkling red grinder. The clerk selected our blend and cranked the shiny chrome dial to grind our coffee to perfection.

I found the percolator.

Before too long, the aroma of coffee filled the entire house and coaxed Pappy to poke his nose into the kitchen.

"How yuh doin' this mornin', daughter?"

"Scared, but I'm better . . . ready for some coffee, Pappy?"

"Yeah . . . reminds me of those times when yo' mammy got up way 'foe me and had the coffee all nice and hot when I woke."

"I remember."

"Been thirty years some odd, and I still 'pect her tuh walk through the door."

I poured him a cup of coffee, which he laced with cream and sugar until it held the color and sweetness of Mammy.

"Yeah, sometimes when I'm home alone, I jump because I think I've seen Thad out of the corner of my eye. I'd turn, and nuthin' faces me but an empty chair. Then there are some mornings when his scent fills the air suddenly. That's when I draw a deep breath 'cause I know it's gonna be gone as quickly as it came."

Pappy looked at me and shook his head with recognition.

He blew his coffee cool, took a sip, and asked, "What's this mess 'bout Floyd, Margaret?"

I placed my cup on the table, breathed, and told my story.

"Right in the broad, open daylight?"

"Yeah."

"The man's touched in the head."

"He told me if I screamed, he'd slit my throat, said nobody cared if he killed a nigga woman."

Pappy took to his feet—the way he did during my childhood when something irritated his craw.

"Nate saved me. Pappy, yuh should'ah seen the boy fight. He beat Floyd wid'in an inch of his life."

"Somebody should'ah. Looks like all of us gonna haf tuh face this thang tuh'gether. Yuh cain't hold up here forever."

"I know."

"When William comin'?"

"Today, but jest tuh look in on us."

"Whut did'ja wanna do?" Pappy asked.

"Not sure, but I've got a feelin' the Lawd gonna be showin' us de'reckly."

The front door slammed, and Pappy said, "Who in the world . . . ?" but it was just Fannie. "Y'all ain't scared, is yuh? Why y'all held up in here?" she asked.

"Fannie, girl, whut'ja doin' over here?" I asked as Pappy kissed her on the cheek.

"I done been by yo' house, lookin' for my husband. He'd been out wid William all night long—I finds him laid up in one of the children's rooms."

"Whut have they been up to?" I asked.

"I axed 'em the same thang; said it wan't none of my business."

"*Whut?*"

"I pulled Robert's narrow behin' out that bed and sniffed his breath. He had tuh be drunk!"

"Robert dud'en drink, and neither does William," Pappy said.

"Well, I figured they *must've* been drunk, talkin' tuh *me* like that."

"Huh, sump'tem got'tuh be afoot," I said.

"Well, they ain't sayin' nuthin' tuh nobody. Allst William muttered was he brung yuh over here. So, I had tuh make sure my baby sister was all right." She gave me a hug. "Pappy, whut'cha thank 'bout this mess?"

"Snip, snip," Pappy said.

"Whut?" I asked.

"He ortah be a geldin'."

"Wish I had been there," Fannie said, pouring herself a cup of coffee.

"Y'all think we need tuh worry 'bout Robert and William? You don't think they went lookin' for Floyd last night, do yuh?" I asked.

"I hope they ain't that crazy. Why, they'd string 'em up 'foe we could spit," Pappy said.

"Shhhhhh! Whut was that?" I asked.

"Whut?" Pappy asked.

"On the radio." I got up and turned the knob.

" . . . of Hollis Demmings. We interrupt this program to bring you this important news. In the early evening last night, authorities found Hollis Rhodes Demmings murdered in his home. The investigation, headed by Sheriff Toler of the Hampton County Sheriff's Department, has revealed no suspects in the death of the seventy-eight-year-old Demmings, a long-time resident of New Harmony. We will continue to keep you informed as developments arise."

"Lawd. Did'ja hear that?" I asked, lowering the sound.

"Guess where he headed?" Pappy said, with his finger pointing down, almost touching the floor.

"If'n yuh ask me, it wan't soon uh'nuf. 'Bout time somebody done kilt that old sorry son of a bitch. Should'ah been dead a long time ago. Much trouble he done give colored folks 'round these parts," Fannie said.

"Yuh don't think Robert and William had anythang tuh do wid this, do yuh?"

We eyed each other, and Fannie said,

"Nah. Folks done been waitin' in line by the droves tuh kill his sorry behin'. I wonder who done got the gumption tuh do it. I say Hallelujah and good riddance, and I hope the devil snatched his tail as soon as the last breath left his sorry-ass body. That cracker was mean as a snake, and he ain't deserve tuh live no ways . . . that old, white-headed, cigar-chewing, flat-ass cracker."

How does she think up this stuff? I wanted to laugh, but I stopped myself.

"Fannie. We best git back tuh the house and check on Nate and the uh'ther menfolk."

"'Spect yuh're right. Go git yo' stuff."

"Pappy, you gonna want sump'tem tuh eat 'foe we leave?" I asked.

"I'll git sump'tem later. Y'all go on."

When we got home, William and Robert slept like their names were John D. Rockefeller and Cornelius Vanderbilt.

"Why y'all still in bed?" I asked.

"Whut'ja doin' back? I thought I told'cha tuh stay at yo' pappy's."

"Wait jest a cotton-pickin' minute, William Butler. Whut are y'all still doin' in bed?"

"I'm tired, Margaret—been up all night."

"Doing whut?"

"We went lookin' for Floyd."

"Git up! Both of y'all better git up! NOW!" I ordered.

Fannie's eyes got right big. "Margaret, is that you?" she asked, amazed at my tone.

"Hush up!" I said. Fannie side-stepped toward the door.

"And did'ja find him, William Butler?"

"Now Margaret, calm down. Whut'ja so flared up 'bout anyway?" By then, Robert stood in the doorway with his arms around Fannie.

"Somebody killed Hollis last night. Y'all ain't have anythang tuh do wid that, did'ja?"

Their eyes flashed shock.

Robert said, "Nah. We didn't do it."

William jumped up. "We swear 'foe God."

I looked at both of them.

Fannie went to the door. "Is Nate up there? Margaret, yuh best call and see."

The phone stayed busy, but I finally got through.

"Who are yuh?" the voice on the other end asked.

"This is Margaret, Margaret Butler."

"Sheriff Toler, Margaret. Are yuh friendly wid Nathan Demmings?"

"Yessir."

"When did'ja see him last?"

"Yesterday."

"'Bout what time?"

"Oh, in the afternoon."

"Huh. Well, it seems like Nathan done disappeared. We've got a whole mess of questions for the boy.

"Margaret, if yuh hear from Nathan, call us at the courthouse."

"Yessir."

I flopped in the chair, flabbergasted. "They're lookin' for Nate."

"Nate ain't kilt nobody," Fannie said. "Why would he wanna kill his daddy? Nate ain't have no . . . what'cha call it?"

"Motive," Robert said.

"That's right. He ain't got no motive tuh do such a thang. Nate and Marlene prob'ly the onliest people who loved that old fart."

"Fannie, but—"

"But nuthin'. We done known that boy all his natural-born life, and he ain't mean that way."

"Fannie's right," William said. "Nate didn't . . . couldn't do anythang like that. Ain't in his nature."

"Then, William, who did?"

———— •◦• ————

The radio and television carried nothing but coverage of Hollis's death. They said Hollis and his kin were aristocrats, not from here, but from Georgia. That was news to me; I thought the money came from Miss Ophelia's family. Hollis's mammy, Gwendolyn Rhodes, was from Atlanta and had met Hollis's pappy there. His daddy, George, served as a captain in the Confederate army, and his family had plenty of money, too.

Then I remembered that Marlene's last name was Rhodes. Did Hollis's mother's folks buy Marlene before the war ended, and did Marlene continue living with 'em after emancipation? That would clarify a mess of issues.

They said when George and Gwendolyn married, the family moved to Hampton, where he opened the First Bank of Hampton in eighteen and seventy-six. Hollis was born the next year. They showed a picture of the family right after Hollis's birth. It was one of those old-timey pictures. George stood all straight and Gwendolyn sat in a chair wearing a long white dress with ruffles fitted tight around her neck. On the floor, sitting at Gwendolyn's feet, looking like a baby doll in her Sunday-going-to-meeting outfit, was a little colored girl. I got closer, and I about fell out of my chair. It was Marlene. Why didn't Marlene ever say anything? She had known Hollis all her life!

For Marlene to be in the picture meant that Hollis's mammy considered her part of the family, and by her dress, she sho' wan't the family servant. But how and why did Marlene become his servant and appear to have nothing? How do you explain that? Marlelne didn't seem to be lettered either, but if you went by the way they dressed her, you'd think they would have educated her, too. And what about the lock of braided hair, the feather, the pressed rose, and the wedding ring? I suppose we'll never discover the meaning behind those either. They sho'nuf took that stuff with them to their graves.

Then two timid taps on the screen door broke the train of my speculations. It was White Candy. She had snatched her hair into a bun. A strand of pearls hung around her neck and rested just below the scooped neckline of a plain black dress with matching stockings and shoes. I couldn't remember when I'd seen her last, and with some surprise, I said,

"Candy?"

"Margaret. I'm sorry tuh intrude, but somethin' awful has happened."

"I'm sorry for yo' loss," I said.

"Thank you, but it is worse than that. May I come in?"

I opened the screen door. She glanced around the room, spotted Tilda's family pictures on the mantlepiece, and froze but regained her composure.

"They arrested Nate."

"Nonsense. He wud'den kill a fly. Why would he kill his daddy?"

"The servants heard Nate and Daddy arguin', and—"

"That dud'en mean a thang. They always fought like cats and dawgs 'bout sump'em or the other."

"But this differed from the rest. They say Nate was furious; kept sayin' he was gonna kill Daddy."

"Oh, that was jest talk. Nate didn't do it. Not to his daddy."

"Sheriff Toler found a gun right outside the parlor's French doors. They believe it's the same weapon that killed Daddy."

"So?"

"Nate's fingerprints are on the gun."

"Oh, my Lawd. Lawd Jesus." I took to a chair.

"They have him in the jail in New Harmony, but they're movin' him tuh Hampton."

"We haf tuh do sump'em."

"Well, I came home as soon as I got the call from Sheriff Toler."

"Did'cha talk to Nate?"

"He was on his way tuh Atlanta when they stopped him b'foe the state line. He says he's innocent, but the sheriff thinks otherwise."

"Lawd. Whut are we gonna do?"

"I came here tuh . . ." She swallowed and straightened herself. "Alexander Bouchard is the finest lawyer who has ever set foot in a courtroom. We need him tuh represent Nate. I don't know of anyone 'round here tuh whom I would entrust Nate's life. If yuh asked, Alexander would consider doin' it for you and yo' daughter."

"Oh, I don't know. Floyd and yo' daddy ran him out'ah here, and I think he's scared tuh come back. Whut about gittin' Leroy?"

"A colored lawyer cain't represent him. They'd hang Nate for sure. Alexander is his only chance."

"When William comes home, I'll send a telegram."

"We cain't wait. We need to send a telegram now. Besides, Nate says he needs tuh talk tuh yuh right away."

"Lemme git my things."

Candy went on out to the car. I fumbled around, got the children's address, and left a note for William. When we were halfway to town, Candy stopped the car and turned to me, damming back the tears.

"Margaret, there's somethin' I've wanted tuh tell yuh. I'm so sorry for how I treated yuh b'foe and for my actions after losin' Alexander. Hatred and bitterness consumed me; I was so lost and filled wid so much sadness that I finally sought help. When I found a church home and relied on my pastor and prayer, I found peace in Scripture and felt brand new. Nate was there for me, too. I regret sayin' those dreadful things when William Alexander was a baby. I hope yuh can find it in yo' heart tuh forgive me."

"Lawd, honey, that's been twelve long years ago. Wid the Lawd in yo' heart, we are sisters in faith, and we haf tuh stay strong and focused if we're tuh win this fight. So, let's git on in town and send this telegram. We haf tuh git our boy out'ah jail."

"You're right." She reached for my hand, and I shook hers.

When we got to the Western Union office, I crafted the telegram, signed my name, and showed it to Candy.

-alexander-

in desperate need of help—nate arrested for killing his father. he's innocent. you're our only hope. please come quickly.

-margaret butler-

Candy paid for the telegram, and we headed to the jailhouse, but Nate wasn't there. They had moved him to the county jail in Hampton.

Lord, how did we ever get here?

TWENTY-EIGHT

Unto Every Season

On the way home, the deceptiveness of Indian summer intrigued me. Trees showed hints of fall's blood-red and yellow hues peeping through the green. But the lingering heat diverted folks' attention, and they were less likely to notice the first crinkle of brown adorning leaves just before they fell into their demise. As we drove to New Harmony, the sun and the shadows it birthed raced across the countryside. Rolling fields of grass floated like rivers pushed along by an agitated wind. Meadows of wildflowers bobbed their faces of color to the sky, while the pines, so tall and dark, anchored their roots deep and punched holes skyward. Up there, a white-kissed moon hung like jewelry. Clouds disappeared, then reappeared to dance their shadows across the flat lands, hills, and valleys.

It wasn't enough to lift the doldrums surrounding my heart, but I remembered what Mammy used to say:

"Yuh gots tuh remember tuh seek beauty and love even when you's in the middle of sorrow. Rejoicin' when yuh needs it most."

My thoughts turned to Tilda and Alexander, wondering how they would react when they received the telegram. Would they be willing to return? If they did, I suspected our little Curly Top wouldn't know how to behave in New Harmony after spending years in France. But I suppose he felt free over there, and having wetted his whistle on freedom, backsliding to all the *yesssir, nossir* of Southern life as a colored person would be difficult—dropping his head and fixing his eyes on the floor when he talked to white folks.

The phone rang throughout the night. We weren't home for anybody. I balled myself up in one corner of the bed and made a nest for my nagging thoughts. I recalled the wind on Pleasant Ridge, the sun setting behind the river valley, and the light shifting to darkness. Marlene came to mind. I considered how her and Hollis's lives intertwined, and I wondered about the secrets they carried to their graves. Images of Tilda and Alexander emerged. Did they still love each other? I thought about my dead son and remembered those years when Nate and Thad played together. How did Nate become so close, like a son? But I reckoned that's what love is. If you only love folks like you, it hasn't challenged you much. You may as well be loving yourself, and that was enough to fling me into tomorrow and prepare me for my jailhouse meeting with Nate.

The next day, Nate, escorted by a deputy sheriff, entered a room containing a table and two chairs. We sat across from each other. A single fixture hanging from the ceiling illuminated the table. I surveyed his face, and while I had seen him countless times and had been familiar with his facial expressions, the one he wore fascinated me. The wisdom of the ages rested there, and I longed to hug him, but they wouldn't let me.

"How yuh holdin' up, Nate?"

"Strange . . . I don't know how, but . . . I've been filled wid such peace," he said. "A dream revealed somethin' to me this morning. I heard a voice from deep within and recalled words I'd learned as a child.

"To everything there is a season, and a time to every purpose under the heaven:

"A time to be born, and a time to die; a time to plant, and a time to pluck up that which is planted;

"A time to kill, and a time to heal; a time to break down, and a time to build up;

"A time to cast away stones, and a time to gather stones together; a time to embrace and a time to refrain from embracing;

"A time to get, and a time to lose; a time to keep, and a time to cast away;

"A time to rend, and a time to sew; a time to keep silence, and a time to speak . . ."

Then I finished it:

"A time to love, and a time to hate; a time of war, and a time of peace."

He cleared his throat.

"I have something to tell yuh that might break your heart; you might not love me after you hear it."

"Nuthin' can do that, boy."

He closed his eyes. As his eyelids met, he said, "I can see his face now . . . I can feel his breath." His chair squeaked as he shifted his weight. He said, "I loved Thad, Miss Margaret, wid all my heart." From the weight of it, his chin drifted to his chest.

"Well, of course," I said.

"But yuh don't understand."

"What?"

"The affection yuh share wid yo' husband, I shared wid Thad," he said, staring at my lips.

My hands surrendered the table; they fell and stiffened in my lap. "Whut are yuh sayin'? Do you mean . . . are yuh sayin' . . ." I couldn't bring myself to say the word . . . but neither could he. Nate mumbled,

"Yes, ma'am."

I fell back into the chair. A rush of air filled my chest. I felt it striving to push my soul out of this darkness. In wrestling with his revelation, and given my world and considering my raising, I was only able to stammer. I floundered in this unchartered territory. I labored to say something—to find the proper words to chain into a sentence, but perplexity snatched my wits. So I cheated and said,

"If a man also lie with mankind, as he lieth with a woman, both of them have committed an abomination: they shall surely be put tuh death; their blood shall be upon them."

My eyes shifted from the table to his. I said, "Love should only exist between women and men. It ain't natural for two men to feel that way 'bout each other."

Choking down some angry tears, I continued, "Boy, why yuh wanna tell me this? Why yuh tryin' tuh taint my baby's memory?"

"I hesitated to tell yuh, but it's bound tuh come out in court. They're gonna use it as my reason tuh kill daddy. I would rather yuh learn this from me."

"Did'ja kill yo' daddy?"

"No, ma'am. I didn't.

"After yuh told me 'bout Floyd's telephone call, I went tuh Floyd's, and he was full of liquor.

"The first words out of his mouth were: 'You're a goddamn sissy, a fuckin' faggot. If I'd known yuh twisted that way, yuh could'ah pulled on mine. But shit, boy . . . even bein' one of them wan't uh'nuf for yuh! Yo' sorry ass had the gall tuh fornicate wid a nigga.' Then Floyd chuckled and whispered, 'I told Daddy,' all in my face."

"How did he know?"

"Floyd said he had seen us. He asked if I'd felt any eyes spyin' when I was wid Thad b'foe. But that night, him and Daddy, after huntin', stumbled upon us. They saw us kiss each other. 'Boy, yuh're disgustin' . . . an abomination,' he said, and he said he had never seen anythang so vile."

"So, you met Thad 'foe the killin'?"

"Yes. When you told Thad you wanted him tuh take somethin' to Sister Jamison, he asked me tuh wait for him . . . said he had somethin' he wanted tuh give me. I walked a bit, yuh know, waitin' for him. As he approached, I saw a truck parked in the distance but I didn't think about it. He took somethin' from his shirt pocket and gave it tuh me but told me not tuh read it until later. We hugged and kissed good night. I was near home when I heard a noise, soundin' lac'uh car backfiring."

"What else did Floyd say?"

"He said that neither of us deserved tuh live, but Daddy spared me. Then, wid his eyes stretched wide, he insisted Thad was back, hauntin' him, but he pumped his chest full of air and shouted he had never feared niggas. Then he said, 'I'm tellin' yuh, boy, like I tried to tell . . .'"

Nate dropped his head.

"Whut did he say?"

"He said, 'Like I tried tuh tell that sweet, pretty Margaret.'"

The chair caught my back. "The thought of him soilin' my skin . . . I'd rather jump from this buildin' than think 'bout that anymo' . . . but Floyd and yo' daddy—*tuh'gether*? *Huntin'*? I thought they fell out over Vivian. Did'ja ask him 'bout that?"

"I did."

"And whut did Floyd say?"

"Got puffed up and said, 'We ain't like you, boy. We're men! But we're blood, too. Blood *always* thicker than water. That's why Daddy saved yo' sorry ass. Yuh got that?'"

"I reckon that's true."

"He said Daddy might have gotten mad 'cause he had relations wid Vivian, but Daddy wasn't gonna let no son of his have relations wid the likes of a nigga boy. That, he said, was uh'nuf reason for Daddy and him tuh come tuh'gether.

"'Besides, wid a woman like her, I did what any man was *'posed* tuh do,' he said. 'Fucked her!' Then he threw his head back and laughed; 'But yuh and yo' nigga ain't deserve any kind of forgiveness.'

"Floyd said our fornicatin' was unnatural; that demanded somethin' altogether different. He said he and Daddy could unite tuh combat that kind of wickedness."

"Whut happened?"

He replayed the events for me, and my boy's murder spun out like something reported by Edward R. Murrow on television.

The night was hushed—even the birds trembled their songs into silence.

"They had parked their truck down the road, and when they came out of the woods, they saw us embrace and kiss."

Hollis and Floyd waited for Nate's departure, and when Thad got farther down the road, the truck raced toward him; its headlights hit my boy in the back of the head.

My heart raced, and I took a deep breath.

The tires dug their treads to a stop.

"They got out of the truck, and Thad walked faster. He musta seen Floyd's shotgun.

"They called tuh him, but he didn't reply."

I imagined Thad's thoughts of panic. *He wanted to run, but he had that damn pot of soup.*

"When they caught up tuh Thad, Floyd spun Thad around; the soup spilled, splashin' onto Floyd. He glanced at me and said, 'Now, Nate. You know how I dislike gittin' soiled.'

"Floyd cursed Thad and sent him tuh the ground wid his fist."

Oh, my God! Please tell Nate to stop.

He didn't.

"Thad tried tuh git up, but Floyd planted his foot on his chest; he unzipped his britches and told Thad to suck it. He grinned at me and said, 'Ain't that whut y'all did for one uh'nuther?'

"Thad struggled tuh his feet and told Floyd tuh go to hell. Daddy saw red and snatched the gun from Floyd's hands."

I imagined Hollis's mind shifted, remembering when he had to kill another nigga, that Gator who killed his sweet little Selma, his baby. The shotgun blast from both barrels exploded into sparks of fire and a puff of smoke. It unleashed pellets that ripped open Thad's red-plaid shirt, opened his chest, spewed his blood onto one Oxford shoe, and knocked the other shoe from his foot.

It laid sideways.

Untied.

In fallen leaves.

"Then Floyd said, 'Yeah, Daddy got rid of that no-good sorry nigga, and both o' yuh fairies . . . pansies . . . don't deserve tuh foul the air that us decent folks breathe.'

"He grabbed himself, looked at what he held in his hand, and said, 'I used my hose on him.'"

Tears stood in Nate's eyes. "He peed on him, Miss Margaret."

The backs of his hands wiped away tears.

He went on.

"Floyd said, 'Hell, I'm gonna make sure yuh die, too. Daddy didn't know my intentions, but yuh're gonna die. I learned 'bout the will. Watch what I tell yuh.' He laughed and said, 'Boy, yuh're gonna swing just like the niggas swing when we strin' 'em up.'

"Miss Margaret, I had no idea he hated me so much. I stumbled toward the front door wid him pressed up behind me. He got in front of me; I dodged 'round him. We played tag 'til we reached the door. When I got outside, I puked, but he laughed and said, 'Watch out, boy. You're next.' He kept laughin' and sayin' that: 'Watch out, boy. You're next!'"

I slumped in the chair.

"Now we know," I said.

He dropped his head and asked, "Why did he haf'tuh die like that? Why? 'Cause we loved each other? Why did Daddy haf'tuh kill him and leave me here all alone?" Nate sobbed. "When they killed Thad, I didn't wanna live. How can yuh live when somebody steals the person who makes yuh whole?"

His words stunned me, and shock trampled my feelings, but I asked, "Whut did'ja do when yuh got tuh the Big House?"

He sat straight up, as if a puppet master had pulled the right strings, and wiped his eyes with the heels of his hands.

He sniffled and said, "I drove home tuh confront Daddy. He was in the parlor. I walked in and slammed the door behind me. Daddy said, 'Nathan. You seem a little edgy, son.'

"'I've come from Floyd's, and he told me everything.'

"'Nathan, Floyd always likes tuh stir up trouble. He exaggerates.'"

I imagined the scene with Hollis's slow, deliberate speech up against Nate's fury.

"I asked, 'Why did yuh kill him?' He looked puzzled and asked, 'Killed who, son?'

"'Thad Butler,' I said, and I screamed, 'Yuh son-of-a-bitch!' as loud as I could. I told him not tuh hide behind his goddamn Southern smile." I slapped his face, but Daddy grabbed me by the shirt collar and pulled me close.

"He told me we had a perverted love. I pushed him away, and I reminded him about Marlene and the two babies he fathered—one of 'em born when he had a wife. I told him he didn't even give Burton or Leroy a dime's worth of attention. '*That's* perverted!' I said."

"'Boy, whut do yuh know 'bout my life?' he said. 'Sides, I tried to tell Margaret.'"

"Tried tuh tell me what?" I asked.

"He said he chooses the time and he decides the payment, and that *y'all*, the Butlers, had to pay up. I screamed, '*For what?*'

"I will *never* forgit his tone, Miss Margaret." Nate's back pressed against the chair, and he said, "'You wanna know? All right. For the land and the money Ophelia left them; for the courthouse bein' full of nigga-lovers, allowin' those high-minded niggas in white-face tuh keep it; for Jake, thinkin' his color ain't matter—gittin' so *uppity* that he couldn't work my fields anymore; for their whore, Tilda, breakin' my precious baby's heart, seducin', *stealin'* her husband; for Tilda havin' Alexander's bastard and havin' the *audacity* to brang it back here, for the *whole* town tuh see; for Alexander *ownin'* that, that little curly-head bastard, the seed of their fornication. Most of all, for you, Nate; for whut that nigga, Thad Butler, did tuh my *blood* . . . the disgrace.'

"'And if *that* wan't uh'nuf . . . tuh see both of yuh kissin', and then the disrespect he flung at Floyd . . . well, those thangs screamed *settlin'-up time*. That shotgun blast dealt wid *all* them insults. Hell, after hearin' the thud of his body meetin' the ground and seein' him sprawled out in that ditch, I finally felt pacified. I took sump'tem them niggas prized: their precious little Thad. 'Sides, that nigga never knew his place either.'"

Nate continued, "He walked towards me and said, 'Ain't no need tuh thank me for settlin' the score . . . no need tuh thank me for savin' you from *that!*'

"Daddy shoved his hands in his pockets and fumbled wid some loose change. He told me he had hoped the army would make me a man, and that's why he didn't interfere when they drafted me; thought I'd 'git that foolishness out of my head.'

"B'foe he walked away, he said, 'Walk carefully. I won't always be able tuh protect yuh.'"

Nate continued, "I tried tuh git him tuh realize that Thad was a human being. He sneered and said, 'Look here, boy. Don't preach tuh me 'bout no niggas. What's the value of a nigga's life? Huh! Ain't worth these two copper pennies.'" Then he tossed them at my feet.

Nate said he thought about Thad then, and his passions rose.

"We slugged it out until we ended up on the floor. I was so furious I didn't even know what I was doin' . . . I had my hands locked tight 'round his throat, and when I came to myself, I realized that hatred had brought us to this place. I jumped up, and I left through the French doors off of the parlor. I was confused at first, but I decided tuh drive tuh Atlanta and see Candy. They arrested me b'foe I crossed the state line."

"Was he alive when yuh left?"

"I swear."

Placing my hands on the table and taking a breath, I said, "We sent for Alexander, and I'm waitin' on a response from the telegram Candy sent. We've done all we can do for now."

"There's one more thing, Miss Margaret. Floyd isn't the only one tuh have seen Thad."

I leaned closer.

"Whut?"

"In my dream, right after hearin' the Bible piece, somethin' touched my shoulder, and I woke up. I wasn't groggy either . . . I was wide awake just like that, and I recognized a familiar scent, like rain hittin' the earth when it's hot and dry."

He closed his eyes.

"I swear it was him. Thad sat on the edge of my bed and kissed my forehead; he fingered the scars left on my wrists. 'That's when you cried for me,' he said. He kissed my wounds closed. I cried, and Miss Margaret, he caught each one of those tears, and he held them in his hands. When he opened his hands, he blew on 'em, and my jail cell filled wid stardust, like cascadin' flecks of light. They sparkled for a while, and then they disappeared.

"'Take me wid yuh,' I said. 'It's too hard livin' wid'out you.' Then he said, 'B'foe we were born, we revel in heaven. But as yuh were 'bout tuh depart, I cried and lamented so. Yuh heard me, and yuh prayed tuh God that I'd be born and incarnate wid you.'"

Nate opened his eyes.

"That's part of what he had written in his tablet just b'foe they murdered him. I memorized it a long time ago. It's in my wallet, wid the uh'ther things they took when they arrested me. If anything should happen tuh me, I want yuh tuh have it." I nodded; he picked up again.

"I understood it all when he crawled up beside me and I held him in my arms. No matter what happens tuh me, his love waits for me."

He closed his eyes and whispered,

"I don't want yuh tuh hate me."

"Boy. How could I hate yuh? I've loved yuh all yo' life, and I know whut kinda heart yuh have. If yuh want forgiveness, yuh'll haf'tuh git that from the Lawd. I need time tuh wrestle wid this.

"Thad was my heart, and I loved him until the day Hollis took him 'way from me."

"I love you, Miss Margaret."

"And I, you."

I left burdened by Nate's words, unsure what to say to William and the family.

TWENTY-NINE

Cain't Build No Bridge

Night stretched its fingers through the daylight it had not yet consumed, and unfamiliar shadows sprouted alongside the road as William and I made our way back home. William accepted the quiet. He sensed that I sat overwhelmed. I tried to embrace what I had learned, but the thought of my son being one of "them" felt like an affliction. I wrestled with saying *that word*, the one I knew some folks use to mock them. I tried to reconcile Thad loving a man instead of a woman. His "truth" challenged everything I knew about love. If he had lived, having no grandbabies to spoil would have been another kind of loss.

Twilight still lingered when we got home, and I grabbed William by the hand.

"We need tuh talk."

"Best go on up tuh the Ridge," he said, placing his arms around me as we walked in twilight's ebb to Pleasant Ridge.

The Big House loomed in the distance, and I wondered what occupied Candy there. They hadn't had Hollis's funeral yet. They were waiting for Candy's daughter, who lived in England. I kept staring at the Big House, lamenting what happened that night. As twilight disappeared, darkness enveloped us. Yet a radiant moon illuminated our faces.

"I cain't remember when I was here last," William said. "Whut did Nate say that got'cha so twisted up inside?"

"He didn't kill his daddy. I believe him one hundred percent."

"But that ain't whut's troublin' yuh."

"Nah."

I couldn't pull my words together. I took a deep breath and, seeking to prepare the ground, I said, "Yuh remember when Thad was born, and how yuh sobbed when he cried his first whiff of air. Remember how much love flipped in yo' chest when yuh held him that time? Hold on to that."

He took a long breath, surrendering it with a tentative "Okay."

I cleared my throat and said,

"Thad and Nate loved . . ."—I shut my eyes—"one uh'nuther."

"Everybody knows they were like brothers."

"More than that. William, they loved each other, lac'uh man and a woman." The words stuck in my throat like a man's last sighs at the end of a hangman's noose.

William sat speechless. When he couldn't hold it any longer, he coughed up, "*Sissies*. You mean they were sissies?"

I closed my eyes and nodded.

"*Nah! Nah!* Not my boy! Not my Thad! Nah, you wrong!"

"Yes, William. It's the truth."

"Stop!"

He jumped up like he wanted to run.

"That's why they killed him."

"Well, I'm glad somebody else did, so I wud'den hafta."

I took to my feet, spun him around, and said, "He was yo' flesh! Made with yo' seed, and he came out my body! Don't'ja *dare* say that. Who do yuh think yuh are, William Butler? Hollis murdered our boy, and Floyd peed in his face. He had none of us tuh protect him, nobody who loved him when death took him. But we cherished his birth, and we ached when you . . . you, William Butler, laid his blood-soaked body on the bed where he was born.

"We married over thirty-two years ago, but I never thought *shame* would describe you. Don't'ja *dare* say that 'bout *our* son!"

With the stars adorning the heavens and the moon anointing his head, William kissed the earth. He howled,

"Oh God!"

I knelt beside him, pulled his hands from his face, and lifted his chin.

Tears streaked his cheeks, mucus coated the ridges of his lips, and anguish fueled the heaving body I embraced.

"Does it change the feelin' in yo' heart for yo' baby? Does it erase the love yuh had for yo' son? Is he less handsome in yo' eyes?"

"I'm sorry," he said in a whisper.

My voice quivered, but I didn't fumble for the words.

"Yuh didn't mean it. It's all right." I rubbed his back and kissed his neck. He pulled away.

"For six years, I've blamed myself for not being wid him that night. A man is expected tuh protect his family." He wiped his eyes. "I didn't cry for my boy either. Oh, I grieved, but I didn't cry like I was 'posed tuh. I didn't 'cause my manhood got in the way."

But William cried on Pleasant Ridge. I reckoned he wept over the missed opportunities and the part of Thad that William would never comprehend. He acted like a lot of folks would, but us colored folks should know better. Empathy and compassion should be second nature since we've had enough meanness heaped on us. We ought to understand what it means to have your face in the sand with somebody's foot on your neck stifling your breathing. Besides, William should have known that his thoughts about Nate and Thad would be like two burrowing ticks. They would demand he do a whole heap of scratching before they fled.

We stayed on the Ridge late into the night, trying to understand everything we had learned. When we returned to the house, the Western Union man had just entered the gate, and upon seeing us, he handed William the message.

"Thank you," William said. It was from Alexander.

Will arrive hampton tomorrow at 3:30 p.m.

    Love,

Alexander

"He didn't say anythang 'bout the children or Tilda. Wonder if they're comin'," I said.

It was late afternoon when William came back from the airport with Alexander. My heart sank as I glanced from the chair and saw only him in the car. He still was one of the best-looking white men I had ever seen. I walked to the middle of the yard, and he greeted me with a hug and smile.

"Miss Margaret, wonderful to see you."

"Whut's wid this Miss Margaret stuff? Yuh're family now. Call me Margaret." His immense smile lit me up.

"Where are Tilda and the children?" I asked. "I'd hoped they'd come, too."

"Tilda wasn't able to reschedule some of her engagements, but she and the boys will come later. I brought plenty of pictures."

"Come on in the house. Yuh stayin' wid us?" I asked.

"You think it's—"

"Yuh're comin' tuh defend a Demmings. That's uh'nuf for folks tuh forgit the rest, at least for a spell."

"Well, I just wondered."

"Yuh can stay in Thad's old room," William said. "So, yo' limp's gone, 'long wid that cane."

"My leg is much better. Thank God."

William took Alexander's bags and placed them in Thad's room. When he joined us in the kitchen, I sat at the table, flipping through the pictures Alexander had brought. William stood close to the back of the chair with his arms draped over my shoulders.

"Oh, Margaret. Ain't they big now."

"William Alexander is twelve, you know, and Thad is six. He's Thad's idol; they are so good tuh'gether."

"How's Tilda?" I asked.

"Oh, she's making quite a name for herself. We can't go down the street these days without somebody coming up asking for her autograph."

"Git out'ah here!" William said.

"They're talking about her being in a movie."

"My word! William, we raised a star."

Then Alexander asked, "How's Nate?"

All the joy left.

"He's fine. He said he didn't do it. It's gonna be hard tuh prove, 'cause he and Hollis had a whale of an argument that night; sheriff claims tuh have the murder weapon."

"Dud'en look hopeful, does it, Alexander?" William said.

"No, but speaking with Nate is crucial. I need to talk to Candy, too. What should I expect from her?"

"She has changed, Alexander," I said. "Candy begged me tuh send for yuh. She said yuh were the only one who could save Nate."

"It's been a long time since I've represented anyone. Has Christine arrived?"

"A few days ago," William said.

"She came over from London to visit earlier in the year. Allowed us to talk and afforded her the space to spend time with William Alexander."

"I'm glad 'bout that," I said.

"Well, yuh got'cha work cut out for yuh here. Margaret, should we tell him 'bout Nate and Thad?"

"Yeah."

Alexander didn't appear shocked about Nate and Thad's relationship but expressed his concerns.

"It's going to be harder than I thought." He took a deep breath. "Maybe I should see Candy tonight."

"Well, call her first. No need tuh walk up there if she ain't home," William said. I gave Alexander the number. Candy told him to come on up.

When Alexander returned, he dropped into the chair at the kitchen table.

"Floyd—why, I thought the old man was . . . "

"Evil," I said.

"Yeah."

"Both of 'em ain't worth pig snot. Never held even the value of a plug nickel," William said.

"So, he was up there?" I asked.

"Floyd arrived as I reached for the doorknob. Is he a heavy drinker?"

"Zora Mae, their housekeeper, says so."

Alexander stood up and stuck his hands in his pockets. "Well, when he saw me, he said, 'Alexander Bouchard. I thought the boys ran yuh out'ah town. So, why yuh back here? Ah, that's right. You's uh lawyer . . . came to save a nigga-lover and a murderer, did'cha?'"

"Oh, Alexander. That sounds jest like him," I said.

"I didn't open my mouth. Then he said, 'Seems like Candy has forgiven you. I don't hafta.' Stuck the cigar in'tuh his mouth, took a long draw, and blew smoke in my face."

"Oh, it was the way he sounded when he had me in the alleyway . . . when he tried to . . . ain't he an evil thang?" And the thought of it shot through me like a dose of castor oil.

William draped his arms around my shoulders and asked, "Whut did Candy say?"

"She's willing to spend and do whatever it takes to help Nate. She gave me the names of several investigators, and she suggested I contact Leroy."

"Leroy?" William asked.

"She told me using Leroy would git Nate hung for sure," I said.

"He can't argue the case in court, but she thinks, and I agree, that Leroy could assist me; he's familiar with the lay of the land. Besides, they are half-brothers, and when Marlene passed, Candy said the boys became very close."

"Yeah, they did," I said.

"They'll have the preliminary hearing in a few days," Alexander said.

"Whut's that?" William asked.

"That's where the district attorney attempts to convince the judge there are reasonable grounds to believe Nate killed Hollis. We'll also learn something about the strength of their case, but we'll enter a plea of not guilty."

"Of course," I said.

"Anything we can do?" William asked.

"Pray. It's been a long time since I've been in a courtroom."

———— ••• ————

The following day, Alexander was bright-eyed and bushy-tailed.

"Alexander, yuh want some coffee?" I asked.

"Oh, that smells mighty good. Tilda has gotten hooked on that French coffee. It's a bit too strong for my taste. Give me A&P any day of the week."

"Are yuh ready tuh go slay Goliath?" William asked on his way to the barn.

"Seems like we only have a slingshot," Alexander said.

"The Good Book says that's plenty," I said.

"It's going to be very difficult. I couldn't sleep a-tall last night," he said, taking a sip of coffee. "I need to talk to Nate; get some answers to my questions. I better get out of here."

"But you didn't eat any breakfast," I protested.

"Men!" I said as he dashed out of the house with practically nothing in his stomach. He didn't get too far because William raced from the barn, stopping him before he reached the car. He was animated, and his head bobbed while he talked. Alexander did a right good bit of nodding, too, but Alexander's bright smile became the concluding rite. He got in our old car and drove off. William eyed the house but avoided coming near it. He suspected I'd ask him what they had talked about, and he was right, but before I could pursue him, Robert pulled up.

——— ◆ ———

Since our trip to the Ridge, William had said nothing about his feelings about Thad and Nate, but about a week before the trial, he dreamt about Thad. That Sunday, he and Thad wrestled. Monday night, they fished. On Tuesday, he and Thad worked in the mill together, but on Wednesday, they flew kites. I told him he should talk to Thad.

On the evening before the trial, I felt Thad's presence. I took a deep breath and held it for a long time. I wondered if Thad would appear in William's dreams that Thursday night. Curiosity buzzed in my mind that Friday morning when I found William sitting at the kitchen table.

He spoke softly at first.

"Yuh remember when yuh told me 'bout the two of 'em."

"Yeah. Whut uh'bout it?"

"I ain't never been able tuh git shed of it. Don't reckon I ever will. I thought what they did wid each uh'ther wan't right. They ain't have no business lovin' each uh'ther like that. I thought uh'bout us and how I love yuh tuh pieces. How could he love Nate that way? I wished he had never

335

been born. That's how I felt.

"I didn't care 'bout Hollis and what he had done tuh the boy. I didn't want no sissy for a son, havin' him shamin' our family. And I didn't wanna look in Nate's face. Couldn't bear it.

"You cain't be no man and be one of them. Cain't have babies, and cain't even feel deep like womenfolk do. They ain't no man, and they ain't no woman. They're just a bunch of . . . freaks. Last night when he came tuh me in my dream, I told him this."

"Whut did he say?"

"Oh, he held quiet . . . kept his head down whilst I told him these things. When I finished, he lifted his head, and I seen . . . I seen . . ." but William dropped his head.

"Whut?"

I asked again and again, but William locked his mouth tighter than a diamondback terrapin.

Finally, he lifted his head, cracking his lips to say, "Thad said, 'Look at whut God made.' He smiled at me like nobody had ever smiled b'foe. Then his face . . . his face—"

"Whut about his face, William?"

"It changed."

"How?"

"It changed from his face to my face, then yours, and then I saw every member of our family's face, one after the other, but then I saw uh'nuther face. It smiled, and sump'tem passed through me that spoke, 'Love.' But there were no words. It spoke, but there were no words, cain't explain it, but alls it said was, 'Love.'"

"Who was it?"

"I ain't . . ."

He smiled in recognition but lowered his head and, refusing to answer, he said, "I don't know."

But then I smelled my baby, and when William came over and pulled his pajama top to my nose, Thad was all over him. We fell into each other's arms.

But even this wasn't enough to carry William forward. He still had one more river to cross.

It was November 11th, a month to the day after Hollis's murder, when the trial started, and folks packed the courtroom. All the colored folks sat in the balcony. Leroy couldn't sit with Alexander and Nate. They didn't want Nate getting hanged because he had a colored lawyer at his table. He sat with me, William, and Fast Fannie. Vivian and Floyd sat near the front, on the right side. Candy and Christine sat on the other side, behind where Nate sat. You should've seen Floyd. He seemed sad, looking worse than a whimpering dog who had suffered for years before meeting his heavenly pack. Floyd, however, feigned misery, but he held neither the dog's character nor its disposition.

In his opening statement, the district attorney said Nate killed his daddy because of the homosexual affair Nate had with Thaddeus Butler. A tremendous gasp swelled up from the folks in the courtroom. Everybody, all the colored folks, looked at me and Fannie, but we didn't turn or drop our heads in shame. He said,

"Nathan Demmings sought revenge, ladies and gentlemen. From the evidence, it will become apparent that the defendant went home that evening to confront his father, accusing him of murdering his lover some six years before. The testimony will reveal that during this confrontation, an enraged Nathan Demmings argued, fought with, and murdered his father, Hollis Rhodes Demmings. The motive is clear, ladies and gentlemen—revenge!"

He retrieved a gun and held it up.

"The murder weapon . . . the gun Nathan Demmings used to kill his father."

Then he talked about the witnesses he would call and how they would prove Nate was a cold-blooded murderer. And Nate had another motive; he would inherit a fortune upon Hollis's death. When he waved the gun around again, he said, "The defendant's fingerprints are on the murder weapon," and folks set the courtroom abuzz.

The judge's gavel hushed them so Alexander could address the court. Lord, if looks could save a man from the noose, Alexander's appearance would ensure Nate's freedom. You should have seen the five women in the jury box almost faint when he walked over and cast a smile to set the blood flaring up in their cheeks.

Alexander said it didn't matter if Nate was a homosexual. The question of his innocence didn't hinge on whom he loved. The jury needed to consider whether Nathan had the capacity and the means to kill Hollis. He said he would prove Nate had killed nobody, which meant the killer still ran free, and there were plenty of folks who had a motive. People feared Hollis but didn't love him.

How was he gonna prove those weren't Nate's fingerprints on that gun the district attorney had waved around? How was he gonna dispute that?

He said he would prove Nate was nowhere near the house when someone killed Hollis.

"I hope you will not let the way you feel about homosexuals and homosexuality cloud your sense of justice," Alexander said. "I know you understand a man's life is at stake. Upon hearing the evidence, you'll do the right thing and clear Nathan Demmings of these ridiculous charges. He is innocent."

Alexander smiled, and I watched the women in the jury box as he walked to his seat. They kept their eyes all over that fine white man. Yes, it was lust and licentiousness, but I thought, *Tall order, Alexander. Your looks ain't gonna be enough to make 'em forget Nate's homosexuality and their outrage that he laid up with a colored boy. Let's entrust this to the Lord.*

The judge adjourned the court; the trial would resume on Monday. Alexander conversed with Nate, and Candy reached over the railing to shake Alexander's hand. She hugged Nate. Christine hugged her daddy, but Floyd came over and said something that caused Candy to turn blood red. Floyd just walked away, smiling, as cool as you please.

William left as soon as the judge's gavel fell, and Fast Fannie and I waited outside the courthouse for Candy, Christine, and Alexander. Floyd watched from across the street, standing at the edge of the park, puffing on his cigar and blowing smoke rings into the sky.

Alexander, Christine, and Candy joined us, and I expressed my concerns until Leroy arrived and whispered something in Alexander's ear.

Alexander placed his hand on my shoulder and said, "It's too early for worry, Margaret. This is just the first round. Leroy and I are embarking on God's work."

"We're prayin'," Fannie shouted.

"We're going to need it," Alexander yelled as he ran off. Floyd waited until Alexander and Leroy were out of sight before he walked over.

"Margaret, yuh're lookin' rather stunnin' today. Is that dress new?"

I rolled my eyes, but Fast Fannie had clenched her fists. I grabbed her by her dress. He smiled, shoved the cigar in his mouth, and took a puff, caving in his cheeks. He blew a smoke ring into the air and settled his eyes on Christine.

"Christine, darlin'. Every time I feast my eyes on yuh, I'm stunned. Yuh're lookin' so . . . European. When I first laid eyes on yuh at Pleasant Bluff, I didn't recognize yuh." Christine didn't say one word. Then he turned his attention to Candy.

"Candy, for the life of me. Why trouble yo'self over this no-good who killed our father? Oh, darlin', is this yo' feeble attempt tuh git yo' husband back after he done run off wid that *colored* woman?"

He looked at me and smiled again.

"Y'all have a nice day." And with that, he strutted away.

THIRTY

He's Gone, Good and Gone

As Thanksgiving neared, there was little reason to celebrate. Nate was in jail, Tilda and the boys were in Paris, and Alexander and Leroy, who worked hard to defend Nate, seemed exhausted. Burton visited Nate as much as possible but was busy at Doc Rosenthal's clinic.

Nate's homosexuality didn't fret either Burton or Leroy. But if Nate did get through this rough spot, he would have to leave New Harmony. How could he have a life here? If he stayed, every time he turned around, somebody would rumor the creek bed gold: "Oh, he got away wid killin' his daddy 'cause he's rich." Or "Yuh know, he's one of them thangs." They'd treat him like a leper, pulling their children to the other side of the street, afraid Nate would turn them into sissies.

I wondered what folks said about my child behind my back. William hadn't gotten there. He hadn't crossed his river Jordan, you know. If William harbored such feelings, how would other family members feel about Nate, Thad, and the love they shared? I pondered on who approached whom first. Did my baby turn Nate into one, or was it Nate who seduced Thad? My voice whispered: *Perhaps they were two souls finding peace in each other's embrace.* I embraced that and reckoned that wisdom came from what Aunt Sarah called "the silent times."

Fast Fannie and I sat up in the balcony and watched every move the district attorney made during the trial. He called all kinds of folks to testify: the sheriff, the pistol expert, the colored people who worked for Hollis, the medical examiner, and Candy.

Floyd was his last witness.

You should've seen how he strutted to the witness stand with his head all reared back—a stallion about to mount a mare, full of himself.

He placed his hand on the Bible and swore to tell the truth.

"So help me God," he said.

Oh, he practiced real good. *A fully polished, practicing liar,* I thought.

He sat in the chair.

"Mr. Demmings, what happened the night Nathan arrived at your home, the evening they found your father murdered?" the district attorney asked.

"Oh, my word . . . that evening? Well, whilst I'm havin' a nightcap of brandy, the boy nearly broke down the door. He rambled on, accusin' me of doin' sump'em tuh the Butler woman, Margaret Butler. I told him he was bein' foolish. Of course, I had seen her in town. I remembered tippin' my hat tuh her and sayin' have a pleasant day as she walked on Market Street."

"What was Nathan's response?"

"The boy called me a liar and slapped me 'cross the face. I saw red, grabbed the boy, and told him I knew what he was. I spoke the truth: he was a no-good faggot, and he'd better be glad he had'en ended up like his colored lover, Thad Butler. Daddy took care of that disgrace, and the only reason Daddy spared him . . . well, he's kin."

"Did he accuse you—believing you were involved?"

"Why, of course. But I didn't have anythang tuh do wid the Butler boy's killin'. Everyone knows Daddy and I fell out a long time ago over uh'nuther indiscretion, which we don't need tuh discuss. Besides, everybody is aware of what happened. Ain't no sense in belaborin' the matter here.

"I 'pose the shame and losin' his lover, the colored boy he'd been sleepin' wid, was jest too much . . . he snapped, I think."

Floyd remained cool as a cucumber but slippery as an eel—*definitely* a practicing liar.

Alexander just stood, reserving the right to recall Floyd to the stand, which set everybody to muttering. I looked at Fast Fannie, and she read my discontent and whispered,

"Oh, Floyd is 'bout as slippery as greased goose shit."

"Alexander knows Floyd is lyin'. Why didn't he do sump'tem?"

Fannie shrugged her shoulders.

The court stood in adjournment, but my concerns were not. When I met Alexander and the rest of the family outside the courthouse, I sounded more like Fast Fannie than myself, with my jaws stuffed full of wind.

"Why didn't yuh say anythang tuh Floyd?" I demanded. "He had his hands in killin' my boy as sure as yuh were born, and he tried to *rape* me. You didn't *open yo' mouth!* Whut kinda lawyerin' is that? Do yuh know whut'ja doin'?"

"Miss Margaret, it's going as we expected," Leroy said.

"This is difficult," Alexander said. "But it isn't over yet. There's more here than you realize." He placed his hand on my shoulder. "Nate didn't do this. The truth will prevail. Please believe that."

I blew the rest of the air out of my jaws and nodded in agreement.

Alexander and Leroy headed off somewhere, leaving Fannie, Christine, Candy, and me standing there with the November air beating its ache into our faces.

When Fast Fannie and I arrived home, every light in the house was on.

"Did'ja fasten the door?" Fannie asked.

"Never do, and William is at work. Who's in our house?"

We sprang from the car as if we were ready to tear their heads off, but if they said, "Boo!" we'd jump as high as a jackrabbit, catching the smell of a cougar's fart. The screen door opened before we took two steps, and Curly Top and Bubba dashed out. Tilda stood in the doorway.

Lord, I cried so, the tears met under my chin. I picked up Bubba; I had him in my arms, but I couldn't pick up Curly Top. He had grown so. I walked to the door with Curly Top holding my waist, and I held Tilda for the first time in . . . Lord, how long had it been? Four years? Five years? I put Bubba down, and I threw my arms around her.

"Lawd child, lemme see yo' face."

I kissed her on the cheeks and said, "Baby, you haven't changed a bit. Alexander didn't say one word."

"Oh, he doesn't know, either. This is both of y'all's Thanksgiving surprise. Where's Daddy?"

"Workin', and I cain't wait to see William's face when he gets home." Fannie came up on the porch, and she hugged them, too.

"Lawd, y'all, it is too cold out here. Let's go in the house and sit where it's warmer," I said.

When we got inside, Tilda asked about the trial.

"Didn't yuh git my letters? I wrote yuh every day."

"In the last one I got, you told me about Thad and Nate."

"Well, whut'ja think 'bout that?"

"Many friends of mine are like that. In Paris, it's '*C'est la vie.*' You know, 'That's life.'"

"Listen tuh yuh, speaking French."

"Oh, you should hear the children. Their French is better than their English. It's been a constant struggle to keep their English going, particularly for Bubba. Oh, it's all right to call him Bubba in private, but, you know, not in public, at least not in France."

"Girl, hush. Ain't that a mess," Fannie said.

When Alexander walked through the door, he dropped his stuff, and those children ran around him like nobody's business. You should've seen it. They called him Pappa, you know. He reached for Tilda; he took the palm of his hand, ran it down her face until his fingers touched her lips, and caressed their ridges with his thumb. They kissed.

"I love you," he said. "I've missed you."

When William came home, the merriment resumed. I asked Fannie, "Whut'ja think 'bout this now?"

"Never thought much 'bout no white boy, but if you haf tuh have one in yo' family, I 'pose he'll do."

"Oh, Fannie. Yuh're gittin' soft. Yuh might as well admit it: you love Alexander, too."

"He all right . . . for a white boy." We laughed.

Fannie left, saying, "I'll see y'all in the morning. Glad y'all home."

We celebrated that night, and for the weekend, I took the troubles concerning Thad and Nate and chunked them out the window. We laughed and rejoiced, and William found some peace.

On Sunday, Leroy came by the house after church and got Alexander. They chatted in the yard until Alexander invited William to join them. They talked for a long spell; then William went to the barn. When he returned, he carried a crocus sack and gave it to Alexander. After taking a peep, he handed it to Leroy. Their heads set to bobbing again, and I wondered what they were up to. Leroy smiled, got in his car, and took off. The other two entered the kitchen as if they possessed nuclear secrets. I asked, "Whut y'all doin' out there? Plotting?"

All Alexander said was, "Trust. Margaret, trust." William winked at me.

"So, you aren't gonna tell me?" I said, directing my disbelief toward William.

"Nope. Cain't. Swore I wud'den, and I ain't never broke no promise. You know that."

"William Butler. I'm yo' *wife*!"

"That won't work this time. Like Alexander said: trust."

William's refusal shocked me, but I still had enough outrage and gumption to spew "*Well!*" to his departing back.

On Monday, Tilda stayed with the children so Fannie and I could watch the trial. We found our spots in the balcony. When the judge entered, we stood up like before, and everybody except Alexander took their seats.

"May I approach, Your Honor?" Alexander asked. The judge motioned for him. They talked, and then the judge motioned for the district attorney. They had a lengthy conversation until the judge ordered them to step back.

"The court stands in recess for one hour," the judge said.

Before we piled out of the courthouse, Alexander and Leroy talked to Nate.

Fannie and I got some coffee at the colored diner way on the other side of town, but by the time we took two sips, we needed to rush back. We returned just as the judge said, "Mr. Bouchard. I've considered your request. It's unusual, but considering its implications, the court grants the defense's petition. Court stands adjourned until Wednesday."

"Lawd. Whut's happened?"

"Guess us gonna haf'tuh trust . . . the white boy must know what he doin'," Fannie said.

———•◈•———

It didn't seem as if Wednesday would ever come. When it did, we rode together to the courthouse. Miss Bessie agreed to stay with the children.

A different tension hung in the air when we took our seats in the front row of the balcony. The judge entered, and Alexander asked if he could approach. They talked for a long time; the judge motioned for the district attorney again. More talk. Then, the judge motioned for a deputy. More talk. Then the judge said, "Step back."

They scattered.

"Mr. Bouchard, are you ready to proceed?"

"I am, Your Honor."

"Call your first witness."

"The defense recalls Eleanor Simms, Your Honor."

"You're still under oath, Miss Simms," the judge said.

"Yessir," she said.

The district attorney had already called Eleanor Simms to the stand.

"So, you heard the defendant and Mr. Hollis Demmings argue just as Hattie Starks, Burt Hanley, and Mason Miller have already testified." (They were the other folks working in the house, and Hollis had hired them when he employed Eleanor.)

"Yessir. Us in the kitchen workin', jest lac I tell the sheriff and the district attorney. We heard 'em arguin' sump'tem awful that night."

"I see, but I'm curious about one thing, Miss Simms."

"Yessir."

"Who left first?"

"Sir?"

"Who left the house first?"

"Well, let's see. Hattie and Mason left tuh'gether; Burt picked up and went tuh the attic. He said he wanted tuh rest. I left last."

"Did Hattie and Mason leave while Mr. Hollis and Nathan argued?"

"Nossir. They didn't leave 'til way later. Burt be in the kitchen for quite a spell, helpin' me put thangs away whilst we talked; then he left."

"Did you see him any more that evening?"

"Yessir. 'Bout ten minutes 'foe I leaves. Burt come tuh fetch sump'em he forgit."

"Did you see Mr. Hollis before you left?"

"Nossir. Didn't lac botherin' him, yuh know. He was uh' stickler 'bout thangs lac that."

"Did you hear any more arguing before you left?"

"Nossir."

"You were in the kitchen. Is that correct?"

"That's right."

"The kitchen, that's near where Mr. Hollis was?"

"Yessir, the kitchen be's close by."

"Did you leave the kitchen for any reason?"

"Nossir. Burt stayed right there wid me. Lac I said, he helped me put thangs away."

"Did you hear Nathan Demminngs leave the house?"

"Sho' did . . . caused quite a fuss when he did, too."

"I see. How much time elapsed between the argument's ending and you leaving the kitchen?"

"'Bout twenty minutes."

"During those twenty minutes, did you hear any gunshots before leaving the house?"

"Nossir."

"So, is it your testimony the house was quiet and you didn't hear any gunfire prior to leaving Pleasant Bluff that evening?"

"Yessir."

"Are you certain?"

"I am."

"One more thing. Did you notice Nathan Demmings's car in the driveway when you left?"

"No cars in the driveway then, but . . ."

"Yes?"

"There was a car, though. Parked tuh the side near the avenue's end."

"But it wasn't Nate Demmings's? Is that right?"

"It wan't his car."

"Thank you. I have no further questions."

The district attorney threw up his hands along with "no questions."

"Mr. Bouchard, yo' next witness."

"Mr. Burt Hanley."

"Let me remind you that you're still under oath," the judge said.

"Yes, Your Honor," he said.

"After Marlene Rhodes's death, you took over her living quarters in the attic when you became Mr. Hollis's butler. Is that correct?"

"Yessir, that's right."

"After you returned to your room, after leaving Miss Simms the second time, when did you hear gunshots?"

"'Bout thirty or forty minutes later."

"So the house was quiet for about fifty minutes, give or take?"

"I'd say so."

"When you ran downstairs after hearing gunshots, did you see Nathan Demmings in the vicinity?"

"Nah, he was long gone."

"Did you see anyone?"

"Allst I seen was a car hightailin' away in a ball of dust."

"Did you recognize the car?"

"Too dark."

"Thank you, Mr. Hanley."

"Your witness," Alexander said to the district attorney.

"No questions," he said.

So the house was quiet; there was an unknown car. So what? Nate still could have come back during those fifty minutes and killed Hollis. Alexander still ain't done nothing to disprove that. What about the gun? The fingerprints? That's what will send the boy to the electric chair.

"I call Julian McCutcheon." (He was the gun expert the district attorney had already called.)

"Mr. McCutcheon, I have questions about the State's exhibits: the murder weapon, the bullets retrieved from Mr. Demmings's body, and the one recovered from the parlor wall. Can you clarify something for the court?" Alexander asked.

"I'll try," he said.

"What troubles me is there's no report linking those bullets to the so-called murder weapon. Were tests conducted?"

"No, sir."

"Why not?"

"It didn't appear necessary."

"Because?"

"We found Nathan Demmings's fingerprints all over the weapon."

"The defense will prove that was an error, a faulty assumption," Alexander said. "I have no further questions." He swung around and shot, "Your witness," to the district attorney.

"The State has no questions."

"The defense calls Samuel Hawkins."

I turned to Fast Fannie. "Ever heard of anybody wid that name from 'round these parts?"

She shook her head. We were on the edge of our seats.

"For the record, Mr. Hawkins, please state your name and address."

"Samuel Hawkins, 06 Mellow Lane, Montgomery, Alabama."

On showing Hawkins the pistol, Alexander asked, "Have you ever seen what the district attorney calls People's Exhibit Number One before today?"

"Yes, sir," he said.

"Could you share your knowledge about this gun?"

"As yuh can see, it has a walnut grip. It's a Colt 1851 Navy revolver. General Lee carried one, but other soldiers purchased them b'foe goin' off tuh fight in the Civil War. In those days, it was a favorite."

"Why was that?"

"It's among the earliest belt-worn single-action revolvers. Folks like Jesse and Frank James, and the Youngers also fancied it as their favorite six-shooter."

"Please tell the court how you're acquainted with this weapon."

"It's one of a pair of pistols owned by my family."

"You mean there is another pistol identical to this one?"

"Yes, sir."

Alexander turned to the judge and said, "Your Honor. I'd like to recall this witness—unless there are objections."

"None, Your Honor, and I have no questions."

The judge turned to Hawkins and said, "You may step down, Mr. Hawkins, but please remain in the courtroom." Looking at Alexander, he said, "Mr. Bouchard, please continue."

"The defense calls William Butler."

Fast Fannie looked at me, and I looked at William. William winked at me and threw me a smile. I whispered to Fannie, "The sack . . . the one I told'cha about. That must be whut was in the crocus sack."

"Mr. Butler, please state your name and address for the record."

"William Butler. RD 33 New Harmony Road."

"Mr. Butler. Where were you the night of Mr. Hollis Demmings's murder?"

"Me and Robert Gardner searched for a no-count who had been threatenin' my wife. He tried tuh hurt her once b'foe, but he'd called on the phone, harassin' her again."

"She received the call prior to someone killing Mr. Demmings. Is that right?"

"Yeah. That's right."

"What did you and Mr. Gardner do, Mr. Butler?"

"We tracked this scoundrel down and followed him a ways, the best we could, but he must've got a whiff of us 'cause he managed tuh slip away."

"Mr. Butler, after that, what did you do?"

"We drove to that snake's den . . . found a spot in the woods opposite his place."

"And?"

"He drove up, right slow-like, then stopped; we seen him git out'ah his car and go in the house."

"How long did he stay in the house, Mr. Butler?"

"Never comes out. She did, wid Kearns. He jumped in his car and left.

She threw sump'em in her passenger seat. She grabbed a shovel and sack from the house and placed them in the trunk, then she takes off."

"And what did you and Mr. Gardner do, Mr. Butler?"

"We thought it mighty funny, peculiar. So, we followed her . . . uh . . ."

"Yes, Mr. Butler."

"Jus' felt sump'tem was wrong, yuh know. Cain't explain it, though."

"I see. And then what did you do?"

"We followed her. We seen her go tuh and from Mr. Hollis's house. She sneaks 'round on the side of his house, then she hightailed it down the avenue."

"Did you and Mr. Gardner continue following her?"

"We did."

"Mr. Butler, what did she do?"

"She drove way 'cross town. Well, 'tween here and New Harmony. She parks her car, gits out carryin' uh small box, opens the trunk, and hauls out the shovel and the crocus sack she had thrown in there. She puts the box in the sack and went in'tuh the woods a piece. I tracked her and watched her bury the sack. Mr. Gardner waited 'til she was out'ah sight, and then he found me in the woods; we dug up whut she buried."

"For the court, please identify what you and Mr. Gardner found, Mr. Butler."

"We found the sack lyin' over yonder."

"This sack, Mr. Butler?"

"Yeah. That's the one. We didn't touch what was inside. Jest left every-thang in the sack, you know, but we figured it was sump'em important if she went tuh all the trouble tuh hide it in the woods. But we were . . ."

"What, Mr. Butler?"

"'Fraid."

"Of what?"

"Colored men claimin' tuh find a gun that could've killed somebody, well . . ."

"And?" Alexander asked.

"We figured we needed tuh do the right thang. It's Nathan Demmings's life, you know. Seein' the district attorney waved the uh'ther gun, knowin' what we found, I figured we needed to tell somebody."

"At which time I informed the court.

"Mr. Butler, can you identify the woman you saw?"

"Sho'. There she is. Miss Vivian, Miss Vivian Demmings."

Well, honey. A gasp went up in that courtroom like nobody's business.

I dropped my head and whispered to Fannie, "She gon' lie and say William or Robert did it."

"Oh, hush up, Margaret. We gots they sorry asses now."

The judge's gavel fell, and he promised to clear the courtroom if there were any more outbursts.

Alexander said, "I have no further questions for this witness."

The district attorney didn't say one word. He shook his head and threw up his hands as William left the stand.

Alexander said, "Your Honor, I'd like to recall Mr. Julian McCutcheon."

"Mr. McCutcheon, please be mindful, you're still under oath," the judge said.

"Yes, sir."

"Mr. McCutcheon, please confirm that the weapon Mr. Butler and Mr. Gardner found is identical to the one identified as People's Exhibit Number One?"

"Yes, that's correct in some respects. They look the same on the surface, but they are different weapons."

"Since the second gun appeared, have you since conducted the tests to determine which gun is the actual murder weapon?" Alexander asked.

"We have."

"Please tell the court your findings."

"Your Honor, we conducted several tests yesterday, and we determined the weapon found wid the defendant's fingerprints is not the murder weapon. The second weapon, found by William Butler and Robert Gardner, is the actual weapon that killed Hollis Demmings."

"Are you sure on this point, Mr. McCutcheon?" Alexander asked.

"We're positive. Although the guns look the same, the second one has slight barrel irregularities. These irregularities produced distinct markings on the projectile as it left the gun. It's impossible for the gun found wid the defendant's fingerprints to be the murder weapon."

"Your cross," Alexander snapped.

"No questions," the district attorney said.

"Your Honor, the defense wishes to recall Mr. Samuel Hawkins to the stand."

"Mr. Hawkins, can you tell us about these weapons?"

"Sho'. The pair was in a burgundy velvet-lined case."

"Please inspect this case. Do you recognize the case found by Misters Butler and Gardner as the case that housed those revolvers, and how can you be certain it's the same one?"

"Because my daddy had his name inscribed on the underside of the case; there's a plaque wid his name, city, and state on it."

"Would you read it to the court?"

"Yes. It reads Josiah Samuel Hawkins, Montgomery, Alabama. The case holds the revolvers, the Colt London Agency instructions, which are still intact and legible, and a good stock of spherical and conical bullets from the original Colt .44 caliber mold. The revolvers are in excellent condition."

"And how did these guns leave your possession?"

"A gentleman, along wid his wife, visited one day. I had known her since we were children. Well, us menfolk got tuh talkin' 'bout shootin' and huntin', and I showed him the case. He took a shine tuh those revolvers and begged me tuh sell 'em. Well, they had been in the family for so long, I didn't wanna sell 'em, but his wife and her family have been so close tuh ours. I broke down and let him buy the pair."

"Can you identify the man and his wife for the court, Mr. Hawkins?"

"Yes, sir. They're right there. Mr. and Mrs. Floyd Demmings."

Well, folks were beside themselves. Everybody was having a tizzy fit. The judge's banging gavel didn't quell the situation. When folks stopped talking, the district attorney had nothing to say. I reckon he knew what was coming, just like the rest of us.

Alexander said, "The defense would like to call Mrs. Vivian Demmings."

The courtroom broke out into whispers and again the judge attempted to stifle the crowd.

She walked as if she had nothing to hide, and she was dressed to kill, with black patent leather shoes and a matching pocketbook, a small one she clutched under her left arm. She wore a two-piece burgundy suit; the jacket fitted tight in the waist and flared out over a matching skirt. It was too tight for her. Oh, she twisted her little tail on up there.

She took the stand.

"Wiggle yo' sorry ass outta this, Missy," Fannie whispered to me.

They swore her in, and she promised to tell the whole truth and nothing but the truth. But the truth wasn't in her; she was a practicing liar, too.

"Mrs. Demmings. How are you related to the defendant?" Alexander asked.

"Nathan is my son."

"How would you describe your relationship with your son?"

Silence.

"Do you want me to repeat the question?"

She still said nothing.

"Mrs. Demmings, we're waiting for a response. How would you describe your relationship with your son?"

"Hollis raised Nathan . . . and I had . . . a limited relationship."

"Do you love your husband, Mrs. Demmings?" She looked startled, answering as if surprised by the question.

"Yes, I love my husband."

"Do you love him more than you love your son?"

She shifted her eyes in Floyd's direction, but her chair creaked as she twisted to find support from the chair's back.

"Would you do anything your husband asked you to do, Mrs. Demmings?"

The chair creaked louder, but her chin fell to her breast, and her eyes scoured the floor.

Alexander got right in her face.

"Mrs. Demmings, did you drive your car, as Mr. Butler testified, and did you bury this sack containing this case and gun in the woods?"

He held the gun up and shoved it right in her face.

Her teeth dragged over her bottom lip, and tears waterlogged her eyes.

"The court is waiting, Mrs. Demmings."

Her chair screeched louder against the hushed courtroom.

"Did you, on the night of October eleventh, *kill* Hollis Rhodes Demmings in cold blood?"

Tears started down her face. Then suddenly Floyd jumped up, flung himself through the gate, grabbed Nate around the neck, and threw a gun up beside Nate's temple. Folks began screaming. Some of them hit the floor, and Floyd said, "Oh,'nuf of this shit! I did it. I killed that old fool!

"Daddy's lawyer told me he was gonna leave every penny to his *perverted, nigga-loving son!* Even everythang Mama said was gonna be mine."

Vivian screamed, "Floyd, please don't!"

Floyd yelled out the corner of his mouth,

"Bitch, shut the fuck up! It's all yo' fault."

Pulling Nate closer as he moved to the left side of the courtroom, he said, "I told'cha, boy. Remember? Told'cha that night I was gonna make sure you see the Lord . . . I'm gon' keep that promise."

Smiling and inching backward, he said, "Come on, boy. Death's waitin' for all of us . . . this ain't yo' time tuh struggle."

He stepped backward, licked the side of Nate's face, smiled, and said, "Didn't know you smell so sweet.

"Hush! Boy, yo' skin . . . it's soft, lac'uh woman's," licking Nate's cheek once more.

Then he addressed the stunned audience, with his lips curled into a smile.

"I know y'all don't wanna see me blow this freak's brains out . . . not right here, in front of y'all nice Christian folks.

"Ain't that right, boy?"

Nate's face flamed crimson as Floyd dragged him across the floor, shoving chairs and tables out of the way. But the path he had cleared led to nowhere, so he said to Nate, "Say goodbye, boy," as he pressed the gun tight to Nate's temple and prepared to squeeze the trigger.

But then, Vivian screamed,

"Floyd, *no!* Nate is yo' son!"

Distracted, Floyd loosened his grip and looked in her direction.

The sound of a gunshot exploded through the courtroom.

I closed my eyes and threw my hands to my mouth as screaming erupted all around.

Bodies scrambled below us. Folks were running, screaming, and crying. Somebody said, "Oh, my God. He killed him?"

I opened my eyes and saw Floyd and Nate sprawled on the floor.

I screamed through my hands and tears fell from my eyes.

William held on to Tilda.

Folks huddled over the dead.

Then the crowd parted a bit, and Alexander reached over and pulled Nate to his feet.

Lawd. If Fannie and I didn't run from that balcony, God don't sit in heaven. We didn't care about segregation. We flew down those steps.

Seemed like everybody was in tears. I brushed past a deputy who placed his gun into his holster.

Floyd had a bullet in his head.

Vivian collapsed crying over Floyd's no-good body, but the judge's shouting "Arrest that woman" didn't hold a smidgin to Fannie's "Yeah, carry that heifer—that redneck cow—carry her old sorry ass to the jail-house, jest where her belongs!"

All of that happened the day before Thanksgiving, 1955.

THIRTY-ONE

Searching for Symbols

The sheriff arrested Vivian, and the judge ordered Nate's release. Christine and Candy were so happy that I think they would have carried Nate on their shoulders if they had been strong enough. After the commotion of clearing the courtroom, William and Tilda headed home, but Fannie and I spoke with Christine and Candy while Alexander and Nate had to take care of things concerning his release. When we reached the house, William had dinner on the stove, and the "Empress of the Blues," Bessie Smith, sang "Tain't Nobody's Bizness If I Do" on the radio. It was one of Fannie's favorite songs, which prompted her to grab William, who spun her out like a ballerina. Then she announced her departure. She said,

"Thank God this is over," she said. She hugged me before leaving.

"How yuh feelin' this evenin'?" William asked me.

"At peace. You?" I replied.

"Had a talk wid my soul; got some ways tuh go, but I've made some progress."

"Yuh sit on down, and I'll git yuh some dinner. Where Alexander, Nate, and Leroy at?"

"They'll be here soon … needed tuh wrap up some things. Where's Tilda?"

"Resting."

Tilda appeared in the doorway right then. William looked up from the frying pan and said,

"Oh, there she is. Want sump'em to eat?"

"Yeah," she said.

"Grab a seat next tuh yo' mama," he told her. He went on, "It's hard tuh believe how much weight got lifted wid us learnin' who did all this killin'. I didn't think knowin' would make a difference. Whut do yuh think, Margaret?"

"I feel like I can breathe and live full again. But . . . how yuh feelin' 'bout Nate now, William?"

"Ah, Nate. He's family, lac'uh son . . . gon' always be part of this family."

"Whut happened tuh you, William?"

"I done finally crossed that river."

"I wonder how Nate's feelin' 'bout Floyd and Vivian," I said. "Didn't have the heart tuh ask him."

"'Spect the boy's tryin' tuh catch his breath right about now," William said. "The haints will git tuh swarmin' when the quiet comes."

"But whut possessed Vivian?"

"She kept that secret for so long," Tilda said.

"Think it was hard on her?" William wondered.

"Scared," Tilda said, like she had laid with it her entire life.

"Maybe some shame too," William said.

"But how could she?" I said. "Willin' tuh send her son tuh the electric chair! Whut sort of woman . . . whut kind of parent is that?"

"Well, Fannie would say, 'She uh redneck heifer who ain't never been a damn.'"

"William, that's about right," I said.

"I feel for Nate," Tilda said. "He lost Thad, his grandfather, his father, and his mother. Who does he have now?"

"Us," William said. "The boy gots us."

"And Candy, too," I said. "She fought tooth and nail to free him."

Tilda and I had finished washing and drying the dishes when the door opened. Alexander escorted Nate, Leroy, Christine, and the children, who had stayed with Miss Bessie. With their arrival and into our celebration, we learned Vivian had gone crazy. Nate had always been kindhearted, and he asked Alexander to see what he could do for Vivian. Alexander visited her in jail, hoping to help her. But Vivian, swept up in delirium, ran to the corner with her fingers in her ears, stammering and asking "it" to stop. Something or someone was tormenting her unrelentingly. That was another piece of our justice.

We showered Nate with affection, but the weight of Thad's death lingered and the troubles stirred up by Floyd and Hollis were enough for Tilda and Alexander and the children to depart earlier than planned. They realized that even when you were "almost" white—lighter than a brown paper bag—there was always the potential for danger. Lord, I wished they would have spent Christmas with us, but they intended to leave for Paris the following Friday.

I stayed up late, long after the house had fallen silent. The thoughts of Thad and the trial kept my mind racing, but I dozed off in the rocking chair. Lying somewhere between knowing and slumber, cradled between pressed sheets and a goose down quilt, William awoke in the darkness of our room, startled by my absence. In distress, he sought after me and found me asleep. His gentle kiss bespoke of gratitude and nudged me from my dreams.

"Come tuh bed, baby," he said. He pulled me to my feet, and with the grace of princes and kings, he kissed me once more, lifted me into his arms, and carried me to bed as he did on our wedding day when he reminded me of cotton candy.

I woke early and headed to the Ridge to wait for sunrise. I wanted to let my heart rest in thanks and praise that Thanksgiving morning. When I got there, a smoky mist shrouded the earth. Mountains of fog pushed up by hills, rocks, and other hard things. Fingers of mist crawled, sought cracks, hugged the ground in low spots, and made dew until the sun appeared and took my side, winning the dawn and kissing the sky orange, pink, and then purple.

A rooster crowed.

Once.

Twice.

Three times, then I said the psalm.

> *Be merciful unto me, O God, be merciful unto me;*
> *for my soul trusteth in thee;*
> *yea, in the shadow of thy wings will I make my*
> *refuge, until these calamities be overpast.*

I will cry unto God most high; unto God that performeth
  all things for me.
He shall send from heaven, and save me from the
  reproach of him that would swallow me up. Selah.
  God shall send forth his mercy and his truth.

I lifted my head toward heaven with gratitude and pride surging in my chest. I thanked the Lord for teaching me compassion and wisdom through my identity as a Negro and woman.

I prayed He'd let me see my baby one more time.

After that prayer, lines from books came to me, and I considered colored and white folks' sufferings. We seemed to be as separate as wintertime's freezing chill and summertime's roaring heat, and no other season existed where temperateness might meet. Some colored folks hid their sorrow and hatred all up in a smile and a laugh. Even decent men got stuck in the tines of the white man's folly. Others believed a grin from someone white masked deception because experience taught them that white folks had perfected scheming and manipulation.

I came to understand part of what Fast Fannie ranted over. She said Negroes needed to stop chasing after what white folks dreamed up as happiness. "It'll lead us all tuh hell in a handbasket," she said. Fannie believed all their longings were tricks of perversion. She raved about how Mr. Charlie's fork-tongued deceptions had broken plenty of colored backs, bloodied plenty of colored heads, and busted a whole heap of Negro dreams. Fannie fumed about deceit and manipulation—how they had unleashed a bunch of colored heartaches among colored men.

But I had taught my children another set of aspirations. They should fix their plow deep and scoop a wide path, and I prayed they'd understand how we bear the lessons of history. I wanted them to be authentic in their words and actions, and I asked them to consider that most folks spent too much time crying over their own pain and gave too little consideration to the heartaches they caused. I hoped my brood grasped how the mockery of others exposed their own unhealed wounds, mistakes, and losses. I wanted them to understood that they couldn't conceal their ridicule of others by saying, "It's just a joke." I wanted them to love everything and everybody.

The words I gleaned from reading told me what I always understood:

black folks could slap their knee and laugh because we knew everyone's sorrow was one or two chuckles away. We could jump and dance with no compunction to call it art—'cause dancing was what you did when joy grabbed at your heart.

From those books, I figured Hollis had conjured deception and spun illusions to propel him through life to appear as something he was not, and no matter how you diced it, his tricks stemmed from greed and violence. Did he love Marlene, Nate, Candy, little Isabel, or Miss Ophelia? I can't say for sure but I reckoned they were all just property to him. However, I suspected his youngins held more value—fared better than the horses he owned because they were from his loins.

And when we learned the truth about my baby's murder, I saw that Floyd and Hollis were cut from the same piece of cloth. People like Hollis were the arch-demons, but men like Floyd were their thugs. If I were forced to split hairs, I would say the only distinction between them was that Hollis had a heaping helping of old-fashioned Southern gentility, with its proper manners and plenty of money. Hollis used his refined behavior and wealth to take what he desired and snatch what he didn't need. A pristine life for Hollis and his kind meant they conspired with the devil in secret and performed their deeds with unsoiled hands. They lurked behind the scenes, taking names and reconciling debts. The difference between Hollis and Floyd, you see, lies in the division of labor.

Eventually, the sun vanquished the morning fog, bringing warmth to a chilly Thanksgiving dawn. A breeze swept across my face in the charity of that sunniness, and my prayer became flesh.

I looked up, and Thad sat facing me.

He didn't say a word but broke out in a gigantic smile, smiling until I came to myself, and then he moved toward me. The fluidity of his movement transported me to the lake near Pleasant Ridge. He was the lone swan whose arched neck slid between lily pads, rippling the dark, brackish water with perfect grace and agility.

Harmonious.

Seamless in its simplicity.

He laid his head on my lap, and speaking not with tongue and mouth, he wound up in my heart and crawled up in my head. He nestled there as the whisper of his voice fell into my ear.

"Mama, I rejoiced when yuh healed . . . when yuh didn't cry after me any longer."

"Oh, baby, I've been dreamin' 'bout holdin' yuh in my arms one mo' time."

I rubbed his back and stroked his head.

"Thank you, Mama."

"For whut?"

"For bein' my mother."

Joy broke loose, and I spoke.

"I want you tuh know how thankful I am that God allowed yuh tuh come in'tuh my life as my baby, as my son. When yuh left the house that night, I missed the opportunity tuh hug yuh . . . didn't receive the pleasure of showerin' yuh wid affection and love. And when yuh disappeared in'tuh the spirit realm, I lost any chance tuh tell yuh how proud I was of yuh."

"Mama, you cried for so long. I worried 'bout you."

"Son, I came through it . . . I wish I had known 'bout yuh and Nate, but I hope feelin' the way yuh did for Nate didn't cause yuh tuh suffer."

He tried to interrupt, but I said,

"Shhhhh. Hush now. Jest lemme hold yuh a little longer."

I didn't need to look down. The mass of his body had grown light. Disappeared. I kept right on patting. Not his back, but the misty gray of my dress and the softness of my thigh, while his scent covered me.

The crackle of twigs snapped by a rhythmic footfall roused me, and turning in that direction, I saw Nate approaching.

"Whut'ja doin' up here?" I asked him.

"Went by yo' house, lookin' for you . . . couldn't sleep a lick. Mr. William told me you might be here, and I wanted tuh see yuh."

"I reckon decipherin' all yuh've been through is lac'uh monkey tryin' tuh crack a math problem."

"Yeah, I couldn't stop the cyclone of thoughts. So last night and this morning, I rummaged through Granddaddy's things. I discovered a chest full of some things that might give us some answers. I found a bundle of correspondence between him and Marlene that just makes him more of an enigma. Even after all I've been through, I'm baffled by what he placed in her coffin . . . cain't stop thinkin' 'bout it. I left part of what I found at your house."

"Let's explore those things tuh'gether," I said. "Perhaps we can figure it out . . . give yuh some peace 'bout all of this."

"There's one more thing," he said.

He knelt before me.

"The night of the murder, Thad gave me this sheet of paper. I told'cha 'bout it when I was in jail. I didn't think I'd survive then, but since I did, I want you tuh have it."

"Oh, I don't know . . . I don't think it would be—"

"It's all right. He wud'den mind, and I want you tuh have it."

From the sight of it, Nate had carried it around the world and back, and its tattered edges confirmed he had pulled it out countless times to recall the strokes made by Thad's hand. Even when I opened it up with the reverence it deserved, its deep folds crackled.

I held it a little sideways, read it, and said out loud to Thad,

"Baby, I'm so thankful tuh read yo' last words."

Nate sat next to me on the Ridge.

I looked to heaven, and envisioning the plot of ground where I sat as his, I patted love to the earth and whispered,

"Rest now."

And then it seemed as if God exhaled and a gust of wind collected, spun, soared, and sent leaves full of joyful autumn colors into my lap.

Thad's presence covered me.

I took a deep breath, gathered autumn's delight into my fists, placed my arms across my chest, and closed my eyes.

———◦◦———

May the positive actions accomplished here, and their merit,
be dedicated to the flourishing of the peerless wisdom of all
pure paths and for the benefit of all sentient beings.
—SARVA MANGALAM![1]

---

1 Sanskrit for "May all be auspicious."

GENEALOGY

The Long and Butler Family Tree

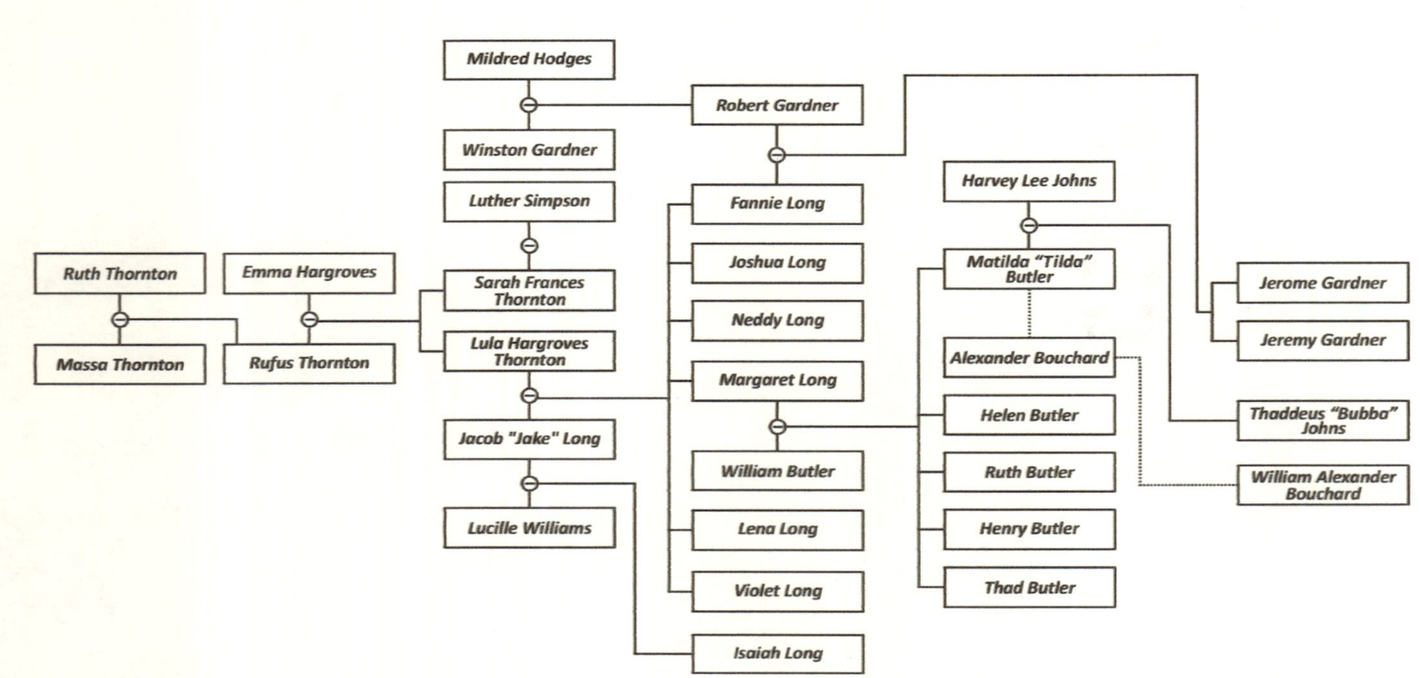

The Weatherby and Demmings Family Tree

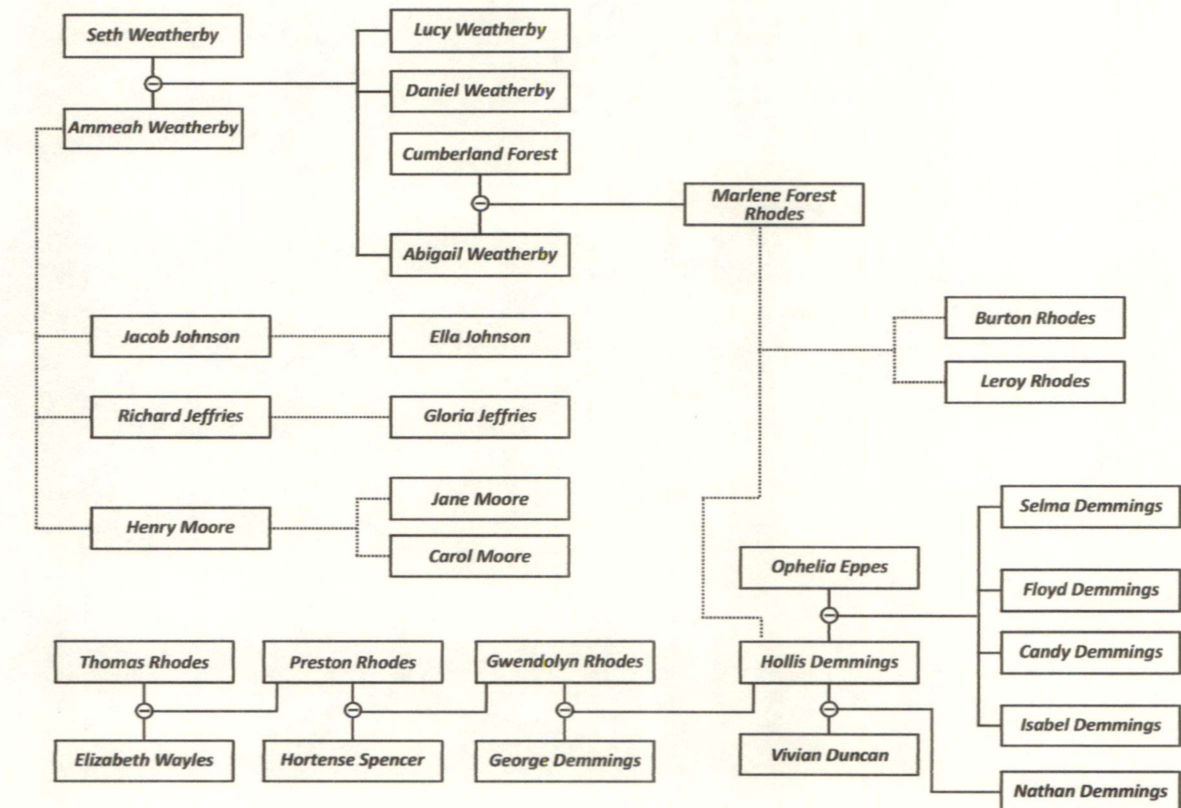

GLOSSARY

Southernisms

'bacca	tobacco
'cept	except
'cross	across
'em	them
'foe	before
'head	ahead
'long	along
'longs	belongs
'magine	imagine
'mancipation	emancipation
'member	remember
'nuf	enough
'nuther	another
'pend	depends
'pose	suppose
'preciate	appreciate
'round	around
'suade	persuade
'sides	besides
'strubance	disturbance
'ticularly	particularly
'twas	it was
'tweren't	were not
'tween	between

'way . . . . away

a'tall. . . . . at all

allst . . . . all

axes . . . . ask

axed. . . . . asked

b'foe . . . . before

bet . . . . best/better

bet'cha . . . . bet you

cain't . . . . can't

cain'tja . . . . can't you

call'cha . . . . called you

cu'dha . . . . could have

de'reckly . . . . directly

did'ja . . . . did you

don'tcha. . . . . don't you

dud'en . . . . doesn't

git . . . . get

gittin' . . . . getting

glad'ja. . . . . glad you

gon'. . . . . going to

got'cha . . . . got you

got'tuh . . . . got to

gwine . . . . going

haf'tuh . . . . have to

has'tuh . . . . has to

if'n yuh . . . . if you

if'n . . . . if

ig'rant	ignorant
in'tuh	into
Jaw'ja	Georgia
jest	just
lac.	like
lac'yuh	like you
lac'uh	like a
must'uh	must have
mo'	more
nah	no
nome	no ma'am
ortah	ought to
out'cha	out of your
out'ah	out of
parti'lar	particular
partic'ly	particularly
po'	poor
prob'ly	probably
ruut	root
sho'	sure
sho'nuf	sure enough
sump'tem	something
t'eat	to eat
thank	think/thought
taught'cha	taught you
told'cha	told you
tuh	to

tuh'gether . . . . together
uh . . . . a
Uh'lanta . . . . Atlanta
uh'nuf . . . . enough
uh'nuther . . . . another
uh'ther . . . . other
us'es . . . . us *or* ours
use'ta . . . . used to
wan't . . . . wasn't
wender . . . . window
whut'ja . . . . what are you/what do you
whutever . . . . whatever
wid . . . . with
wid'out . . . . without
wu'dha . . . . would have
wud'den . . . . wouldn't
yessum . . . . yes ma'am
yestiddy . . . . yesterday
yo' . . . . your
yo'self . . . . yourself
you's . . . . yours *or* you are
you's uh . . . . you are
yourn . . . . yours
yuh . . . . you
yuh're . . . . you're

About the Author

Leon E. Pettiway is Professor Emeritus at Indiana University, Bloomington, and a fully ordained Buddhist monk in the Gelug tradition of Tibetan Buddhism. As a lifelong scholar of crime, justice, and social inequality, he focuses on the lived experiences of society's most marginalized individuals, particularly in relation to race, urban life, and the structures that shape human behavior. He is the author of *Honey, Honey, Miss Thang: Being Black, Gay, and on the Streets* (1996) and *Workin' It: Women Living Through Drugs and Crime* (1997), both from Temple University Press, as well as *Only for the Brave at Heart: Essays Rethinking Race, Crime, and Justice* (Meishin Press, 2023).

New Harmony: A Mother's Story of Love and Loss is Pettiway's debut novel and the first in a series of thematically linked fictional works that explore resilience, community, and the quest for love and acceptance.